Taken

BOOKS BY SHALINI BOLAND

SHALINI BOLAND

Taken

SECOND SKY

Published by Second Sky in 2023

An imprint of Storyfire Ltd.
Carmelite House
50 Victoria Embankment
London EC4Y 0DZ
United Kingdom

www.secondskybooks.com

ISBN: 978-1-83790-020-6
eBook ISBN: 978-1-83790-019-0

For my family

PROLOGUE

'Ben, you need your hat and gloves!' Madison Greene called to her younger brother as he stepped out through the door of March-wood House into the freezing December night.

'I'll be fine, Mads,' Ben called back as he hurried to catch up with Freddie and Jacques.

Maddy grabbed a spare pair of woollen gloves and a bobble hat from the basket next to the coat stand. She'd lay bets on him complaining he was cold by the time they reached the ice rink. That was the trouble when you lived with five vampires – you sometimes forgot you had to worry about mortal concerns, like freezing to death, starving to death, falling from the top of a tree to your death, or, well, things that wouldn't trouble a vampire, but might kill you.

Maddy and Ben had inherited Marchwood House last year from distant ancestors, two of whom – Leonora and Freddie – also happened to be vampires. She smiled as Alexandre came up behind her, put an arm around her shoulders and kissed the top of her head.

'Are you ready?' he asked in his disturbingly gorgeous nineteenth-century French accent. Alex was also a vampire, along with his younger siblings, Jacques and Isobel.

'Think so,' Maddy replied, tilting her head up to kiss his delicious lips. He'd been brooding all afternoon, but she wasn't sure why. Things were great at the moment. Had been pretty much perfect ever since the end of summer, so why was Alex so distracted today?

'It will be busy at the rink this evening,' he said, fixing her with his dark gaze. 'We should try to stay together while we're there.'

'Alexandre, Maddy...' Isobel strode past them, arm in arm with Leonora. 'Are you coming? Stop dawdling. I cannot wait to get out on the ice. It has been too long!'

'We're coming, we're coming,' Maddy promised. 'You go out, I'll lock up.' Once all seven of them were finally on the driveway, Madison pulled the huge wood-panelled front door closed and turned the key in the lock.

'Are you okay?' she asked Alex as she slid the cold iron key from the lock and slipped it into her pocket.

Alex didn't reply straight away. 'I'm fine, it's just... a feeling.'

'Do you want to talk about it?' she asked, a stab of worry bleeding into her excitement. Headlights from their taxis were sweeping up the driveway and she covered her eyes against the glare.

'Thank you, but no,' Alex declared, giving her a soft smile. 'We will have fun and enjoy the ice-skating tonight. We must live in the moment, no?'

'Yes!' Maddy agreed with a skip in heart, pushing out her anxiety with relief. 'Living in the moment is a very good idea.' She took his hand and they walked down the steps towards the others. Towards whatever the night might hold for them.

CHAPTER ONE

CAPPADOCIA, AD 571

The stream tickled her heels. She pointed her toes and wriggled them under the cool clear water, watching the red dirt swirl away from her feet. She was pleased with herself for giving the others the slip. *I mean, what would they do?* Scold her possibly... warn her never to go off again. She would say she had fallen asleep, lost track of time, something or other. She just needed a few moments alone, that was all.

It was funny how she couldn't stop smiling. So, this was what it felt like. She had never in her life felt anything like this before. This was the secret that the women would not speak about in front of her. But now she knew. She was part of it now. She didn't need to eavesdrop anymore.

She shouldn't have done it. It was wrong and dangerous and she couldn't even guess at the trouble she would be in if anyone found out. But it had felt so right and so... beautiful. Yes. She had felt very beautiful. She bit her lip to stop herself from laughing. She glanced over her shoulder, making sure no one was around. Her thoughts were so loud, she almost worried someone would hear them.

It was not really such a terrible thing to have done. They

would be married of course and then it wouldn't matter. He had assured her that they would wed as soon as they were able. And then they could be together whenever they liked. But for now, it would have to be kept secret. A stolen moment. Like this, here, sitting alone on the bank of the stream. A moment in time to treasure and keep safe.

Aelia narrowed her eyes against the glare of the sun and looked down at her toes again. She frowned. Something had brushed up against her foot. Oh! A bird. Dead and bloated, its beady eye unseeing. She shuddered and pulled her feet out of the water. Time to go home before someone missed her.

She slipped her wet feet into her sandals, stood up and smoothed down her tunic. The sun had not yet dipped behind the hill, she could relax; she would not yet be missed. Aelia picked up the water urn and headed back towards the village. She wished she might catch a glimpse of him this evening, but that was a near impossibility. They lived at opposite ends of the village.

She had grown up with Lysus. He was the strongest, the funniest and certainly the most handsome boy in the village. He was older than she, but had recently started to pay her some attention, which had caused her friends to tease her and some to cast envious glances her way. His father was the village leader, and so Lysus would be a good catch.

Yesterday, he had sought her out during the hot afternoon when everyone was asleep. He had dared to sneak into their courtyard, had jerked his head towards the lane and left as quickly as he had arrived. She had followed him. She was such a model daughter that nobody would ever think her capable of doing something so daring.

He had been waiting for her, had drawn her around the side of a house, had stroked her cheek and teased out a blonde curl of hair from beneath her headcloth. She had blushed and tried to brush away his hand, but he grasped her fingers and put them to his cheek and then to his mouth. His eyes were gentle, but his grip was quite firm, making her grow weak with some feeling she couldn't identify.

She supposed the mere act of leaving her house unaccompanied had given Lysus a signal. He had assumed something and she had not dissuaded him of those thoughts.

'You have grown pretty, Aelia. Don't think I haven't noticed.'

She bowed her head, not knowing what to say.

'Will you walk with me, away from the village for a while?" He still held her hand and his eyes twinkled.

'I cannot. I will be missed. I must return to—'

'Just for a short while. We'll return before anyone wakes up.'

Aelia had been flattered and nervous and so had let herself be persuaded. She followed him along the back lanes, terrified and excited, her headcloth pulled across her face in case she was recognised. What was she doing? She knew it was madness, but some unknown force was pushing her on.

She still couldn't work out how it had happened. They had been walking and then they had sat and talked about the heat and about some of her friends in the village. He had said she was the only one he could think about. That she was driving him to distraction with her unblemished skin and graceful hands. That he would give up everything for just a glimpse of her wrist, her ankle, her neck...

She had become dizzy under his warm gaze and had raised her hand to her face, letting her sleeve drop to reveal the honey skin of her arm. He had smiled and bent to kiss the flesh on her forearm. The rest was a haze of heat and feeling.

Unable to believe it had happened, she had cried afterwards and he had soothed her with kisses and promises. They would be married. Her parents would be thrilled at the match.

Either through her own eyes or those of a stranger, her

childhood had been idyllic. A cocoon of love, warmth, joy and innocence. Born to a family poor in money but rich in happiness, Aelia had thrived and blossomed, secure in her skin. Her village was small and remote with its own customs and traditions, strong family values, but no tolerance for any other way. Thus, village life had been blissfully uneventful – until now.

Her father was an artisan, the village potter, and she was the eldest of four daughters. She didn't doubt that her father would be thrilled at the match, as long as he didn't guess what had already happened. But Lysus's parents might not be so happy. She doubted that *she* was what they had planned for their only son.

Of all of her friends, she was probably the least likely to have done what she had done. Verina or Licinia – she could imagine them giving into a boy. She had heard them talk immodestly on more than a few occasions. But they would never in a million years believe that she could be so... so wanton. Well, she would never tell them, never tell anyone. It was her and Lysus's secret; one they would laugh about once they were married.

And now a fingernail of sun slipped behind the hill as Aelia walked into the village carrying the heavy jug of water. Something felt different. She glanced around and strained her ears. There was no chatter, no clacking of pots as meals were prepared, no children playing outside. The dwellings were silent and still.

She tiptoed cautiously up the main path and turned left as the eerie silence followed her. Had everyone fled? Had some foe attacked their peaceful village? Should she knock on someone's door to ask? She walked up to a house, set the jug of water on the ground and raised her hand to rap on the door, but then lost her courage and lowered it again. Too scared to make a sound in the echoing silence. Her throat felt dry. She scooped some water from the urn and drank a few sips. Then wiped her wet hands on her tunic and resumed her course towards home, along the silent road. A dog barked twice and a startled bird cawed. Her heart beat loud in her ears. The sun was halfway behind the hill now.

Suddenly she made out a murmur of voices. As she walked, the murmur grew louder. It became a buzz and a hum, like a chattering crowd. She sensed... fear? No, more like agitation and anger. The closer she got to home, the louder the noise. A new seed of worry began to grow in her chest.

Aelia quickened her pace, a pearl of sweat formed at her breastbone and slid down towards her navel. She rounded the last corner and saw a gathering of people. It looked as though half the village was standing outside her house. Shafts of evening sunlight striped everyone with swirling dust motes. As she approached, the crowd gradually grew silent and all eyes gazed at her, but Aelia couldn't read their expressions. 'She could still hear a couple of voices, though, one of which was the croaky sound of her father. His normally quiet tones now raised loud and angry.

What on earth was going on? She tried to find a face in the crowd, a friend who might smile and tell her what was happening. But each time she tried to catch someone's eye, their gaze slid away to the floor. Her fear was really taking hold now, squeezing itself around her ribs and numbing her thoughts. As she walked woodenly towards her house, the crowd parted to let her through. Whatever had happened, she and her family must be at the centre of it. Within seconds, she was outside her dwelling where she saw her father arguing with Praetor Garidas, the village leader. Her mother caught sight of her and stumbled over to where she stood.

'You stupid, stupid girl!' her mother shrieked, grabbing hold of her arms and shaking her so that she dropped the water urn. It shattered, the liquid soaking quickly into the parched ground.

But now her mother was clutching her tight and sobbing into her shoulder.

Only a thin slice of sun was left sitting on the top of the rocky hill, its light now a heavy orange glow. Aelia suddenly realised what was happening. She understood the reason for the crowd, for the argument between her father and Praetor Garidas and for her mother's inconsolable disappointment. Aelia understood that it was her fault and that her life would never be the same again.

CHAPTER TWO

PRESENT DAY

Sitting on her ass on the freezing ice after having skidded into an inelegant tumble, Madison thought that if there was ever a perfect moment to remember forever, this was it. The tears streamed down her cheeks as she tried to think of insults to hurl at the others, who were almost puking with laughter, but she couldn't get the words out because she couldn't stop laughing either.

It had been Leonora's idea to come ice-skating because she'd said that she and Freddie used to go skating a lot before they were vampires.

The others had been enthusiastic too, but Maddy wasn't keen at all. She'd never ice-skated in her life. She'd never even roller-skated, or bladed or whatever the hell else kind of skating there was, due to the whole 'being in care and then fostered' and 'never having any fun' thing. She'd been worried she would look like an idiot. And now, here she was on her ass, looking like an idiot. But the funny thing was, she didn't care, she really didn't.

Gloucester Cathedral had turned its cloisters' garden into a temporary ice rink for the whole of November and December.

In one of the cloisters, a brass band played 'Good King Wenceslas' and in another, chestnuts roasted on a brazier. Right at the centre of the glistening ice floor stood a twenty-foot Christmas tree studded with teeny-tiny white lights which echoed the stars in the inky blue night sky. It was so beautiful here; like something on a Christmas card. The rink was only small, but it had been large enough for her to get up enough speed to completely and utterly embarrass herself.

After nervously skate-walking around the edge, Madison had finally plucked up enough courage to let go of Alex's hand. She had soon found her rhythm, but had become over-confident, flying off with no control smack bang into Miss Look-at-me-aren't-I-gorgeous-and-can't-I-skate-way-better-than-any-of-you-plebs. This girl, that none of them knew, had been off in her own world doing some fancy spinning ballet number until Maddy had barrelled into her and grabbed the girl's waist to steady herself, like some illegal rugby tackle, sending them both skidding across the rink and taking out random skaters on their way. If this was ice-skating, Maddy thought she might be addicted.

Now Alexandre glided up to her and held out his hand. Maddy gave him a fake glare, took his hand and let herself be helped up.

'That was quite something,' he said.

'Didn't you know? I do all my own stunts.'

He held her face and kissed her lightly on the lips.

'Are you all right? Did you hurt yourself?'

'Bruised, but I'll live.'

'Hey, Maddy!' Ben shouted across the rink. 'That was awesome!' He shuffled towards her, holding on to Isobel to steady himself. 'Wish I'd videoed it. Could've got loads of YouTube hits with footage like that.' He collapsed into fits of laughter.

'Yeah, and the YouTube sequel would've been "Sister murders her brat of a brother",' Maddy retorted.

'Are you all right, Madison?' Isobel asked. 'I have never seen anything quite like that before.'

The others skated over to see if Maddy was okay and to laugh some more.

'That girl looks very angry,' Leonora said.

They all turned to see the girl in question skating towards them, her glare fierce enough to melt the ice.

'You shouldn't be on here if you can't keep yourself under control,' the girl snapped as she spun to a halt.

'I'm really sorry,' Maddy said with an ill-concealed smirk.

'It's not funny. You could've killed someone.'

'Sorry,' Maddy repeated, trying not to laugh.

'Calm down, it was an accident,' Ben said.

The girl gave them all a dirty look and skated off.

'Say cheese,' Isobel said, holding out her phone to take a photo. They all tilted their heads together and pulled silly grins.

'Will you show up on there?' Ben asked.

'What do you mean?' Freddie replied.

'Well, I didn't think vampires could show up on photos.'

'Yeah,' Freddie said, 'and we're also allergic to garlic, crosses and daytime TV.'

'Okay, okay,' Ben replied. 'I didn't know. Just asking. You always see it in films, don't you – no reflections in mirrors and stuff.'

'Don't scare Isobel like that,' Jacques said. 'She'd die if she couldn't see herself in a mirror. She wouldn't be able to do her hair properly.'

'Oh, Jacques,' Isobel replied. 'You're so funny, you should be a comedian.'

'I know. I crack myself up.'

'No, really, you should.' She pushed him off balance, so he skidded across the rink. Isobel smirked.

'Anyone want a hot chocolate? Ben?' Maddy said, knowing the others wouldn't be interested. 'I need something sweet to take the edge of my humiliation.'

'Yeah, Mads. Can I have whipped cream and marshmallows on mine? And a chocolate flake?'

Maddy raised her eyebrows. 'Shall I see if they can fit a jacket potato and a tub of ice cream on there too?' She turned away from her brother, wrapped her arms around Alexandre and kissed him again.

'Urgh, you two are so gross,' Ben said, pretending to throw up. 'Don't forget the flake,' he shouted, attempting to skate off.

'I won't be long,' Maddy murmured into Alexandre's ear.

'I'll come with you,' he replied.

'No, stay and skate. I'll only be a few minutes.'

'Make sure you are.' He held her mittened hand and kissed it before letting her go.

Maddy skate-walked to the edge of the rink where she sat on a bench, stuffed her mittens in her pocket and began to unlace her boots. God, Alex was so amazing. Life was so amazing. She smiled to herself and gave a small snort of laughter as she pictured herself flying into that girl.

'I'm such an idiot,' she said out loud.

A man standing nearby raised his eyebrows and gave her a friendly smile.

She smiled back and carried on unlacing her boots.

'Very impressive,' he said.

'Huh?'

'Your skating manoeuvre out there – very impressive.'

'Oh. Yeah. Thanks. I mean, God, so embarrassing.'

'We all have to start somewhere.'

'I suppose. But most people don't start by taking down half the population of Gloucester.'

'True.'

'Well, see you round,' she said, standing up, her boots in her hand.

'Sure. See you round,' he replied.

Maddy scanned the area until her eyes landed on a signpost to the café and she headed away from the cloisters towards the alleyway.

Alexandre watched Madison as she slipped and slid across the ice towards the edge of the rink. He was suddenly overcome with a feeling of such intense happiness, it scared him. He loved her so much. Too much. All those years ago, when he and his siblings had become these creatures, he had accepted that he would never know happiness again, that his life was effectively over. But here, now, he felt as though he had reached the pinnacle of everything. This was what life was about – this place, this time, this girl.

The night air was crisp and sharp and the scent of blood was sweet in his nostrils. He would hunt later, but he could ignore the call for now. It was something he didn't enjoy thinking about too much – their need to feed on human blood. For his part, he always took from those who were close to death. Despite the blissful relief that feeding gave, he didn't think he would never delight in it. On the contrary, it shamed him.

'Come on, Alex!' Jacques called, skating over, his blonde hair tousled by the breeze. 'Stop mooning about after Maddy. You're embarrassing yourself.'

It was incredible how quickly his younger brother had adapted to twenty-first-century life. It was as though Jacques was made for this era. He already had a full vocabulary of contemporary British slang, and he, Freddie and Ben were a regular little clique or, what was the word? *Crew?* Ugh. Alexandre cringed. He preferred his own colloquialisms and felt foolish attempting to use modern-day terminology, like he was trying too hard. It just didn't sound right.

He narrowed his eyes. Madison was sitting on a bench removing her skates while a stranger spoke to her. A man. He felt a rush of anger and jealousy but squashed it down immediately. He knew he had nothing to worry about. He and Madison were above such petty emotions. Their love was true and steadfast. Unbreakable. It was almost a year since she had woken him from his sleep on Christmas Day. And six months since their first incredible kiss.

'Alex, come on, bro,' Jacques said, grabbing his arm. 'Have some fun.'

'Better come on, Alexandre.' He heard Leonora's soft voice behind him. 'I think the boys want to impress you with their tricks.' She took his other arm.

'All right, all right, I get the message,' he said, shaking himself out of his reverie. 'I bet you can't skate backwards without knocking anyone over.' He moved away from them and glided backwards, pulling stupid faces as he went.

Leonora rolled her eyes and followed him, graceful as ever. They skated across to the others who were jumping and twirling on the ice with ease.

'That's so not fair,' Ben said. 'You vamps get to do way more cool stuff than me.'

'Yes, but when you do it, it is much more impressive,' said Isobel. 'We can do these things in our sleep, but it takes proper skill for you to master them.'

'I suppose.'

Jacques and Freddie took Ben in between them, pulling him along while weaving expertly through the other skaters. Ben's grin lit up the cloisters and Alexandre smiled. Ben was such a wonderful boy and so similar to Jacques it was like having a second brother; a third if he included Freddie.

Freddie and Leonora were Madison and Ben's ancestors.

Like Alexandre and his siblings they had all been transformed into these immortal creatures over one hundred years ago during an archaeological expedition in Cappadocia, Turkey. Now they lived here, in England, in Marchwood House to be exact, with Madison and Ben. And life was... *complicated*, but good.

Ben had welcomed them all into his life with eager acceptance, no drama or resentment at all – and that was something. Not many people would welcome five vampires into their life, into their home. And Madison, well, she was something else – brave, beautiful, kind, funny... and stubborn. He smiled and looked over at the bench. She'd disappeared to get the drinks. Maybe he should go after her and check she was all right. But then the others would moan at him.

He skated around for ten long minutes and still Maddy hadn't returned with the drinks. Alexandre knew he was being irrational, but he couldn't relax. That unknown feeling he'd had all afternoon was back.

The ice rink was busy, town bustling with late-night shoppers, so there was no reason for immediate concern, but there was still a shadow hanging over all of them. Much as they were enjoying themselves right now, they had enemies out there who might not be so keen for them to live out their lives in peace.

'I'm going to find Maddy,' he announced to the others.

'She'll be back any minute,' Leonora said.

'I'll help her with the drinks. She won't be able to carry her skates and hot chocolate at the same time.'

'Oh, let him go,' Isobel said. 'He can't be more than two feet away from her at any given time or he'll turn into a pumpkin.'

Alexandre ignored their good-natured jibes and skated over to the edge of the rink. He swiftly removed his boots, put on his shoes and headed down the alley which led to the café. A long queue coiled out of the door, but Maddy wasn't part of it. Perhaps she had seen it and decided to go to a different café. He did a quick scan of the area, but she was nowhere. Alexandre's senses were sharp – if she was in the area, he would have found her straight away. Something was wrong. He cursed himself for not trusting his initial instincts to accompany her. Then he saw the man.

'You,' Alexandre said.

The man was just about to climb into his car, a midnight blue Audi, when Alexandre stood in front of him, blocking his entry to the vehicle.

'What the—'

'Where is she?' Alex said.

'Who? What are you talking about? Who are you? You're not getting my wallet and you're certainly not getting my car.'

The man was rubbing at a dirty mark on his coat sleeve. He was broad shouldered and tall. Now, he squared up to Alexandre, not intimidated in the slightest.

'I don't want your money or your car,' Alex replied. 'The girl you were talking to at the ice rink – where is she?'

'What girl?'

'I saw you talking to her while she was unlacing her boots.'

'Oh, that girl.' The man smiled.

Alexandre grabbed the man's coat collar.

'Easy,' the man said. 'She's *your* girl, I take it.'

'That's none of your business. Where is she?'

'How the hell should I know. We just spoke a couple of words and then she left. Let go of the coat.'

Alexandre released him. 'Did you see her again after she left?'

'No.'

'Are you sure about that?'

'Look, man, I don't know what your problem is, but I don't know that girl. I spoke two words to her and then she left. Maybe she doesn't like possessive psycho boyfriends, and decided to take off.'

The man was an arrogant idiot, but Madison wasn't here. Alexandre left the man and decided to return to the ice rink. Maybe he had missed her somehow. He doubted it, but there was a slim chance. The car door slammed behind him and the Audi roared away down the street.

Alexandre remembered his phone. How could he have been so stupid? He should have called her straight away. But now as he held the phone to his ear, willing her to answer, it just went straight to voicemail.

'Madison, where are you? Call me.'

He pressed redial a few times, but it was the same message.

Back at the rink, Alexandre scanned the crowd. Everyone was here except Maddy. It had been at least thirty minutes since she'd gone for the drinks. Something was definitely wrong. Leonora caught his eye and smiled. He beckoned her over.

'She's missing,' he said.

'Missing?'

'Maddy. She's nowhere to be found. Something's happened. Get the others and tell them I'm going to search for her.'

'Wait a minute... what do you mean?'

But Alexandre didn't hang around to reply. Something had happened to Madison and he had to find her. All kinds of scenarios raced around his head. Was she ill? Had she collapsed? And then more sinister thoughts came to him. What if this was something to do with Blythe? The lawyer for those powerful vampires who wanted Alexandre and the others dead. He knew he should have made more of an effort to track that miserable solicitor down and kill him, but life had been so good recently, so peaceful, he hadn't wanted to go looking for trouble. Well, now it seemed trouble had come looking for him. Or perhaps he was getting ahead of himself. Maybe there was a perfectly logical explanation and Madison would appear any second to tease him about his overactive imagination. Please, God, let that be the case.

Alexandre spent the next three hours scouring the whole of Gloucester and beyond. Isobel had taken Ben back home to Marchwood House in case she showed up there and Alexandre rang his sister every fifteen minutes to check if Maddy had arrived home yet. They had also called all the local hospitals and the others were out searching for her too, but nothing yielded any results. Maddy was gone.

CHAPTER THREE

CAPPADOCIA, AD 571

All Aelia heard was her heart booming in her chest and the ragged bleating of someone's goat. Her mother had been pulled away and her father made a move towards her, but Praetor Garidas put an arm out to stop him.

'No,' he said. 'You know the law. She cannot go with you or speak to you. She will go with them.' He pointed to two women dressed in black robes. 'She will lodge with them until we have decided.'

'But she has never spent a night away from us. She is only sixteen. Still a child...'

'We will determine the truth of that tomorrow,' Praetor Garidas replied.

Aelia's mind was a blur of thoughts. How could this be happening? The whole village outside her house, her father shouting at Praetor Garidas and her mother in tears. How had they found out about what she had done? And where was Lysus? He had said it would be all right, that they would marry. She glanced around wildly. She had to find him. He would make it right. His father was the Praetor after all.

Was it her imagination or could she hear whispers and

hisses in the crowd? No, not imagined. 'Whore,' someone muttered. 'Slut.' Tears pricked behind her eyes. The women in black now had hold of her arms and were trying to lead her away, but her legs didn't want to work.

Then she spotted him standing on the step of her neighbours' house. *Lysus.* His dark eyes bored into hers and she stared at him, a silent plea. She could feel the desperation in the twist of her mouth and the strength of her gaze. He shook his head and briefly put a finger to his lips. He mouthed the words *don't worry* and then he stepped down and was gone, hidden by the crowd. Did that mean there was nothing to worry about, that he would sort it out and make things right?

Aelia found a little strength to walk and so let herself be taken, unresisting, barely even registering her mother's rising screams and her father's useless pleading. The women gripped her arms too tightly and she stumbled along the path, trying to match their pace. She didn't dare look up now, too ashamed and terrified to see the stares of disgust, pleasure and pity.

Was it only a few minutes ago that she was happy? It didn't feel like the same year, let alone the same day that she had dipped her toes in the stream and felt such joy. How could things have changed so quickly?

'Where are we going?' Aelia managed to choke out the words, but neither of the women replied and she didn't have the courage to repeat herself.

Fear had never been a part of Aelia's life. Only love, happiness and a feeling that nothing bad could ever really happen. She was a good girl, never ungrateful or dissatisfied, never one to make trouble or mischief. As the eldest daughter, her sisters looked up to her – Aelia, the steady one. Maybe she had been saving it all up for now – for this one spectacular fall from grace.

She realised they had stopped walking. Raising her gaze from the ground, it now rested on a faded wooden door. The women let go of her arms and she automatically reached up to massage the bruised spots. The door swung inwards and they prodded her inside a dark room that smelt damp and disused. One of the women walked past her, over to a table where she lit a stubby candle. It flickered to life and illuminated all but the shadowy corners. Next to a rickety table, sat two roughly carved chairs and three straw pallets lay on the floor against the far wall.

'Get some rest,' one of the women said, pointing at one of the pallets.

'What's going to happen?' Aelia asked.

'You'll find out soon enough, foolish girl.'

Aelia coloured. The words hurt her. Everybody seemed to know what she had done, but Lysus didn't seem to be in trouble. She didn't understand it. She walked across to the pallet and sat down. Her parents must be so disappointed in her. She hoped her sisters didn't know what she had done. What would be the punishment for her sin? She had heard the rumours of punishments for past sins, but they couldn't be true, could they?

She leant back against the wall and closed her eyes. Aelia didn't even feel like herself anymore. There was a hollow feeling where her insides should be, but the hollowness felt heavy, which made no sense at all.

The women ignored her. They barely spoke to each other and when they did it was in half-whispers and swallowed murmurs. They sat at the table like a couple of huge ravens, sharp-eyed and aloof. After a while, Aelia gave up trying to glean anything from them. She lay down on the prickly straw and turned to face the wall. The humiliation and shame was almost worse than any possible punishment. Lysus had said not to worry. His father was the Praetor. He would surely make it right for her. Aelia's mind kept circling around the same things. Her poor parents, she had let them down. They would be devastated.

She still wasn't sure how she could have let it happen, how

she could have given herself so easily to a boy. It had all been so fast that she hadn't had time to think. The soft caress, the kiss... How had everyone found out? That was what really puzzled her. She and Lysus had been alone. Maybe someone had seen them go off together, but that was not enough for such an accusation. No doubt she would discover the answer tomorrow. She hoped she would have the courage to face whatever she needed to.

Tiredness suddenly overwhelmed her. The blur of thoughts in her head grew more shapeless and worrying, becoming a solid mass, like an unwelcome creature she couldn't shake loose. She realised she'd had no food since noon. The women had eaten something earlier but had not offered to share any of it with her. In any case, she didn't think she would be able to stomach food, even though her empty belly gurgled in disagreement.

Despite exhaustion, sleep was slow to come to Aelia. Each time she thought oblivion was about to take her, she would be startled awake with the strangeness of everything. When sleep finally did arrive, she dreamt of birds in flight and of a sunset so beautiful it made her weep.

CHAPTER FOUR

PRESENT DAY

Mmm. Maddy smiled to herself at the thought of hot chocolate. Her footsteps echoed along the narrow cobbled alleyway and her breaths came out in little frosty puffs. It was quiet down here, away from the laughter and music of the ice rink. These days she felt as though her life had really begun. It was like she'd been on hold for years, living a half-life, waiting for this life, waiting for Alexandre. They were so different from each other – he came from a loving family and a life of privilege and she'd been brought up in foster care with nothing to call her own.

Before Alex had come along, everything had been a battle and a struggle for Maddy. It had just been her looking after Ben. Worrying about him and worrying about herself. Angie and Trevor had been okay, but when it came down to it, their foster parents hadn't really cared about her and Ben. Not really. Not when it mattered. Even when she inherited the money, she still felt insecure. There was always that nagging fear in her stomach like she was responsible for everything and she constantly felt like she was about to make a massive mistake and ruin her and Ben's lives.

But Alex made the world make sense. He knew her and she knew him. She couldn't explain it. They fitted together. He made her feel confident and capable. Like she could do anything.

Madison emerged from the alleyway, walked through the car park and followed the signpost to the shops. She saw the café she was looking for – a warm yellow glow in the dimly lit street. She opened the door and felt the heat of the place and the noisy chatter of happy people. The takeaway queue almost reached back to the door, so she scooched in and took her place behind a red-cheeked family who were loosening scarves and removing woolly hats.

'It's boiling in here,' a little girl said to Maddy.

'It is,' she replied, smiling down at her serious face.

'I can ice-skate,' the girl said. 'Daddy said I was really good.'

'I'm not very good at all,' Maddy said. 'I fell over.'

'You have to practise if you want to get better.'

'Okay. I'll practise some more.'

The girl's mother smiled at Maddy. The door opened behind her, letting in a welcome blast of cold air.

'Hello again.'

Maddy turned to see the man from the ice rink standing behind her.

'Looks like we had the same idea,' he continued.

She gave him a small smile and turned back around. He was probably harmless, but she couldn't help thinking he'd followed her in here. She should never have spoken to him back at the rink. She'd probably given him the wrong idea. He didn't look like a nutter, but you could never tell.

'They do great coffee in here,' he said.

Oh no, he was trying to strike up another conversation. Could she get away with ignoring him? Probably not. 'Great,' she said in her least-enthusiastic voice.

'Are you a tea drinker or a coffee drinker?' he asked. 'I bet you like tea.'

It grated on her nerves that he was right. Maddy gave him what she hoped was a discouraging smile.

'Tea? Am I right?'

The queue moved forward and she pretended she hadn't heard him. He was quite good-looking, broad shouldered and well-dressed, but she wasn't remotely interested in anyone other than Alex. Plus, there was something a bit *off* about him.

She felt a tap on her shoulder. Maddy flinched, wanting to turn around and push him away. Instead, she looked at him with unconcealed annoyance, but her expression didn't seem to faze him.

'You're a tea drinker, right?' he repeated.

'Look, I don't mean to be rude, but I'm not really in the mood to chat.' There, that should shut him up. The queue was moving pretty quickly, thank goodness, and the family in front of her was being served now. She would order the hot chocolates and get back to the ice rink before the man had a chance to catch her up. Once he saw her with Alex, he'd get the message.

After a complicated order and lots of changing of minds from the children and frayed tempers from the parents, the family left with their drinks and snacks and it was Maddy's turn to order.

'Two hot chocolates to take away, please. One with cream and marshmallows. Oh, and a chocolate flake.'

She waited while the woman behind the counter prepared her order,

'They look great,' the man said as the woman put the drinks on the glass counter.

Maddy ignored him. She felt like a bit of a cow, but she really didn't want to encourage him.

'I'll put them in a little tray for you, love,' the woman said.

Maddy paid and headed to the door, avoiding any eye

contact. Someone thoughtfully opened the door for her and she began walking as fast as she could, back to the rink. It was a little awkward, as she had the skates in one hand and the tray in the other. The mittens were still in her pocket so her hands were freezing, and now her wrists were beginning to ache too.

'Here, let me help.'

Maddy gritted her teeth and rolled her eyes at the sound of the man's voice.

'I thought you were getting coffee,' she said.

'Their machine's broken. Just my luck.'

Maddy didn't believe him.

'Here, I'll carry those for you.' He took hold of the cardboard tray, but she didn't let go.

'I'm fine, thanks.'

'It'll be much easier. We're walking the same way. Come on, let me help.'

'I said no thanks.'

They had reached the car park now and a few people were milling around, but no one paid them any attention. The man kept step with her as she decided whether to make a run for it or not. There was something definitely creepy about him and he was starting to scare her with his persistence.

Maddy jumped as a van door slid open to her left. The man put his arm around her shoulder and pushed her towards the vehicle.

'Hey!' She brought the skates up to hit him, but someone pulled them out of her grip. She dropped the drinks on the ground and was shocked to realise there were people in the van who were trying to pull her inside. And they were succeeding. The man let go of her as she was forced into the interior, a dark piece of cloth rammed over her head. Maddy tried to yell, but no sound came out other than a useless moan.

The van door slid shut and the engine started up. She struck out with her fists and feet, but they restrained her, pinning her arms while someone else held her legs. The cloth smelt funny, like sweet glue. She felt odd, woozy. Voices filtered into her head as though from far away.

'Did anyone see you?'

'No.'

Men's voices. *Shit.* Her heart was racing. That bloke had deliberately pushed her into the van. Who was he? Why was she here? The others would find her. Alex would find her. She couldn't stay focused. Her eyes were closing.

'Is she out yet?'

Maddy lost consciousness.

Alexandre and the others met back home at midnight to discuss a plan of action.

'But where could she be?' Ben asked for the hundredth time.

'I don't know, Ben,' Isobel replied. 'Don't worry. We'll find her.'

'Maybe we should call the police?' Ben suggested.

'Do you really think they'll do a better job than us?' Freddie replied.

'It can't hurt to have as many people looking as possible.'

'We can't involve the police,' Leonora said, stroking Ben's hair. 'We're vampires. It will raise too much suspicion and things could get very awkward.'

'I don't care if things get awkward,' Ben replied, ducking away from her. 'I just want my sister back.'

'Don't worry, Ben,' Alexandre said, understanding the boy's fear. 'You'll get your sister back. I promise you now, you'll get her back. I would never let anything happen to Madison.'

'It already has happened!' Ben cried.

They were in the kitchen, standing around the scrubbed

pine table, the back door to the utility room wide open, letting in the freezing night air.

'I think this is something to do with Blythe,' Alexandre said. He should have heeded the uneasy feeling he'd had earlier today. He had sensed something bad in the air, but he had pushed aside his fears.

'Is that the solicitor who tried to kill you?' Ben asked.

'Why would he take Maddy after all this time?' Isobel said. 'That happened back in July and we haven't heard anything since.'

'I assumed all that was over,' Jacques added.

'Why would it be over?' Alexandre replied. 'Blythe told us his clients didn't tolerate fledgling vampires. That they wanted us dead. That hasn't changed.'

'But you killed them all,' Jacques said.

'I killed a lot of them,' Alex replied, 'but I don't know if they *all* perished. And you're forgetting about the one that got away – the Cappadocian vampire who turned me. He's still out there somewhere and I've a feeling he's the most powerful of them all.' Alexandre hadn't let himself think too deeply about the Cappadocian vampire who had changed his life forever all those years ago, because even the thought of him was terrifying.

Back in the nineteenth century, Alexandre had been a young man with his human life ahead of him, but he and his friends and family had been attacked by blood-drinking demons, and the creatures had killed his parents. It had been terrifying, a nightmare from which he thought he would never wake. And when he finally did wake, he had become... this.

'So if Blythe's vampires have got Maddy, how are you going to get her away from them?' Ben cried.

'Be calm,' Leonora soothed. 'We still don't know this is even the case. Alexandre is just guessing. There may be a more simple explanation.'

Like what?' Ben snapped.

'It will be quicker if we split up,' Alexandre said, needing to act rather than stand around answering all these questions. 'We have to find her before daybreak. Ben, you wait here and call us if she arrives home.'

'I'm not waiting around while you're all out—'

'Ben,' said Freddie, 'we can cover more ground than you. It makes more sense for us to go.'

'But I can go too. I can take the bike.'

'You have to stay at the house in case she comes back,' Alex said gently. 'We'll need to know if she shows up here.'

'I'll stay with you, Ben,' Leonora offered, her pale blue eyes full of worry.

'Fine.' He looked like he was going to cry.

'It will be okay, Ben,' Alexandre said. 'Do you doubt me?'

Ben stared at Alex, a scared bewildered expression on his face.

'Do you?'

'No. But you'd better keep your promise. She's my sister. She can't be...' His voice cracked.

'Shhh,' Isobel said. 'We'll find her.'

Alexandre stood on an iron motorway bridge watching the eastbound traffic below. If Maddy's disappearance *was* Winston Blythe's doing, he would have arranged for her to be taken to London, maybe to his solicitors' offices in Marylebone where Madison first discovered that she and Ben had inherited Marchwood. If that were the case, they would probably be heading east towards the capital. So he stood on the bridge, trying to see if he could sense her in any of the speeding vehicles, their blurred tail lights like blood trails. He caught the chatter of children, the banter of youths heading for a night out, the companionable silence of couples and the music of a thousand radio stations. But no Madison. She wasn't in any of the vehicles that passed below him.

Something niggled at Alexandre. A memory he couldn't quite grasp, that he knew was important. Something to do with the smell in his nostrils, but he couldn't think clearly. He was too angry and scared. This danger which dogged him – it meant Maddy had never been safe, *would* never be safe. If only he hadn't been so complacent. He should have sought out Blythe and put an end to this back in the summer. It was his own stupid fault. He gripped the metal rail in front of him and savoured the icy burn against his fingers. When he'd been human, such cold would have been painful, stripping the skin and seizing up his joints. Now, it felt like a sharp pleasing tingle, clearing his mind and giving him a jolt.

Suddenly he recognised the lingering scent in his nostrils. It was warm milk and cocoa – hot chocolate! That man who had talked to Madison, he'd had a stain on the arm of his coat. It was hot chocolate! How could he not have noticed that at the time? He was such an imbecile. Alexandre leapt off the bridge and onto the central reservation below. The traffic roared past him, but he ran across to the hard shoulder without interrupting its flow. Alexandre was sure now that the man had lied to him about not seeing her again. Maddy had gone to buy hot chocolate and the man had hot chocolate on his coat, which meant something must have happened between them.

Alexandre almost flew back to the cathedral. It was silent now. No skaters, no music, no lights, only a dull glow from the ice rink where a sliver of crescent moon shone down. The arches of the cloisters surrounded him like dark gaping mouths. He slowly retraced his steps from the rink towards the café. The alleyway was deserted apart from a small black and white cat that darted away into the shadows.

A few vehicles remained in the car park. Alexandre stopped. Something caught his eye. From a couple of hundred yards away it looked like some random trash on the ground, but Alexandre knew what it was. He crossed the space in less than a second and knelt down to pick up the cardboard tray. Ben's chocolate flake lay squashed into a frozen puddle of milky chocolate. Maddy's scent was all over the area. So, she had made it back this far and then something had happened. Something had caused her to drop the drinks. Something to do with that man. Alexandre remembered the car, the blue Audi. He would find it and he would question the man. He would rip his arms from their sockets if he needed to.

He searched the area using his vampiric senses of scent, sight and sound, moving quickly, unseen, almost spirit-like through the dark city. He discovered the Audi in the grounds of a disused warehouse at Gloucester Docks. The car was still smouldering, a burnt-out shell, the number plates removed. But it was the same make, model and colour. Too much of a coincidence for it to be anyone else's vehicle. Alexandre wanted to yell out in frustration. He wanted to find that man and throttle him until he could no longer breathe. He was a damn good actor whoever he was. When he'd questioned him earlier, Alex hadn't detected any duplicity in his answers.

What could he do? What use was this immortal life if he could not protect the one he loved? How could he bear it if she was gone forever? That mix of vulnerability and spikiness, of humour and bravery. Madison had suffered greatly in her life, yet she was the most generous person he had ever met. If anything had happened to her it would destroy him more thoroughly than the sun ever could. It would obliterate him. But he couldn't let his mind wander down such desolate paths. He must continue to act. He would locate Madison, his love, and kill whoever was responsible.

But dawn was only about an hour away and Alexandre couldn't believe he would soon be powerless to act, impeded by daylight, his enemy. He had to find Madison *now*, but how?

The man was gone, a shadow. The car had been his only link. Alexandre was out of ideas. The obvious thing would be to confront Blythe but there wasn't enough time. The sun would soon be here. And Blythe's offices in Marylebone were lethal for vampires with all that UV installed throughout the building. No. He would have to visit the solicitor at his personal residence. He would do it tonight.

CHAPTER FIVE

CAPPADOCIA, AD 571

Aelia awoke to darkness and hunger. She glanced about the unfamiliar gloom. This was not the room she shared with her sisters. This was somewhere else. Then she remembered everything, and her empty stomach lurched. Had it all really happened?

The windows were shuttered making it impossible to tell whether morning had arrived yet. But it must not be far away, for the darkness was not absolute. No one sat at the table and no one lay on either of the other straw pallets. It appeared she was alone. This realisation made her a little less terrified and she closed her eyes again, trying not to think about what the day could bring.

'There is a little bread and cheese if you want it.'

The voice made her jump and her eyes snapped open. One of the women was sitting on the end of her pallet, staring at her. Aelia instantly drew her knees up. How had she not noticed her before?

'I would eat if I were you. You may not get the chance later.'

'Thank you,' Aelia whispered.

The woman pointed to a covered platter on the table.

'Take what you want,' the woman said.

Aelia stood and shook the creases from her clothes. She had slept in her headcloth and now attempted to straighten it. Her mouth tasted stale and dry.

'Please, may I have some water?'

The woman pointed to an urn and some cups resting on a ledge on the wall. Aelia walked across the room, lifted the heavy urn and tipped it towards one of the cups. She misjudged the angle and splashed water onto the ledge and floor.

'Oh! I'm sorry,' Aelia said, feeling like she wanted to cry.

'*That* is not something you need to be sorry about,' the woman replied.

'Shall I mop it up? Do you have a cloth?'

'Leave it. Sit. Eat.'

The door swung open and a sharp flood of light swept into the dwelling. The other woman entered.

'It is time,' the woman said.

'Better eat quickly,' the first woman said to Aelia. 'We leave now.'

Aelia gulped down her cup of lukewarm water, tore off a chunk of bread and stuffed it into her mouth. At the women's beckoning, she followed them out of the door and into the hot morning.

Yesterday, she had taken little heed of her surroundings, but now she saw they were in a little side alley which she did not recognise. That was nothing strange, as she was only familiar with the immediate vicinity of her dwelling and the well-worn route to the stream. Aelia was never supposed to leave her house unaccompanied. It was only during these last few weeks that she had felt a pull from outside, a need to be away from the claustrophobic confines of her house and village. She wished she had ignored those rebellious feelings, for look where they had led her.

The two women resumed their positions from yesterday

and stood either side of her, gripping her upper arms. They looked straight ahead and began walking while Aelia stumbled along in between them, their black robes swirling about her. She chewed her mouthful of dry bread, trying not to choke, wishing they had offered her a little oil to moisten it. Where were they going? Were they taking her home? Probably not.

They emerged from the quiet alley into a wider lane and Aelia couldn't help but notice everyone staring. She recognised a few faces, but today they were either hostile or embarrassed. She saw those she had played with as a young child, those she had laughed and run and teased and argued with, but they had no words for her now. No morsels of comfort or smiles of reassurance.

She briefly locked eyes with one of her father's friends. He came often to their house to chat or to purchase pottery from her father's studio. When she was younger, he had ruffled her hair with twinkling eyes and pinched her soft cheeks. But the look he threw her today almost made her stagger backwards as if he had struck her, for it was a stare of pure hatred and loathing. Aelia took a breath and told herself she did not care that they showed her the other side of their faces today, for hadn't Lysus told her not to worry? He would make things right. He had to.

Her two escorts paid no heed to the stares or the taunts but marched relentlessly forward. By now, a small crowd followed them. She felt a sharp stinging pain at the back of her head and realised someone had thrown a stone at her. The two women stopped and turned. They shouted at a group of young boys who laughed and made no move to leave. As her keepers resumed their walk, Aelia cringed, expecting more stones to strike her. It was an awful feeling. Everything was spiralling out of control. Her calm and peaceful existence was disintegrating into fear and uncertainty.

Approaching the village square, she saw a long trestle table had been erected, behind which sat Praetor Garidas and three other village elders. A space had been left clear in front of the trestle, but all around, the whole village was gathered and people had now begun to notice her. Aelia's cheeks flamed and she felt light-headed. The women hoisted her up between them, as her knees gave way.

The mood of the crowd was one of tension and expectancy. What were they going to witness here today? Aelia didn't know either. As soon as she set foot in the square, the noise level erupted. The sun beat down on her covered head and she thought she would faint with the terror of it all. This crowd was here for *her*. She was the cause of this gathering. It was like a terrible, terrible nightmare.

The women led her through the parting spectators. Again, Aelia dared not lift her head for fear of seeing more hatred etched on familiar faces. More friends to spit at her or curse her name. She felt she might die of shame. Soon, the women came to a halt and Aelia found herself standing in a clear patch of sunlight. She risked raising her face a little and found herself squinting into the eyes of the village elders. She quickly lowered her eyes again at the sight of their stern expressions.

She was shocked and a little dismayed to see the women in black had melted away from her sides and she now stood alone. Although they were her keepers, there had been some small comfort in having them either side of her – a barrier between her and the hostile crowd.

A hush swept across the square, like a dying breeze. Where were her parents? Why weren't they at her side? And Lysus... where was he?

'Aelia Laskarina, you are an unwed maiden accused of sinning in the worst way, with a man.' The Praetor's voice filled every pore of her body. It rang out across the square and up into the sky. Aelia felt the tension around her increase even more, if that were possible. 'Are you guilty of this crime?' he asked.

She was expected to speak now, but what should she say?

Should she admit her sin or should she plead ignorance and pretend she did not know what they were talking about? Where was Lysus?

'Well?' Praetor Garidas said, after a few seconds of silence. 'Have you nothing to say? Are we to answer for you?'

'Where are my... where are my parents?' she stammered.

'Your parents cannot help you. They cannot answer for you. Only *you* can know what you did or did not. And only *we* can determine if you tell the truth or if you lie.'

She heard the crowd hold its breath. The silence was absolute. She knew that whatever she said now would determine the rest of her life. If she told the truth, she would be condemned, but if she lied and they already knew the truth, her fate would be a thousand times worse.

'I... I did this,' she whispered.

'Speak up.'

'I did this. I am guilty of this, but—'

The crowd erupted in a frenzy of jeering and shouting, drowning out the rest of her words. One of the elders rang a large hand bell, calling for silence.

'Sir,' she said. But she still could not be heard above the angry crowd. Once they had finally quieted, Aelia raised her voice, tears streaming down her face. 'Sir, he promised me we would be married, that we would—'

'Quiet, girl. Silence, everybody.' The Praetor stood and waited for hush to descend again. He spoke directly to Aelia who had begun shaking and sobbing. 'I am sorry to hear you say it. I am sorry to pass out this sentence, but it is the law and we must abide by it or we will descend into chaos and heathen ways.'

'But please, Praetor Garidas,' she wept. 'He has promised to marry me. It is—'

'Promises are not the issue, girl. You have sinned. That is all that matters.'

'But if I tell you who I was with! It was your—' Aelia froze
as a stone struck her cheek. She put her hand up to the stripe of
pain, then gazed at her red-stained fingertips before staring into
the crowd, to where the stone had originated. Her gaze landed
upon a pair of guilty eyes and she caught her breath as realisation punched its way through, like a blow to her gut. For it was
Lysus.

Up until now, Aelia had prayed that Lysus would halt her
humiliation and make everything right. But now, as she locked
eyes with him for a second that lasted an eternity, she realised
his loyalties were to himself. He would do nothing. Even if
Lysus *had* intended to marry her, he certainly would not help
her now. She knew nothing anymore, cared not if she lived or
died. The gentle security that had cloaked her childhood had
been ripped from her shoulders and used to suffocate her. She
turned away from Lysus in disbelief and surrendered herself to
the Praetor's judgement.

'Enough!' His voice silenced the crowd once again. 'It is a
straightforward case. The girl has pleaded guilty. The sentence
is death.'

Aelia's blood stopped cold. The air emptied from her lungs
and her legs turned soft. There was a ringing in her ears and a
feeling like she might float away, a severing from the solid earth
beneath her feet. There came a low murmur from the crowd
and then a high-pitched wail as a small, cloaked figure emerged
and threw itself onto the floor in front of the elders.

'Please, please!' the woman shrieked. 'Not death. Please!'

Aelia felt the world snap back into focus.

'Mother?' she whispered, still rooted to the spot.

The woman knelt on the ground sobbing. 'Please, Praetor
Garidas, I beg of you! Do not kill my eldest girl. It is not her
fault. It was me. I did not raise her properly. Blame me.'

Loud mutters emerged from the crowd now.

'What is she doing here?' the Praetor said. 'What are you doing here, Madam Laskarina? You should not be here.'

'Where else would I be? This is my daughter. And you have known her from childhood. You cannot do this to her. Have mercy.'

'Mother,' Aelia croaked, and staggered across to the kneeling figure. 'Mother!'

Her mother turned and flung her arms around her daughter, pulling her down to where she knelt. Aelia breathed in deeply and allowed herself a stolen second of relief. It felt so good to smell the scent of her mother. To feel such love after the hatred of the crowd, the dispassion of the elders and the betrayal of her lover.

'There is another way,' her mother said to the elders, shrugging off her recent hysteria. She rose to her feet and stood to face the four displeased men. 'You remember it. You must remember it. There was a trial when we were children. You know how that ended. You could pass the same sentence today. It is within the law. It is within your power to make it so.' She pulled Aelia to her feet and held her close.

Aelia did not dare look up but buried her face into the soft space between her mother's shoulder and collarbone.

The Praetor lifted his hand to silence Aelia's mother and to still the crowd. He turned to the other elders and they stood in council for a few long moments. Aelia couldn't think of anything but the word 'death'.

The elders soon returned to their places behind the trestle. The crowd became completely silent once more.

'Madam Laskarina, you were given strict instructions not to attend this trial today. You have disobeyed the elders and there will be a punishment.'

Aelia's mother did not react.

'However, you have brought to our attention a precedent

which we cannot ignore. And we are relieved to have an alternative to the sentence of death.'

Aelia's mother prostrated herself on the ground and cried out her thanks. The crowd reacted noisily with booing and jeers, but there were also a few cries of relief above the general displeasure. Aelia stood above her mother's cloaked body. She wondered how Lysus was reacting to this. Then she told herself she should not care.

The Praetor's voice cut through her thoughts and through the noise of the crowd. 'Aelia Laskarina, you can thank your mother, for we have decided your fate and it is to be *banishment*. You have been lucky today.'

Lucky? Mingled in with the terror, and the vague relief of having escaped death, she felt an urge to laugh at his word choice – *lucky*. She heard him still talking and struggled to concentrate on his words.

'You may not say goodbye to those you know. You may not take anything with you but the clothes on your back. You may not return to this village during the course of your natural life.'

Banishment. Sent away from everyone and everything she knew. So, it may as well have been a death sentence. Her mother rose to her feet and embraced her once more.

'My darling daughter,' she murmured in her ear. 'You will survive. You will find a way, I know it.'

Aelia clung to her mother as they were prised away from each other by the rough guards surrounding them.

'Be strong!' her mother shouted as she was dragged away out of sight. 'Be strong, Aelia!'

CHAPTER SIX

PRESENT DAY

A strange engine-like hum filled Madison's ears and she had the odd sensation of weightlessness. The lingering gluey smell made her remember. She snapped her eyes open and her eyelashes brushed against cloth. She'd been blindfolded... no, some kind of hood had been pulled right down over her face. She panicked and suddenly breathing became hard. She tried to move her hands but they were tied and so she struggled against her restraints, crying out.

'Hey!' Her voice sounded hoarse and muffled. 'Hey! What's going on?'

'She's awake.' It was a bland male voice without an accent.

'Yeah, I think we gathered that,' came the reply.

'Why am I tied up?' Maddy croaked. 'Take this thing off my head.' She pulled again against her restraints, but couldn't move at all. Her ankles were also bound together and as she struggled the ties cut into her skin.

'Calm down. You'll hurt yourself.'

Maddy's temper flared, her initial fear momentarily forgotten at the amusement in the man's voice. 'I might be a bit calmer if you hadn't snatched me, tied me up and shoved a bag over my head.'

'I'll need you to be quiet now,' the man said.

'You can go—' But then Maddy felt a wetness seep through the material over her face. There was that cloying smell again blocking everything out. The engine sound grew faint, there was a whooshing noise in her ears and her thoughts turned fuzzy and then blank.

In the early hours of the morning, Ben and the vampires gathered in the basement where no daylight could harm them. This was no normal basement, but a lavish suite of apartments furnished in the late nineteenth-century style. They all sat, except for Alexandre who paced the sitting room as he filled them in on his discoveries.

'Do you think she's dead?' Ben asked, wild-eyed and exhausted.

'No, I do not,' Alexandre replied. 'It is not even a possibility so do not think it.'

'You can't know that, Alex.' Ben stood up and tugged at his hair. At fourteen, he was no longer the naïve young boy Alexandre had first met a year ago. 'How can you pretend you know that? She could be lying dead in a ditch somewhere.'

'Don't ever talk like that again,' Alexandre replied.

'I'll talk how I want. It's my sister out there! And it's your fault she's gone missing. It's because you're vampires. You attract trouble. You're not safe to be around.'

'Calm down, Ben,' Jacques said.

'No, Jacques,' Alexandre said. 'Ben is correct. It *is* our fault Madison is missing. We have put Ben's and Maddy's lives in danger, but we will make it right. We will find her. Tonight, at first dark, we will go and confront Blythe.'

'We can't go to that place again,' Leonora said. 'We're defenceless against those lights.'

'We won't go to his offices. We'll find out where he lives and we will kill him. Madison will be there, I am sure of it. Then I'll hunt down the other vampires and I will kill them too. We cannot live like this any longer – under threat all the time.'

'Sounds good to me,' said Freddie.

'You make it sound so simple, Alexandre,' said Leonora. 'But you don't even know if she will be there. This may be nothing to do with Blythe or his vampire clients. Perhaps she simply needed some space away from us and has gone off for a few days.'

At this, everyone began talking at once, telling Leonora what a ridiculous suggestion that was and how Maddy would never go off without telling them.

'Fine, I'm wrong,' she said. 'I'm just exploring all the possibilities.'

'I guarantee it is Blythe behind her disappearance,' Alexandre repeated.

'Well then, we need to find out where he lives,' Isobel said. 'And, Ben, you need to sleep. You've been up all night.'

'How d'you think I'm ever gonna sleep?'

'Then go upstairs and read or watch television or just lie in bed awake. You need to rest.'

'But I—'

'If you don't, you'll be no good to anyone,' Isobel said, smoothing Ben's hair.

Alexandre turned his head at a knock on the basement door.

'Only me, love.' It was Esther, the housekeeper.

'Come in,' Isobel called out.

They had no secrets from Esther and Morris Foxton, the caretakers of Marchwood House. That summer, they had discovered that Esther was the great-granddaughter of Refet, the Turkish guard who had accompanied Harold Swinton

(Leonora and Freddie's father) back to England in 1881. That was the year Alexandre and the others had become vampires. Esther and Morris had known about the vampires long before Maddy and Ben ever had. It was a secret their family had been entrusted with for over a century, along with the care of Marchwood House.

But none of them mentioned to her that Madison was missing.

Esther's gaze went straight to Ben.

'You look like you could do with some food and some sleep, young man.' Then she faced the vampires. 'It's not good for him, keeping him up all night like this. He needs a proper night's sleep. He's a growing lad. Come upstairs. I'll make you a nice bowl of soup and then you can go and have a lie-down.'

Ben looked as though he might cry.

'And I thought at least *you'd* know better,' she said to Isobel. Esther put her arm around Ben and began to lead him out of the room. 'Oh, nearly forgot. This came for you, Alexandre.' She handed him a white envelope with his name handwritten on the front.

'It's been hand-delivered,' he said. 'I'll bet it's from Blythe.'

'That solicitor?' Esther said.

'Did you see anyone dropping it off?'

'No, it was on the doormat this morning.'

Alexandre growled. 'If only I could get out of here, I'd be able to catch up with whoever delivered it.' He ripped open the envelope.

'Has something happened?' Esther asked.

'What does it say?' Ben walked over to Alex and ripped the paper out of his hand. He began to read:

If you wish Madison to survive, the five of you must return to Cappadocia to the underground city. You must be there after sunset on the shortest day or she will die.

'What's happened?' Esther asked. 'Is Maddy in trouble?'

'No!' Ben shouted. He punched the door and then bent his head in pain and brought his fist up to his mouth.

Alexandre felt anger and terror sweep through his body. Everything was disintegrating. Madison was missing, her life in danger. She might be hurt. She would definitely be scared, even though she would never admit it. And now his family was also going to be put in danger. Why was this happening? Why couldn't they be left in peace? He didn't want to harm anybody. All he wanted was to live his life. He felt so caged in right now. He needed to run, to shout, to feed. Alexandre understood why Ben had punched the door. He wanted to destroy the whole house.

Everyone began talking at once.

'Quiet, everyone! Please,' Alexandre said. 'Esther, did either you or Morris hear a car coming up the drive? Are you sure you didn't see who delivered the letter?'

'No. I didn't see anything. Like I said, all I saw was the envelope on the doormat.'

'We need to get some security cameras fitted,' said Ben.

'Good idea, but a bit late now,' said Alexandre. 'So if they didn't come by car, they must've come on foot and it would've taken them at least fifteen minutes to walk across the grounds. Esther, maybe you and Morris should drive around and see if you can find who dropped that letter off.'

'Yes,' she replied. 'We'd better be quick before they disappear. Ben, you need some ice on that fist.'

'I'll come with you, Esther,' Ben said.

'No, I don't think...' Esther started to reply.

'Yes,' Alexandre interrupted. 'That's a good idea. Take your mountain bike and scour the grounds. But don't engage the person. Just follow them, see where they go. Are you all right to ride... with your hand?'

'I'll be fine,' Ben replied. 'I'll ice it first.'

'Go quickly.'

Ben returned the note to Alexandre and left with Esther.

'He's just a boy,' Leonora said. 'You should not have sent him.'

'He's fourteen, not that much younger than our human ages, Leonora,' Isobel said.

Alexandre raised his eyebrows at his usually overcautious sister.

'What?' Isobel replied. 'It's true. We can't treat him like a weak child. He's been through too much with us.'

'Fine,' replied Leonora.

'But I cannot go back to Cappadocia,' Isobel said, her blue eyes suddenly wide with fear, 'to that underground place. I just cannot.'

'Don't worry, Belle. We'll sort this out before it comes to that.'

'How?' she replied, her voice becoming shrill.

'I thought Harold and Refet destroyed the entrances to the underground city,' Freddie said.

'They did, according to Harold's journal,' Alexandre replied. 'But we know Hamilton Blythe found a way down there – they found the Cappadocian vampires, didn't they?'

'So what are we supposed to do now?' Jacques said. 'We can't just sit around like nothing's happened. This daylight thing sucks.'

'Jacques,' said Isobel. 'Must you speak like that? But I do agree with you. It is truly frustrating.'

'We should go online and find Blythe's house,' Freddie said. 'That man needs to be stopped.'

'Yes,' said Alexandre. 'Yes, he does. And that is just what we shall do.'

Ben's fist throbbed as he hopped onto his mountain bike, but he barely registered the pain. Esther had put a small bag of frozen peas inside one of his gloves to bring the swelling down. She hadn't asked how he'd done it, and he was glad not to have to explain how he'd punched the door in fear and frustration. Which way should he go? He should probably head down to the woods. If *he* was going to sneak into Marchwood, that was where he'd do it. He pushed off and headed across the front lawn to the meadow beyond.

Maddy. She was all he had. Sure, Freddie and Leonora were his ancestors, so they were technically family. But they weren't like Maddy. Freddie was awesome, like a cool vampire cousin or something, and Leonora was all right, a bit serious and boring, but all right. But Maddy had always been there for him. She'd lay down her life for him and he would do the same for her. She was his sister, his mother and his father all rolled into one, and he wouldn't let anything happen to her. He pedalled faster, his mind creating unwanted scenarios which he tried to block out. If he could catch this person who'd left that terrible note, then he could get Maddy back. His eyes watered and he brushed a gloved hand across his face. Stupid cold wind.

Within minutes, Ben had reached the woods. He rode along the perimeter, peering into the leafless gloom. There was no movement aside from the shiver of branches and the occasional startled bird. He turned his bike and entered the woods, weaving expertly through the trees, hopping over tree stumps and constantly scanning for any sign of a person. He wished he had the vampires' heightened senses. If they were here, they would've caught up with the person already. Maybe he should get a dog. A dog would come in very handy right about now.

Even as Ben searched, he realised it was useless. Whoever had delivered the note was probably long gone and, even if they were still in the grounds, there were acres and acres to cover. It was a waste of time. He felt a spurt of anger at the futility of his search and suddenly skidded to a halt, flinging his bike against a tree. It lay twisted on the ground, one wheel spinning in the air. Ben stood there for a moment, breathing hard. Then he sank down onto the frosty ground and wept.

Winston Blythe's home address was not so easy to come by. They had been searching online, but had so far come up blank. If only night would fall so Alexandre could travel to London and track him down the old-fashioned way. He had no need of sleep, but these interminable minutes of daylight ticked by at a snail's pace. And he would also need to feed soon.

What had that note said? He reached into his pocket and pulled out the crumpled piece of paper. It said they were to arrive there on *the shortest day* – that was December 21st. Today was December 15th. That gave them six days to get her back. Well, he did not intend to wait six days, he intended to find her tonight and then those who were responsible would pay. He balled up the note and put it back in his pocket. Where was Ben? Maybe he had found the person who delivered the note or perhaps Esther and Morris had had some luck. It was so infuriating having to wait around for others. He felt a hand on his shoulder.

'Be calm, brother,' Isobel murmured. 'We will find her. You know we will.'

'There cannot be any other outcome,' Alexandre replied.

'Have you had any luck locating Blythe's address?'

Alexandre shook his head.

'Leonora is still looking online. If anyone can find it, it's her. She has a knack for this modern technology.'

'Who would have thought it,' Freddie said. 'My sister, the twenty-first-century techie.'

'Well, I haven't had much luck so far.' Leonora lifted her

head from her laptop and Alexandre thought for the hundredth time how uncanny the resemblance between her and Madison. The same fair skin, only Maddy had freckles; the same pale blue eyes, only Maddy's sparkled with humour whereas Leonora's glittered with... disdain. She hadn't always been so cold. He felt sorry for her. She was a good person, but she wasn't easy to like.

'There's nothing on Blythe that I can see,' she said. 'Sorry.'

'Then keep looking,' Alexandre said.

Leonora scowled at him, then sighed and carried on. Alexandre felt bad for snapping, but he didn't apologise. She would only glare at him if he did.

He'd had a hard time adjusting to becoming a vampire. Last year, when he had awoken to this new century, his vampire family had still had the sleeping sickness. He had been alone and bewildered, trapped in this strange new era where nothing was familiar. Madison had been his only bright spot. She had made him laugh, had teased him out of his black humours and comforted him when it all became too much. With her help, he had almost reconciled himself to living for an eternity, but to live for an eternity without her would not be possible. A life without Maddy would be no life at all.

For a moment, a choking panic gripped his chest. He sat down heavily in one of the armchairs and stared glassily at his knees. He felt as though he was sliding into the deepest blackest hole in the universe, deeper than the caverns in Cappadocia, deeper than the oceans, blacker than any moonless night. He tried to steady his breathing. As soon as night fell he would claw his way out of here and then nothing would prevent him from getting her back. Heaven help the people who had made him feel this way, for he would show them no mercy.

CHAPTER SEVEN

CAPPADOCIA, AD 571

She lay face down in the dirt. The dry red soil filled her nostrils and she tasted metal and chalk on her tongue. She felt it caked beneath her fingernails and baked into every pore of her dried-out body. How long had she been lying like this? Her eyelids scraped open a fraction, to snap back shut immediately against a sun that scorched. She dare not try to swallow for she knew her throat was beyond parched. It was a brittle dried-up cavern and to swallow was to invite a pain that she wasn't yet strong enough to bear. If only dark unconsciousness would consume her again; anything but this unyielding, cruel light.

She tried to stop thinking, to go back to oblivion, but something fluttered and twittered deep inside. Something insisted that she face the pain and humiliation. That she draw on her pitiable reserve of strength and not give in to easy surrender – it was the voice of her mother, telling her to be strong. To survive.

There was a single drop of moisture left in her body and Aelia could feel it slowly evaporating into the thirsty air. Was this the third day or the fourth? She wished never to see another, but now here was that thin, insistent voice again, telling her something completely different. Willing her to face the unfaceable. *Get up, move, do something*, it said. *Don't give up. Death will not come quickly, you have time. Death is too busy to claim you this day. Life is yours for the taking if you want it. But you have to try.*

Lying in the silent heat, she only wanted to block out everything. But the pain and the fear were oozing and seeping, slow and unrelenting through her clogged veins. Had she really been expelled from her home?

They had covered her eyes with a cloth, taken her out of the village and left her in a place she did not know. There had been no familiar landmarks and no stream to quench her thirst. Only barren rock, dry red earth and hot sun. By day, she had been terrified that she would run into bandits, and by night, the thought of ghouls and demons had tormented her mind. But after a couple of days all alone, she prayed she might see someone, anyone who could help to find her way out of the unending wilderness. She walked until she could go no further. And now here she lay. Finished.

'My dear, the vultures are circling. Are you getting up, or do you fancy yourself a banquet for the birds?' Aelia heard a woman's raspy voice, as if in a dream. Yet, it was like no dream she'd had before.

'My dear? Can you hear me?'

She felt her shoulder being roughly prodded by something sharp and it hurt – a separate kind of hurt to the other overwhelming ache she felt throughout the rest of her body. She groaned.

'Ahh, alive!' The woman chuckled. 'My lucky day. Come along, my dear, get up. You'll come with me. No need to thank me today, you can do that later.'

Aelia turned her head and forced her eyes to open. She saw a dark shape looming and gradually a pale wrinkled face came into focus. The face wore a smile, but the smile was not kindly. It was... mocking. Aelia closed her eyes again.

'Up, up. Get up,' the woman said. 'I saw you open your eyes. It's no good pretending to be dead. Come on.'

Aelia felt more sharp stabs of pain on her back and shoulder. She gasped and opened her eyes again. The woman was prodding her with a wooden cane.

'Please stop,' Aelia croaked. 'You're hurting me.'

'Good, you can talk. Now, get up, my dear, before I lose my patience.'

Aelia didn't know how she did it, but she managed to struggle to her knees and then to her feet. Her head throbbed and her throat felt as though it was being stabbed with tiny little needles as the thirst hit once again.

'Water. Please.'

'Come with me and I'll see what I can do.'

The old woman limped ahead, using her wooden cane to walk. Aelia staggered in her wake, almost wishing she'd stayed on the ground to let the earth take her.

They walked for a good long while. The old woman did not offer to help her, nor did she even turn around to see how she was. But Aelia kept following regardless. Vegetation appeared around them. They passed by some low scrubby bushes and a couple of hunched trees. Clumps of plants dotted the ground and a sudden breeze cooled Aelia's cheek for a blissful moment, before melting into the heat again.

In the distance, Aelia saw a dark shimmering hill and, as they drew nearer, it rose up as a steep, grey rock face. The woman walked right up to the jagged wall and sidestepped into it before disappearing from view as if by magic. Aelia followed, too tired to be puzzled. As she came closer, she saw there was a simple explanation – an outcrop in front of the rock face concealed a narrow gap. The old woman had entered a hidden cave. Aelia stopped for a second and then followed her inside, away from the relentless sun and into the cool gloom.

It was a relief to be out of the sun's glare, but Aelia felt so weak and thirsty, she barely registered her surroundings. All she saw was darkness and all she heard were their hushed slow footsteps. Suddenly, she felt a claw-like grip on her arm.

'Sit here,' the woman squawked at her. She pulled Aelia down onto a chair-like boulder before shuffling off into the darkness.

Aelia felt no curiosity; only the need to close her eyes and block out the knives of thirst in her throat. She was going to die here in the darkness. This was the end. Seconds later she felt a cold sting of water trickle down her lips and chin.

'You're no good to me dead,' the woman cackled, pressing an earthenware cup into Aelia's hands.

Aelia ignored the woman's words and concentrated on the cool liquid. Maybe she wasn't going to die after all.

CHAPTER EIGHT

PRESENT DAY

Ben returned to the house at midday. Esther and Morris were already there, sitting in the kitchen sipping tea. None of them had seen anyone who might have been the deliverer of the mysterious note. Esther insisted that Ben eat something and then go to bed.

'You'll be needed later, and you won't be any good to anyone if you don't get some rest. Don't worry, I'll go down and tell the others we've had no luck.'

Ben glared at his empty bowl and dragged himself up the stairs to bed. He was exhausted, but it felt wrong sleeping while Maddy was missing. He crawled under the bed-covers in his clothes and closed his eyes. He meant to lie there and think about what they should do. But sleep came for him straight away.

The afternoon passed uneventfully and all Alexandre and the others could do was to wait for night to fall. Luckily it arrived shortly after 4.30 p.m. and Alexandre was straight out of the door with Jacques, Leonora and Freddie close behind. Isobel was to stay at the house with Ben and Esther. Ben wouldn't like it, but he was still asleep and they had all decided not to wake him.

Alexandre took in a lungful of night air and headed over to his motorbike, a BMW S1000RR. Morris had topped up the fuel tank and parked it on the driveway ready to go. Alex would be faster without it, but once he found Madison, he might need the transport to get her away quickly. The caretaker was standing next to the bike and it looked like he wanted to speak to Alex. Alexandre didn't want to waste a single second chatting, so he nodded to Morris, making straight for the bike. However, the caretaker had already started speaking.

'I'll ask around town this evening. See if anyone's seen her. You never know.'

'Thanks, Morris. That would be great.'

'I'll speak to 'em down at the Bell. Anything strange happens round here, they'll know about it.' Morris was referring to his regular haunt, the Old Bell. Nowadays it was a luxury hotel, but it had once been a normal pub where Morris and his friends would sip a pint of bitter and have a chat. The décor and prices had changed dramatically over the last thirty years, but Morris and his cronies had carried on frequenting the place, nonetheless.

'Let me know how you get on,' Alex said, not really listening to the caretaker and itching to be off. He didn't want any undue police attention, so he wore his leathers and crash helmet like a good little human, jumped on his bike and sped off. The others would follow in Leonora's silver Audi RS6 – comfortable but fast.

As he rode, Alexandre tried not to think, but everything flashed through his mind at once. He ripped up the miles, avoiding the cop cars and speed cameras, taking the bike as fast as it would allow, weaving in and out of the traffic in a blur of shiny noise.

During their last fateful meeting, Blythe had told him that

his ancient vampire clients wanted him and the other 'fledgling' vampires dead. But why? Were they really that much of a threat? Was this why they were being summoned? To be killed? He would gladly give his own life for Madison's, but he could not give up the lives of his siblings, or Freddie's or Leonora's.

In less than an hour, he hit London and came to a halt outside the offices of Hamilton Blythe, in the affluent area of Marylebone. The others would have traffic to contend with. They could call him when they arrived, but he didn't plan on waiting around. He would manage Blythe himself. They knew it was a risk going into his offices after the last time. But what choice did they have? They had still found no home address for that wily lawyer.

Alexandre swung his long legs off the bike and removed his crash helmet. Then he flexed his fingers and combed them through his hair as he stared up at the huge building in front of him. The white mansion block was the epitome of respectability. No one would have guessed that beneath its traditional façade lay a state-of-the-art underground facility dedicated to reviving dormant vampires as well as destroying them. But Alexandre didn't plan on going down there. All he needed to do was discover Winston Blythe's address and he would find that easily enough, even if it meant coercing the information from someone.

The offices were closed, but Alex didn't have long to wonder what to do as, within a couple of minutes, the black painted front door swung open and two smartly dressed women emerged. Alexandre slipped past them, like a cool breeze. One of the women shivered and frowned, but at that moment her colleague said something funny and she laughed, dismissing the shadow she thought she'd seen from the corner of her eye.

Once inside the building, Alexandre scanned each room, until he reached the fourth floor where the partners' offices were situated. Once he had Blythe's address he would be done

here. And then he caught a familiar scent – an odour of fake
respectability and greed that he remembered from before. Well,
it was actually the odour of a certain cologne, but the smell
conjured up the man – Blythe.

A door lay ahead of him and beyond the door sat Winston
Blythe. Alexandre had to get himself under control or he might
just tear this man limb from limb before he had a chance to find
out where Madison had been taken. He needed to extract every
last piece of information out of the man and that would require
a more composed Alexandre than the one currently snarling in
the wood-panelled hallway. He breathed in through his nose
and out through his mouth, sliding his fangs back behind his lips
with great difficulty as he collected himself, preparing to deal
with this traitorous snake.

A few seconds later, he stood in front of a walnut desk
staring at the lawyer's bent head. He was handwriting a letter
and hadn't yet noticed Alexandre. The room was large and
opulent, all polished wood, leather and glass – a gentleman's
office.

'Writing another of your mysterious notes I see,' Alexandre
said softly.

Blythe looked up, shocked for a second before hastily
composing his craggy, but handsome features. His white hair
had thinned somewhat since their last dramatic encounter, and
Alexandre hoped he might have had something to do with that.

'Alexandre, my boy. I've been expecting you. Do sit down,
won't you.'

'I prefer to stand and I am not "your boy".'

'Just a figure of speech. No offence meant, I'm sure.' Blythe
set his pen down on the desk.

'What game are you up to this time?' Alexandre asked.

'No game. I'm merely helping to move things along. After
our last encounter, you surely can't have thought that would be
it. No, alas, there are people far more powerful than you or I

and they have deemed that things must be brought to a conclusion.'

'Things?'

'Yes. Such as the question mark hanging over you and the other Marchwood vampires. You are inconvenient, that's all. You must go to Cappadocia and be accounted for.'

'Accounted for. Why?'

'It is not for me to know the reason why. I am but a humble servant in all this. A servant to carry out orders and document history.'

'A servant?' Alexandre gave a short laugh. 'That is ridiculous! You may try to deny any responsibility, but you are more than a servant; you are a facilitator of evil. A parasite.'

'That is a little harsh, but I can see why you might think that. Your view is limited. You look at the world through a sliver of glass instead of a wide-angle lens. Alexandre, you are a tiger cub nipping at the heels of kings. They do not like it. They do not care about your good heart or your lack of ambition. They will not take the risk. They know you have eternity to change your character from passive to aggressive. They want you dealt with *now*.'

'But that is nonsense. I do not nip at anybody's heels.'

'Nonsense to you maybe, but it is the nature of things.'

'Well then "things" will have to change.'

'Things already have changed.'

Alexandre opened his hands in a gesture asking for explanation.

'My clients, my fourteenth-, fifteenth- and sixteenth-century clients, are tigers; they are kings. But they have recently discovered an Emperor.'

'Stop talking in riddles. For a "servant", you have too great a liking for the dramatic. Speak plainly for once.'

'Very well.' Blythe paused and Alexandre had to restrain himself from leaping across the desk and choking the words out of him. Eventually, the solicitor continued. 'Your Cappadocian vampire is awake. He is over two thousand years old, the most powerful being ever to walk this earth, and he demands obedience.'

Alexandre went cold at the old man's words. His worst fears had been realised – the Cappadocian vampire was behind this.

Blythe continued, 'The kings have bent their knees to him. Now he is rounding up the princes.'

Alexandre's mouth hung open. He recalled the under-ground city where he had been turned, more than one hundred years earlier. He pictured the dead, kohl-rimmed eyes of this so-called Emperor who had torn into his flesh and stripped him of his mortality. And then he remembered the opportunity he had missed earlier this year when he'd stumbled across the Cappadocian's unconscious form but had not the foresight to destroy him. Now it was too late. The creature had captured Madison. It held her life and their happiness in the palm of its hand and was preparing to make a fist.

Alexandre realised that Winston Blythe had not been lying when he said he was nothing more than a servant, that he had no real power or influence. The rage he felt towards Blythe was dissipating, turning into a creeping despair. The most Alexandre could hope for was that Blythe might know where Maddy was being held.

'Where is she?' he whispered.

'You know where she is, Alexandre.'

And he realised he did know. He had known all along that she would be under the ground, deep in the belly of the Cappadocian earth. In the place he had prayed he need never return to. Coming to London had been a fruitless exercise. Madison was already out of his reach.

'I should kill you for your part in this,' Alexandre said without conviction.

'But you won't.'

'No.'

They appraised each other for a moment or two, a ticking clock the only sound in the room.

'Do you even possess an opinion about what's going on?' Alexandre asked. He still couldn't determine Blythe's true character. Was he ambitious? Greedy? Weak? What was his true agenda?

'I'm not paid to have an opinion. Let's just say I enjoy being a part of this secret history. It thrills me.'

'So, you are a voyeur.'

'A documenter of important historical events,' Blythe replied with a self-satisfied smile.

'A coward.'

'I like you, Alexandre, but you're too judgmental. You have the righteousness and arrogance of youth. Maybe I'll seek out your company in a century or two.'

Alexandre paused at Blythe's last sentence. Could he really mean...

'Don't look so surprised, Alexandre. They have made me a promise.'

'A promise?'

'Yes.'

'You mean... to be turned?'

Blythe nodded.

Alexandre stared at Blythe for a moment and then he laughed. 'If you believe that, you're more of a fool than I thought. They will not turn you.'

'I have their word, but more than that, I have a legally binding contract.'

Alexandre laughed again. 'You think the law means anything to an immortal? To a cold-blooded killer? Mr Blythe, even *you* do not respect the law.'

'It does not matter what you believe. It is what I believe that counts and I believe they will keep their promise.'

'And you would actually choose to be like this?' Alexandre tapped his own chest.

'Who wouldn't want to live forever?'

'Me. I would never choose this. Never.'

'I don't believe you. You are thriving as a vampire. You love the power it affords you.'

'No!'

'Tell me, what was your life like before you were turned? Was it exciting? Were you fulfilled?'

Alexandre tried to banish the traitorous memories of his human frustrations, of his feelings of inadequacy and boredom.

Blythe smiled. 'You'd better go. You have a plane to catch.'

Alexandre glared at the smug lawyer.

'All this is nothing personal. You know that,' Blythe added, getting to his feet. 'I meant it when I said I liked you.'

'That is not something to make me happy. You're a vain old fool,' Alexandre growled.

'Goodbye, Alexandre. Good luck. I sincerely hope you make the right decision. A little knee-bending is not the end of the world you know.'

Alexandre turned and left the room, unable to listen to the man any longer. As he hurried down the stairs, he could sense the others in the street below. They had just pulled up outside the offices. He would fill them in and then they would have to plan their strategy well. He would not be drawn into ancient vampire politics; it was nothing to do with him. He and his family must be able to live freely, *peacefully*, not governed by barbaric laws at odds with his own morality. Bending the knee was one thing, but he wasn't stupid, he knew it wouldn't end there. These creatures were devoid of humanity. There was no reasoning with them, no negotiating or bargaining. They would require him to submit. This eternal life would never be his own again.

There was only one option – the Emperor had to die.

CHAPTER NINE

CAPPADOCIA, AD 571

Some days, Aelia thought her old life must have been a dream. Everything was so different now, here with Widow Maleina. But for all her sharp words and harsh looks, the old woman wasn't all that bad. There was no affection, no softness, nor even politeness, but neither was she deliberately cruel. Aelia wasn't a prisoner, she was free to leave at any time, but then where would she go? She was an outcast and knew no one else outside her village. The widow had asked her no personal questions and for that Aelia was grateful. It would be too humiliating and upsetting to have to recount everything. Equally, the widow offered up no information about herself.

A rhythm had evolved in their daily lives. It was Aelia's job to sweep their dwelling and keep it clean and she would also wash their garments every week. The cave had its own underground spring and so trips to and from the distant river were unnecessary. Aelia missed the communal ritual of fetching water, but there were other opportunities to taste a little freedom. She would spend hours gathering firewood and sometimes she hiked the eight-mile round trip to shop in the markets. Something else she enjoyed doing was collecting the wild herbs and roots which the old woman used in her medicines. For Widow Maleina was a healer.

Aelia had a basic knowledge of plants, but nothing like the wealth of information the old woman had begun to share with her. Every morning, before breakfast, they went out early to gather ingredients. Aelia was gradually learning how to cool fevers and soothe headaches; how to clean wounds, treat snake bites and even knit broken bones.

Visitors came to the cave every day and paid Widow Maleina to cure them of their sicknesses. At first, Aelia was the subject of scrutiny as each visitor eyed her with undisguised curiosity.

'My niece,' the widow barked at each of them until the stares grew less intense.

Inevitably, Aelia's thoughts often turned towards the family and friends she had left behind. She hoped her parents had forgiven her and she prayed her sisters had not been tainted by the shameful shadow she had cast over them. The other person she thought about was Lysus.

Aelia had been surprised by her feelings. She had thought she would be devastated by his casual betrayal. She had expected to sob and wail and be heartbroken at his treatment of her. But for him to throw that stone was the final insult. She had looked up to him, trusted him and had never doubted his word. Growing up, she had heard all the stories of grand love and how painful it can be to experience longing and rejection. But, after the initial shock, all Aelia felt towards Lysus was cold hatred. She cringed when she remembered how willingly she had followed him, like a trusting puppy. She had been weak-willed and gullible. How had she let him make such a fool of her? She had allowed him to destroy her life and ruin her family's good name. One day he would feel her anger. One day he would pay.

Over the course of several weeks, Aelia became aware of the rumours. She overheard fragments of conversation in the market place and she was puzzled by odd questions from some of Widow Maleina's patients. They were all talking about barbarians. About an invasion of some sort.

One evening, as they sat cross-legged on the floor finishing their supper, Aelia plucked up the courage to ask the widow about it.

'Is it true?' Aelia asked.

'What?' the widow snapped. 'Speak clearly or don't speak at all.'

Aelia raised her voice. 'Is it true the barbarians are coming? Everyone is talking about it. They're saying that—'

'Those gossips are all fools,' Widow Maleina interrupted. 'And so are you if you believe such rubbish.'

'So why would they say it?'

'Fetch me some more water.'

Aelia picked up the widow's cup and hurried over to the spring at the back of the cave. She dipped in the vessel and scooped up some of the crystal-clear liquid, hoping this wasn't going to be the end of the conversation. She desperately wanted to know what was going on. She returned to see the widow mopping up her food with a scrap of flatbread. Aelia set the cup on the floor, unsure whether to sit back down or retire to her place at the back of the cave.

'Stop looming,' the widow said. 'Sit down. You're irritating me.'

Aelia did as she was bid, pleased she wasn't being sent to bed yet.

'Something bad is coming,' the widow said. 'Something we haven't seen for centuries. It's happening again.'

Aelia felt a chill across her shoulders.

'I saved your life once before, my dear, and it seems I shall save you twice.'

'Is it the invaders?' Aelia asked.

'I already told you, that's nonsense. Weren't you listening? You can be so dim-witted sometimes. Perhaps your brain was damaged when I found you on the ground that day.'

Aelia bit her lip and lowered her head, ignoring her rudeness. It was like the woman didn't know how to be any other way. She spoke in the same manner to her patients and they didn't pay any mind to it either. So, if not invaders, then what? What was Widow Maleina talking about? Maybe she was mad. But Aelia didn't think so. In her opinion, the woman was sharp as a crow's beak.

'What is coming, then?' Aelia asked. 'If not barbarians, then what is it that is so terrible?'

The widow eyed Aelia for a moment. 'Demons.'

So she *was* mad after all.

'You can doubt me, but it won't change the fact,' the widow replied. 'Demons are among us and soon there will be more. Your family will perish along with everyone else.'

'My family will perish?'

'I wouldn't have thought you'd be worried. They cast you out, did they not?'

'How do you know about that? Anyway, it wasn't my family who cast me out, it was the Praetor.'

'Doesn't matter. They didn't prevent it. They didn't come with you to make sure you were all right. They watched as you were sent out into the wilderness to die.'

The widow's words stung.

'That's not true. My mother saved me from death.' The thought of her mother squeezed Aelia's heart, made her eyes prickle with emotions she hadn't allowed herself to feel for a long while.

'Pssht.' The widow waved her hand to dismiss Aelia's protests. 'It's not important. What is important is that we are safe here. Everyone else is doomed. They will all die.'

'What!' Aelia got to her feet. 'How? Why will they die?'

'You're making me tired with all of your questions. I thought you were a good girl, a quiet girl. I don't want all this questioning. You want shelter here? Or you want to take your chances with the demons?'

Aelia took a breath. 'I'm sorry. I didn't mean to—'

'I am tired now,' Widow Maleina said. 'All this chatter. I don't like it.' She stood and limped across to her sleeping quarters.

Aelia cleared away the supper things and retreated to her corner of the cave. None of the widow's words made any sense. It must be nonsense. So why did she have such an uneasy feeling? Why did she believe every word the widow said?

CHAPTER TEN

PRESENT DAY

Madison shivered and reached for the quilt. She needed to pull it up to her chin to get warm. Where was the stupid thing? But as she felt around, she realised there *was* no quilt, there were no covers at all. And what was that smell? The air smelt damp and musty... horrible. And then she remembered.

She didn't want to open her eyes for fear of what she might see, but they opened anyway. The bed she lay on was narrow and covered in a grubby white sheet. Sitting up, she took in her surroundings and her stomach lurched. A concrete floor, bare stained walls, no windows and a flickering, whining strip light. The room was small with two doors. Her head pounded and her mouth tasted disgusting, like six-month-old milk. Her wrists and ankles hurt where they had been tied together. She gave them a rub and winced as she saw the red raw flesh.

Sliding off the bed, Maddy staggered across the three feet required to reach the nearest door. It rattled in its hinges as she tried the handle – locked. She gave the base of the door a half-hearted kick before heading over to the second door. This handle creaked and the door opened inwards to darkness. Maddy patted the wall until she found the light switch.

Another strip light buzzed on, illuminating a sink, a toilet and a blackened shower head protruding from the ceiling. Everything was caked in layers of grime, rust and other stuff which she'd rather not think about. Shallow pools of liquid lay on the floor. She wrinkled her nose, turned off the light and closed the door. Where the hell was she?

She strode across to the locked door and rattled it again, harder than before.

'Hey!' Her fist pounded against the peeling paintwork. 'Open the door! Hey! Is anyone out there?'

She put her ear to the door and listened hard but all she heard was her own ragged breathing. No sound came from outside. Either there was no one there, or they were ignoring her. Well, they couldn't ignore her forever, could they? They had brought her here for a reason and she'd probably find out what it was soon enough. Maddy shivered. She was still wearing the same boots, jeans and sweater she had on at the ice rink, but it was freezing in here. Scanning the room, she spied a dark shape on the floor near the end of the bed. Her parka. She picked it up and shrugged it on, then checked for her mittens, but the pockets were empty. Never mind. The coat was toasty and she zipped it up to her chin and shoved her hands back into her pockets.

Suddenly, the light spluttered and went out. Darkness. Silence. Maddy's skin crawled and fear clutched at her belly. She took a breath and told herself that whoever had taken her hadn't harmed her. They obviously wanted her alive. For now, at least. She shuffled over to the low bed, climbed on and brought her knees up to her chest, hugging them in tight to her body.

Alex would find her soon and then her captors would be sorry. She wouldn't like to be them when he arrived. She remembered what Alex had done to that slimy solicitor, Vasey-Smith, when he'd held her at gunpoint – Alex had broken his neck with a flick of his wrist. She wished he'd hurry up and find her now because she was beginning to freak out and this place was rank. She was cold, hungry and felt so grotty that the vain part of her almost didn't want Alex to come and see her like this with her hair all greasy and her gross breath.

Images of warm bubble baths, crisp cotton duvets and tooth-paste floated into her head, followed by the picture of one of Esther's home-cooked roast dinners with mountains of crispy potatoes and treacle tart for pudding. Her stomach gurgled and she banished the image from her mind. No, she couldn't waste time wishing for the impossible; she needed to work out how she was going to get out of here. Part of her brain was telling her to crumple down onto the bed and sob her eyes out, but Maddy refused to give in to it. She needed to be strong and clear-headed; she couldn't dissolve into tears.

A whirring noise broke the silence, followed by a crackle and a pop and then the humming sound of the strip light flared into life again. Once more, Madison was forced to take in her depressing surroundings and she decided she would have preferred to remain in darkness.

Maddy dozed on the bed, leaning back against the wall. Sometime later, she didn't know how long, she was startled awake by a jingling sound. Maddy opened her eyes and imme-diately sat upright. It was dark. The power must have gone again. Was that the sound of the door opening? Of someone entering the room? Maddy's heart began to race.

'Hey,' she croaked. 'Who's there? Why am I here?'

The light flickered on and off a couple of times illuminating a slim girl just a little taller than Maddy – maybe 5'3 or 5'4. She wore her hair in a French plait.

The girl didn't look at her. She put something down on the end of the bed and made to leave. The room plunged back into darkness.

'Hey, wait a minute. Where are you going? You have to help me.'

The girl ignored Maddy, her dim outline heading towards the door. Still groggy with sleep, Maddy jumped off the bed and stumbled across the room.

'Hey! I'm talking to you. Why have you got me locked up? Who are you?'

But the girl had left the room. Maddy groped around for the door handle and pulled, but she wasn't quick enough. The girl had already locked the door.

The generator kicked in and the strip light came on properly.

'Oh yes, *now* the light decides to stay on.' Madison could've screamed. How had she allowed herself to miss such a perfect opportunity for escape? She could've kicked that girl's ass easily and bolted out of the door. What a total idiot. She didn't even think the girl had any kind of weapon and all Maddy had done was gawp uselessly at her.

Next time she'd be totally prepared, as long as there *was* a next time. But she knew it wouldn't be as easy as all that. There had to be more people outside the door somewhere. Back at Gloucester Cathedral there'd been several men in that van. That evening at the skating rink seemed like weeks ago. But it couldn't have been more than a day or two. The others must be worried sick. Poor Ben, he'd be going crazy by now.

Maddy looked at the bed: the girl had left a bottle of water and a plate with a couple of slices of bread and a pear. Not exactly one of Esther's roast dinners, but she was starving and it looked pretty good to her. Soon the plate was empty and Maddy felt hungrier than ever. She sipped at the water and thought about how she could overpower the girl. Her eyes rested on the plate. It was cheap pottery and should break easily enough. She walked into the vile bathroom and turned on the light. Then she closed the door behind her.

Tentatively, Maddy banged the plate on the chipped tile floor. It didn't break, so she brought it down a little heavier. It was vital it didn't smash into tiny pieces. She wanted a pointed shard which she could use as a weapon. This time, the plate broke in half. She held one of the pieces and banged it against the wall. Part of it dropped on the floor and shattered, but Maddy was left holding a large triangular piece which would be perfect. She allowed herself a grim smile.

Maddy had been in a few scraps before but never anything like this. Well, not unless you included the time she'd tried to kill Alexandre with a pickaxe. But that was before she knew him. She wasn't going to try and kill the girl anyway; she would just try to incapacitate her. Should she stab her in the arm or the leg? The eye would be good, but she didn't think she had the stomach to do it. She'd better decide quickly and decide well, because this might be the only chance she'd get to escape.

They had arranged to transport themselves to Turkey in packing crates. Not a particularly glamorous or comfortable way to travel, but there wasn't enough time to arrange passports and this way it meant they could travel safely by day. As usual, they were all gathered in the large living area of their beautifully furnished basement where no sunlight could reach them. It was late morning and the marble mantel clock showed twenty past eleven.

'But how will we ensure the aeroplane people will not open the crates? What if one of them opens a crate in daylight?' Isobel said.

'They won't open them,' Alexandre replied.

'But how do you know?'

'Easy,' Ben said. 'Just mark the crates: "Light-Sensitive Artwork – Do Not Open in Daylight".'

Jacques grinned. 'Would that work? It sounds a little strange to me.'

'We did it at school,' Ben explained. 'Light damage is called "photochemical deterioration". That's why they don't let you use flash photography in art galleries.'

'Interesting,' said Leonora. 'Do you think that's what happens to us? Photochemical deterioration? Maybe vampires have an extreme version of this condition?'

'Maybe,' Ben said. 'Let me see if I can remember what our teacher said...' He screwed up his face in concentration. 'Light energy is absorbed by the molecules of an object and this can start a chemical reaction. Each molecule needs a certain amount of energy to begin a chemical reaction with other molecules. It's called something like activation energy. Different types of molecules have different activation energies. Maybe a vampire's activation energy is really weak or something.'

'Wow, Ben. You're really quite clever,' Jacques said.

'Yes,' Freddie agreed. 'That is very enlightening.'

'Don't sound so surprised,' Ben said, flushing under their admiring stares.

'So will this labelling of the crates work?' Isobel said.

'I'm pretty sure it will,' Ben said. 'Just make sure you write it in big letters.'

'I'm nervous,' Isobel said. 'I have horrible images of them opening my crate on the airfield. The pain of daylight is not something I ever wish to experience again.'

'We'll be fine, Isobel,' Alexandre said.

'Perhaps you should stay here, Isobel,' Leonora said. 'I'm sure we can manage.'

'No. Of course I'm coming with you. I just want to be sure we'll arrive safely.'

'So,' Ben said. 'You'll all be travelling as priceless sculptures.'

'Perfect,' Leonora replied, giving Ben a rare smile.

He basked in its unexpected glow, but his happiness was short-lived.

'And don't worry, Ben,' Freddie said. 'We will keep you informed of everything.'

'What do you mean, "keep me informed"?'

'Just what I said,' Freddie replied, a puzzled expression on his face.

Alexandre sensed trouble. 'Ben, you do understand you are staying here with Esther.'

'You are not doing this to me again,' Ben said.

'Ben, we're not doing anything to you. We've talked about this. You have no passport.'

'*You* might have talked about it, but *I* didn't.'

'The passport issue is one we cannot avoid.'

'Then I'll travel in a packing crate.'

'You'll die in a packing crate.'

'But Maddy's my sister!'

'I know. I'm sorry,' Isobel said, reaching her hand out to his face.

He jerked his head away in anger. 'You all treat me like I'm some stupid kid whose opinion doesn't matter. You went off to London without me and now you're going to Turkey without me. It's not fair. It's not—'

'Ben, Ben,' Isobel interrupted. 'It's not as though we want to leave you behind. It's just that you cannot board an aeroplane if you have no passport.'

'Why can't I just... get one?'

'There is not enough time.'

'You could drive me to London. Alex, we could go on your bike.'

'If I could, I would. But it's not as simple as that. You are only fourteen. You're a minor. We cannot manage all the paper-work in time.'

Ben stormed out of the basement, slamming the door behind him.

'He's just worried,' Isobel said. 'He's not angry with us, he's angry at the situation.'

Alexandre rubbed his sister's shoulder and they smiled sadly at each other. Jacques and Freddie stood there awkwardly and Leonora seemed oblivious, tapping away on her small blue laptop.

Back in London, Alexandre had filled them in on his conversation with Blythe. They had agreed there was no other option than to go to Cappadocia. Alexandre had offered to go alone, but they had shouted him down.

'We're all going and that's final,' Freddie had said.

Now it was two days later and they were in the Marchwood basement preparing for their imminent departure. Alexandre's eyes rested on the back of Leonora's head. Her hair was pinned up in a loose bun, tendrils escaping in wisps across her white neck. Even from the back she looked similar to Madison, but her bearing was so much stiffer, more controlled. Maddy was infinitely more relaxed than her ancestor. But they were both as strong-willed as each other.

'How is everything coming along?' he asked.

'Fine. I'm just printing out Morris's flight ticket. I'll be done in a few minutes.' They needed Morris to accompany them, to manage the crates at the other end in case of any problems, and to deal with anything that might arise during daylight hours.

'Play something for us, Isobel,' Jacques said. 'You never seem to play anything these days. I miss it.'

'You want me to play the piano?' She arched an eyebrow at her twin.

'Yes.'

'But my playing always used to irritate you.'

'I know I gave that impression,' Jacques said. 'But I wasn't entirely serious when I made those comments. I'm your brother, it's my job to annoy you.' He grinned.

'Yes, Belle,' Alexandre said. 'Play something.'

'I don't believe I've ever heard you play,' Freddie said.

'There is no time. We have too much to do,' Isobel replied.

'There is time,' Alexandre said. 'We have two hours before we leave for the airport.'

'Well, with all this encouragement, how can I refuse?' Isobel crossed the room, sat at the tapestried stool and lifted the polished piano lid. She closed her eyes and took a breath before opening them again and bringing her slim fingers down over the keys.

Alexandre heard the notes as if listening from far away. It was one of Chopin's Nocturnes. As a mortal, Isobel had always struggled with this particular piece, but now the notes floated from her fingers and Alexandre became immersed in them as if the music was swirling inside him and he was a part of the melody.

Memories of Paris flooded back to him so quickly they almost knocked him from his feet – the drawing room at home, Maman's laughter, Papa frowning and concentrating on the music, Jacques clowning around, and he, Alexandre, longing to be gone, bored and wishing he was anywhere else. If only he had savoured those rare times. He should have clung to those moments, not brushed them away like stale crumbs. Now they were over, just images in his head, memories of that vivid life, a life so close he could almost touch it. Almost...

CHAPTER ELEVEN

CAPPADOCIA, AD 574

Over the next few months, the rumours of invasion grew stronger. It was all anyone talked about, not that Aelia ever got the chance to speak to anybody. But when she was in populated areas, the atmosphere was alive with the chatter and buzz of preoccupied people. There was an urgent energy in the air, an energy made up of purpose and excitement and fear. People were preparing for the invasion, but they were not discussing weapons or defences – they were talking about digging.

'Excuse me,' Aelia said to a young slave girl, whose attention was being held by a performing dog in the market place. The little creature was selecting coins according to which emperor's face they bore. Of course, it was all a trick and anyone who attempted to outguess the dog would invariably lose his money.

The girl turned to Aelia, a look of panic on her face. 'Oh,' she said, relaxing. 'You gave me a fright. You sounded like my mistress.' She looked Aelia up and down and turned back to watch the entertainment.

'Sorry if I startled you,' Aelia said. 'I was just wondering what's going on.'

The girl reluctantly turned around again, forming an insolent question mark with her eyebrows.

'The digging...' Aelia continued.

'What digging?'

'Everyone is talking about digging up the earth.'

'You don't know about the barbarians coming? Are you simple?'

'No,' Aelia said, biting her tongue at the insult. 'I've heard about the invasion, of course I have. But why is everyone digging?'

'I can't believe you don't know.' The slave girl smirked. 'I'll tell you, but you'll have to make it worth my while.'

'I'll make it worth your while,' Aelia said, suddenly feeling angry with this sly-looking girl. 'How about this – tell me what you know and I'll make sure your mistress doesn't hear how you spent the morning idling about watching cheap entertainment, instead of getting on with your work.'

The girl scowled. 'All right. No need to be like *that*. But how do I know you're not a barbarian spy from the east?'

'Do I look like a barbarian spy from the east?'

The girl sighed. 'All right, all right.'

'The digging?' Aelia prompted.

'We're all to move down there,' the girl said.

'Move where?'

'Where d'you think? Down there, below the ground. They're moving all the villages underground. We're going to live down there so the invaders can't find us and slaughter us in our beds. Apparently, they're the most vicious race in the world. They keep their women in chains and eat babies as a delicacy.'

'They eat babies?' Aelia gasped.

The girl nodded. 'The mistress says living underground will be fun. Fun for her maybe, swanning around with all her fancy friends. Won't be much fun for the rest of us, lugging all their stuff miles under the ground. Cooped up for weeks on end until the barbarians have gone. And what if they don't go? What if they stay forever? We'll be trapped. It's a stupid plan, if you ask me.'

Aelia had to agree with the girl. It sounded like a ridiculous plan. Did that mean her old village would be moving under the ground too?

The crowd broke into raucous laughter as the dog selected the correct coin yet again and another punter lost his money.

'Have you heard of Selmea the village?' Aelia asked.

'Yeah, of course. Everyone's heard of Selmea.'

'Are they also moving underground?'

'They were the ones who came up with the idea in the first place.'

'Really?'

The slave girl glanced around and then leant closer to Aelia. 'My mistress heard that Selmea had some travellers from the east who warned them about the barbarians coming. They said we've got to get the underground villages built as quickly as possible or we'll all be slaughtered.'

'Why don't we stay and fight them?' Aelia asked.

'Apparently the capital won't arm us and there aren't enough men to fight since the plague took most of them.'

'When will the invaders get here?'

'Oh, it won't be for ages yet,' she said airily. 'They're hundreds of miles away to the east, slaughtering and conquering as they go. At the rate they're moving, it'll be a few years till they get here. That is, if no one stops them first.'

Aelia thought the whole thing sounded dubious. Why would you build an underground city because of a possible enemy that might never come?

'My mistress says it's just an excuse. A few timid old councillors are being overcautious and think it's a good idea to build the city as a precaution. And it keeps the people busy in work and out of trouble. She thinks it's all great fun. But then everything's fun for *her*. She doesn't have to do any of the work.'

'So where's the entrance to this city?' Aelia asked.

'It's a secret. We won't find out until nearer the time. The workers are being lowered down through ventilation shafts for now.

'Musa!'

Aelia saw a hairy arm thrust its way through the crowd, its hand gripping the slave girl's scrawny shoulder. She stared up to see a male slave with irritation in his eyes.

'Musa, you'll get a whipping if you don't hurry up.'

The girl rolled her eyes at Aelia and let herself be led away. Aelia stared after her, pondering on what she had heard. Widow Maleina had said rumours of the barbarians were nonsense, but how could she possibly know that? Whatever the real truth was, she hoped her family was going to be safe.

CHAPTER TWELVE

PRESENT DAY

The shard of plate felt smooth and slippery. She worried she might lose her grip on it, that it might slip and slice her own hand instead of cutting into the other girl's flesh. Maddy had decided to wait behind the door. She would have to aim for the girl's face because she wasn't sure the shard was sharp enough to pierce clothing. She would go for her cheek – that would be soft enough. Maddy touched her own cheek and wondered what it would feel like to have someone rip it apart. But she couldn't afford to think like that, couldn't be squeamish or senti-mental. The girl was holding her here against her will. If she got hurt, it would be her own fault.

She'd been waiting by the door for hours now. She crouched down to give her legs a break from standing. Out of the corner of her eye, she saw something scuttle under the bed. It was either a very small rodent or a massive spider. Maddy decided she'd rather not know which. She gave a shudder and then suddenly heard the unmistakable rattle of the lock. Here was her chance. She only hoped it was the girl and not some larger, more powerful captor. As the door opened, Maddy stood and took a step forward so that she was just at the edge of the open door. Her heart raced and she held her breath. Adjusting the pottery shard in her hand, she raised her arm up high.

Maddy saw the smooth thick braid at the back of the girl's head and as the girl turned to face her, Maddy brought her arm down swiftly, aiming directly at her cheek. There was no way she could miss. But the girl didn't even register surprise. She just stepped neatly backwards out of harm's way. *How?* It was as though she'd moved lightning fast, but in slow motion. Then realisation hit Maddy as she remembered where she'd seen that type of movement before – at home. Alexandre and the others could move in exactly the same way.

The girl was a vampire.

Maddy couldn't believe she hadn't it realised earlier. Of course she was a vampire; no human being was that beautiful. The girl had clear hazel eyes and perfectly smooth skin. Her braided hair was a thick and lustrous chestnut colour and she had the aura of a film star. Maddy must really have been half-asleep last time not to have noticed all that. Although the light had been flickering on and off, so it had been difficult to get a proper look. Her shoulders slumped as she understood there would be no escape. That it was hopeless. The girl smirked. She *actually* smirked at her. Maddy's disappointment was replaced with blazing anger.

'Why am I here?' she yelled. 'Who are you? Yeah, laugh it up – the stupid human's far too slow to catch out the vamp girl. So? What's going on?'

The girl held out her hand for the piece of plate. Maddy grudgingly passed it over. In her other hand, the girl held a plate piled high with something which smelled delicious. She dumped it on the bed before striding into the bathroom to gather up the other pieces of plate.

'This place is disgusting, you know,' Maddy said. 'And I've been starving all day. How long am I supposed to stay here?'

'I can't tell you anything,' the girl said softly. 'So there's no point asking.'

'So you do talk, then.'

There was that smirk again.

'Why am I here?'

The girl shook her head and walked past Maddy to the door.

'Hey!' Maddy tried to grab her arm.

The girl evaded her grasp and thrust her face up close to Maddy's. 'I wouldn't try that again if I were you. You know what I can do. Don't be stupid. I don't want to hurt you.'

'So what *do* you want?'

The girl gave her a strange look and left, locking the door behind her. Maddy sank onto the bed with a sigh.

'Well, that went well. Not.'

So... the girl was a vampire. She was a *vampire*. What was going on? Could Winston Blythe, that other solicitor, have something to do with this? Of course he could. But then again, maybe it was nothing to do with him. Maybe... Oh, what was the point in all this guessing. She didn't know. She really had no clue why she was being held here, other than it must be something to do with Alex and the others. She hoped they were okay, that they weren't in any danger. And Ben! Please, God, let him be all right. What if they'd abducted him too? What if he was locked up in one of these hideous rooms? If they'd laid a finger on him she'd... she'd what? What could she possibly do against one of them? Nothing.

She had to get some information from somewhere. This 'not knowing' was sending her loopy. She had to calm down, but being in this concrete cell wasn't helping. It felt as though the walls were closing in on her, squeezing the air from her lungs. Her vision blurred. Maddy swung her legs over the edge of the bed and let her head hang down between her knees. She was having a minor panic attack, that was all. If she just breathed slowly, she'd be fine. In through her nose and out through her mouth. The floor was tilting. No. She couldn't give into this stupid panic, that wouldn't help at all.

Gradually, the giddiness passed and she lay on her side, curling into herself. She'd been in bad situations before and she'd managed to come out of all of them. She would come out of this one too. The horrible musty smell of the sheet made her want to cry.

Maddy closed her eyes and pretended she was back home at Marchwood House, lying on her huge bed, the French windows open and an evening summer breeze ruffling the curtains. Darkness had just fallen and Alexandre was on his way to see her, to wrap her in his arms and kiss her lips. She sighed, her breathing calm, her mind no longer racing through dark tunnels. She would have this dream again, but next time it would be real.

In Gloucestershire, the weather had turned miserable. Iron-grey clouds took up residence in the sky, sporadically shaking out vicious drops of sleet. The wind blew from the east and the temperature hadn't risen above two degrees.

The basement already felt neglected and sad without them here, but it smelt of them – a faint scent of vanilla. It made him feel hungry. Ben bounced down onto a cream chaise, swung his feet up and lay back against the firm upholstery. He still had his shoes on. Good thing Isobel wasn't here, she'd go mad. Maddy and Leonora didn't get so stressed about stuff like that.

He pulled his phone out of his pocket – no new calls or messages. He'd ring Morris soon to see if they'd landed in Turkey yet. Ben's eye rested on the TV remote. He picked it up and hopped through five or six channels before turning it off again. The sudden silence made him nervous for some reason.

It would be Christmas soon, next week in fact. She'd better

be home by then. They couldn't have another terrible Christmas like last year. Ugh, this was useless. *He* was useless. What could he do to help? Surely there must be something...

What was the name of the hotel they were staying in? It was close to the underground city, he knew that much. Maybe he could look it up online. He glanced around the room.

Leonora's dark blue laptop sat on her writing desk in the corner. Ben wandered across, lifted the lid and pressed the power button. A green light blinked and the machine began to hum. Ben settled himself in the carved oak swivel chair and gently spun himself around while he waited for the laptop to fire up.

Their hotel was in a place called Ayvali. Ben googled the place, found the hotel and clicked on the room images. They were proper caves, done out like posh hotel rooms. He clicked on some of the links. It looked like Cappadocia was a full-on tourist resort now. They had hot-air balloon trips and horse riding tours, cave expeditions and all sorts of other cool stuff. Lucky no one had discovered the vampire city yet. Well, if they had, they probably wouldn't be around to tell the tale.

'What are you doing mooching down here all by yourself?'

Ben turned to see Esther poking her head round the door, frowning at him.

'It's no good you hanging about down here. Come on upstairs, you can give me a hand.'

'But I'm just—'

She'd gone before he had a chance to reply, her feet clomping back up the stone steps. Ben grumbled to himself and powered down the laptop. He dragged himself up the stairs and into the kitchen where Esther was unloading the dishwasher.

'With Morris gone gallivanting, I need a bit of muscle to help me out.'

Ben waited for her instructions. He knew she was

humouring him with her talk of 'muscle' – even though Esther was small and trim, she was as strong as an ox.

'How's that hand of yours?' she asked.

'Fine.' It was a bit bruised that was all. He was a bit embarrassed about the whole 'punching the door' thing.

'Good. There's a pile of wood in the shed that wants bringing in. And when you've done that, the bins need emptying. I'll make us a spot of supper for when you've finished.'

Ben wanted to argue, but he couldn't be bothered. What else was he going to do? And she'd never asked him to help out around the house before. He supposed he was lucky really.

'Morris's gloves are in the shed. Put them on so you don't get splinters.'

Ben trudged out to the hall.

'And don't forget your coat! It's freezing out there!' she called after him.

Ben grabbed his parka off the peg. She treated him like a two-year-old, but he didn't mind too much. He knew she meant well. She drove Maddy nuts, though, and he sometimes worried that Maddy would be so rude that the Foxtons would leave. He opened the front door and a sharp gust of wind hit him full in the face. God, it *was* freezing and he'd lost his hat. He zipped up his parka, lowered his head and battled through the wind towards the outbuildings round the side of the house.

The shed smelt of creosote and wood shavings; a great smell in Ben's opinion. He spied Morris's work gloves on one of the shelves, picked them up, pulled them on and grabbed a wheelbarrow. He headed back out to the wood pile and spent the next forty minutes filling up the huge log baskets in the four main reception rooms. It was warm work, but his face, hands and feet still felt like slabs of ice.

'Can I take the rubbish out *after* we've had dinner?' he asked Esther, shrugging off his coat and putting it on the back of one of the kitchen chairs before plonking himself down at the table.

Esther pointed to the coat and then to the door. Ben sighed and took his coat out to the hall when he shoved it back on the peg. He came back into the kitchen where a haze of delicious cooking smells made his stomach gurgle.

'It'll take you two minutes to empty the rubbish, by which time supper will be ready.'

'Okay,' he replied, and went into the utility room. 'Where do I put it?' he called out.

Esther came into the utility room. 'Put the normal rubbish in the wooden store outside the back door and put the recycling in the green box next to it.'

Ben picked up the first of the trash bags and lugged it outside. He wished he'd kept his coat on. He flipped open the lid of the wooden store and heaved the bag inside, wrinkling his nose at the sour smell. He chucked the last two plastic sacks in and then moved on to the recycling, dragging the box outside. Nearly done and then, at last, he'd be able to eat something.

A piece of screwed-up paper stuffed down the side of the box caught his eye and made him suck in his breath. It looked like the note from Maddy's kidnapper. But Alexandre wouldn't have thrown that away, so what was it doing in the recycling? Maybe Alex had misplaced it. Ben reached down and picked it up. He flattened it out against his leg. It was blank. He turned it over, but that side was blank too.

Ben frowned and examined the paper. There was no doubt in his mind that it was exactly the same kind the note had been written on – a small rectangle of white mottled paper. It didn't make any sense for the paper to be here in their recycling box. Had the kidnapper written the note here? And if they had, why would they have bothered to put this blank page in the recycling? What did it mean? Ben didn't know what to do.

'How are you getting on?' Esther called from inside. 'Supper's ready!'

Ben stuffed the paper into his pocket. 'Coming!' he shouted.

———

The first thing Alexandre saw when he opened his eyes was the grey felt roof of the van. He sat up and gazed beyond the open van door at a quarter moon, its surface pockmarked with orangey craters. He still had difficulty believing that Man had walked upon it. Imagine that.

Morris Foxton stood to the side of the van door and then leant forward, holding out his hand. Alexandre didn't need the caretaker's help but took his hand anyway out of politeness.

'Thank you, Morris,' he said, lightly exiting the vehicle. 'I trust everything is going according to plan?'

Morris gave a nod.

Alexandre glanced around. The night was cold and still, the air cleaner and sharper than in England. Morris had parked their silver hire van behind a stand of trees set back from the main road. Mounds of cliffs and lumps of rock jutted out behind them. He remembered this strange, jagged landscape from his last visit. It was like nowhere else. One hundred and forty years had passed since he was last here. That long-ago time had turned out to be the most eventful few months of his life. So much excitement and adventure, before the terror of that awful night.

He and Morris set to work opening the other crates. This morning they had flown from Birmingham Airport to Istanbul and had then taken an internal flight to Nevşehir Airport in Cappadocia. Morris's plane had landed at seven o'clock in the evening, but it was ten fifteen by the time he had collected the hire van and loaded the five crates. They had decided it would be wise for Morris to drive to a secluded spot before opening up the crates.

'We're about half an hour from the hotel,' Morris said.

Alexandre glanced at his watch. It was already 11.20 p.m. The night was rushing past. As they levered open each crate, Alexandre was relieved to find everyone safe.

'Sunrise is at half past seven,' Freddie said, hopping out of his crate.

'So we still have most of the night,' Isobel added.

'Come on, let's get back in the van,' Alexandre said. 'We can't afford to waste any time. I'll drive.'

Morris didn't protest. He climbed into the back with Freddie and Jacques, while Leonora and Isobel sat up front with Alexandre.

'Do you think they know we're here?' Isobel asked.

'I am sure of it,' Alexandre replied.

He drove quickly along the empty road. He didn't speak, although he could hear Jacques and Freddie chattering in the back. Lights glowed in the hillsides. It didn't feel like the Cappadocia he knew. This place felt tamed with its tarmac roads and electric lights. Soon, however, they crossed a small bridge and he took the turning for the village of Ayvali. Here, away from the main road, their surroundings became more rustic. The road narrowed and soon it became apparent that the van wouldn't make it. Alexandre swore, reversed and got out of the van. He opened the back.

'We'll have to find somewhere to park. The road's not wide enough.'

'You go up on foot,' said Morris. 'I'll park it and join you later.'

'Thank you,' said Alexandre, handing Morris the keys.

The five vampires walked up the lane towards the hotel. A large squarish building at the base of the hill gave way to rising tiers of rock behind which housed a honeycomb of rooms carved out of the side of the steep hill. Winding staircases crisscrossed in front of the caves and skinny trees shivered on the slopes.

They would check in and then scout out the area. This place wasn't what he had expected. It felt like a beautiful tourist resort, not like the wild and strange place it had once been. But if Madison was here, he would find her.

CHAPTER THIRTEEN

CAPPADOCIA, AD 575

The months blurred and Aelia's life took on a pattern which she accepted. This was her life now. The days and nights grew chillier, and soon, another bright, cold winter was upon them, polishing the air and giving the barren landscape a sparkling clarity. Widow Maleina thrust a handful of blankets in Aelia's direction and in amongst them was an extra thick woollen tunic and hood, for which Aelia was very grateful. She had been with the widow for over three years now and, although she wasn't exactly happy, she wasn't exactly sad either.

Aelia had learnt a great deal from the widow and she enjoyed the freedom she'd been given. Her only causes for concern were thoughts of her family and the loneliness of her current life. She was lucky if she spoke more than a sentence to the widow in a day and she rarely spoke to any of the patients who visited the cave. If anyone addressed her directly, the widow would interrupt them, or send Aelia off to do a task elsewhere. She often ended up talking to herself for comfort.

One morning, she awoke as usual, but something felt slightly different. It was always quiet in here, but today it felt more so. There was a hush. The widow had already left, so

Aelia stretched her body and hurriedly dressed. She splashed her face in the icy spring and walked down the narrow passageway towards the entrance. Feeling a crunch beneath her foot, she looked down – snow. It had drifted into the passage and as she stepped outside she was greeted by a world in white. Swirling wet flakes melted onto her cheeks. She smiled and pulled her hood up. Then she set off to catch up to the widow, whose small footprints were barely visible.

She hadn't walked very far when she heard a shout. Aelia turned to see a cloaked figure standing near the cave entrance. A man. He had called out her name. Aelia's heart sped up. She recognised that voice. She ran towards him, her heart full of joy.

'Father!'

He looked hesitant for a moment and then he opened his arms to her. She fell into them, warm tears streaming down her cheeks. She had tried not to think too much about her family as it only made her sad. But now, faced with her beloved father, she let herself give in to the feelings she'd been trying to block out – a mixture of loneliness, humiliation and anxiety.

'Come now,' he said, holding her close and then stepping back from the embrace. 'What are these tears? I thought you would be pleased to see me,' he said, trying to lighten things.

But Aelia could see the emotion in his eyes. 'How did you find me?' she asked.

'That's not important,' he replied. 'But I promised your mother I would find you and now I have. My little Aelia, you have grown into a beautiful woman. A little thin, but beautiful nonetheless.'

'Come, Father. Come in out of the snow and warm yourself.'

What did it mean that her father had come to find her? Had she been forgiven? Would she be allowed back into the village? She busied herself stoking up the smouldering fire and put some water on to heat. Her father drew closer to the flames and held his hands out to warm them.

'I was told you live with a healer,' he said.

'Yes. She found me after... after...' She swallowed. 'Father, I'm so sorry for everything. I'm ashamed of what I did. I hope you and mother and my sisters didn't suffer for my actions.'

'That is in the past. There are now more urgent matters to attend to.'

Aelia handed her father a cup of tea and he cradled it in his hands, blowing on it.

'How did you find me?' she asked again.

'It took me a while. I asked around and picked up a little gossip here and there. Does the woman treat you well?'

'Yes. She is strict, but not too unkind.'

'I trust you've heard about the barbarian invasion?'

'Widow Maleina says it's nonsense.'

'Well, it's a good thing Widow Maleina isn't in charge.'

'I think she knows things others do not,' Aelia said, surprised to find herself defending the widow to her father.

'That's as may be, but there is no time to debate the wisdom of your wise woman. Everybody knows the barbarians are coming. They are close now and will be here before a year is up. We have almost finished our preparations and I have come to tell you there will be a space for you when we descend.'

'A space?'

'Yes. Below the ground we will have our own room and there will be space for you.'

'For me? But I was banished. How did you manage it?'

'Never mind how I managed it,' he said. 'You must come at the appointed time and we will all descend together. The entrance to the underground settlement is located outside the village, at the cave with the chimneys. You must be there at sunset on midsummer's day. That is the hour we shall descend.'

Aelia knew the cave well – an eerie place surrounded with rumours. As children, they had all believed it to be haunted. She had only seen it a few times, but everybody knew about the cave with the five stone pillars. It was said they were the chimneys of an ancient god who had been banished underground for all eternity.

'So am I to stay here with the widow in the meantime?'

'Yes, I'm sorry, little one, but I could not manage to persuade them otherwise. Here...' He handed Aelia a piece of crumpled parchment which she unfolded. 'A map from here to the cave. It is a straightforward journey and should be no more than a day's walk. You must set off early that day.'

'Only a day's walk? But when I left, it took so long to get here. I must have wandered in circles.'

Her father set his drink down and cupped her face in his hand. 'I'm so sorry you had to face that alone, but I knew you would survive it. You have always been a brave girl.'

'Really? You think so?'

He laughed. 'Yes, really. Don't you feel brave?'

'Not at all. I always seem to be terrified of everything.'

'Courage is all about continuing on despite your fears. And you, my little Aelia, you have continued on.' He kissed her forehead.

'Widow Maleina must come too.'

'I don't think so. It was hard enough to get a space for you. I'm not sure they will allow it.'

'But I can't just leave her to the mercy of the barbarians. Not after she took me in.'

Her father sighed. 'Very well. Bring her along, but I can't guarantee they will let her descend. Every space has been accounted for. There is a list.'

'We'll manage it. That is if she'll agree to come. She doesn't believe in the invasion.'

Her father looked distracted.

'What is it?' Aelia asked. 'Is there something you're not telling me?'

'I know it was Lysus Garidas,' he said quietly through gritted teeth.

She gasped. How could he know? She was too scared to ask. She didn't want to speak about this with her father. He was talking to her like an adult and it made her feel uncomfortable.

'You were both seen,' he continued. 'But the girl who followed you neglected to mention that she also saw *him*. Only *your* name was given to the Praetor.'

So someone *had* followed her and Lysus? Aelia felt mortified. Who could it have been?

'It doesn't matter who it was,' her father said, reading her thoughts. 'But I got the truth from her, and now Praetor Garidas knows it too. His son is the one to blame but he escaped punishment. That is how I got the Praetor to relent and save you a space below the ground.'

'What did... what did Lysus have to say about it? Back then, he told me we would be wed.' A torrent of unpleasant memories began to surface and it was all Aelia could do to stop the tears from flowing. She was determined not to cry over him.

'Praetor Garidas sent him to live in the next village on some pretext or another,' her father said. 'And it is a good thing too, for I don't think I could have looked at the boy without...' He gritted his teeth and clenched his fists.

'Father, I'm sorry.' She placed a hand on his arm.

'Let us not dwell on it further. We will all be together soon and we can find you a suitable match. You are nineteen now – a little old to be a bride.' He gave a sad smile. 'But you are pretty enough for your age not to matter. We will put all that business behind us.'

A suitable match? The reality of going back home was starting to sink in. How would she be able to face her friends and neighbours? Surely they would shun her.

'Much as it pains me, I must leave you now, daughter. I have been gone too long.'

'Already? But you must meet the widow. She'll return before noon. You must stay for a few hours at least.'

'I wish I could stay a while longer. I've missed you so much and it is wonderful to look upon your sweet face after all this time. But I promised your mother I would return with news. She'll be sick with worry.'

'Very well.' Aelia looked down, desperately trying not to cry. 'Will you at least stay for breakfast?'

He smiled. 'That I can do.'

CHAPTER FOURTEEN

PRESENT DAY

How long had she been shivering in this damp, terrible place? There were no windows so she couldn't even gauge what time of day it was. Maddy's earlier panic had quickly morphed into boredom and frustration. She paced the floor, stamping her feet to get some warmth into her chilled bones. She was desperate to know if Ben was all right. She missed him and Alex so much, it was a physical ache.

'Come on!' She hammered on the door with her fist. 'What's going on!' If anyone was outside, they weren't answering. What else could she do? She thought for a while, trying to decide on the best strategy. Well, maybe she could try and get friendly with the vampire girl. Didn't they say it was a good idea to try and make friends with your captors? She was sure she'd seen that in a documentary. Or was it a movie?

Several hours later, the door finally opened again.

Maddy tried to catch the girl's eye as she walked in, but she stared straight ahead.

'Hi,' Maddy said. 'What's your name?'

Nothing.

'I'm Madison. You probably already knew that. My friends call me Maddy.'

No response. Maddy felt a bit stupid, but she was determined to plough on. The girl carried a tray with a bowl of what looked like soup and a big hunk of bread.

'That looks really good. Thanks.'

The girl flicked her eyes across at Maddy. Maddy felt slightly encouraged.

'Don't you get bored just bringing me food and then taking it out again? It can't be that interesting.'

The girl gave her a glare as she dumped the tray on the bed and picked up the empty bowl. *Oops*, Maddy thought. Criticising her job probably wasn't the best move.

'I mean, as a vampire, you can do really amazing stuff. Why don't they just have a human doing the meal deliveries?'

'Because a human might get stabbed in the face with a piece of broken plate,' the girl replied.

Maddy smiled. 'Fair enough. So, what did you say your name was?'

The girl rolled her eyes at Maddy and left the room.

Maddy grinned to herself.

Over the next couple of visits, Madison kept up her plan to befriend her vampire captor.

'When did you actually become a vampire?'

The girl didn't respond, but Maddy was getting used to being ignored. She didn't let it put her off.

'Let me guess... hmm... you've got that French plait going on and you talk pretty normally, but that doesn't necessarily mean anything. Okay, my guess is, you were turned three hundred years ago. Am I close?'

The girl tried to suppress a smile.

'Aha! You're smiling. I reckon I'm right. Am I right? Just nod once for yes.'

The girl left the room.

'Spoil-sport,' Maddy called after her. 'And I'd kill for a cup of tea. What are the chances?'

She felt like she was slowly getting somewhere. The girl wasn't hostile. If only she could get her to talk, she could trick her into revealing some useful information about where she was and who was behind her abduction. She also needed to know if Ben was safe. Maddy was desperate to get out of this place. What if Alex and the others couldn't track her down? She'd been here for ages already and there was no sign of a rescue. She knew it was down to her to escape. She had to try harder to befriend the girl.

How long had she even been here? She made a guess that when the girl brought her bread and fruit, it was probably meant to be breakfast. She'd had that three, no, four times now, so that must mean she'd been here for at least four days – four days! It felt like she'd been here four months. Wait, the door was opening again. That was quick. There was normally several hours in between each visit.

This time, the girl was carrying a mug.

'Is that...' Maddy took the mug in her hands. '... tea! Oh, that's amazing. Thank you. I've been dying for a cuppa since I got here. I usually have it with milk, but hey, I'm not complaining.'

The girl turned and headed back towards to the door.

'Please don't go just yet,' Maddy said, really meaning it. 'It's lonely in here. And it's always nice to drink tea and chat. You don't have to say anything, just stay for a minute or two. *Please.*'

The girl hovered in front of the door, her back to Maddy.

'So, you never told me when you were made into a vampire. Was I right? Was it three hundred years ago?' Maddy sipped her tea. 'Mm, great cuppa.'

'No,' the girl said softly.

'No? So not three hundred years ago. How about Victorian? You look quite like a girly girl, no offence meant. Just, your high heels and your clothes are very... perfect and pretty. Are you from the Victorian times?'

'No.' The girl left the room.

Maddy sighed and blew on her tea.

The journey had been uncomfortable, but they had finally made it to Turkey. Alexandre didn't allow himself to think about the last time he was here. Instead, he gave a cursory glance around his hotel accommodation, a suite of sumptuous rooms hewn out of the honey-coloured rock and linked by elaborately carved archways. Turkish rugs, wall hangings and tapestried furniture adorned the sitting room, and in his bedroom the columns and canopy of the four-poster bed were actually carved from the rock. But he had no time to appreciate the splendour on offer. They had to find the entrance to the underground city and rescue Madison.

There was no way he was going to hang around for two days until the 21st to hand themselves over like trussed-up turkeys to that Cappadocian creature. He may call himself an Emperor, but to Alexandre, he was a monstrosity, a stealer of life. And he wasn't to be trusted.

Morris had already gone to his own room. He would sleep now, but had arranged to meet them at six in the morning in case there was anything they needed him to do once day broke. Isobel, Jacques and Freddie were now busy covering the windows with blackout material, but Leonora had gone hunting. She had said she wouldn't be long, but Alexandre was impatient. Why on earth hadn't she fed before the journey?

Before the sleeping disease had taken hold, the vampires had been very open with each other about how they took their sustenance, sometimes even hunting in twos or threes. But since their long sleep, they had all become more solitary. They no longer discussed it.

Of course, Alexandre told Madison everything. She didn't berate him for it, but he could tell it made her squeamish, no doubt remembering the time he had unwittingly taken blood from her and from Ben. He appreciated the fact that she didn't sweep this aspect of him under the carpet. Instead, she quizzed him, wanting to know exactly what he needed to survive: Yes, he drank blood, but no, he did not kill anybody. He could take blood from animals, but it didn't have the same effect. Their blood tasted bad and did not give him enough energy to function properly. He tried to feed on only those humans who were already close to death. Unfortunately, his victims would probably suffer fevers and delirium, but he ensured they would not remember what had happened. It was a part of who he was. He could either starve, or live with the guilt. But he could go days between feeds and he always stretched it out as long as he could.

Aah, here was Leonora, her cheeks flushed and her eyes bright. She gave him a dazzling smile, beautiful in its unexpectedness.

'This place agrees with you,' he said. 'You're glowing.'

'Blood agrees with me,' Leonora replied. 'I was so ravenous in that crate. I could smell the customs people and it was all I could do not to break out of the box.'

Alexandre laughed nervously at the thought of it.

'Well, I'm glad you didn't break out,' Freddie said. 'Or you would be a little pile of ash right now.'

'Oh, don't even joke about it.' Isobel shuddered.

'Are we ready to go?' Alexandre asked.

'What exactly do you need us to do?'

'We must stick together. This is their territory and if they know we are here, they will be watching out for us. We are stronger together and they are less likely to attack.'

'Do you think they will?' Jacques asked.

'In truth, I don't know. But I hope not. If they had wanted us harmed, they would have tried to do it before now. Blythe told me they want us to join them.'

'So tonight is just a little look-see?' Jacques said.

'Exactly,' Alexandre said. 'If we can locate Maddy's whereabouts, we can plan her rescue.'

'Will we go to the place where the old ventilation shaft used to be?' Leonora asked.

'Not yet. I have a feeling that is where we are supposed to go at the appointed time. They will have guards posted.'

'So what do we do?' Leonora said.

'We go to the river where the cave is.'

'But the cave is gone,' Freddie said. 'Harold and Refet blew it up.'

'Yes, but we can walk the city from above. See if we can sense anyone below.'

'I suppose so...' Jacques sounded dubious.

'Well, do you have a better idea? We cannot attract their attention. We have no idea how many of them we're facing.'

'I think we're screwed.'

'Jacques!' Isobel cried.

'Thanks for your input, brother. But thankfully I have a little more optimism than you.'

'Sorry, Alex,' Jacques said. 'But now we're here, I'm just starting to realise this isn't going to be easy.'

'Of course it isn't! But what do you suggest? Should we repack ourselves into our crates and go home? Would you leave Maddy to her fate?'

'Of course not, Alex. I'm sorry. Ignore me, I was just talking nonsense.'

'It's not nonsense, Jacques,' Isobel said. 'We all feel nervous.'

'Come on,' Freddie interrupted. 'Let's go. Talking about it is making me doubt everything.'

'You're right, Freddie,' Alexandre said. 'We won't know what's out there until we go.'

They went out onto the terrace of their suite which perched halfway up the side of the cliff and gazed out across the landscape. The valley and cliffs beyond were dotted with more cave dwellings – some dark and empty, others glowing with warm yellow lights. Thankfully, it was too cold for the other hotel guests to make use of the outdoor areas. They were all cosily tucked up in bed or lounging beside crackling fires. So the vampires stood there unobserved.

'We must head north,' Alexandre said.

'I remember.' Isobel sighed. 'As if I could ever forget.'

Alexandre clasped his sister's hand. 'We will finish this thing here. We will end it once and for all and put it behind us.'

'I hope you are right,' she said, closing her eyes and stepping off the terrace. The others followed and Alexandre watched them drop down the side of the cave-studded rock face and move up and over to the top of the opposite cliff. They stood on the grassy summit, four dark shapes against the blue-black sky. Alexandre paused, took a breath and joined them.

Esther bustled around the steamy kitchen for a few minutes, before finally putting two plates on the kitchen table. She sat down in front of one of them.

'Don't mind if I join you, do you?' she asked Ben. 'Keep you company.'

'No, course not.' He sat opposite the housekeeper and eyed his plate: a cheese and mushroom omelette, chips and salad. 'This is great. Thanks.' But he couldn't stop thinking about the piece of paper in his pocket. It had taken the edge off his appetite.

'Eat up, then,' Esther said, looking across at him.

He still hadn't even lifted his knife and fork.

'What's the matter? Too tired to eat?'

'No, no, this is great.' He grabbed his fork and speared a chip. Was he just being paranoid? Maybe the notepaper wasn't the same at all, maybe it was just his memory playing tricks on him. But no. He knew it was exactly the same. So, why then had it ended up in the recycling box in their house?

Uncomfortable conclusions kept springing to the front of his mind and he tried to shove them away. It was Esther who had brought them the original note in the first place. But it couldn't be anything to do with her... surely. Why would she have written it? She had no reason. Yes, she and Maddy clashed a bit, but not so much that she would betray her like that. No. Esther was a good person. She had nursed Maddy and Ben back to health after their first vampire encounters and she and Morris had come to their rescue in London when Maddy and the others were trapped in Blythe's underground facility. She wouldn't have looked after them only to sell them out in the end.

Anyway, it had been Esther who had asked him to empty the recycling box and she wouldn't have done that knowing he might find the notepaper in there. Not unless she was really stupid, which she wasn't. He felt ultra-disloyal even thinking about it. How could he even look her in the face. He stared down at his omelette.

'Worried about your sister?' she asked. 'Don't be. Morris will bring her back safe. And don't eat if you don't want to. You can always heat it up later. I expect you're tired out after all those chores I gave you.'

'I'm okay.' He blushed, convinced she must know what was going through his mind.

'Your face is a bit flushed. Hope you're not coming down with something. Although I wouldn't be surprised after all the dramas we've had going on around here.'

'I'm fine. Honestly.'

'I shouldn't have got you doing all that work. It was probably too much, what with your bruised hand and all. Just thought you could do with taking your mind off everything.'

Ben let her ramble on. It was no good disagreeing, or even agreeing for that matter. When Esther spoke it was like a force of nature, you just had to let it run its course. She said what she said and that was that.

Maybe he'd give Jacques or Freddie a call later. See what they made of the fact that he'd found similar paper to the note in the recycling box. Alex might not take it seriously; he was probably too busy with too much on his mind. He might think Ben was being over paranoid. But maybe Freddie would have an idea about it. Ben chewed on a piece of omelette, but it was no good. His appetite had completely deserted him.

'D'you mind if I go upstairs?' Ben asked. He knew she wasn't his mum or his boss or anything like that, but he thought he'd better ask. He didn't want to offend her, not after she'd gone to all that trouble of making him dinner.

'I think that's a good idea,' she replied. 'You go on up and have an early night. I don't know what I was thinking getting you to do all that work. I didn't want you to brood, that was all.'

'It's okay. I kind of enjoyed it.'

'There! I knew you would. Took your mind off things for a little while, didn't it.'

Not really, he thought.

'Good. Right. Well, you go on upstairs and hopefully you'll feel better tomorrow.'

Ben got up from the table and left the kitchen. He took the stairs two at a time and pulled his mobile from his jeans pocket. There was a message from Morris. How had he missed that? As he entered his bedroom, he opened the message and sank down onto the floor to read it. He leant back against the bed and sighed. All it said was that they'd landed. Ben hadn't really thought they'd have any news yet, but part of him had hoped for something more.

He tossed his phone onto the rug and eased the crumpled piece of paper from his pocket. The paper was quite thick. He smoothed it out on the floor. It was rectangular shaped, smaller than A4. Maybe it was A5. Ben held the paper out in front of him, his head tilted to the side. No, not quite A5. It looked like one side was uneven, at an angle like it had been cut. Ben wished he had the real note to compare this one against. Why would one side have been cut? Had this been part of the actual note and they had cut off this blank piece? But that wouldn't make any sense. He stuck out one side of his bottom lip and puffed his fringe out of his eyes. Maybe it was just an innocent piece of paper which happened to look like the paper the note was written on. Maybe it was just as simple as that.

CHAPTER FIFTEEN

CAPPADOCIA, AD 575

Winter melted into spring, and spring soon became summer. Aelia's days with the widow had a reassuring rhythm and she had mixed feelings about returning to her village. She wanted to see her family, of course she did, but how would everyone else feel about her return? Would her friends be allowed to associate with her? Did her sisters even know what she had done? And what about Lysus? Would he be there too? Her father had said he now lived in the next village, but all the villages were moving below ground, so surely that meant he would be joining everyone. Part of her didn't ever want to see him again, but another part of her wanted to look him right in the eye with the full measure of scorn and hatred he deserved.

Today, Aelia and the widow were negotiating their way down a narrow goat track cut into a steep gorge. At the bottom, in the relative shade of the valley, they would find wild mushrooms and asparagus. As well as being edible, asparagus was used for treating jaundice, toothache and as an antidote for venomous spider bites.

The sound of running water grew louder and Aelia spied

flashes of silver at the foot of the gorge, where the river peeked out from beneath its canopy of poplars and pistachio trees. The way down was precarious and took much concentration. Aelia was aware that one misplaced step might have her plummeting to her death, but in front of her, Widow Maleina seemed sure-footed and confident, jabbing her stick into shallow crevices for balance.

Aelia sighed as she thought about the widow. She was being contrary and refusing to talk about the invasion. Every time Aelia tried to broach the subject, she would either snap at her or pretend she hadn't heard her speak. Aelia didn't know what to do. How could she leave the old woman alone to be slaughtered or enslaved? She was a crotchety old thing, but the widow had saved her life and given her a home.

The morning sun grew stronger and a trickle of sweat ran down Aelia's back. Only a couple of days now remained until Midsummer, the day she was to travel back to her village and begin living underground. Aelia hadn't thought to ask her father how long they were all supposed to remain down there. It would surely be for several weeks, maybe even months. How strange it would be to live in darkness, to never see the sky or the trees. She felt a little frightened by the whole idea of it.

Growing up, Aelia had always pictured a simple life for herself – a dutiful daughter who would marry and have children. Now she realised nothing was ever certain in life. Perhaps she might eventually have those things, but it was getting harder and harder to imagine. Who would want to marry her now? Perhaps she would end up like the widow – living alone in a cave on the fringes of society. It wasn't such a bad life. At least you got to be independent. But then, to live for so long without love must be a terrible thing. Maybe that's why the widow was so cantankerous – she had no one to soften the edges. Did Aelia still believe in love? Her parents certainly had a loving marriage.

Would she ever have anything like that? A small part of her still dared to dream it.

'You're dawdling.' The widow's voice cut through her thoughts. 'I have no use for idlers and layabouts. Do you think you're a princess surveying your lands? You are an outcast, girl. Do not forget it.'

Aelia flushed, lowered her eyes and picked up her pace. Over the past few days, Widow Maleina had said some particularly hurtful things to her. Aelia thought it might be because of the approaching invasion. Perhaps the woman was frightened. But Aelia dismissed the thought as soon as she had it. She didn't think the widow would be frightened of anything. She had a suspicion that these digs were supposed to put her off returning home. Words like 'outcast' were stark reminders of what she had left behind.

'So will you come with me?' Aelia asked, not put off by the widow's jibes.

'To your underground tomb?' The widow cackled.

'It's not a tomb. It's a refuge. It's only temporary.'

'That's what you think.'

'What do *you* think?' Aelia said.

'I think you talk too much.'

And so, as always, the conversation ended.

Back home, later that evening, Aelia began preparing the evening meal. They had collected an abundance of herbs and vegetables and Aelia was excited to cook something new for the widow – a summer vegetable dish she remembered helping her mother with.

'I'll prepare the food tonight,' the widow said, shuffling over to the spring, where Aelia was washing some lettuce leaves.

'Oh, no that's all right. I was going to make us—'

'I said, I'll prepare it.' The widow snatched the lettuce out of Aelia's hands, causing her to drop most of it into the spring where it was carried away underground.

Aelia was shocked and more than a little angry. The woman was getting ruder by the day. She stood up, dried her hands on her tunic and stalked off. It was a good thing she was leaving in a couple of days and if the widow didn't want to come along, well that was just fine. She could stay here to be savaged by the barbarian horde. No, she didn't really mean that, but the woman was impossible.

Aelia stepped outside the cave, holding up her hand to shield her eyes from the sun that threw out bright shafts of light as it slid down into the rocky landscape. Only two more days and she would be back with her family. She'd just have to grit her teeth and put up with the widow's moods a little longer. She sat cross-legged on the dusty ground and watched a few birds streak across the sky, trying to make it home before nightfall. A warm breeze swirled about her and she closed her eyes for a moment. She sat there like that for a while, trying to rid herself of her annoyance at the widow's behaviour.

'Supper is ready.'

Widow Maleina's voice interrupted her meditation. She turned around, but the widow had already returned to the cave. Aelia sighed and got to her feet. She wouldn't even attempt a conversation this evening. It was too exhausting and a complete waste of time.

Aelia saw that the widow had made a stew. In Aelia's opinion, it was far too hot for such a meal, but at least it smelled good. She realised she was starving, sat down and took a huge spoonful.

'I didn't mean to be quite so abrupt with you earlier,' Widow Maleina said.

Aelia almost choked on her food. *Was the woman apologising?*

'I am grateful for your help these past years,' the widow continued. 'You have earned your keep quite well. I would like you to know that.'

'Umm. Thank you,' Aelia murmured, before spooning in another mouthful.

'You are a good girl,' the widow said with a sad smile.

And that was the last thing Aelia heard before the world went black.

CHAPTER SIXTEEN

PRESENT DAY

Okay, there was nothing else for it – Maddy was going to have to brave the shower. She felt so disgustingly grimy and vile that even a cold shower in the most rank bathroom in the universe was better than feeling this gross. And, anyway, the thought of Alexandre seeing her like this when he came to rescue her was too much for her ego.

She was freezing to start with, so stripping off her clothes was not enjoyable. Her teeth chattered and her grimy flesh broke out in goose bumps. Maddy steeled herself for the squalor and stench of the bathroom, opened the door, turned on the light and strode in. She ignored the feel of the slimy floor, trying not to gag, and stood under the rusty shower head. Bracing herself for a freezing onslaught, she turned the metal dial on the wall.

Cold brown water dribbled out onto her hair and skin. Too late, Maddy realised she should have tested the water before standing under it. She'd have to make the best of it now. But to her surprise and delight, the water gradually grew warmer and clearer until, after about twenty seconds or so, the muddy trickle had turned into a steaming hot jet of heaven. Oh my God, this was exactly what she needed. Her bones thawed out and her skin glowed with warmth and cleanliness. She could have quite easily stood there all day. Even without soap or shampoo, she felt a million times better.

Eventually, Maddy felt sufficiently scrubbed, and so reluctantly turned off the water and returned to her room or cell or whatever it was. She used her vest top to dry her body and sighed as she stepped back into her dirty clothes. Now, she just had to wait for that vampire chick to come back in again and then she could work on befriending her. She felt like it was only a matter of time before the girl came around. She'd brought her a cup of tea and spoken a couple of words already. Next time, she'd get a whole sentence from the girl if it killed her.

It wasn't long before the girl came back. She walked in and smiled at Maddy. It was small and quick, but it was an unmistakable smile. Maddy returned it with a hundred-watt version of her own.

'Come on then,' Maddy said. 'How long have you been a vampire? A hundred years? Fifty? Five hundred? Put me out of my misery, ple-e-ease. At least tell me your name.'

'My name's Zoe Marshall and I've only been a vampire for a year.'

Maddy was shocked that the girl had answered. What a result. If she was honest, she hadn't really expected her to reply.

'Zoe... Hi... A year? Well, I was totally off the mark.'

'It feels like forever.'

'I bet.' Maddy was sitting on the bed, leaning up against the wall, her legs stretched out in front of her. Zoe put the tray of food on the bed and made to leave.

'You can't go now,' Maddy said. 'You have to tell me how you got to be a vampire.'

'I don't have to tell you anything.' Zoe's face darkened.

'I didn't mean... I just meant, it would be interesting to hear your story. Sorry if I made you angry.'

'No, I'm not angry with *you*.'

'Angry with who, then?'

'I'd better go,' Zoe said.

'No. Please.'

'Sorry.' The door slammed.

'Shit. Nice one, Maddy,' she muttered to herself.

Suddenly the door burst open again and Zoe appeared, sitting next to Madison on the bed in that disconcerting way that vampires have of materialising right next to you as if by magic. She leant back against the wall and began to talk.

'I don't really get why they told me not to talk to you. I mean, it's not like I'm going to tell you where you are or why you're here or anything. And, even if I did, what are you going to do about it? You can't escape. This place is serious.'

'Wow,' Maddy said.

'Yeah,' Zoe replied.

Although Maddy hadn't said 'wow' in response to what Zoe had said. She said 'wow' because it was weird hearing all those words come out of Zoe's mouth. Zoe, the quiet vampire chick who never spoke.

'You have no idea how serious this place is.'

'Serious in what way?'

'Oh, you know,' Zoe said airily, waving her hands in a dismissive gesture.

'No, tell me,' Maddy replied.

'Well, it's ultra-secure. It's not like a normal building or anything.'

Maddy suddenly remembered her journey here when she'd woken up to that strange engine sound. Something occurred to her. 'Am I still in England?'

Zoe laughed. 'I guess it won't hurt to tell you that much. Nope, we're not in the UK.'

So that engine noise must have been a plane. That wasn't how Maddy had pictured her first trip abroad. She'd had dreams of travelling first class to some exotic destination with Alexandre, just the two of them for a few weeks of uninterrupted bliss. Instead, she'd been drugged, blindfolded and abducted to the Costa del Grotty Bathroom. At least the room service was all right.

'Can you tell me what country we're in?'

'Better not,' Zoe replied. 'I've probably said too much already.'

'Thanks for bringing me that cup of tea before.'

'I used to love a cuppa,' Zoe said. 'That's the kind of thing I really miss about being human. It's weird, the blood thing is amazing, but it kind of takes over. Whereas with food you have these little rituals and treats. It's more interesting. More varied.'

Maddy glanced sideways at Zoe. It was odd how comfortable she felt in her presence. She supposed that was because she was in love with a vampire who was the funniest, most generous person she knew. A wave of emotion pricked at her eyes. She took a breath.

'I hope you don't mind me saying, but you don't seem like the kind of person who would keep someone else locked up.'

Zoe pursed her lips and stared at the wall.

'Zoe?' Madison prompted.

'You know, you're not the only one who's here against her will. I'm not exactly—'

Suddenly the door opened. A man swept in. Except it wasn't a man. It was another vampire.

'Out,' he hissed.

Zoe moved out of the door so fast she was a blur. Maddy stood, her heart hammering in her chest. The vampire was medium height with thick dark hair. His face was that of a teenager, but his black eyes and bearing were much older. He stared at Madison for a moment. She wasn't usually lost for

words, but the man had such a presence she felt fear like a
palpable thing on her shoulder. Was he going to drink from her?
The thought made her want to scream in terror. Then, just as
suddenly as he had entered, he turned and left the room.

With a thud of dread, Maddy realised that he was probably
going to be her new jailor. And what about Zoe? He'd looked
really angry with her. Would she get into trouble? She hoped he
wouldn't hurt her. What if Zoe didn't return? What would she
do *then*? That male vampire didn't look like the sort you made
friends with. He was one scary dude. She was never going to get
out of here. *Think. Think, Maddy. What are you going to
do now?*

This was more like the Cappadocia Alexandre remembered,
only now he was seeing it not as a mortal, but as a vampire. Last
time, he had viewed the countryside from the back of a camel,
gently swaying through the rocky landscape along a man-made
trail, his eyes wide with naïve wonder. This time, he skimmed
the dark surfaces of stone and rock and jumped any obstacles in
his way. He climbed up rock faces, freefalling down valleys and
stepping across streams as though they were small puddles.

The others travelled close by and they matched each other's
speed, silently covering the dark miles. There were more settle-
ments now and new roads stretched smooth and wide, where
before had been only dusty tracks or nothing at all, but most of
the terrain was still as it used to be. They were nearing the
village of Zelmat and Alexandre thought back to the old woman
who had originally told him the legend of the blood demons.
What was her name? *Havva Sahin.* She would be long dead of
course, as would her sweet grandchildren. Perhaps her descendants still lived here.

Before long, they reached the rushing river where

Alexandre had dived down into the cave all those years ago. He hoped he would still be able to recall where the entrance used to be. The fairy chimney markers were no longer standing and so he would have to trust to his memory. He scanned the river bank.

'Is this it?' Leonora asked, coming to rest at his side. 'Is this the place?' Her hair had come loose and she began pinning it back into place.

'This is the river, but I'm not sure if this is the exact spot. Wait here a moment.' Alexandre travelled along the river bank for a few miles. It only took him a minute or two. He suddenly remembered the cave had been located at a particularly wide section of the river and also, there had been a cliff on the opposite bank. Here, there was flat ground opposite, so this was not the spot. He retraced his steps and called to the others to follow him. Soon he came to an area which looked promising.

'I think this is it,' he said. 'It may not be the exact location, but it's near enough.'

'So what do we do now?' asked Isobel.

'We walk. We listen. We scent the air and the ground. We use all our senses to find her.'

'Let's spread out,' said Jacques. 'We'll cover more ground if we—'

'No,' Alexandre interrupted. 'We stay together as agreed.'

'How about if Freddie and I go together and you and—'

'I said no!'

'Fine. We'll stay together,' Jacques grumbled.

'We stay in sight at all times.'

'I said *okay*.'

They travelled more slowly this time.

Alexandre concentrated on everything around him. He smelt the frost on the ground and the fresh tang of pine needles in the wind. The earth beneath him felt solid and dense.

Insects, lizards, snakes and rodents moved below him, but he could not sense anything more.

'I cannot get a feel for anything below the surface,' Isobel said, giving voice to his thoughts. 'I just feel the rocks beneath my feet. Nothing more.'

The others murmured their agreement.

'Perhaps the rock is too thick for our senses to penetrate,' Leonora said.

'I think you're right,' said Freddie. 'It just feels like normal ground to me. I can't tell if there are any caves below or not.'

'And I definitely can't tell if there are any people down there. Human or vampire,' said Isobel.

'Shh.' Alexandre held up his hand for silence. 'We have company.' He tensed his body. There were four of them coming this way, travelling quickly. He knew they were about to have a confrontation with these creatures and he wished he could send the others away to deal with it on his own. The fear for his siblings and friends was worse than his apprehension at meeting these powerful beings.

They came to a stop only a few yards away. Four male vampires dressed in modern clothing.

'No need to be nervous,' one of them said. 'We don't bite.'

The other three laughed at their companion's humour.

'Where is she?' Alexandre asked, praying his voice would remain steady. It did.

'Hello, pleased to meet you. My name is Sergell.' He looked young, but Alexandre knew this vampire was old. Older than him. Much older.

'Where is she, Sergell?'

'And you must be Alexandre,' he continued.

Alexandre took a step forward.

'Now, now.' Sergell held up a hand. 'We are soon to be family. We don't want any unpleasantness.'

'You started this unpleasantness when you took Madison.'

'I can see this is not getting us very far. Return to your hotel. Relax, enjoy the scenery and come to the city in two days' time as agreed.'

'Nothing has been agreed,' Alexandre snarled. 'Nothing!'

Leonora put a warning hand on his arm. 'We will return on the 21st,' she said.

'Very good,' Sergell replied.

The four strangers left as quickly as they had arrived.

'Why did you say that?' Alexandre growled at Leonora.

'To avoid trouble. We don't want to fight them now, not without having found Madison.'

'Yes. I know you're right, but to give in so easily...' He threw up his hands in frustration.

'They were the real deal,' Jacques said. 'I thought *we* were scary. But those vampires are like...'

'I know,' Freddie agreed. 'You could feel the power coming off them in waves. And they knew it too.'

'What are we to do, Alexandre?' Isobel asked. 'We cannot go up against these creatures. They will crush us.'

Alexandre shook with anger and impotence. He knew the vampires had been laughing at them. He and the others were way out of their depth here. They would not be able to take them by force. Not for the first time, Alexandre wished he had destroyed the Cappadocian back when he'd had the chance. Now that evil creature had set himself up as leader once again, with layers of protection surrounding him, gathering vampires from the London facility as well as reviving those who had remained trapped in Cappadocia. It made Alexandre crazy to think that Madison was beyond his reach. He couldn't bear to think of her alone and afraid, not knowing what was going on. And it was all his fault. If he couldn't keep her safe, what good was he to her? She was in danger because of him, because of what he was.

He couldn't let Maddy down. Already, he missed her so

much that nothing felt right. His world felt bleak and empty without her and it hit him again just how much he loved her. He and the others would have to rethink their non-existent strategy to get her back. With a fresh lurch of despair, he realised they would need a miracle.

CHAPTER SEVENTEEN

CAPPADOCIA, AD 575

The blackness was heavy, pushing down onto her face and chest until she couldn't breathe anymore. The terror of not being able to take a breath made her forget who she was. The air was leaving her lungs, sweat prickled all over her body and a rushing sound filled her ears. She couldn't talk or see or move. This wasn't real, was it?

She heard a murmur. It was a rasping, dry sound that made no sense. Aelia felt a pain in her throat and realised it was she who was making the murmur. She tried to remember what had happened. She lived with the widow... had been with her for years. There was a trip to the valley to gather mushrooms and wild vegetables. They had returned home and the widow had treated a couple of patients. They had sat down to eat their evening meal and, for the first time ever, the widow had been quite pleasant. And then... she couldn't remember anything else.

'Awake?'

Aelia recognised Widow Maleina's voice. As she opened her eyes, the widow's face shimmered into focus.

'What happened?' Aelia croaked.

'You had a fever. But you'll be fine.'

'I feel awful.'

'You look awful.' The widow laughed.

Aelia attempted to roll her eyes, but she was too weak even for that.

'Here, drink this.' The widow helped to hold her head up and Aelia felt a dull pounding above her eyes. She opened her mouth and sipped at the warm liquid. It tasted bitter but soothed her throat a little.

'Thank you.' She lay back down and her stomach gurgled. 'Why do I feel so hungry?'

'You've been asleep for two days.'

Two days? Midsummer! She was supposed to meet her family. 'But... but I should be at the cave today!'

'It is too late for that.'

'Maybe if I leave now I'll be able to make it in time. Surely it won't matter if I'm a little late.' Aelia tried to sit up on her own. Her head felt as though it contained a huge, sharp boulder and she thought she might throw up or pass out. Gingerly she lay back down.

'It would take you all night to get there, by which time it would be too late.'

'But my family will be so worried. They'll think I've been attacked on the road, or that I'm ill or dead. My mother—'

'It's too late for them. But you will be safe here.'

'Too late for them? No, they'll be safe underground. We're the ones in danger. We'll have to hope the barbarians don't find us here.'

'There aren't any barbarians. How many times do I have to tell you. I know you're not stupid, even if you sometimes act it.'

'But—'

'But, but, but... no buts. Your family and friends are probably all dead by now. And if they're not, you'd better pray for them because they will wish they were.'

'Why are you saying these things? You're scaring me.'

'Good. You should be scared. I've saved you from a fate far beyond what you can imagine.'

'*You? You've* saved me?' Aelia suddenly realised that the widow had never intended to let her go and join her family. She had kept her here intentionally. 'Why? How could you let me miss my chance at happiness? Are you so twisted and bitter that you would deny me a chance to make my life right again? Did you drug me to keep me here?'

Widow Maleina scowled and walked off towards the back of the cave, muttering to herself. Aelia felt a wave of helplessness wash over her and a tear rolled down her cheek. She would probably be stuck here forever. A flash of anger overtook her sadness.

'Why did you do it?' she called across the echoing cave. 'Is it so you can keep me here as your servant? Is that it?'

No reply came. She turned onto her side and closed her eyes. Before her father visited the cave, Aelia had been prepared to remain with the widow. It had been her only option. But after his visit, she had allowed herself a glimmer of hope for the future. Of course, she'd also felt a certain amount of fear at the thought of returning to the people who cast her out, but at least she would have the opportunity to start again. But now... now, she just saw years of the same thing stretching out in front of her. That was if the barbarians didn't slit her throat first.

A rich smell permeated the air and Aelia's mouth began to water.

'Broth,' the widow said, standing next to her.

Aelia still lay with her back to her and remained silent.

Widow Maleina sighed. 'I know you are angry now, but in time, you will come to see that I am right.'

The smell of the broth was driving Aelia mad. She was so hungry but didn't want to give the widow the satisfaction of seeing her drink it.

'I know the demons are here because I have seen them,' the widow said. 'And I remember them from before.'

'Before?' Aelia replied before she could stop herself.

'They have travelled here from a long way away. From a cold country in the north. The country where I was born.'

'You mean you're not from here?' Aelia turned and sat up, forgetting her anger for a minute. The widow handed her a bowl and Aelia took a sip of the warm clear soup. As she drank, the splinters of pain in her head seemed to melt away.

'No,' replied the widow. 'I was brought here as a slave when I was a girl. In my land, everybody knows about the night demons. And now they are here and they will wreak terror and destruction because you are all unprepared and ignorant.'

Despite the heat of the soup, Aelia felt a chill.

'We knew all their tricks,' the widow continued. 'We endured centuries of their evil ways. But we knew how to deal with their kind. Your people are ignorant. They don't know what they have done.'

Aelia saw sadness in Widow Maleina's eyes. 'So if that's true, why didn't you try to warn them? Why didn't you tell them?'

'Do you think your councils would listen to a half-mad crone? Don't look at me like that. I know what everybody thinks of me. Because I am old and live alone, they think I am some kind of demented witch. They are happy to take my medicines, but that is all.'

'If there are demons, where are they?'

'Right now, they are leading your people into the under-ground city. The demons have fabricated this invasion. They cannot stand the light of day. They need darkness and blood to survive. Below ground, in the newly constructed city, they will have both.'

Aelia didn't know what to think. The widow sounded convincing, but she could just as easily be the mad old crone people thought she was. Either way, Aelia knew she would have to find her family and make sure they were safe. Demons or no demons, Aelia was going to travel back home to see for herself.

CHAPTER EIGHTEEN

PRESENT DAY

Ben awoke to the chime of a text message. With his eyes still shut, he reached across to the bedside table and bashed about trying to feel for his phone. After a few seconds of no success, he remembered it was on the floor. He groaned and sat up, sleep still clinging to his body.

Gathering his quilt around his shoulders, he slid off the bed and onto the floor. His mobile lay face down on the rug. There were two texts – one from Alexandre and one from Freddie. Suddenly, he was wide awake. Please let them have found her. Please.

Alexandre's message was short and unenlightening:

Hi Ben, Checked out the area but no sign of Maddy yet. Don't worry. We'll find her.

Ben got that sick feeling back. They had been there for a whole night and had found nothing. If Ben was honest with himself, he had been convinced they would have rescued her by now. After hearing all about their amazing escape from the underground facility in London earlier this year, he'd let himself believe there wasn't anything Alex couldn't do.

Freddie's message was a little more honest but a lot more worrying:

Confrontation with 4 scary vamps last night. Too powerful for us to do anything. We're working out a strategy. Will get back 2 u as soon as we have a plan.

So if the Cappadocian vampires were too strong for even Alexandre and the others, what were they going do? How would they rescue Maddy? Ben felt so useless. He texted Freddie back:

Be careful. Is there anything I can do from here?

But Ben knew they wouldn't ask him to do anything. His stomach growled and he remembered he hadn't had anything to eat last night. He did still feel slightly sick, but his stomach also felt like it had a massive hole in it. He needed food. Quickly, he pulled on yesterday's socks, some jogging bottoms and an inside-out sweatshirt before going downstairs to get some breakfast.

Esther was in the hall, picking the mail up off the doormat.

'Hi, Esther,' he said, heading into the toasty warmth of the kitchen.

'Morning.' She followed him into the room.

Ben grabbed a box of cereal from the larder and a bowl from the cupboard. Esther passed him a spoon.

'Thanks,' he said. 'I had a text from them. They haven't got her back yet.'

'I know, love. Morris called me first thing. It might take some time, but they'll do it, don't you worry.' She passed him a bundle of letters. 'It's Maddy's post. Maybe you should open it while she's away. In case there's something important.'

'Really?' He felt a bit uncomfortable about opening his sister's mail. And wasn't it illegal to open someone else's letters?

'Well, I wouldn't normally tell you to open someone else's post, but these are exceptional circumstances.'

'Okay then.' Ben put the letters on the table and shook out some cereal. It was some horrible muesli crap, but he couldn't be bothered to change the box. Anyway, he figured he was hungry enough to eat just about anything. He sploshed on some milk and started eating. Hmm, not as bad as he'd thought it would be.

As he chewed muesli, he sliced open the first letter with his finger. It was from the garage to say Maddy's Land Rover was due a service. That could wait. Next letter was a dental check-up for both of them and the third was a confirmation letter from the Cappadocian hotel where the vampires were staying. He opened the rest which were either junk mail or boring appointments.

'Nothing interesting,' he said.

'Good,' replied Esther. 'Things have been a bit too interesting around here lately. We could do with a bit less of it, if you know what I mean.'

Ben did know what she meant. He'd give anything to go back to boring routine if it meant having Maddy back home.

———

Maddy was jolted awake by the jingling of the lock and now the door swung open. She remembered the male vampire, the way he had stared at her, and fear crept up her spine. Her mouth was dry and her neck stiff where she'd fallen asleep leaning against the wall. Her body and mind were sluggish with sleep, unable to cope with any kind of confrontation. But she needn't have worried, as the person walking through the door was Zoe.

'God, he's a pain in the ass,' Zoe said, sitting cross-legged on the end of the bed.

'I was worried I wouldn't see you again,' Maddy said, relief sweeping through her. 'Who was he? He was scary.'

'That was Sergell. And yes, he is scary. You do not want to mess with Sergell Elioreg.'

'Did you get into trouble? For talking to me?' Maddy asked.

'What? No. They tell me not to talk to you, but they're too busy to worry about stuff like that. They're not bothered. As long as I do my job and make sure you stay put and don't die.'

'Oh.' Maddy hadn't expected that. She'd thought they would be... stricter or something. Although, you couldn't get much stricter than abducting someone and locking them up. She let out a snort of laughter.

'What's funny?' Zoe asked.

'Oh, I don't know,' Maddy said. 'Just *all this.*' She spread out her hands. 'In a weird and twisted way, it kind of reminds me of being at school. You and me slagging off the "teachers".'

Zoe smiled wistfully. 'Yeah, I s'pose.'

'Where are you from anyway? You're English, right?'

'Yeah. I'm from Newcastle.'

'Up north?'

'Mm-hm.'

'You haven't got much of an accent.'

'My accent always comes back when I'm visiting family. Not that I can do *that* anymore. They think I'm dead.'

'I'm sorry,' Maddy said.

'Nothing's normal anymore,' Zoe replied. 'Everything is dark and serious and scary all the time. My life's changed beyond anything I could've ever imagined.'

Maddy reached across and took Zoe's cold hand in hers. She gave it a squeeze. 'I know you probably don't think it, but I do know what you mean. I haven't always had it good. My life was pretty bleak and hopeless a couple of years ago, but it's turned right around. I never thought it would be possible, but I'm so happy right now.' The words came tumbling out before she remembered she was stuck in a cell.

Zoe gave her a look. 'You *are* joking?'

The ridiculousness of her words hit them both, and they dissolved into hysterical laughter.

Maddy held on to her stomach. 'Oh, oh, I can't breathe...'

'Yeah, like I need a pep talk from the girl I'm holding prisoner in a locked cell.' Zoe snorted and squealed. 'Too funny.'

'*I'm so happy right now,*' Maddy mocked herself, tears streaming down her cheeks.

When they'd calmed down a bit, Zoe gave a sigh.

'I meant it, though,' Maddy said. 'I might not be delirious with joy at this precise moment in time, but it is possible for your life to get better.'

'Thanks, but I seriously doubt it,' Zoe replied, getting to her feet.

Maddy sensed that their temporary closeness had faded for now.

'I'll be back tomorrow with your breakfast,' Zoe said.

'Great. Thanks. Night.'

'Goodnight.'

Maddy felt the loneliness wrap itself around her again. God, she missed Alexandre. It was like a physical ache in her chest and throat. He had become her whole life. How had she coped before he'd come along? She couldn't even remember how she'd *been*. She knew she used to be constantly angry, always fighting against some injustice in hers and Ben's lives. But now with Alex, she had an ally, a best friend, and she loved him so much she didn't know what she'd do if she never saw him again. Her new life was perfect and she wouldn't let it be stolen from her. She had to get back to him.

The sick feeling in Ben's guts intensified, his appetite dulled by worry. Only one more day until Alexandre and the others had to be at the underground city. If they hadn't managed to rescue Maddy by tomorrow night, what would happen? Would they turn up on the 21st as arranged and then would the Cappadocians let Maddy go? Would they hurt his friends? Kill them even?

As he lay on top of his bed, a thin winter light creeping in through the window, he turned the blank notepaper in his hands. Over and over, feeling the ridges where it had been crumpled, staring at its mottled surface, listening to the rustle of it. There was something crucial he was overlooking, he was sure. This paper was similar to the letters he'd opened this morning, but it was a nicer quality, thicker. And it was a different shape. No, it was no good; he couldn't think what it was he might be missing.

Esther had tried to get him involved in the housework again today. He knew she was only trying to help, but he really couldn't face it. What was the point? But doing nothing was turning out to be just as bad. His bedroom felt oppressive; in fact, the whole house felt as though it might suffocate him. He needed to get out. Maybe a ride would clear his head a bit. It was funny, even though Maddy had bought him that amazing trail bike last Christmas, he still preferred his mountain bike. He liked the silence around him and the resistance of the pedals as he pushed.

Ben stretched, yawned, sat up and put the notepaper on his bedside table. He'd been lying next to this morning's mail and, as he slid off the bed, he accidentally knocked the letters onto the floor. He swore and crouched to gather them up, straightening them out as he did so. Then he dumped the blank notepaper on top of the pile, returning the whole lot to his bedside table.

It would be cold out, but he didn't care – the ride would warm him up. He clattered down the stairs, grabbed his coat from the peg in the hall, took his gloves out of his pocket and left the house. As he walked over to the bike shed, the cold air blasted his face and shook him out of his lethargy. He was looking forward to a hard cycle through the woods. He unlocked the shed and saw his Trek in front of all the other bikes. Maddy and the others hardly ever used theirs, so Ben's was always right by the door where he left it. His beanie hat hung off one of the handlebars.

'There it is,' he said. He'd been looking for his hat for a few days. He pulled it down over his ears, wheeled his bike outside and locked up the shed.

Seconds later Ben was pedalling hard across the front lawn, his fears behind him for a brief moment as his muscles worked and fresh oxygen flowed through his body. He wished his mind would stay blank for longer, but the worries soon jostled and fought their way back in, coming at him like stabs of a knife or twists to the gut.

He suddenly skidded to a halt, his back wheel spinning out in a muddy arc. Something important had just occurred to him. Ben pointed his bike back towards the house. He needed to look at the piece of paper again to double-check his theory.

Once he reached the house, he left his bike outside the utility room door, kicked off his trainers and ran up the stairs. The notepaper was where he'd left it, on his bedside table, on top of this morning's mail. He pulled off his gloves and picked up the pile of letters.

The notepaper was exactly the same size as the other letters, *except* it was shorter in length. Every single piece of mail he had opened this morning had been written on headed paper, but the blank notepaper had no header. Maybe that was because originally it *had* been headed paper and someone had cut the header off. That would certainly explain why the top of the paper was uneven. But why? And who would've done it? And headed paper from where? What did it mean? Did it even mean anything?

The letter lying immediately behind the notepaper was the reservation confirmation from the Cappadocian hotel. The paper was similar to the blank note – thick and expensive looking; a heavier weight than the other letters. So, maybe the note came from a hotel... that would make a lot of sense. Blythe had said that Maddy was taken by the Cappadocian vampire. If that were true, he would've had to come over to England and he must have stayed in a hotel. Well, not necessarily him, but his vampire followers or staff or whatever. So, maybe they had used the hotel's paper to write the note but had cut the top off. It would be a local hotel, he was sure of it. Somewhere posh probably.

Ben began to get excited. This could be his first proper lead. This could really be something. He knew he was making a lot of leaps. Maybe he was way off the mark, but he didn't think so. And, anyway, he didn't have any other leads to follow. This might be a wild goose chase, but then again it might not. It could be a breakthrough. But it still didn't explain what the paper was doing in the recycling. Anyway, Ben realised his appetite had suddenly come roaring back. He would eat and then he would go into Tetbury and check out the local hotels.

CHAPTER NINETEEN

CAPPADOCIA, AD 575

Aelia recovered quickly and, by the following morning, she felt almost completely well again. Widow Maleina's attitude seemed to have changed and softened. She wasn't what you would call *friendly*, but at least her tongue had lost some of its serrated edge. She didn't care how pleasant the woman was being, all Aelia could think about was trying to find her family.

'If you go, you will be inviting death in one form or another,' the widow said. 'I know you don't entirely believe me, my dear. But I am speaking the truth.'

'I need some fresh air,' Aelia said. The cave felt oppressive and warm.

'Come. Let's go outside.' The widow picked up her walking cane and hobbled to the cave entrance. Aelia stood and followed her. She would rather have been alone with her thoughts, but it seemed there was no chance of that happening. The air outside was heating up, the sun already high in the sky, almost bleaching out the rocks below. It was hotter out here than in the cave and Aelia instantly wished she had stayed inside.

The widow was already a few steps ahead so Aelia sighed and followed on behind. They threaded their way through the parched shrubs and junipers, occasionally receiving some much-needed shade from the tall stone outcrops that punctuated the landscape.

After about ten minutes of walking in silence, the widow stopped and thrust her cane into the dusty earth. Aelia sat on a low rock and picked up a handful of fine brown gravel. She let it run through her fingers and watched as it bounced and slid off the rock. The widow handed her a pouch of water and she took a grateful gulp.

'I'm going back to my village,' Aelia said quietly, defiantly.

'Yes,' the widow replied.

'What? You're letting me go?' Aelia was surprised. She had expected the usual mocking resistance. As long as she didn't plan on drugging her again.

'Yes, you can go. I think you may have a part to play in this,' the widow said.

Aelia didn't know what the widow was talking about, but she wasn't going to argue. She felt nervous and excited that she was finally going to be reunited with her family.

'I'll rest today and travel tomorrow,' Aelia said, a nervous smile curling at her lips. 'Will you come with me?'

'No,' the widow replied. 'But I'll help you. We must go back and prepare. There is much to do and much you need to know about the risk you are taking.'

Aelia still didn't know if she believed Widow Maleina's warnings, but at least the woman wasn't going to stand in her way anymore. Aelia decided she would humour her and take whatever precautions the widow thought necessary.

Back home, Widow Maleina began working on her medicines. She called to Aelia to pass her the various powders and herbs she needed.

'I'm preparing this for you, my dear.'

'What is it?'

'I have been experimenting for a number of years and I am sure it will work. But it may also end up killing you.'

'What do you mean?' Aelia asked, alarmed.

'These demons drink human blood. Pass me that cup.'

Aelia handed her the vessel and noticed her hand was shaking. She made a fist to stop the tremble.

'If you enter that cave,' the widow continued, 'they will want to drink *your* blood. Of that, there is no doubt.'

'So you're saying they will kill me and drink my blood?'

'No. I am saying they will drink your blood. It is not certain they will kill you. They may keep you human or they may kill you or they may turn you. Make up a fire. I need to reduce this mixture.'

'*Turn* me?'

'... into one of them,' the widow replied.

Aelia felt numb. The widow was speaking so certainly and surely. In all the years Aelia had been here, Widow Maleina had never lied. So why should she make these horrific things up now? She set to work making a small cooking fire, trying to decide what to believe. The wood was so dry that the fire caught instantly with a whoosh, making Aelia start and jump back.

The widow's voice rose above the crackle and roar of the flames. 'Now I must ask you if you are certain this is the path you wish to take? Once we embark on this journey, there is no going back. And you must understand there is a very strong likelihood you will die a slow and agonising death.'

Aelia tried to block out the widow's melodramatic words. 'But is there also a chance I could save my family?'

'There is some hope. There is always hope.'

Aelia paused for a moment before speaking.

'I was almost sentenced to death three years ago. This second life I live now is a blessing, but I will risk it to save my family. There's no other choice.'

'Then it is decided. And who knows, perhaps you will also

live a third life. But now you must leave the cave, my dear. This next part is too dangerous for you to remain.' Widow Maleina tied a square of material over her mouth and nose. 'Do not re-enter the cave until nightfall.'

Aelia's heart beat loudly now. This was all becoming too real. What was Widow Maleina going to do that was so dangerous?

'Why are you still standing there?' the widow snapped, her voice muffled by the cloth. 'Out!'

Aelia backed away, stumbled out of the cave and began walking. The best scenario would be if the widow was crazy, then Aelia would reach her village to find her family safe underground and she could start to rebuild her life. The worst scenario... Aelia did not want to think about the worst scenario. It was like a nightmare. Murdering barbarians or night demons and death. And what was the widow *doing* in there? She would no doubt find out soon enough.

CHAPTER TWENTY

PRESENT DAY

As the hours dragged by, Maddy switched between fear, frustration and mind-numbing boredom. She would have to ask Zoe for a book or a magazine or something. Madison had even attempted to do a few sit-ups and push-ups, which was a sign things had become truly desperate, but her heart wasn't really in it. She didn't need to get fit, she needed to get out of here, to get back to Alex and Ben.

Whenever she tried to formulate an escape plan, she got as far as: 'ask Zoe to help' but then her mind would wander or go blank. And the chances of Zoe helping her were pretty slim anyway. Even if she agreed (unlikely), the other vampires would probably kill them both or worse. She would have to find out why she was actually here and who was behind it. Maddy's heart gave a lift as she heard the lock rattle.

'Hi.' Zoe entered the room with lunch which she deposited, as usual, on the end of the bed.

"Hey, Zoe.'

'Hey.'

'I just have to ask – do you know if they're keeping my brother here? Or Alex? Or the others?'

'No, it's just you.'

'Are you sure?'

'Pretty sure.'

'So you don't know for definite?'

'Let's say I'm almost ninety-nine percent sure they're not here.'

'Good.' Maddy exhaled. 'That's good.' At least that was something Maddy could stop worrying about. 'So, what's going on?'

'The usual.'

'Which is?'

'Look, Maddy. All you need to know is, you're not in any immediate danger.'

'Great.'

'Don't be like that.'

'Well, how would you be if you were being held against your will and didn't know why?'

Zoe sat on the floor and leant back against the grimy wall. 'Maddy, I'm not here for the fun of it. I've got no choice either.'

Maddy raised a cynical eyebrow. 'Just because you're a vampire, doesn't mean you have to stay here with the rest of them.'

'Where else would I go? Sergell turned me into this. He thought he was doing me a favour, but he got that wrong.'

'What do you mean?'

'I mean... I was as good as dead, but he changed his mind and turned me into this.'

'How did you nearly die? If you don't mind me asking.'

'My life was normal. Some people might've called it boring, but I was happy. Married with a beautiful son, lots of friends. The usual.' Zoe spoke the words robotically, with no hint of emotion.

'Believe me,' Maddy interrupted. 'That is not the usual. I'd say you were lucky.'

'Oh, I know I was lucky. My life was as near to perfect as it could be.'

'So, what happened?'

'Sergell happened.' Zoe sighed.

Maddy waited, hoping she'd continue.

'I was on a day course in London for work. I missed my train home and had a couple of hours to kill until the next one. I didn't want to hang around the train station, so I went for a walk.

'It was a warm night with loads of people around, so I didn't feel nervous about being on my own. I thought I'd find somewhere to eat, take my time and then head back to the station. I was going to call my husband to let him know I'd be late home. But as I pulled my phone out of my bag, I accidentally knocked my lip gloss onto the ground. It was one of those little pots you dab your finger into, you know the sort?'

Maddy nodded.

'Well, it fell onto the ground and rolled down a side street. I didn't think twice, I just followed it. It was expensive stuff. It rolled along the pavement right up to these shiny black shoes. I looked up and saw this amazingly handsome man. Not as lovely as my husband of course, but this man... he was out of the ordinary. He picked up my lip gloss and handed it to me. I couldn't even speak to say thank you or anything. The man made me feel odd. Nervous. But at the same time, I felt like I knew him.

'I took back my lip gloss and turned to go, but then I felt his breath on my neck. Part of me wanted to scream, but the other part...' Zoe stood up. 'Sorry, my story is probably the last thing you want to hear.'

'*What?*' Maddy cried. 'No. Carry on. Please. Of course I want to hear your story.'

'Well, if you're sure...'

Maddy gave her what she hoped was an encouraging smile. It really did show how deceptive appearances were. When

Maddy had first seen Zoe, she'd assumed she was an ancient vampire with no real feelings. How wrong could she have been. She was just a normal person who had been in the wrong place at the wrong time. Like Alexandre.

'So I felt his breath on my neck.' Zoe closed her eyes and clenched her fists. She was now standing in front of the bed and Maddy reached out her hand and took one of Zoe's in hers. 'I felt a sharp pain and then a warm glow through my body. I lost consciousness pretty quickly.' Zoe opened her eyes again and looked at Maddy.

'So when you woke up you were a vampire?' Maddy asked.

'Pretty much, give or take a few days of brutal agony. Sergell said he hadn't planned on turning me, but I reminded him of someone he knew. Someone special from his human life. He treats me well.'

'So are you and he...'

'God, no! No. He treats me like a daughter or a sister. It's weird, because even though he looks so young, he acts like my father, only much, much stricter. I suppose I'd be dead by now if he hadn't turned me. But I don't know if that would've been better than this. He said I wasn't to see my human family again because they would be put in danger. And I miss my son so much it's like someone stabbing me in the heart every day.' Zoe's breath caught in her throat and two blood tears slid down her cheek.

'I'm so sorry.' Maddy tried to squeeze her unyielding hand.

Zoe wiped the tears across her cheek and sat next to her. 'Life's a bitch and then you die and death's a bitch too. Only my life was lovely, and I miss it so much.'

'Then go back to it,' Maddy said.

'How exactly?'

'What Sergell said – about how seeing your family would put them in danger – well, yes, maybe he's right. But don't you think they'd prefer that to thinking you're dead?'

'But I—'

'No!' Maddy said, anger flaring. 'I grew up without a dad and then my mum went and died on me. If I found out she was out there but hadn't come to see me because it would've put me in danger, I would've said "stuff the danger". Do you honestly believe your family would be happier thinking you'd died rather than becoming a vampire?'

'But it would freak them out. How could I turn up like this? And what if Sergell's right and something happens to them? What if they get hurt by all this?'

'Why would they get hurt? You're a vampire, you can protect them from anything.'

'I don't know...'

'Don't be such a coward! Your son needs you.'

Zoe's eyes flashed and she put her face up close to Maddy's with a snarl. Then she crossed over to the other side of the room and hung her head. 'It's too risky. Look at you. You're involved with vampires and you've been abducted and locked in a cell. And these vampires, they won't just let me walk out of here and go back to my life.'

'Well, it doesn't look like you've tried very hard. Maybe your perfect life wasn't so perfect and you'd rather stay here and deliver room service to prisoners for the rest of your eternal life.'

'You're quite a bitch, you know,' Zoe said.

'No, I'm not. I'm just telling it how it looks.'

Zoe flashed her a dirty look and left the room.

Maddy was too cross to call her back in. If she'd been in Zoe's situation, she knew she would do anything to get back to her family. Saying that, wasn't she jeopardising her own chances of getting out of here by making Zoe angry? She was supposed to be befriending her, winning her trust and getting her to help her escape. Instead, she was giving her a hard time. The trouble was, Maddy was genuinely starting to like her and wanted to reunite her with her family. Poor Zoe. Maybe she had been a bit harsh on her. She'd had the courage to spill her guts and all Maddy had done was criticise. Maybe she *was* a bitch.

'I think we should take our chances and attack tonight,' Alexandre said.

Morris and the vampires were gathered in the sitting room area of their hotel suite, the blackout material firmly secured against the large window. Tension and worry painted across their faces.

'I agree,' Freddie said, his blue eyes glittering. 'We have to attack.'

'Well, I do not agree,' said Isobel, rising to her feet. 'We risk Madison's life if we rush in with no real plan.'

'And we risk her life if we do nothing,' Alexandre replied.

'May I suggest something,' Morris interjected.

'Of course,' Isobel said.

Alex and the others turned towards him. He was sitting at the dining table, his thick fingers drumming the polished table top.

'Why don't you just go and talk to them,' he said.

'We tried that last night,' Alexandre said. 'It didn't work. They want us to present ourselves tomorrow night, like obedient servants.'

'I think it's a good idea, Morris,' Leonora said. 'Maybe a couple of us could go tonight and see if they will talk, tell us what they want from us.'

'But whoever went would be putting themselves in greater danger than if we all went together and attacked at once,' Freddie said.

'No,' Isobel said. 'We should only attack as a last resort.'

'I will go and "talk" to them.' Alexandre drew imaginary quotation marks in the air. 'And while I am there I will attempt a rescue. Maddy will be in that place and once I've located her, I will get her out.'

'But you'll need our help,' Jacques said. 'How can you hope to—'

'No.' Alexandre cut his brother off. 'If we all go, they will expect an attack. If I go alone it is less suspicious. More... conciliatory.'

They all began to talk at once, voicing their objections and putting forward alternative suggestions. But Alexandre couldn't listen. He left the sitting room, went into his bedroom and closed the door. He couldn't think clearly with everyone chattering, trying to press their opinions on him. He sighed. He supposed he was doing the same – trying to impose his will. But Madison was his responsibility. It was up to him to get her out of there.

He sat on the end of the huge four-poster and rested his chin in his hands, his mind spinning this way and that, not able to settle on any semblance of a watertight plan. Every choice involved a massive risk, with Madison at the centre of it. At least if he went alone, it would be the simplest way. The least messy.

'Are you all right?' Leonora came in.

Good, she had closed the door behind her. He couldn't face another planning committee session with everybody talking at once. It was too exhausting and confusing. Leonora sank into a leather armchair and gazed up at him.

'It will turn out well,' she said. 'I know it.'

'You cannot know it. We are caught in an impossible situation and I feel responsible for you all.'

'You are not responsible for me,' she said with a sad smile.

'You are all my responsibility whether you like it or not. And I refuse to allow any harm to befall any one of you.'

'Why don't you and I go to the city tonight?' she said. 'We

will talk to them and find out what it is they want. Morris is right. It is the simplest way.'

'Let me think about it,' Alexandre replied. 'There are many hours between now and nightfall. Perhaps another solution will present itself between now and then.'

CHAPTER TWENTY-ONE

CAPPADOCIA, AD 575

As the bats emerged from their places of darkness and the cicadas began their evening chorus, Aelia returned to the widow's cave. She hesitated outside. What if she was too early? The widow had said not to return before nightfall. She turned and looked up at the velvet sky. Milk white stars emerged before her eyes, growing larger and brighter as she stared. It was time.

Inside, the cooking area was clean and tidy and the floor and fireplace had been swept, but there was no sign of Widow Maleina.

'Hello!' Aelia called into an echoing darkness.

No reply.

She lit the lamps, fumbling in the darkness, and she searched all around the back of the cave, but the widow wasn't there either. Aelia felt bemused and a little concerned, but she was also hungry and thirsty. She dipped a cup into the spring and took a long drink. The idea of cooking did not appeal, but she managed to find a stale piece of bread and an apricot. Curling up on her pallet, Aelia chewed the bread and waited for the widow to return. Before long, she was asleep.

A low droning sound woke her up. Or was it someone

muttering? Aelia strained her ears and realised it was a sort of tuneless humming. She opened her eyes and sat up. The pale waxy light told Aelia it was morning. The cave always descended into absolute blackness at night. She stood and saw Widow Maleina sorting out her medicines; putting some into a leather bag and arranging the rest on the thick stone ledges of the cave. This was not such an unusual sight. What *was* unusual was the manner in which the widow was moving around – she seemed almost light-hearted and was she... *singing?* Yes. The tuneless humming was emanating from the widow.

'Good morning,' Aelia said, unnerved by the widow's strange behaviour, but pleased to see she had returned to the cave after last night's absence.

'You're awake,' the widow replied. 'Good.' As Widow Maleina turned, Aelia noticed she still wore the cloth tied over her mouth and nose.

'I suppose I'd better leave soon,' Aelia said, feeling trepidation at the thought of the journey ahead. 'It will take me most of the day to reach my village and I don't want to travel after dark.'

'No need. You can leave a bit later.'

'But I have t—'

'I have something for you,' the widow interrupted. 'Come.'

Aelia followed. As they entered the narrow passage which led to the cave entrance, she smelled the earthy warm scent of an animal. Tethered just inside, she saw a small grey horse.

'He's yours, so there's no need to leave just yet.' The widow briefly locked eyes with Aelia before heading back inside.

'What?' Aelia hurried after her. 'Mine? But—'

'There's no time to change him so it's hard luck if it's not what you wanted.'

'Change him? Why would I want to change him? He's beautiful. Thank you so much. A horse of my own. Not even a mule. Why would you do that for me?'

'I did it to stop *them*. It is safer to travel on horseback than on foot. This beast is fast. He will carry you away from danger if you meet it. We must keep you safe until you are able to do what you need to do.'

'I don't understand.'

'Of course you don't. I will explain, my dear. Come, sit.' Aelia had a flash of déjà vu as the widow pointed to the same chair-like boulder Aelia had sat on when she'd first arrived. She sat now, almost as confused as she'd been all those years ago.

'Have you heard of the blood plague?' Widow Maleina asked. She shuffled over to her medicines and continued fiddling about with the various jars and bottles, her back to Aelia.

'I've heard of the plague,' Aelia replied.

'The blood plague is similar but worse. The symptoms are terrible, agonising. Brutal.'

'You said before that the demons drank human blood. Is the blood plague carried by the demons?' Aelia asked.

'No. The demons are immune to all human disease. The blood plague is a human disease which poisons the blood. There is no cure and it is very contagious.'

Aelia digested this information. Widow Maleina turned to face her and, in her hand, she held a small box. Her hand shook as she held it out.

'What's that?' Aelia asked, although she thought she knew the answer.

'This is the blood plague.'

'In that box?'

The widow nodded.

Aelia looked at the small brown box. 'How can you have a plague inside a box?'

'From the tiniest, most insignificant insect, I have taken this plague and changed it into something else and I have sealed it inside this box.'

Aelia didn't really want to hear the rest of the widow's explanation. Truthfully, she dreaded it. This talk of plagues and blood was bad enough, but somehow she knew it was going to get worse.

'As I said before, the blood plague is fatal to humans, but the demons are immune to any human disease. Now I have changed the disease. Now it will affect those demons. We can infect them with this plague.'

'So it will infect demons and not humans?'

'No, it will affect both, but it can now only be transmitted through the blood.'

'How can you be sure it will work on the demons too?'

'I can't be sure,' the widow snapped. 'But it is the best I could arrange and it will have to do. Now, listen to me, my dear. Listen very carefully and I will tell you what it is that you must do.'

CHAPTER TWENTY-TWO

PRESENT DAY

Tetbury, their local town, was in full Christmas mode. Twinkling lights garlanded Long Street and at the far end, two Christmas trees towered either side of the Market Hall steps. Underneath the Hall, flanked by stone pillars, was a bustling Christmas market, jammed with traders and shoppers as carol singers sang 'Silent Night' accompanied by a brass band. The whole thing reminded Ben of the Victorian-style Christmas card he'd received from Esther and Morris a few days ago.

In the street, shoppers chatted and laughed, jostling each other, red-cheeked and innocent. They flitted in and out of the pretty Cotswold stone buildings where shopkeepers sold beautiful things which would soon be wrapped, beribboned and piled high in living rooms around the county.

Ben viewed it all as if he were watching a movie. This festive cheer certainly had nothing to do with him. He paused and swallowed in front of the imposing building before him – a Georgian hotel on the main street. He told himself this was no time to be hesitant or nervous and walked inside, straight up to the front desk.

'Excuse me,' he said to the man on duty.

'Yes?' The man wasn't exactly hostile, but he wasn't friendly either.

'Do you have any headed paper?'

'Sorry?'

Ben blushed and stammered. 'Umm, head... headed paper. My mum stayed here and I... er... thought I'd get her some. Umm... buy some, I mean.' He sounded like a right idiot.

'I'm sorry,' the man replied. 'But our headed paper isn't for sale to the general public.' He said the words 'general public' as though they were something terrible and disease-ridden.

'Could I have a look at it then?' Ben asked, cringing as he spoke. 'I just want to check something.'

'No, you can't.' The man began to look around for someone and Ben knew he'd cocked the whole thing up. 'I'm going to have to ask you to leave,' the man said.

'But I'm not doing anything wrong. I just want to—'

'Now. Or I'll have to call security.'

'Security? You are joking.'

The man lifted the phone and poised his index finger over the buttons while looking pointedly at Ben.

'Fine,' Ben harrumphed. 'I'm going. Don't know why you had to be so snotty about it.' He turned and slouched back out into the chilly street. Dickhead. What was his problem? Well, that tactic obviously wasn't going to work. He hoped that wasn't the hotel notepaper he was looking for. If it was, he'd have to wait for that twat to finish his shift. And he'd have to think of a better line next time. A much better line.

He felt more confident as he marched up the steps of the next hotel. A young girl sat at the curved black reception desk, talking in a business-like manner on the phone. A noisy family had followed him through the entrance doors, a concierge heaving their bags up the steps and through the lobby. As Ben waited by the desk, their son slid across the marble floor with some style. The dad was tickling the little girl who giggled and squealed while the mum rolled her eyes and laughed at them. Ben experienced a pang of something. Not quite envy; more a longing tinged with regret for something he'd never had.

'Can I help you? Hello-o! I said, can I help you?' Ben looked up to see the receptionist smiling down at him. 'You were miles away.'

'Oh sorry,' Ben replied. 'I was... er... wondering if you had a piece of paper I could borrow, or... er... use. My friends are staying here and I need to leave them a message.'

'Yes, of course,' she said. 'Hold on.'

The newly arrived family had also approached the desk, the children bouncing around while their mum tried to calm them down.

'Won't be a minute,' the girl said to them before handing Ben a sheet of headed paper and a pen.

'Thanks,' he said, and went over to sit on one of the sofas in the wide bay window. The headed paper was smooth and creamy, nothing like the notepaper he was trying to match. Ben stayed on the sofa for a few seconds, disappointment making him frown. Then he heaved himself up and returned to the front desk.

'It's okay,' he said, holding up the pen and paper. 'My friend just called. I don't need these anymore.'

The girl was preoccupied with the new arrivals and so just mouthed a quick *okay* at him.

Ben placed the pen and paper on the side and left the hotel. He picked his way through the shoppers and joined the steady stream of people on the zebra crossing, ignoring the exasperated glares of the stationary motorists. The end of the crossing brought him to a stop outside the Old Bell, his next port of call.

The lobby was packed and Ben had to wait in line at reception as various people checked in. He kept getting jostled out of the way. None of the staff on the desk would catch his eye. He guessed it was so busy because it was Christmas. Everyone was here to spend time with their loved ones, their friends and families. Where were *his* family and *his* friends? In another bloody country trying to rescue his sister from evil vampires. It sounded like a bad B movie. And what was he doing? Looking at headed notepaper in hotels. It was pathetic. *He* was pathetic.

He turned to go. This was a waste of time. He was just a stupid deluded kid who thought he was doing something useful. No wonder the others had left him behind. As he walked out of the door, he passed a wooden lectern with a pen and notepad resting on it. Ben stopped and backed up. The paper was a mottled white colour with a blue-inked header. The lobby was still busy. No one was looking in his direction. He swiped a few top sheets and stepped outside.

It had started to rain, slanted sleety bullets which had driven the shoppers inside. The choir and brass band had stopped and the only sound now was of spattering rain, muffled car engines and wet tyres. Ben paused under the stone-canopied hotel entrance.

'You can't wait here,' a uniformed bellboy said.

'Yes, I can. I'm a guest,' Ben retorted. 'I need a taxi.' Ben didn't know where his confidence had come from, but it worked.

'Oh, sorry. I'll call one up for you. Two minutes.'

As he waited, Ben pulled the original notepaper out of his pocket and compared it to the hotel paper. He held his breath. The original was pretty crumpled, but as far as he could tell, they were a perfect match, apart from where the header had been snipped off. Ben's heart beat faster. Now what? How could he find out who had been staying here?

This hotel, the Old Bell, was Morris's local. It had once been a normal pub but had since been converted into a posh hotel. Morris and his drinking buddies still came here on a regular basis. A horrible thought crept into Ben's mind. But surely... no. It couldn't be. No. Not *Morris*.

The others would not be happy with him. No, they would be furious and they would be worried, but it was a small price to pay to keep them safe. Alexandre had lied to them. What other option had there been? He had already tried to tell them he wanted to go to the underground city alone, but they hadn't listened. They didn't realise it was the best plan for everybody. And so when they had argued, he'd pretended to capitulate. He told them they were right. That he would wait until tomorrow and then they would all go to the city together.

Isobel, in particular, had been relieved. She'd been working herself up into a bit of a frenzy, but now she was calm again. Well, as calm as she could be here in Turkey where the memories threatened to suffocate them all. He'd told them he wanted to be alone tonight, to give him a chance to plan tomorrow's meeting. It had sounded a weak excuse to his own ears and he wasn't sure the others would buy it. But they had been so relieved that he wasn't going to do anything rash and foolish, that they hadn't questioned him further.

And now here he was, about to do something rash and foolish. Alexandre smiled grimly to himself. He just hoped the others wouldn't do anything stupid, like follow him. He was so annoyed with himself. He should've done this on day one. As soon as Blythe had confirmed where Maddy was being held he should have arranged to fly straight here. Why had he spent so much time deliberating? He was an idiot. He didn't need to work out a plan; he just needed to get the love of his life back. But he had allowed the others to talk him out of it. Well, no more. Tonight he would act.

The scent of snow hung in the air, an expectant hush which cleared his mind and calmed his body. Tonight he felt invincible. The Cappadocians would not prevent him from reaching her. He would tear them apart. He knew he was capable of it.

They might be older and more powerful, but they didn't have his motivation. To them, Madison was merely part of a larger plan, but to Alexandre, she was everything. He was running on anger, desperation and love.

Would they try to stop him before he reached the city? He expected so, but as yet he could detect no scent of them. And now here came the silent snow. Sparse at first, but then thicker and faster, settling on the rocky earth and smoothing the landscape into soft curves.

Despite the snow-changed scenery, Alexandre knew the way. He remembered intimately the place of his hopes-turned-to-nightmares. It was the last place he had seen his parents alive. Afterwards, Leonora and Freddie's father, Harold, had destroyed the entrance to the city, blowing it to hell with dynamite and concealing its hidden danger from the world. But Alexandre was confident there would be another way in. He would dig down with his bare hands if he had to.

He quickly arrived at the place, but there was still no sign of another vampire. Was it a trap? But even as he scented the area for signs of life, he was overwhelmed with memories. Everything here was as he remembered it. How strange. He had thought to find it changed – modernised somehow, perhaps even paved over by a new town. But here was the same stand of trees, now leafless and snow-covered. The small hillock over there, behind which their tents had been pitched. And here was the area where the fire pit had once sat, everyone huddled around its warmth on those long ago chilly spring evenings. The delicious smells of a well-deserved supper curling into their nostrils after a hard day's work. He recalled the good-humoured banter, the disagreements and the endless planning of the two archaeologist families and the fearless Turkish guards who soon became their friends. But tonight, the snow fell onto silence.

Alexandre remembered it all as if it was yesterday. How his human self had been so full of ambition and excitement at what treasures they might discover here. But all those hopes and plans had come to nothing, turned to dust and death and destruction. And still it continued. Would there be no let-up? Would the taste of ash follow him across the centuries forever?

No time to dwell.

The snow had blanketed everything, but he quickly found the place where the ventilation shaft had once been. The secret entrance to the underground city. Now all that could be seen of it was a deep depression in the ground. And still no scent of another vampire came to him. How curious. He had expected nothing less than a heavy guard in this place. The shaft was long gone and so Alexandre began to dig.

Beneath the thin layer of snow, lay a swathe of thick ice and he smashed it with his heel and elbow. Under that sat a mixture of hard earth and soft rock. He tunnelled through it in minutes, using his vampire strength, throwing the earth up and out of the hole as he dug until he finally came up against solid bedrock. Now he changed from digging downwards, to digging horizontally. He tried in several directions, each time meeting the same solid rock. Eventually, he found what he was looking for – rock, but hand-carved to a smooth finish. He cleared an area, exposing a wall of this smooth rock. Then he placed his hands on the centre of it and he pushed sideways.

Alexandre hoped this would work. If it didn't, he wasn't sure what else he would be able to do. The slab of rock he was pushing against was one of the old stone wheels used to seal off the underground passageways. No human had the power to wheel it open from the wrong side, but Alex was sure he could do it. And now he felt a slight give. There was a rumble and he was showered with yet more earth and stones as the millstone rocked aside.

The passageway on the other side was clear and Alexandre stepped through, spitting dirt and wiping mud from his eyes and ears. He was in. But there was no time to congratulate himself, for suddenly he could sense them coming from all directions. They would be with him in a matter of seconds.

Alexandre glanced around and weighed up his options. He couldn't run now and he didn't want to. A friendly conversation would be the best approach; one in which he could glean as much information as possible.

The corridor stretched out in front of him, with rooms and other passageways branching off it. There was no light, but Alexandre did not need it. He could see, hear and sense everything clearly.

They arrived, fangs gleaming and then instantly sheathed. There were six in all and he recognised none of them. These were younger than the others, less controlled, but not as strong. Hostility radiated from each of them.

'Who are you?' a young female demanded.

'Alexandre Chevalier. I have come for Madison Greene.' His voice was low and calm. 'Sorry, I'm a little early,' he added.

The vampires stepped aside as another appeared. This one Alexandre knew. It was Sergell, from last night's encounter.

'Actually,' Sergell replied. 'Although you are unfashionably early, you are also too late.'

A chill like a cold stone dropped into Alexandre's stomach.

'What do you mean, "too late"?'

'I mean, you are too late. She is gone.'

CHAPTER TWENTY-THREE

CAPPADOCIA, AD 575

The horse was fast and Aelia felt safe on his warm back. Lowering her head into his mane, she savoured the mix of sweet fresh air and horsey scent. She tried to enjoy the speed and freedom, to ignore the fate she was riding towards, willingly. She could end it now. Turn around and return to the widow's cave. But no, it was too late even for that.

After Widow Maleina had explained what Aelia must do, she had banished her from the cave and told her not to return. Aelia had wanted to say thank you, to say goodbye properly. The widow had turned away and made to walk off, but Aelia had grabbed her sleeve to make her stop. When the widow faced her, Aelia saw her eyes were heavily bloodshot and that she had glistening beads of sweat on her forehead. She let go of her sleeve as she realised – the widow had been infected. She had the blood plague.

Aelia had cried out and tried to think of something to say, but words failed her and all she could do was stare in horror.

'I am an old woman,' the widow had mumbled through the cloth she still wore over her mouth and nose.

'But surely you must be able to cure it.'

'I could not make the new infection without exposing myself. And I told you there is no cure. It is unfortunate.'

'But this is my fault,' Aelia cried. 'If I had not insisted on going—'

'This is nothing to do with you, my dear. This is time and fate and happenings far beyond your influence. Come now, you have much to do and very little time to do it in. You must leave this place or all our plans will be for nothing. God be with you, child, and remember everything I told you.'

Aelia wanted to rail and cry. To fling her arms around the woman who had sheltered her for so long. To beg her to do something to save herself, but she knew it would be fruitless. The widow did as she pleased, and she did not want or enjoy displays of affection.

'Thank you!' Aelia called uselessly after her. But the widow did not respond.

Now, on her way back to her village, guilt swamped Aelia and she urged her horse ever faster to try to shake off these heavy feelings. As if the wind could blow away her regrets and fears. But soon her horse would stop and she would reach her destination and there would be no getting away from her destiny. She would have to face goodness knows what. There was still the chance that Widow Maleina was mistaken, but Aelia had to prepare herself for the worst. And aside from the demons, there was still Lysus to face and the rest of the village who would all be passing judgement, no doubt.

Her father's map was detailed and easy to follow. It took her away from the main routes, through narrow rocky passes and desolate stretches of scrubland. Her main concern was for bandits and she constantly scanned the horizon for dust clouds and movement. She silently thanked the widow for providing her with a horse. It made her feel so much safer and not so alone.

They stopped at a shallow stream where they both drank

and rested. For a brief moment, as she stood, staring at the wide blue sky and listening to the birds chirping, she felt all right. Not frightened or panicky about what lay ahead. She patted her steed's neck.

'What's your name, boy?' she murmured.

The horse blew out through his nose and stamped his foot.

'I can't think of a fitting enough name for you. You're my hero anyway, my horsey friend.' She kissed his velvety nose and sighed. She should be terrified, but instead, she just felt anxious to get there, to know what the future held for her. This not knowing was awful. 'Ten minutes rest and then we'll go,' she said. According to the map, they were a little over halfway there.

The miles were falling away now and dusk was creeping up to meet them. It was lucky she hadn't come across anyone on her journey. Perhaps they were all below the ground. Maybe she and the widow were the only ones left on the surface. That was a strange thought. As her horse's hooves flew across the dusty ground, Aelia couldn't help picturing the thousands of people down there below them. Were they all contentedly settling into their new home? Or were they trapped and terrified? She had to reach her family before it was too late.

It was dark when she neared her destination. Aelia dismounted and tethered her horse to a tree out of sight a few hundred yards away. She decided she would sit and rest for a few moments before approaching the cave. She needed to gather her nerve and go over the plan in her mind once more. During the journey, her mind had either been a jumbled mass of thoughts or empty of everything. Now she needed to order her brain and steady herself. The horse nickered softly and she stroked his mane.

'I'll have to leave you soon,' she whispered. 'You'll be fine.'

Aelia sat cross-legged on the ground, leaning against the tree. Earlier, before she left, the widow had given her a small leather bag containing a few provisions and now Aelia loosened its drawstring. She pulled out her waterskin and took a long drink. Again she reached inside the bag and felt around until her hand closed around the small brown box. She drew it out and stared at it under the moon's bright glow. Such an innocuous-looking thing, but the widow's plan hinged on its contents. Aelia shuddered at the thought of what it contained. So many things could go wrong. She tucked the box inside her robe and secured it against her body with a long piece of cloth which she tied in a knot.

A rush of air flew past her face, and then another – bats. Aelia didn't mind the tiny fluttering creatures. She thought of them as large moths or night birds. Harmless. Aside from their swooping antics, the night was silent. No chirruping cicadas or other animal cries. Just the quiet night.

'Hello.'

Aelia jumped, startled to her feet by the voice which was calm and amused. She turned and glanced around, but could see no one.

Then, out of the gloom, a man stepped forward. Her horse whinnied and Aelia held onto his rearing head to calm him.

'It's late for a girl to be out on her own,' the man said. He kept his distance and made no move to come closer.

Aelia's first instinct was to jump onto her horse and gallop away. This man was on foot and she could easily outpace him. But she couldn't leave now. She had to get into the underground city. Perhaps the man was a guard, but somehow she didn't think so. He was dressed too richly and spoke with an accent she couldn't place. Was he one of the invaders? He didn't look threatening.

'I'm not an invader. I live here,' the man said. 'You're free to leave. I mean you no harm.'

'Who are you?'

'You first,' he replied.

She hesitated, but could think of no reason why she shouldn't give her name. 'Aelia. My name is Aelia.'

'Pretty name.' He took another step forward. 'I am Mislav.'

Mislav. The name hung in the air like a whispered promise. Her horse whinnied again and Aelia slowly began to untether him, just in case.

'Why are you out here alone?' he asked. 'Are you in trouble?'

Was she in trouble? Yes. She was in a mountain of trouble. 'No,' she replied. She didn't want to mention the underground city in case he was an invader.

'Did you miss the descent?' he asked.

She didn't reply.

'Everyone has descended into the city, but you alone remain above ground. Do you wish to descend?'

Not an invader then. 'Yes,' she replied with a rush of relief. 'Yes, please. I missed the descent. I was ill.'

He smiled. A beautiful smile which filled her with lightness and joy. He was so mesmerising, his hair like a golden crown above noble features. Her horse was untethered now and she held the reins loosely in her hand. Suddenly the creature neighed, reared up and cantered away into the night.

'My horse!' she cried.

'Ah, let him go. He looked like a fine steed, but you cannot bring him with you. There's no room for any more beasts below.'

'But—'

'Let him go.'

She clutched her bag, feeling more alone than ever.

'I...' She didn't know what she wanted to say.

'Come.' The man smiled his glorious smile again.

Aelia took a breath and stepped towards him. She would go with him. This was why she had come here – for her family. She would see them soon.

CHAPTER TWENTY-FOUR

PRESENT DAY

'Been Christmas shopping, have you?'

'What? Er, yeah.'

'Get something nice for your girlfriend?'

'I haven't got a—'

'Here's a tip for you – You've always gotta get 'em something nice for birthdays and Christmases. Keeps 'em sweet.'

'Right. Thanks.'

The last thing Ben felt like doing was making small talk with the taxi driver. He seemed like a nice bloke, but Ben's mind was locked in a downward spiral of doom. *Not Morris. Not Morris.* The words repeated over and over again in his head. Surely it just had to be a coincidence. But it all added up too conveniently.

'Terrible weather,' the driver said. 'I've got the wipers on top speed.'

'Sorry?'

'The windscreen wipers – I've had to put 'em on top speed, but they're not making a blind bit of difference. It's chucking it down out there.'

'Yeah,' Ben replied, staring at the torrents of rain streaming down the windscreen. A snowflake air freshener swung from the rearview mirror, wafting the scent of fake pine needles under Ben's nose and making him feel nauseous.

'Can only do twenty miles an hour. Can't go any faster; not on these bends.'

Stuck to the dashboard, a gilt-framed photo of a woman and two teenage girls smiled up at Ben. The driver's family, he supposed.

'Look at that idiot!'

Ben looked up from the dashboard to see a car overtaking them.

'He'll get himself killed,' the driver said, shaking his head. 'And he won't get there any faster.'

Ben suddenly realised that finding the notepaper in the recycling bin now made perfect sense. If it was Ben, he would've burned the paper, got rid of the evidence. Morris obviously didn't watch many crime movies. But why would he do it? What would he get out of betraying them? Money? Did Esther know? Ben felt sick and shaky and weird. How could he face her now, knowing what he knew? He didn't know what would be worse – Esther being in on the whole thing, or Esther being devastated to find out what Morris was up to. Ben realised he actually felt afraid to go home.

'Stop the car,' he said.

'What's that?'

'Stop the car!' He almost yelled the words.

'Eh? Stop? Hang on, I'll find a place to pull over. You're not going to be sick, are you? I just cleaned the car this morning. You haven't been drinking? How old are you? You're just a kid, surely.' He clicked on the indicator and pulled into a shallow layby.

'Thanks,' Ben said. 'Can we just stay here for a minute? I need to think.'

'Well,' the driver said, looking a bit put out. 'We can. But I'll have to leave the meter running. I can't just sit here indefinitely all night. Not in this weather. I was going to—'

'Look,' Ben interrupted, pulling a wad of cash out of his pocket. 'I'll give you...' He counted out the notes. 'I'll give you sixty quid if we can just sit here, not talking for a few minutes.'

'All right then.'

Ben clumsily handed over the money, as the rain drummed down and cars splashed past. He felt as though he was free-falling. And there was no one there to catch him.

She had wandered around in here a hundred times before, but the layout had somehow changed. What had used to be the exit was now blocked by another high hedge. It was almost dark, shadows loomed large and she couldn't find her way out. Maddy was stuck in the Marchwood maze. She tried to shout for help, but no sound came out of her mouth. A hand grabbed at her shoulder and she whipped around, but there was no one there.

'Maddy. Maddy, quickly, wake up.'

She opened her eyes and the dream melted away. Zoe stood by the bed holding a small rucksack in her hands.

'Get up, quick,' Zoe hissed.

'What's going on? What is it?' Fear eliminated all traces of sleep and Maddy got to her feet, blinking.

'I'm getting you out,' Zoe said.

'What?'

'Well, do you want to go or don't you? It's almost dawn. You'll get a good head start before they realise.'

'Oh my God. Really? You're helping me?'

'Please hurry. And keep your voice down.' Zoe was already halfway out of the door, but Maddy still stood by the bed.

'Sorry,' Maddy replied. 'I'm coming. Of course I am.' She'd

slept fully clothed, with her coat and boots on for warmth, so she had no need to dress.

'This way,' Zoe urged.

Madison didn't give the room a backward glance as she shadowed Zoe out of the door. The room led into a *tunnel* and there were no lights out here. Once the door closed behind her, the tunnel went black.

'I can't see,' Maddy whispered.

'Shh. Here, hold my hand.'

Maddy felt Zoe's cold hand slip into hers. What was this place? She had a feeling she knew the answer and the thought made her skin crawl. 'Is this the underground city? Are we in Cappadocia?'

'For God's sake, shut up please, Maddy. Yes, we're in Cappadocia.'

Zoe moved silently without a footstep, a breath or a rustle. In comparison, Maddy's clumsy footsteps reverberated around the passageway, shuffling, tripping and scraping along the floor. And her breathing was so loud, she sounded like an asthmatic climbing Mount Everest. But that was nothing compared to the clanging rhythm of her heartbeat. And she could literally see nothing.

So, here she was in the darkness, in the place of Alexandre's nightmares. She knew the story of the Byzantine vampires that had attacked him and his family. They were brutal unfeeling creatures and now she was here among them. Why did they want her? Did they plan to turn her into one of them too?

The thought of becoming a vampire had crossed her mind before, of course it had, but she would never willingly do it. She loved Alex, but the way he had to live was not appealing. Never going out in the sun, never tasting food. Yes, there were some benefits, but Maddy didn't think she would like to live forever. It was too scary a thought. To watch everyone else grow old and die, to see the world change beyond all recognition. Mortality was a good thing in her opinion. She understood Alexandre's occasional moments of despair – it wasn't an easy way to live. She knew he often tried to forget what he was.

'We're coming to a flight of stairs,' Zoe said. 'Narrow and steep. Be careful.'

Maddy stumbled upwards, half pulled by Zoe. She used her free hand to try steady herself against the wall.

'This is no good,' Zoe whispered. 'We need to move quicker.'

'But I can't see where I'm going,' Maddy said, blinking furiously and trying hard to focus on anything at all.

Zoe sighed. 'I wish we had a torch.'

'Do they know I'm missing yet? Can you tell if we're being followed?'

'No, they're not following, but it's almost dawn and we only have a short time to get you out. I can't move the stone after sunrise.'

'Stone?'

'You'll see. Come on.'

They eventually reached the top of the staircase and Maddy bumped into Zoe's back as she stopped abruptly.

'This next passageway is pretty straight and even,' Zoe said. 'Do you think you can run?'

'In the dark? I'll give it a go.'

'Good, keep hold of my hand.'

Maddy put one foot in front of another and ran. Zoe matched her speed. It was an odd feeling to move so quickly in total darkness. She kept imagining herself running directly into a brick wall and knocking herself out. Eventually, Zoe slowed down.

'Going round to the right, now,' Zoe whispered.

They carried on like this for several more minutes – running and slowing, running and slowing. It was disorientating and strange. Maddy had thought her eyes would get used to the dark, but she was wrong. This must be what it was like to be blind.

'We're here,' Zoe said.

'Where?'

'Hold on to my hand tight with both hands. We're going up quite high and you'll get hurt if you fall.'

'Going high? What do you mean?' She grasped Zoe's hand with both of hers.

'Ready?' Zoe asked.

'I think so.' Maddy tightened her grip as she felt Zoe clamber skywards, nimbly, like a spider up a wall. Maddy was literally dangling in mid-air, hanging by her arms. She was too shocked to make a noise. Then there was a loud scrape and a bang and a sudden freezing blast of air. In less than a second, they were outside.

Maddy slid her fingers from Zoe's hand, more than slightly shaken up from her mid-air flight. They stood in the dark pre-dawn air, nervous and alert.

'I found that exit a few weeks ago,' Zoe said. 'I think it's an old chute or air vent or something.'

Maddy peered down into the blackness and shivered. The square hole was hidden from plain view in between several rocky outcrops.

'When I first found it,' Zoe continued, 'it was uncovered and sunlight was streaming into the passage. I was pretty terrified. But I came back at night and covered it over with that huge rock.'

'So the other vamps don't know about it?'

'I'm sure they don't. If they did, it wouldn't have been left uncovered. They've blocked up all the other vents down there and every known exit is guarded. I'm not allowed out without an escort.'

'But now you've found this exit, surely you can leave?'

'Look, Maddy. Don't start lecturing me again, please.'

'Sorry. I'm so sorry. I should be thanking you, not having a go. I just want you to be happy.'

Zoe touched her arm and smiled. 'Thank you, honey.'

'No, thank *you*.'

'Sun's coming up. I gotta go. Here...' She handed Maddy the rucksack she'd been carrying. 'Food, cash and other useful stuff. Keep heading east, towards the rising sun. That should lead you to civilisation and away from the underground city. Go as fast as you can. They can't follow until nightfall, but they might send others. Scratch that – they *will* send others.'

'Won't you be in danger? Now you've helped me?'

'I'll make something up.'

'Please be careful, Zoe. You should leave too. Escape with me. We can help each other. And then, when we're safe from them, I can help you get back to your family. Me and Alex and the others.'

'I've got to go. It's almost dawn.' Zoe looked scared. The sun's blush was spreading across the horizon.

'Did you say to go east?' Maddy asked, panicking for a moment.

'East. You'll be fine.'

'Thank you,' Maddy said. But Zoe was gone, just her white hand pulling the boulder back across the entrance with a scrape and clang.

Maddy stared into the deep red glow of the eastern sky. It was barren and cold out here. She hoped the sun would be up soon to give a little warmth. She'd better get moving.

CHAPTER TWENTY-FIVE

CAPPADOCIA, AD 575

As they walked towards the cave entrance, Aelia realised she was clutching her bag so tightly her hands hurt. She relaxed her grip a little and tried to breathe normally. The man, Mislav, smelt of vanilla and moonlight – a warm fresh scent that made her a little woozy. She shook herself lightly. She was just tired from the journey, that was all.

Five natural columns of pale stone rose up before them – three at the cave entrance and two on its roof, like sentries on duty. They were way over head height, cone-shaped, with pointed tips. Aelia had seen the cave several times in her life. As children, she and her friends had dared each other to enter, but none had been brave enough. They had always ended up squealing and running away. The cave was said to be the home of a wicked god who had been banished to live underground for all eternity. The pillars were supposedly the god's chimneys. Now they were someone else's chimneys – but human or demon? That was the question.

'Do you have family below? Friends?' Mislav asked.

'Yes.'

'Where are you from?'

'Here. Selmea.' She wished he would stop asking questions. She didn't want to tell him about her expulsion from the village and she couldn't think straight. She just wanted to concentrate on the task ahead. 'Is it... safe down there?'

'Safe?' he replied. 'Safe from the invaders, you mean? Of course. No one would ever guess a single person was below the ground, let alone a whole city.'

That's not what Aelia meant, but she couldn't very well ask him if there were demons underground. 'Is it really the size of a city?'

'Yes. It's larger than you can imagine. But you'll see for yourself in just a short while.'

They reached the pillars and Aelia reached out a hand to touch one of them, its chalky surface rough against her palm. Mislav gestured for her to go in.

'Wait,' she said, a feeling of panic sweeping through her body. Aelia turned and looked out at the night sky, at the stars and the moon and the dark shapes of the trees and rocks. She breathed in deeply through her nose, a final breath of freedom that might have to last her forever. 'All right,' she said. 'I'm ready.'

Mislav gave a nod and she entered the cave. It was wide and low and cool. No one stood guard. He took a torch from a bracket on the wall and walked to the back of the cave. Aelia followed him as he slipped through a small crevice, again it was unguarded. The silence was eerie. If a city's worth of people lived here, she certainly couldn't hear them. The torchlight flickered across the narrow passageway walls and her breaths echoed like a thousand whispers. She patted the place below her ribcage where she had tied the box in place against her skin, relieved to feel its shape beneath her fingers.

After a few moments, the passageway ended and Aelia stepped out into a huge cavern. The flaming torch was the only light, so it was hard to see the scale of the place. Aelia shivered.

It was chilly in here after the warmth of the summer night outside.

'We're nearly there,' he said.

'I hope my family is safe,' she replied.

Mislav smiled. 'Come.'

She followed him across the cavern. As they approached the far side, Aelia saw three sets of stone steps leading up into the wall. But there were no doorways – just a blank rock face. Mislav ascended the set of steps on the left and, as he did so, there was a rumbling sound and the wall seemed to slide open before him. Was it some kind of magic? She hesitated behind him. He walked through and waited for her to follow.

Aelia stepped through the entrance. They were in another narrow passageway. A man stood to her left, middle-aged and thickset. She caught his eye and he immediately looked down at his feet. He looked scared, terrified. Aelia looked up at Mislav, but his back was towards her. He was continuing on down the passageway. As she looked back at the middle-aged man, she saw he was turning some kind of rod attached to a huge rock-wheel which rolled back over the entranceway. She hurried after Mislav who hadn't waited for her.

It was strange to think she was finally here after all those months of thinking about it. Mislav didn't seem scared or worried about demons. Perhaps the widow had been wrong after all. Aelia hoped so with all her heart and soul. It would be wonderful to be reunited with her family and not to have to worry about plagues and demons. She would be a model daughter and marry whoever her parents chose for her. She would be helpful and kind and would suffer the cruel comments of the other villagers with good grace. She would avoid Lysus and forget any thoughts of revenge. It would be a clean slate, a new start. She only wished Widow Maleina had not been so set on her idea that would now end with her death. The poor widow – to suffer alone after she had helped so many in their hour of need. What had she said about the blood plague? That its symptoms were *brutal*. Aelia prayed for a merciful end for her.

'Do you have need of food?' Mislav's voice floated back down the passageway.

Aelia hadn't eaten since she'd stopped at the stream with her horse. She hadn't even thought about food, but now he mentioned it, she realised she was starving and more than a little light-headed.

'I am a bit hungry. If you could spare some bread...'

'I think we can do better than that,' he replied.

He had stopped up ahead, waiting for her to catch up. As she approached, he continued walking, a fast smooth pace that she struggled to keep up with. The passageway forked left and then right. They came to a crossroads and he went straight on. Aelia looked down the passageways to her left and right, but all she saw was unending darkness. She shuddered. How would she ever find her way out of here if she needed to? As they continued, she tried to concentrate on the route, but it all jumbled in her mind. It was hopeless and she gave up. Everything was so quiet. Where was everyone? They descended a staircase, narrow and winding. The steps were narrow and uneven and Aelia had to put her hands against the walls to steady herself.

When they reached the bottom, the faint sound of music reached her ears. Her heart quickened in anticipation – people! They walked along more dark corridors until Aelia felt dizzy with walking. She worried she might faint. The music was getting louder and she heard laughter and chatter. Happy sounds. She couldn't wait to fall into her parents' arms. She thought she might cry.

Suddenly, the passage opened out into a huge hall. Mislav stopped and put his arm around her shoulders. She gaped in astonishment. The hall was strung about with lanterns and draped with rich tapestries. Enormous carpets woven with golden threads adorned the floor. The tables were covered with platters piled high with fruits and sweetbreads, meat, fish and vegetables. The aromas were mouth-watering. In one corner, musicians played and in another, dancers swayed to the hypnotic tune. And the people... there were so many people, all dressed in sumptuous clothing and happier than she'd ever seen anyone in her life. They were all smiling and laughing. Even though it was late, children also sat and ate, or else played with abandon, chasing each other around the tables and nobody minded or chided them for their boisterousness.

'So how do you like our underground city?' Mislav's voice sounded low and clear in her ears, despite the raucous chatter.

'It's beautiful. So... unexpected. May I eat something?' she asked.

He laughed and directed her to a table. 'Sit, eat.'

She needed no further prompting and positioned herself at the end of a long trestle table. In front of her sat a gleaming dish piled high with spiced meat and figs. She took a piece of the succulent flesh and closed her eyes as she chewed. Roasted goat. Delicious. Mislav poured her a cup of sparkling wine. She took it from his outstretched hand and gulped at the liquid which fizzed on her tongue.

'I need to find my family,' she said with her mouth full.

'Food first, family later,' he replied.

She didn't protest. Mislav took an empty platter and walked the length of the trestle, heaping it with delicacies before setting it down in front of Aelia. She smiled up at him and nodded her thanks. He sat next to her and watched as she ate, the amused expression back on his face.

No one else paid any attention to her. They were too busy enjoying themselves, celebrating. It must be the relief of finally completing the city. After years of hard work, they were finally able to relax. Aelia took another sip of wine. She felt tired but relieved and strangely euphoric. The food and drink had satisfied her body. Now she had to find her family. She stood and as she did so she realised the room had quietened down considerably. The music still played, but the chatter and the laughter had stopped. Mislav got to his feet and she looked up at him. He smiled at her, but this time, his smile was different. It was sharp and terrifying.

Aelia dropped her cup and stumbled backwards against her chair. Mislav gripped her shoulder to stop her falling, bent towards her and pierced the soft flesh of her throat with his teeth. In the instant before she swooned, Aelia realised the widow had been right all along. And Aelia hadn't acted quickly enough. It was too late. Too late.

CHAPTER TWENTY-SIX

PRESENT DAY

The call went straight through to Alexandre's voicemail.

'Alex, it's Ben. Can you call me back? I've got something I need to talk to you about. I hope things are going well. Okay, so call me when you get a chance. Thanks.'

Ben ended the call. Angry rain streamed down his bedroom windows and he closed the curtains against the unfriendly night. He had eventually returned home and avoided talking to Esther by running straight upstairs to his room and shutting the door. He wished she'd leave the house, but she was staying here while the others were away. He could hear her clattering around downstairs and he felt simultaneously annoyed with her, scared of her and sorry for her.

Ben hoped Alex would hurry up and return his call. Maybe he should try Freddie. He called the number, but again it went to voicemail. He didn't bother to leave a message. Ben stood and looked out of the window into the darkness outside. He didn't know what to do. His mind buzzed with unwelcome thoughts and he needed to share them with someone. Maybe Jacques would pick up. He called the number. No luck. Perhaps they were in the middle of a rescue... saving Maddy.

Isobel's phone just rang and rang. There probably wasn't any point even trying Leonora, but he had nothing to lose.

'Hello?'

'Leonora, is that you?'

'Hello, Ben. How are you?'

'All right. Is Freddie around?'

'No, he and the others have gone hunting.'

'Is there any news? Is Alex out too?'

'Yes, Alex is out and I'm afraid there's no news yet. We're going to wait until tomorrow night to go to the underground city and then I'm sure it will all be sorted out.'

'I hope so. Freddie said you'd had a run-in with some of the vampires.'

'Did he. Well, there was no need for him to worry you like that. It wasn't a run-in as such, it was more... a conversation.'

'Well, take care.'

'We will, Ben. You too.'

Ben had been about to hang up, but at the last second, he changed his mind and decided to tell Leonora what he'd discovered. She wasn't his first choice of confidante, but they all needed to know about the possible threat to their safety.

'Leonora...'

'Yes?'

'I think there might be a problem.' He paused.

She waited for him to continue.

'I think there might be a problem with Morris.' Then Ben proceeded to tell Leonora what he knew.

'And you are sure of this?' she asked.

'No. I'm not sure of anything,' Ben replied, the phone hot against his ear.

'But *Morris*? It hardly seems likely.'

'I'm only telling you what I know. It might all be just a big bunch of coincidences. I hope it is. I thought I could trust Morris. He's always been—'

'This is most unsettling,' Leonora said.

'Well, I thought I'd better tell you. Just in case. I mean... he's there with you. Maybe you need to... I dunno... keep an eye on him. See if he does anything suspicious or weird.'

'Yes. Yes, you're right of course. Thank you for letting me know. And well done. That was very resourceful.'

'Thanks.' He blushed, glad she couldn't see him.

'You know, Ben, we are doing everything we can to get her back. You must believe that.'

'I know you are. Thanks, Leonora.'

'Take care, Ben. We'll see you soon.'

'Bye.'

Maddy began to walk. She could have jogged, but she didn't think she'd be able to keep that up for long. Thank goodness there were gloves in her coat pocket – Zoe must have put them in there. She had no hat, but the hood to her parka was fleecy and warm, protecting her ears from the gusting wind. It really was freezing out here. Now that the sun was rising, hopefully, it might throw a little warmth her way. This place looked like the middle of nowhere. Nothing but rocks and stones in freaky shapes. And the sky was massive; a great billowing grey blanket pushing down like it might smother her at any moment.

Heading due east meant walking towards a distant towering wall of cliffs. Did that mean she'd have to climb over the top? She'd try not to think about it until she got there. Hopefully, help would show up long before that. Here, at least, the terrain was pretty flat except for a few rocky outcrops and stunted trees. As much as she was scared and cold, Maddy found she liked the noise of her boots crunching on the textured earth, the uneven ground pebbly with large patches of frost. This was the sound of her escape.

She'd checked the rucksack before setting off. In it were bread, cheese, fruit, raisins, a bottle of water, a box of matches and some unfamiliar bank notes – the local currency she guessed. Hopefully, she'd soon find somewhere to spend it. A nice warm hotel room and a phone call home would be her favourite option right now. There had been no mobile phone in the bag. That would've been too much to hope for, but Zoe probably hadn't been able to get hold of one.

When Maddy had unzipped the front pocket of the rucksack, she had found a knife. A proper glinting sharp knife you could do damage with. It had a serrated edge and measured about the length of her foot. Knowing she possessed such a thing had scared her and comforted her at the same time. She had run her finger along the cold flat metal and then quickly zipped it back up into its pocket. Maddy hoped she wouldn't have to take it out again.

Casting glances over her shoulder, she squinted into the distance to see if she was being followed. No sign yet, but they could come at any moment. She knew she shouldn't waste time stopping to check behind her, but she just couldn't help it. Occasionally, she broke into a little jog, but it was too tiring to keep it up and each time she did she had to stop to recover her breath. If only it wasn't so cold. Each breath felt like ice stabbing at her lungs. Maybe she should have some food. She didn't like to stop, but eating something might give her more energy. Up ahead she spied a smoothish rock she could sit on.

It was properly light now and the top half of the sun was peeking above the cliffs, diamond bright but barely warm enough to feel. Maddy sat on the rock, closed her eyes and tilted her face up towards it, willing some heat to thaw her body out a little. After a moment, she gave up and unzipped the rucksack. She reached in, tore off a piece of bread, stuffed it in her mouth and began chewing. Her stomach gurgled in appreciation. She followed that with a few bites of deliciously salty cheese and a couple of swigs of water. It would be so tempting to gather up some dead wood and light a fire to warm up by, but there was no time and, anyway, the smoke would give her away to anyone chasing her. She'd have to be content with this chilly breakfast.

No time to hang about; she needed to get moving. Shoving a handful of raisins into her mouth, she stood, swung the rucksack onto her back and began walking again. It felt good to put her gloves back on and the food had definitely warmed her up a bit. To her right, the wintry sun glowed. Without it, she didn't think she would be able to bear the cold. The cliffs up ahead still looked as far away as they had when she'd first started walking. Maddy bent her head into the wind and pushed on.

Hopefully, they wouldn't come for her until at least nightfall. With any luck, she might have the whole day to get as far away as possible. Maybe they wouldn't have any humans to send after her during daylight hours. Anyway, Zoe would put them off long enough for her to reach safety. That girl was a legend.

Madison trudged along, one foot in front of the other, beating out a rhythm as she crunched over the loose earth. Her legs began to ache but she ignored the discomfort and kept going. She would see Alex soon, she knew it. Maybe even tonight. It felt like months since she'd laid eyes on him, although it must only have been a few days. The evening at the ice rink seemed like a lifetime away. He must know she was here in Turkey and when night fell he would sense her and come for her. But what if he wasn't here? He could just as easily be back in England, not knowing where she was. The thought made her ill.

Maddy reckoned she'd been walking for several hours now. The sun had risen as far as it wanted before losing heart and sinking a little way back down again, behind her to the west. She wanted to put her hand beneath the pale orb and push it up higher in the sky. She needed more time. How was she going to reach civilisation before nightfall? She didn't dare think of the alternative. She couldn't go back to that dismal cell under the ground.

Hunger gnawed away at Maddy's insides, but to risk stopping would be stupid so she ate on the go. A soft pear, more bread and cheese and some water. It didn't do much. She was still hungry and now tiredness was creeping through her body too. All that remained of the food were some raisins, a small crust of bread and an apple. She could easily have gobbled the whole lot down, but she made herself save the rest for later in case she was stuck out here all night. The thought made her want to curl up in a ball. If she was still out here after dark, she didn't fancy her chances.

What if she kept walking and walking and never reached anywhere? She could die out here. It was cold enough. She thought Cappadocia was supposed to be a major tourist destination – so where were all the bloody tourists? Not here. What she would give to see a group of hikers right now with backpacks full of food and flasks of hot tea. Her stomach growled again and she began to feel faint. The balls of her feet felt raw and blistered, her toes numb with cold. But she couldn't slow down. By now they might have realised she was gone. They might have sent people after her. The thought made her stop daydreaming about food and pick up her pace again. Maddy told herself to stop worrying. If she just kept moving, she'd eventually find someone to help her. She had to.

The sky bleached out, the sun intermittently fading and reappearing behind a froth of icy sky. *Please, God, don't let it snow*, she thought, picturing herself lost in a blizzard, freezing to death. She heard the whine of the wind, but that couldn't be right because the air had become still and hushed. So, where was that noise coming from? Maddy suddenly felt a tremor of fear. Holding her breath, she made herself stop walking and turn around. Staring into the far distance from where she'd come, she scanned the wintry landscape. Her eyes alighted on something – a spot in the distance where a line of dust was being thrown into the air. She saw another line adjacent to it. And another. Squinting, Maddy concentrated on the dust clouds. The lines were moving towards her.

With a thud of dread, she realised she knew exactly what that whining sound was – the sound of distant motorcycles. She told herself not to panic, to think rationally. They might not be anything to do with her. But it was too much of a coincidence that they were coming from the west and heading her way. Her heart pounded. How long would they take to reach her? Ten, fifteen minutes? Longer? She couldn't tell. At the moment, they were still specks in the distance. Her best bet was to hide somewhere. She'd nearly reached the cliffs and the ground was hillier here. There might be some kind of cave she could crawl into. But the problem was, it would be dark soon. And when the vampires came out to play, no cave would keep her safe.

Maddy breathed slowly in and out to quell the panic. The bikes were still specks. Okay, she needed to get further towards the cliffs. Maddy broke into a slow run, ignoring her aching legs and the pain in her chest. If she ever got out of this situation, she was going to get seriously fit when she got home. She was almost at the cliffs now. The rocks at the base were smooth and rounded, reminding Maddy of burnt meringues. If she couldn't climb up them, the only alternative was to go around and there wasn't time for that. Just a few more minutes and she would hit the first set of big rocks. She put in a last spurt of energy. Had they spotted her already? They probably had binoculars. Maybe they were looking at her right now. Don't think about that, just keep moving.

Soon, the sand-coloured boulders forced her to stop. They were too steep, blocking her way and trapping her between the cliff and her pursuers. She stood for a moment, holding her sides and gasping for breath. The motorbike whines were louder now, deeper, more of a roar and she thought she heard a man's voice shout something. She skirted the base of the cliff, desperately searching for somewhere to hide – a cave, a hole... anything.

Suddenly she spied a narrow gap between two boulders. It wasn't very large, but she should be able to squeeze herself in. Once through, she saw it led upwards through the rocks. It was a narrow track. Maddy couldn't believe her luck. She began to clamber gratefully along its path. The track was muddy, studded with stones and thick ice. It looked as though it might be a dried-up stream bed and she traced it upwards, zigzagging through the cliffs. Patches of ice made her slip and stumble, grabbing at the rocks to steady herself.

After a while, she stopped and crouched behind a rock, peering down to see if they were still following. Yes. She could see the motorbikes clearly now. There were four of them, their riders wearing sheepskin coats and woollen hats. If she hadn't managed to find this pathway, they would have spotted her clearly by now. They momentarily disappeared from her line of sight, having reached the base of the cliff. Then she caught sight of them again as they split off into two pairs and rode along the edge. Presumably, they assumed she had gone around and were hoping to catch up to her. She prayed they would keep going and not double back. But even if she lost the bikers, she still had the problem of the fast-setting sun and an even worse set of pursuers.

Her only hope now was that on the other side of these cliffs would be a town, or a village or a hotel or something, *anything*, as long as it wasn't more rocks and stones and wilderness. If she could find someone with a phone, she could call Alex and the others. She continued to climb up the ever-steepening track, her fingers and toes still numb with cold. She wasn't thinking about anything anymore, just the need to move as fast as she could. The need to reach the top and see what lay beyond. She could no longer hear the motorcycles. Good. That was one less thing to worry about for the moment. She must be about halfway up the cliff by now. She turned and looked back, instantly hit by a wave of vertigo.

'Don't look down,' she whispered to herself.

Turning her attention back to the track, she rounded the next sharp bend and gave a short scream of terror. There was a man blocking her path and he had a knife.

CHAPTER TWENTY-SEVEN

CAPPADOCIA, AD 575

The smell was awful – foetid and stifling – and all around her, groans and whimpers mingled with the wails of crying children. She felt hot and cold at the same time, and was so tired and stiff she could barely move. Aelia opened her eyes and instantly panicked. She couldn't see! Was she blind? She blinked furiously, but everything remained black. Stretching her hands out around her, she realised she was wedged in between several bodies. She stifled a scream. Were the bodies alive or dead? She sat up.

'Hello?' she said, hearing the fear in her voice. 'Where are we? I can't see anything.'

'We're in hell,' came a weary reply. A man's voice, quite close to her.

'Were they demons?' she asked. 'Before in the hall.'

'Demons, yes.'

'God, save us from this horror,' a woman moaned.

Aelia began to make out vague shapes, her eyes adjusting to the darkness. 'Does anyone have a light?' she asked.

'Do you think we'd be lying in the dark if we did,' someone replied.

'Why are we still alive?' Aelia asked. 'Why didn't they kill us?'

'They like our blood,' the man answered. 'This is their food store. They're saving us for later.'

Not too late, then, Aelia realised, relief mingling with horror. There was still time to put her plan in motion. 'Why did they bother to feed us?' she asked. 'Why the music and the dancers? Why was everybody celebrating?'

'The celebration was for *them*, not us,' the man said. 'Only we didn't know it, did we. We're being kept like animals, fed and watered and ripe for the slaughter.'

'Shut up, will you!' A woman's voice floated through the gloom. 'The children don't need to hear any of that.'

'Sorry,' the man replied. 'But what does it matter. We're all dead anyway.'

'For God's sake!' the woman yelled. 'Someone shut that idiot up.'

More children began to cry and soon everyone was shouting, arguing. It sounded like there were an awful lot of people in the room. Aelia pulled her knees up towards her body, trying to make herself as small as possible so she wasn't touching anyone else. The bodies next to her were unmoving and she had the horrible feeling they might be dead. Her eyes were still adjusting and she could now make out the outlines of people and the pale curves of their frightened faces.

'Will the demons come back for us?' Aelia asked, facing in the direction where she thought the man was. 'Hello!' She raised her voice above the noise. 'Does anyone know if they will come back for us?'

'We don't know anything,' a woman replied. 'They might just leave us in here to rot. I'm so thirsty. Is there any water?'

'If anyone has any water, please, I'm begging you, let me have a sip,' someone else cried.

Aelia's leather bag was still slung across her body. She still

had the waterskin in it, but she couldn't announce the fact –
there would be a riot.

'Is there anybody here from Selmea?' she asked.

'Selmea?' the man's voice snapped back at her. 'This whole
thing started in Selmea. It was their idea to build this godforsaken place. I'll kill anyone who says they're from Selmea.'

She'd been about to ask if anyone knew her family, but that
didn't seem like such a good idea now. A soft hand grasped hers
and an old woman whispered in her ear.

'I'm from Selmea. Who are you?'

'Aelia Laskarina,' she whispered back with some
trepidation.

The woman was silent for a moment. 'Ahh,' she finally said.
'The Laskarina girl. You're still alive, then.'

'Yes,' she said defiantly. And then more contritely, 'Yes.'

'Good for you. But it didn't make much difference in the
end. Now that we're here...'

'Have you seen my family? Are they down here too?'

'I saw them at the entrance before we descended, but I
haven't seen them since. I haven't seen my family either. I don't
suppose I shall ever see them now.'

Aelia squeezed the woman's hand. 'We can't give up yet.
What about me? A few years ago, I was almost sentenced to
death, but I'm still alive. Tell me something – if you could save
your family by sacrificing yourself, would you do it?'

'I'm going to die anyway,' the woman replied. 'I have two
sons and they have families of their own. I would do anything to
save them, of course I would. But what can I do? A feeble old
woman?'

'I don't know,' Aelia replied. But she did know. And she
would have to do it. She had to do it before the demon creatures
came back for her and it was too late. What Mislav had done to
her was unthinkable. And the look on his face before he had

done it was terrifying. His whole face had changed. And those teeth! She put her fingers to her throat. It felt bruised and tender. There was no time to waste.

She reached beneath the folds in her tunic and untied the strip of material which held the box in place. With shaking hands she took the box out, holding it tightly. If she dropped it in here she might never find it again. She was terrified of opening it, even though she knew she had no choice. But once she did open it there would be no going back.

The widow had told her that if she entered the city and found it inhabited by the night demons, she was to infect herself with the plague. Just a small piece of infected tissue was all it would take. It would surely kill her, but if the demons drank her blood, it would hopefully kill them too. She prayed the widow was right and that it was only transmitted through the blood, otherwise, opening the box would do more damage to everyone here than it would to the demons. But she had to take the risk.

Once a demon was infected, it would also pass on the infection to the humans it drank from. These humans in turn would pass it onto the other demons who drank from them, and so on. This was the part Aelia was worried about – giving the disease to other humans. But what other choice did she have? As the old woman had just said, they were all going to die anyway. Better to die trying to save everyone, than as a meal for demons. If she thought too much about it, she would do nothing and then it would be too late.

The shouting and arguing had faded away now and all she could hear were a few sobs and moans and some hushed conversation.

Aelia manoeuvred herself into a cross-legged position and held the box over her lap in case she dropped it. Stuck to the base of the box was a tiny blade made from bone which she snapped away from the wood. She used her fingers to feel where the box was sealed and ran the blade carefully around the edge. The blade was still sticky, and she re-attached it to the box. Holding her breath, she pried off the tiny lid. She tentatively put her forefinger inside the box and felt something gelatinous and soft. Aelia gagged and tried to steady her breathing. If she threw up in here, she wouldn't be thanked. She rested the box in her lap, pushed up the sleeve of her tunic and picked up the blade again, holding it above her arm.

Clearing her mind of the horror, she thought of her family. Of her sisters' laughter and her mother's comforting arms. Of her father's good humour and of the cosy dwelling where she grew up. She thought of the cool stream where she had paddled in her bare feet and of the beautiful grey horse she had owned for one afternoon. She ran the tiny knife firmly across the soft flesh on her forearm. A warm sting spread across the skin and she dropped the blade. It was lost, but she no longer needed it. Using her thumb and forefinger, she lifted out the contents of the box and rubbed them into her fresh wound. The widow had said this was the quickest way to contract the disease. She also dabbed it onto the sore spot on her neck, but it was so painful she thought she might pass out.

'What have you got there?'

It was the man's voice. Was he talking to her?

'Hey, girl, I said what have you got? Is it water? Have you got water?'

She felt a hand reach out and grab at her. And then another hand. The box and its contents fell away from her.

'No, no. I don't have any water,' she said, and tried to push the grasping hands away.

'What's this?' A woman's voice. 'She has a bag.'

Someone was pulling at the leather bag, still slung across her body. It contained half a skin of water and some food. Aelia suddenly felt really thirsty. But now there were too many people grabbing at her body and her clothes. The bag was wrenched from her body.

'Stop! Leave me alone!' she cried. But the bodies were piling on top of her until she could hardly breathe. They were going to kill her. She was going to suffocate in here. 'Please,' she whimpered. 'Please. *Stop.*'

CHAPTER TWENTY-EIGHT

PRESENT DAY

The man towered above her on the narrow rocky path. Maddy stared at him, momentarily turned to stone by a swift paralysing fear. It was one of the bikers, wearing a tan sheepskin coat and aviator-style sunglasses. The knife in his hand caught the rays of the dying sun and made her blink, shaking her out of her paralysis. She took a step backwards, willing herself to turn and run. The man began to talk, his voice low and guttural, speaking a language she didn't know. And she didn't think she wanted to know it either. Whatever he was saying it didn't sound good or friendly or like anything she would want to hear.

After what seemed like an age, she turned and stumbled away from him. He lunged after her with the knife, but she was too quick. Going back down the way she had come was not as easy as the journey up. For a start, now she was able to see just how high she had climbed and flashes of vertigo almost made her fall. Also, the sun had reappeared from behind its haze of cloud and shone directly into her eyes, half blinding her. After feeling cold for so many hours, now a warm fear swam through her and the sweat prickled down her stomach, her back and under her arms.

Heavy, slithering footsteps from behind made Maddy almost throw herself down the track to get away from her pursuer. She crashed into rocks, half falling down the cliffside. As she ran, she thought that if this giant chasing her was one of the bikers, then where were the others?

She got her answer straight away. Through the laser beam rays of the sun and the mess of boulders, she glimpsed three motorbikes at the base of the cliff. Two figures stood on the ground and one sat astride his bike. All three squinted up. She was being flushed out, heading straight into a trap. It was over.

Her pursuer was slow. She could hear him muttering and cursing quite a way behind. If she was going to do anything, it would have to be now while she was far enough away from the bottom of the cliff for the others to see. Quickly, she ducked behind a large rock, squatting and holding her breath. The temptation to peep out was overwhelming, but she resisted and stayed completely out of sight.

Twenty or so seconds later, she heard him crashing down the path. She squeezed her eyes shut as her heart pounded, sure that any moment she would be discovered. He passed within a few inches of her hiding place, but pretty soon she saw his back disappearing down the cliffside. However, Maddy knew it wasn't over; he would soon realise his mistake, so she came out from behind the rock and began to scramble up the track once more.

Could she outrun them? Were there any more of them lurking behind the rocks? She couldn't worry about that. Madison had to keep going as fast as she could and hope that her luck held. Her breathing was laboured, her legs screamed in pain as the muscles were pushed on and on, up and up. She realised the sun had dimmed, reclaimed by the snowy clouds.

'Got you!'

Madison was grabbed from behind and lifted off the

ground. She squealed with shock and kicked backwards into her attacker's shins.

'Calm down.' It was a man's voice and he had an accent. He had her arms pinned to her sides, so all Maddy could do was use her heels to batter his legs.

'Get... *off!*' she yelled. 'Let me go!'

'Kick me again and I will use this.' The man let go with his right arm, keeping hold of her with his left and she felt cold metal press into the side of her head. Then he dropped her to the ground. 'I'll shoot you in the back if you run. I'm not chasing you around the mountain.'

Maddy didn't move. She didn't look up. She didn't even want to think. What a waste of time. All that effort for nothing. It was almost dark now anyway. Daylight was a distant dream of hope and escape.

'Get up.' The man kicked at her leg.

Maddy took a shaky breath, willing herself not to cry. She wouldn't give the arrogant pig the satisfaction. She stood and turned, staring right into his eyes. It wasn't the man with the knife. This one wasn't as tall and he had a gun which he held loosely at his side. The man pushed her in front of him and prodded at her to start moving down the cliff. As she walked, she tried to project her hatred and defiance by moving as slowly as possible. But the man kept jabbing her in the back with his gun, making her stumble and almost fall several times. By the time they reached the bottom, night had fallen.

'Ben tells me you're a traitor.'

Morris looked up from his English newspaper and stared at Leonora. His face portrayed no emotion.

'Well?' she continued. 'Haven't you anything to say? Aren't you going to defend yourself?'

'Ben must've had a good reason to tell you that.' He folded his paper and set it on the table.

'Well,' replied Leonora. 'To be honest, the evidence isn't overwhelming, but it does pose a worrying question mark over you.'

'What do *you* think?' Morris asked. 'Do you think I've betrayed you?'

'Me? I don't know what to think. It's a dilemma we could do without at this point in time. There's quite enough going on without adding a spy into the mix, don't you agree?'

Morris interlinked his hands and rested them on his lap.

'I think the best thing is if we keep you out of harm's way for the time being. Until we can determine the truth. Is that all right with you?'

'Doesn't look like I've too much of a say in the matter,' he replied.

'No,' she said. 'I'll lock you in the back of the van with blankets. You should be quite comfortable until we can decide what to do with you.'

'Just so's I know, who am I supposed to be spying for?'

'The Cappadocian vampires, I suppose.'

'Right.'

'Come on then,' Leonora said. 'You'd better put on some warm clothes. It'll be cold in the van and I'll have to tie you up so you don't escape.'

'Have you told the others?' Morris asked.

'Not yet. I'd better get you locked up and then I'll let them know.'

Morris stood and pulled a thick jumper from his case. Next, he took his coat from its hanger in the wardrobe. He put on a hat, scarf and gloves, cleared his throat and followed Leonora outside into the cold Cappadocian night.

'What do you mean she's gone? Gone where?' Alexandre took a step towards Sergell who bristled at his approach. The other vampires tensed. 'You'd better not have harmed her...'

'Or what?' Sergell smiled. 'We didn't touch the girl. She escaped this morning.'

Alexandre scrutinised the other vampire's face. He didn't seem to be lying. Sergell appeared calm, not angry or worried by the turn of events.

'How could she have escaped from here? She is a single human. You are a group of immortals.' Suddenly, Alexandre almost felt like laughing. Madison was a constant surprise to him. He allowed himself a small smile. Good for her. He would find her easily, hide her somewhere safe and then he would deal with this 'situation'.

'I'm glad you find it amusing,' Sergell said. 'But she has only made it worse for herself. You see, I cannot now guarantee her safety when they find her.'

Alexandre dropped the smile. 'When who find her? What have you done?'

'We are in pursuit. Night has fallen. It is only a matter of time before my hunters bring her down.'

Alexandre moved quickly. He must find her before they did. But he was forgetting, these creatures were as fast as he, if not faster. Before he reached the exit, two of them had him pinned him against the rock wall.

'You've only just arrived, Alexandre,' Sergell said, walking up to him. 'You can't be thinking of leaving already. And his Imperial Highness will be with us tomorrow. Now that you're here we cannot risk losing you too.'

'You don't need to do this,' Alexandre said, struggling against the two vampires who held him. 'We can work this out amicably. She is of no threat.'

'We have moved past that point,' Sergell interrupted. 'And anyway, I think it's all working out rather well. Your family will be along shortly to see what's keeping you and then you can "meet your maker" as it were.' He laughed.

As Alexandre listened to Sergell's self-satisfied speech, he tried to clear the red mist in his head. 'We had an agreement, Sergell. You said you would release Madison if I came here. You are now honour bound to let her go. Call your men off the chase.'

'We had no such agreement. An order was issued which you are *duty* bound to obey. His Imperial Highness gives the commands and we merely follow.'

'And who is this Imperial Highness? Why should I listen to a word—'

Sergell slapped his face with the back of his hand, a finger-nail cutting into Alexandre's cheek. He was still pinned to the wall by two vampires unable to retaliate although he continued to struggle against his captors.

'Do not use that tone with me, fledgling,' Sergell snarled. 'I am not in the mood for it.'

Alex suddenly realised the seriousness of his predicament. He was also terrified for Maddy's safety. The others had been right to warn him against coming here alone. He had had some naïve notion of talking these vampires around or overpowering them somehow. What a joke. He had to get out of here. He would try to distract them somehow.

'I apologise,' Alexandre said, relaxing his struggle against the vampires. 'I meant no disrespect. But I would like to know who is this Imperial Highness of whom you speak. Were you referring to the vampire who turned me?'

Sergell's face relaxed a little. 'Yes, our Emperor. And as I said earlier, he was your maker. It seems we share a father.'

Alexandre almost gagged. That creature was not his father. The very idea that it was related to him in some way made him feel physically ill. But he swallowed down his distaste and nodded to Sergell in acknowledgement.

Sergell gestured to his vampires to relax their hold on Alexandre. As soon as they did, Alex tried to break for the exit again. But he was not quick enough. Before he was able to step forward two paces, hands seized his upper arms and slammed him backwards. He jabbed his elbows out sideways to try and shake them off and swung forward with his feet, catching one of the other vampires in the stomach and sending him crashing through the recently made hole in the wall. Alexandre had wrestled one of his arms free and now used it to try to pry the other vampire off his arm. But he was instantly surrounded. He knew it was pointless to carry on, but he continued trying to break free, nonetheless.

'Quite impressive,' Sergell drawled. 'You will be useful.' He turned to one of his henchmen. 'Take him.' Then he took a step closer to Alexandre. 'Go quietly with my men and I will person-ally ensure your family remains unharmed when they arrive.'

'And Madison?' Alexandre asked, clenching his jaw and trying to keep his rage under control.

'Alas, as I said before, she is already as good as dead.'

Alexandre tipped his head back and brought it down with as much force as he could summon, head-butting Sergell in the face and shaking himself free once more. The other vampires fell on him, punching, kicking, snarling and tearing at his body until Sergell shouted, 'Enough!' They fell back and silence descended.

From where he lay on the ground, Alexandre looked up through swollen bloodied eyes. His fury kept the pain at bay, but he couldn't move. Bones had been broken and his insides had been pounded to a pulp. Sergell's face gradually came into focus, looming over him and as he came closer Alexandre could feel his metallic breath on his face.

'Anyone else I would kill,' Sergell said, his voice low and cold.

The vampire's face receded and Alexandre was dragged

along the stone floor. But even now, after only a few moments, he could feel his body healing itself. The bones knitting back together, the skin regenerating, his internal organs repairing. Wherever the vampires were taking him, he would escape. They could not keep him here. Whatever it took he would get out. Soon he would return to full strength and there would be no creature or room strong enough to hold him.

CHAPTER TWENTY-NINE

CAPPADOCIA, AD 575

A low rumbling sound filled the room and a wash of orange light flooded in. A brief silence and stillness was immediately followed by whimpers and screams. Aelia felt the grasping, squirming bodies disappear from on top of her. She was able to breathe again. Everyone had scrambled towards the back of the cavern, terror in their eyes. Aelia had been curled into a ball to protect herself from the people who had been trying to grab at her bag. Now, she knelt and lifted her head to look up at the source of the light, staring in fear and fascination at the two demons that stood in the open doorway.

Apart from several inert bodies on the ground, Aelia was now the only human remaining in the centre of the cavern. Everyone else cowered and huddled against the outer walls, as far from the creatures as possible.

The demons in the doorway were blonde-haired female beauties with terrible dark red eyes and sharp teeth, silhouetted in a halo of torchlight. No emotion registered on their faces, reminding Aelia of the blank-faced expression a snake wears when it's sizing up its dinner. The new silence in the room was like a heavy living thing.

'Here, kitty, kitty,' one of them said in a low hypnotic voice. 'Don't keep us waiting.'

'A little child might be nice,' the other said. 'Anyone care to volunteer their baby? Or shall I come and choose?' The demon stepped inside and cast her eyes around the wall. She didn't seem to have noticed Aelia crouched only a few feet in front of her. Sobs and cries now punctuated the silence.

Aelia knew she had to offer herself up to them, although the thought made her insides turn to water. She was infected with the blood plague anyway – as good as dead already. Her body shook as she struggled to her feet. A low gasp came from behind her; someone shocked at her audacity, her foolishness. She forced a smile onto her face.

'I will go willingly with you,' she said.

'How charming,' the demon in front of her spoke. 'It wants to play.'

The two creatures broke into peals of laughter as Aelia stepped woodenly towards them, forcing one foot in front of the other. They linked arms with her and led her out of the chamber and along the passage. Aelia heard the stone roll back into place, sealing her human companions back into their dark chamber.

'Is one enough?' one of them asked the other.

'This one is interesting. I am bored of the taste of fear.'

'Very well. She can be our little secret.' They giggled and walked out of the torchlit corridor into the darkness.

As they continued on, they occasionally passed back into the light which flickered from lamps set into recesses in the walls. Nobody passed them and Aelia felt herself almost being carried along, her feet barely touching the ground. She tried to distract herself from a rising terror by focusing on their beautiful clothes – garments fit for royalty made from sumptuous fabrics in rich jewel colours of golds and blues and greens, the like of which she had never seen before. As they glided through the empty passages and caverns, their hems brushed the rock floor, swishing like the sound of the wind through the trees.

Before too long, they entered a small chamber, fully carpeted with plump brocaded cushions strewn about the floor. If not for the circumstances, Aelia would have loved this room. It was warm and comfortable with a feeling of opulence that she had never imagined could exist. But she realised this room would not be a place to love; it would be a place to fear and tremble.

One of the creatures stroked her cheek with a sharp finger-nail. Aelia closed her eyes. She didn't want to look at the teeth or the eyes. She tried to steady her breathing and think about the blood plague which now coursed through her body and would soon be infecting these two terrible demons. She smiled as she felt the first bite and then she felt a pulsing lightness inside before she fell into unconsciousness.

───────────

'She's awake.'

Aelia opened her eyes to darkness. Even if she couldn't see where she was, she could certainly smell it. She was back in the sealed chamber with the other humans. Her head was on the old woman's lap and now she felt liquid being splashed onto her lips. It dribbled down her chin and she opened her mouth a little to let it trickle onto her parched tongue.

'They gave you food and water,' a man said. 'They said it was just for you. That if we touched it, they'd snap our necks, but surely you can spare some for the children.'

'Leave her be, Marcus,' the woman said. 'She's only just woken.'

'Well, we're all starving and dying of thirst here. There's no time to leave her be. If she says we can have some, that'll make it all right, won't it?'

The water had reached her throat, melting a few of the stabbing blades inside. She swallowed and blinked. Then she smelled the woman's rank breath and coughed.

'We weren't sure if you'd pull through,' the woman said. 'You were shivering in your sleep and muttering about all sorts.'

'What's your name?' Aelia croaked.

'You can call me Nonna.'

'Nonna, is what the man said true? Is there food and water here for me?'

'Yes, it's true,' the man interrupted.

'Give it to the children,' Aelia said.

A grateful murmuring broke out, but Nonna's voice rose up above the rest.

'Wait! We must save some for the girl. If she gets none, *they* will want to know why.'

'Is there any fruit?' Aelia asked. 'I would love a piece of fruit, that's all.' And then she closed her eyes and slept again.

The next time she awoke, she didn't feel quite so bad. It was a relief to feel almost normal again. Widow Maleina had said the infection would work quickly, but Aelia didn't feel ill at all. Just tired. She was surprised to see the others had saved her some food – bread, a little cold meat and a ripe peach. She fell upon it, feeling the others' jealous, hungry stares. Forcing herself to stop before devouring every single morsel, she passed a few pieces of bread and meat to the children, who snatched it wordlessly from her hands.

'Why are *you* so special?' one of the women asked bitterly. 'Why do you get food?'

'Did *you* offer yourself to those things?' Nonna asked the woman.

The woman looked at her feet.

'No,' Nonna said. 'You didn't. Aelia is a brave girl. The demons have left us alone since she came along. You should be thanking her and singing her praises instead of moaning.'

Peach juice dripped down Aelia's chin and she wiped at it with her sleeve. As she did so, she felt a sharp pain in her wrist. Putting her fingers to it, she realised the skin was broken. The demons must have punctured her wrist as well as her neck. Aelia suddenly felt nauseous and had to fight hard to keep the contents of her stomach down. She shouldn't have eaten so quickly.

Her skin felt sticky and filthy with blood and dirt. What she wouldn't give to wash in a nice cool river, to float there and let the current bob her along, rinsing her body clean. But she couldn't afford to think like that. She wasn't going to swim in a river, she wasn't going to get clean, not ever again. What she *was* going to do, was infect these blood-sucking monsters, save her family – she prayed they were still alive to save – and then she was going to die.

CHAPTER THIRTY

PRESENT DAY

As darkness fell, spinning flakes of snow flew into Maddy's face, melting on her skin and sticking to her eyelashes. The lights from the motorcycles shone directly into her eyes as the man with the gun prodded her towards one of them. He made her climb on and sit in front of him, his unwelcome arms around her as he reached for the handlebars. She cast a quick glance at the others, recognising the giant who she'd outwitted earlier on the cliff face. He scowled and she gave him the filthiest look she could manage.

The engines growled into life and they began to move back the way she had trekked. She still couldn't believe it had taken a day to reach the cliffs. What a pointless waste of time. But there was nothing she could do. No way of escape. Anyway, she was exhausted. The snow fell thicker and heavier, the headlights shining into whirling whiteness. Maddy had to duck her head to stop the wind and snow stinging her eyes.

Suddenly, she felt the motorcycle slow and swerve. She was nearly thrown off and she gripped the seat tighter. A dark shape flew low to the ground, hurtling towards them. A vampire. Coming to claim her back and congratulate the bikers on capturing the runaway, no doubt. The riders stopped, their engines still purring. Maddy saw the snow already lay thick on the ground, the motorbike tyres almost buried.

'Another has escaped,' the creature shouted over the loud engine noise.

Maddy looked up to see a female vampire, her face almost covered by a thick black scarf.

'I'll take this one back,' the vampire said. 'You must pursue the runaway. It's another girl. She's headed north, stupid creature. There's nothing for miles in that direction, you'll catch her easily.'

'But the snow...' one of the bikers began to protest.

'Stop whingeing. Your bikes can handle it. We don't pay you to complain. Give this one to me. I'll return her.'

Maddy couldn't believe it. She could barely stop herself from laughing out loud. She knew that voice. *It was Zoe.*

'Get off your bike,' Zoe ordered the man who still had his arms around Madison.

'Off my bike?'

'Yes. I'm not carrying her all the way back. You can ride shotgun with one of the others.'

'But it is—'

'You want to argue about it? Meanwhile, your girl's out there waiting to be caught.'

The man turned off the engine and dismounted, leaving Maddy still sitting there. He climbed onto the back of another bike.

'Get going. And don't come back without her,' Zoe ordered.

They left. As soon as they were swallowed up by the snowy night, Maddy slid off the bike and ran to hug Zoe.

'I can't believe it,' Maddy said.

Zoe pulled the scarf away from her face. 'What were you doing getting caught?' she said. 'Didn't you find the knife?'

'Yes, I found the knife, but I couldn't use it against four huge biker guys. They would've killed me.'

'I suppose so.'

'I can't believe you saved me again. Does Sergell know you're out here?'

'Yeah. I told him I'd bring you back. I said I felt terrible that you'd escaped under my care and that he had to let me make it right.'

'What are you going to do? You can't go back to that place without me. They'll know. Those bikers will tell them. I take it there is no other runaway girl?'

'Don't worry about the bikers.' Zoe gave a grim smile.

Maddy didn't like to think what *that* meant.

'Take the bike and make sure you escape properly this time.'

Maddy glanced back at the dirt bike.

'Well?' Zoe said. 'Do you know how to ride it?'

'Yeah. We've got bikes at home.'

'Thank God for that. We haven't got time for motorbike training. You need to go now.'

'Thanks, Zoe. I mean it.'

'I know you do. Now go. You're not safe yet. Others will come.'

Maddy hopped onto the bike. She didn't think she was scared but her hands were shaking.

'Take my scarf.' Zoe unwound it and put it over Maddy's head, draping it over her mouth and nose. 'Head back towards the cliffs and try to find a way around. There are villages that way.'

'Okay.' Maddy put her hood up over the scarf and started up the engine. 'Bye, Zoe. Be careful.'

'You too.'

Maddy pointed the bike back towards the mountains and took off through the blizzard.

Where was he? Was he dreaming?

'Papa? Isobel?' Were they here in the dark with him? 'Maman? Are you there? Are you all right?' He'd had a strange dream about demons and... but no. It was not a dream. Alexandre's mind began to clear. He must have passed out. He was here, back under the ground in Cappadocia. He was a prisoner. Sergell. They had beaten him. Madison was out there being hunted. He had to get out.

He shook the remnants of sleep and dreams from his brain and stood. His body had healed from the battering and he felt strong again. Alexandre patted his jacket pocket – his phone was gone but hadn't really expected it to still be there. This room, it was one of the underground caverns. A millstone blocked the entrance on the other side. He could shift it easily. Surely there would be guards behind it, but he couldn't sense anyone. Strange. They wouldn't leave him unguarded. Well, there was only one way to find out.

He put his weight against the stone and pushed. As soon as the stone moved a fraction to the side, Alexandre jumped back in shock. Through the gap in the entrance way shone a deadly beam of UV light, scorching his face and neck. He threw himself out of the way, but the light followed him into the furthest corner of the cavern. He took a breath and flew closer to slam the stone back into place, but as he did so the light seared into him again, melting his skin and hair.

Bastards.

Fury pulsed through him and his body screamed in pain. They had well and truly imprisoned him. There was no way past that powerful light. He was trapped.

Maddy glanced over her shoulder as she rode away from Zoe. The snow was easing, but she had to keep a tight grip on the machine to stop it skidding out. It was hard going and took a lot of concentration and energy – energy she didn't have. The cliffs were up ahead, getting blessedly closer again, looming white this time. As the blizzard eased, the moon made sporadic appearances, throwing the winter landscape into focus.

The bike sounded too loud. Surely every vampire within a fifty-mile radius would hear her escape. Hopefully, they would think it was the other bikers. The wind made her eyes water and her hood had blown down, but she couldn't afford to stop just because her ears were cold. She pressed on through the night, skirting the edge of the cliffs and, at last, coming around the other side where the land dropped sharply away to a steep incline.

It was nerve-wracking, riding at such speed through the snow. Potholes nearly jolted her from her seat and the bike got air more than a few times as she hit bumps along the way. She clung on though and kept going. How much fuel did these things have? What happened if it ran out? Her rucksack was still strapped to her back, so she had cash if she needed it. A petrol station would be good about now.

She wondered what the time was and if morning was far away. Where was Alexandre? Surely he would've found her by now if he was in the area. *Come on, Alex. Come and find me.* She willed him to appear in front of her, but the land remained empty and white and cold. Just the roar of the bike and the wind in her ears. A creature darted out in front of her, its eyes luminous in the headlights. Maddy swerved sharply, almost coming off the bike, but she pulled it together and righted herself. What *was* that? A fox or a big cat or something. She kept going.

The intense concentration had made her eyes sore and heavy. She really was exhausted, but there was no way she

could stop now. Please let there be... wait... were those? Yes!
Yes! Lights! She could see lights ahead. Orange and yellow orbs,
winking in the darkness. Adrenaline shot through her body, her
eyes feeling bright and clear again. She angled the bike slightly
to her right and headed directly towards the town or village or
whatever it was. She needed a phone and she needed fuel for
the bike and food for her, although she'd gone past the point of
hunger. All she felt now was a nagging light-headed nausea.

The lights grew brighter and she could see they lay beyond
a narrow valley. She could either head down into it – there did
appear to be a track – or she could go around. The track looked
too treacherous in the snow, so she opted to ride around the top.

Soon Maddy reached a signpost with a foreign name that
pointed down into the village. She didn't stop, but joined the
road which led down a slight incline. It felt good to be on a
smooth surface, after jolting along through that frozen desert out
there, even if the road was still thick with snow. A house clung to
the side of the hill, its wooden door an invitation. Maddy stopped
outside it. No lights were on. She turned off the engine. Silence.
It was unnerving. She got off the bike, her boots squeaking and
crunching on the snow. Maddy found herself swaying a little and
she tried to get her balance. Either the residual motion of the
bike or the lack of food was making her unsteady on her feet.

She rapped on the door, a dull muffled sound. She banged
harder and called out.

'Hello!'

Nothing.

She banged again. 'Please! Can someone help me?'

'Hello.'

Maddy swung around. A man stood in the road. She took a
step back. He didn't look like a vampire. He looked... harmless.
Just a middle-aged man bundled up in a thick waterproof coat,
scarf, hat and boots.

He began to speak. Turkish, she presumed.

'I don't know what you're saying. I don't understand.'

'Ahh, American?' the man asked.

'English,' she replied. 'I need help. Have you got a phone I could use?'

'Yes. Yes, you come this way. I have phone.'

'Have you got a mobile? Can I use it now? It's an emergency. I'll pay you.'

'No, no. Not pay. You use phone. This way.' He began to walk down the track and motioned to her to follow. 'It's cold, yes?'

'Yeah, just a bit.' Maddy took hold of the bike and wheeled it along the road next to the man.

'Good bike,' the man said.

Maddy had a fleeting moment of doubt about following this man into his house or wherever he was leading her, but she banished it quickly. She reckoned she had enough energy to kick him in the nuts if he tried anything funny, but he looked harmless enough and she reasoned he couldn't be any worse than mercenary bikers or angry vampires.

They walked quietly along the road, just the squeak of their footsteps and the soft whirr of the bike's wheels.

'Is it far?' she asked.

He turned to her and nodded and smiled. She didn't bother to ask again. They reached a narrow turning to their left and the man took it. Here, the road was bordered by a wall on one side and a steep drop on the other. Maddy stayed close to the wall. A cluster of small houses crouched at the bottom of the track. Smoke streamed from their squat little chimneys and warm lights glowed in the windows.

'You come, you come.' The man smiled and pointed to the house on the far left. 'My house. You welcome. Leave bike.'

Maddy propped up the bike and followed the man into his

house. He took his shoes off at the door and she hesitated, pointing to her boots.

'Yes. You take off. You come in.'

She removed her boots and touched the ice blocks that used to be her feet. The room was warm, cheerful and cosy. The walls were bare stone but they were hung with wall hangings, curtains and paintings. The stone floor was similarly covered with woven rugs. There were a wooden bench, two armchairs and a couple of low stools. A wood burning stove threw out a tonne of heat and Maddy almost collapsed onto the floor with gratitude at being out of the bitter cold at last.

There were other people in the room, staring at her. Some women and a young boy. They rose to greet her and began jabbering away to the man in their language.

'A phone,' Maddy said. 'I need a phone.' She edged closer to the stove, holding her hands out to the heat. But the older woman took hold of Maddy's arm and propelled away from the stove and into one of the armchairs. Then the woman removed Maddy's gloves, took her hands and rubbed at them firmly. She spoke to the other girl, who then removed Maddy's socks and began kneading away at her feet. The woman said something sharp to the boy who went away and returned moments later with an armful of blankets. The women swaddled her feet and draped blankets over the rest of her.

Maddy realised she was now shivering uncontrollably, her teeth chattering together so she could hardly speak.

'I need a phone. Please. It's urgent.'

The man said something to the woman who snapped back at him. Maddy guessed she was his wife.

Please don't start having a domestic now, Maddy thought. The man shouted at the woman, they glared at each other and then he held out a mobile phone towards Madison. She took her freezing hand out from under the blanket to take it from him with a grateful smile. Finally, finally, she could call Alex. Her heart started racing. If he was in the area, he could be here in minutes. But then, with an inward groan, she realised something... she didn't know Alex's number. She didn't know any of their numbers. She had never needed to know them. They were programmed into her phone. No! How could she contact him now? Think... think. It began with o78, she knew that much. Oh, God! This was hopeless.

Ben! She could ring him at home and he could give her the number, or he could call them for her. Yes. Alex might even be at home himself. He might not even know she was in Turkey. With fumbling icy fingers, she called home and waited, her heart hammering, unable to believe she would get to speak to them. At one point she'd thought she might never see or speak to anyone she loved ever again. There was a funny dial tone and then a foreign woman started speaking down the phone. Maddy removed the phone from her ear and stared at it in confusion. The man took it from her and listened.

'This not good number,' he said. 'Not working.'

'But that's my home number! I need to call home,' she said, almost in tears now. 'I need to call them. Please help me.'

CHAPTER THIRTY-ONE

CAPPADOCIA, AD 575

It didn't take long for the door to wheel open again. This time, Aelia was ready, knowing the others expected her to go instead of them. She didn't mind. It made her feel a little better about what lay ahead. She wasn't cowering in the corner in terror; she was taking control and fighting back, even though her battle was a silent one. Perhaps that was why she had this strength – because she alone knew the power of her tainted blood. Maybe if the others knew the secret war she was waging on the demons, it would give them hope too and with this hope would come courage.

But Aelia's bravery wavered as soon as she saw who had come for her. For standing in the doorway was the man, the demon, Mislav. She remembered the feeling of pure fear she'd had when she'd looked up at him in the dining hall and had seen his demonic face for the first time. Those teeth and the absence of human expression had been like a dream turned into a nightmare. But here, now, his face was soft again with that deceiving friendliness she had almost trusted when she first arrived.

Mislav didn't even glance at the others. He smiled down at

her and held out his hand. She stood and walked across to him, not able to meet his eye, instead staring at a point on his chest. His hand felt cold and hard, like living marble. They walked out into the corridor. No words had yet been spoken. He moved slowly, this time, still holding her hand. He wore a deep blue robe belted over a long dark tunic. The material was a kind Aelia had never seen before and it rippled like a river as he moved. The robe's braiding shone like spun gold as it caught the lantern light and she felt like an insignificant beggar girl by comparison.

They came to a narrow set of stairs which they descended, her feet barely touching the narrow treads. At the bottom, Aelia hesitated as a thin scream pierced the air. Mislav tugged on her hand and they continued on. More passageways, more sealed-off chambers, more steps downwards, more screams, darkness, torchlight. Her head spun with the rhythm of their journey. How far down had they come? Would she spend forever so far away from the light of day? Would she die and be forgotten beneath the ground?

Soon, Aelia sensed a thickening in the air; a warmth and a mugginess which replaced the cool dusty atmosphere that had preceded it. There was a strange heat in this corridor. They were heading towards something. It was as though the air had a fever. Moisture appeared on Aelia's skin. Was this it? Was this the infection making itself known in her body?

'Come,' said Mislav.

Aelia had stopped to wipe the droplets from her brow and chin.

'It's warm,' she said.

'Come,' he repeated.

She took his proffered hand again, aware her own was hot and clammy against his cool skin. Why this should bother her, she didn't know. Why should she care what a blood-drinking demon should think of her sweating palms?

A moment later, the corridor opened out into a large chamber and Aelia realised why the air was so thick and warm. They stood on a slippery wet ledge and in front of them great puffs of steam were billowing up from an underground lake. Shards of rocks hung from the roof of the cavern, like dripping stone and there was some kind of shining natural light covering the walls and ceiling. It glowed and pulsed in blues and greens, like a living thing. Two girls materialised at her side as if from nowhere.

'I'll return later,' said Mislav before turning on his heel and leaving the cavern.

The girls tugged at her clothing and Aelia realised they meant her to go into the lake. The surface was black with just a few ripples where water from the roof dripped down. She didn't know if she should be pleased she had escaped Mislav for a while, that she now had the chance to bathe and wash away the blood and grime which felt as though it were now part of her body. Or whether she should be terrified at what lay beneath the still, dark water.

'Is it safe?' she asked the girls who were peeling away her garments.

They didn't reply.

'Are you human?' she asked.

One of them nodded quickly and then looked away.

'Can you talk?'

The girl put her finger to her lips with a scared expression on her face.

'You're not allowed to talk to me?'

The girl nodded and the other girl gave her a warning look.

Aelia sighed. She felt so set apart from everyone all the time. First, she'd been banished from home, an outcast living on the fringes of society and now, here, again she was separate from all the other humans. What was wrong with her that she never seemed to fit in? She supposed that feeling had been with her

for her whole life. Did everybody feel like this? Or was it just
her who was different? Even as a child she had never seemed to
quite sit comfortably within the crowd. If she ever did, it was
because she'd made an extra-special effort to do things that
hadn't felt natural to her merely to gain acceptance.

One of the girls handed her a thin shift to wear, which she
pulled over her head. The other gave her a small, soft ball and
gestured towards the lake. Aelia sat on the ledge and carefully
dipped her toe in. The heat of the water spread through her foot
and she submerged both legs up to her calves. She looked at the
small ball in her hand, lifted it to her nose and sniffed – soap.
Reaching forward, she rinsed the grime off each foot, in turn,
massaging away the aches and then gingerly, she turned and
lowered herself into the warmth, still gripping onto the side.

The heat of the water was almost unbearable, but after a
moment, she got used to it and enjoyed the womb-like sensation. She'd heard about these types of natural warm springs
before. Her mother had visited an outdoor one as a child, but
this was the first time Aelia had ever laid eyes on such a place,
let alone experienced it for herself.

The wounds on her body burned and stung as the water's
minerals cleansed them, but she hardly cared. In a moment of
bravery, Aelia let go of the ledge and struck out towards the
centre of the lake. She flipped over and lay on her back, floating,
letting her matted blonde hair fan out around her. Closing her
eyes, she tried to block out where she really was and what she
was doing here, but the awful images crowded into her mind, so
she flicked her eyelids open again and stared at the cavern roof
instead. Shards and ridges of glowing rock hung above her like
the seaweed-tangled hair of a water goddess, cascading down
the walls in irregular waves.

Aelia didn't know how long she would be permitted to
remain in the lake and so began to wash herself, using the material from her shift as a wash cloth. It was tricky, as the lake was

too deep to stand and she had to tread water whilst trying to scrub at her skin and hair with the soap. In the end, she swam back to the side and finished off her ablutions from the ledge. Now, warm and clean, she felt much better, almost like a new person, instead of the filthy pathetic creature she had been twenty minutes earlier.

The girls waited for her by the corridor entrance. They led her back into the passageway where they walked for several minutes. Aelia felt warm and sleepy from the hot lake. Soon, a faint whooshing sound came towards her. It grew louder until it became a roar. She looked at the girls, but their eyes were on the ground. Soon the noise was too loud to attempt conversation.

After a while, they reached another cavern, smaller than the previous one, and at last, Aelia saw the source of the noise. There were no glowing green lights in here. Instead, torches lit up the entrance and the walls. Straight ahead of her, a thirty-foot high waterfall gushed out of the rock wall and fell into a small pool below. The cavern was filled with the sound of this crashing water. It was as noisy in here as the lake cavern had been quiet.

Again, one of the girls gestured to her to enter the pool. She did so and gasped at the temperature of the water. It felt like ice after the heat of the lake, but the pool was fairly shallow and only reached up to her waist. Aelia made her way across to the waterfall to let the rushing water batter her skin and untangle her hair. She used the soap again and then just stood under the torrent, her eyes closed. Presently, she felt a hand on her arm and looked to see that one of the girls had come to retrieve her from the waterfall. Together, they waded back to the rock floor and left the cavern.

Now, she was taken into a small chamber – another sumptuous room, this time, decorated in deep blues and silver threads. The walls were painted with a seascape of long narrow boats on stormy waves and the ceiling twinkled with silver stars and a crescent moon. Lamps lit the space, their flickers bringing the paintings to life.

A square of cloth lay on a narrow bench next to a pile of clothes. She presumed they were for her. Aelia removed her wet shift and dried herself with the cloth. Now that she was in a lighted room, she was able to properly examine the gash on her arm where she had rubbed in the infected matter. The skin had knitted together, but it was discoloured and dark with black and red blotches. She gently prodded it with her forefinger and winced at the pain. This was it, then; the infection would move through her body and her blood would infect the demons. Aelia was glad, but she was also scared. Soon she was going to die a horrible death.

To take her mind off what lay ahead, she examined the clothes set out for her. First she put on the white tunic which had long fitted sleeves and fell past her ankles. Next, she picked up a garment of light blue silk, like a billowing sky. She pulled it over her head and belted it, noting how it was trimmed with silver braid and encrusted with tiny sparkling jewels. She was dressed like royalty but was in no state to appreciate it. She may as well be dressing herself in a funeral shroud.

Once robed, Aelia sank down onto a deep floor cushion. The two girls remained outside. A carafe sat on a low table and Aelia poured some of the liquid into a silver goblet. Sniffing at it, she recognised the sweet scent of pomegranate juice. She took a careful sip. Other foodstuffs littered the table and she helped herself to some sticky dates and a small pastry. Why was she here in this beautiful room? She remembered the last time she had been offered the demons' hospitality. Well, if she was going to endure that again, she might as well enjoy the luxury while it was on offer.

But no. What was she doing? How could she just lounge here dressed in fine clothes, eating nice food while her family suffered? She stood and went to the entrance where the girls stood, one either side of the opening.

'Why am I here in this room?' she demanded. 'Why was I given these clothes?'

They said nothing in reply. One looked at her with an apologetic glance, the other looked away. Aelia grabbed the friendlier one by the arm.

'I asked you what I'm doing here. Tell me. Is that demon coming back? Do you know your way around? Have you heard of Selmea? I'm looking for my family.'

The other girl pried Aelia's hand off her friend's arm.

'Well, if you won't tell me, I'll find out for myself.'

The girls both grabbed at her, but Aelia broke free and began to run down the passageway.

'You can't leave!' one of the girls called after her. 'They'll find you and punish you.'

Aelia kept on running. She knew she was at least six floors down from the room she had originally been held in. But if it was true and this place was big enough to house twenty thousand people, she would never find her family. And, anyway, she still needed to infect more demons. What should she do? *What should she do*? If only Widow Maleina was here to advise her. She slowed her pace and finally stopped, sliding to the floor with her back against the sharp rock wall. Tears rolled down her cheeks.

'Why so sad?'

Aelia looked up to see Mislav standing above her. She didn't care. Just lowered her eyes and stared at her lap. His hand curled around hers and she let herself be pulled to her feet. The demon led her back along the passageway. Back to the beautiful room of silver and blue where the bobbing boats sailed away into a never-ending night.

CHAPTER THIRTY-TWO

PRESENT DAY

Maddy was out of options. She didn't know what else she could do. She didn't have Alex's mobile phone number or any of the others' numbers and she couldn't get through to Ben at home. She was in a stranger's house, stuck in a foreign country being pursued by vampires. She hadn't eaten for hours, was freezing her ass off, had no reserves of energy left and all she felt like doing was sinking her head into her arms and crying. But she wouldn't let herself break down in front of these people, no matter how nice they seemed.

'You call England?' the man said.

'Yes. Yes, I tried to call England, but it's not working.'

'You have number for UK? You have code?'

Code? Of course! She'd forgotten to put the UK code in. The man's wife started talking again and the younger woman and the boy, who were sitting on stools near the fire, stared at Maddy with open curiosity. The man shouted at his wife and his wife shouted back. Then Maddy had a thought. She took the rucksack from her back and reached in, groping around until her hand closed around a few rustling notes. She thrust the money towards the woman.

'For the call,' she said, pointing at the phone.

The woman smiled and took the money in her fist. The man went mental, shouting and pointing at Maddy and then at the money. Maddy turned to him.

'Yes,' she said. 'For the phone call to England.'

'No money,' he said. 'You make call. No money.'

'What's the code for England?' she asked. 'The number for the UK?'

The man took the phone from her and punched in some numbers.

'You call now. No zero. No zero.'

Maddy called home, leaving out the zero as instructed. After a couple of clicks, she heard a dial tone. It wasn't a normal ring, but it sounded more promising than before. Behind her, the couple were arguing again, but she tried to tune them out, willing Ben to pick up.

'Hello.'

'Esther!'

'Madison. They got you out, then? You all right, love?'

'Listen, Esther. I need Alex to come get me. I'm being chased. Have you got his number?'

'Hold on a minute.'

'Esther?'

No reply. She'd obviously gone off to get his number. She should've asked to speak to Ben; he'd have Alex's number in his phone. Oh, hurry up, Esther. Any minute, she expected to see vampires crashing through the door. Her bike had left tracks. She'd be easy to follow. She hoped the snow would start falling again to cover them over.

'Right, here we are.' Esther was back.

'Is he in England still?'

'Who? Alex?'

Of course, Alex. Who else do you think I mean? 'Yeah, Alex.'

'No. He and the others have gone to Turkey with Morris to get you back. Me and Ben are holding the fort here.'

Maddy exhaled and gave the faintest glimmer of a smile. Alex *was* here.

'Is Ben okay?'

'He's been moping around a bit, but I got him helping me out with the housework to take his mind off things.'

'Oh, hang on.' Maddy turned to the man who was glowering at his wife. 'Do you have a pen and paper?' Maddy asked, miming a scribbling motion.

His wife beat him to it and handed a small pad and pencil to Maddy. The woman was all smiles now.

'Okay, Esther, go on. What's the number?' Maddy scrawled it down. 'I'd better take Isobel and the others' numbers too, just in case.'

Esther read them out. 'Do you want to talk to Ben? I can fetch him. He's upstairs.'

'I'd love to talk to him, but I can't. I don't have time. Tell him hi and I'll be back as soon as I can.'

'Right you are.'

'Esther, can you take this number down too, in case you need to get hold of me here?' Maddy asked the man for his mobile number and relayed it to Esther. 'You won't forget to tell Ben I said hi... and that I love him.' Her voice cracked as she spoke and she willed herself not to start wailing in front of these strangers and especially not in front of Esther.

'Course I will, love.'

Maddy ended the call. She took a breath to calm herself. At least she'd stopped shivering now.

'I need to make another call,' she said to the man.

'Yes, you make. My wife bring you food. Hungry, yes?'

'Thank you. Only if it's no trouble.'

'Trouble. No.'

'Where are we?' she asked the man as she punched in Alexandre's number with trembling fingers.

He frowned at her, not understanding.

'This place. What is your village called?'

'Ahh. My village Akarsuli.'

Alex's voicemail kicked in and Maddy's chest constricted with disappointment.

'Alex, it's me. It's Maddy. I've been in the underground city, but I got away. They're chasing me, Alex. I need you to come. I'm in...' She turned to the man. 'What's it called again? Your village?'

'It Akarsuli.'

'Alex I'm in Akarsuli. In someone's house halfway down the valley. Please come as soon as you can.'

Maddy ended the call. Maybe he just hadn't got to his phone in time and he'd call her straight back. But she couldn't wait. She punched in Leonora's number. A delicious smell permeated the room. If that food was for her, she couldn't wait to eat it. Leonora didn't pick up either. Nor did any of the others. She left messages for all of them, but this was hopeless. What was she going to do? The phone rang in her hand. She answered it straight away with a breathless, 'Hello?'

'Maddy, that you?' It was Esther.

'Yeah.'

'Thought I'd better let you know that Morris and the others, they're staying in the Vadi Hotel in a place called Ayvali.'

Maddy asked Esther to spell it for her and she wrote it down, thanked Esther and said goodbye.

As Maddy raced through the possibilities left open to her, the wife brought her a bowl of some kind of stew. She took it in both hands, the pottery warm and smooth.

'Thank you so much. This smells amazing.'

The woman smiled and so did her husband. It looked like they'd got over their argument anyway.

'I name Eren,' the man said. 'This my wife, Derya.' Then he pointed to the other woman and the boy. 'My sister and my son.'

Maddy smiled at them. 'Hi, my name is Madison.'

'Nice to meet you, Madison.' They all smiled and laughed.

Maddy spooned in a small mouthful of the stew. It was as delicious as it smelled and she savoured the warmth as well as the taste.

'Amazing.' She turned to Derya. 'This is so good. Thank you.' The woman beamed. 'Where is Ayvali?' she asked Eren.

'Ayvali very far. You want go. I take you tomorrow. You stay here now. Food, sleep. In morning, we go to Ayvali.'

'I have to go now. I have to.'

Eren spoke rapidly to his wife. Obviously telling her of Maddy's plans. She let forth a torrent of words, some aimed at her husband, but most aimed at Maddy.

'My wife too, she say no. You not go tonight. Weather not good. More snow coming.'

'I know, but I'm in danger.'

'Yes. Is danger in snow.'

'No. I'm in... never mind. I have to go.' Maddy slurped down the rest of the stew. 'Do you have any water, please?'

Eren translated and his wife fetched a glass. Maddy downed it and stood up.

'Thank you so, so much,' Maddy said again. 'You saved my life, but can you point me in the direction of Ayvali? I have to find my friends.'

They protested again, but Maddy wouldn't take no for an answer. Eren told her to keep his phone, just in case and she said she would return it as soon as she could – hopefully, tomorrow or the next day. Derya gave her a thick hat and an extra jumper and put some more food and water in her rucksack. Maddy was overwhelmed by the generosity of these strangers she had only just met. She couldn't imagine this happening back in England. She'd be told to bugger off.

Soon she was back outside, more warmly dressed this time, Derya's stew heating her from the inside out. The woman was still protesting, but Maddy couldn't worry about that now. She had to put as much distance between her and the underground city as possible and try to reach the hotel. Eren walked with her to the main track and pointed her in the direction of the closest petrol station, several kilometres away. She would have to hope the bike would get her there and then she would ride on to Ayvali. She must've been in Eren's village for at least an hour, maybe more. That was plenty of time for the vampires to track her.

'Thank you so much, Eren.' She hugged him, swung her leg over the bike and started the engine. Then she set off, alone again, back into the night.

After a while pacing the cavern, Alexandre's skin had finally healed from the UV burns but his heart was still sore and angry. He didn't even know if Maddy was still alive or whether they had recaptured her? He couldn't think like that. Knowing Maddy, she'd be halfway back to England by now. And what about Jacques and Isobel and the others? What would they do when he didn't return by sunrise? He couldn't believe had he had allowed himself to be locked up like this.

Suddenly, he sensed someone outside the cavern. The mill-stone rolled aside and Alexandre backed into the furthest corner to escape from the deadly UV light outside. But the light had gone and instead, a vampire stood at the dark cavern entrance. Alexandre didn't stop to think. He hurled himself at the figure and they both flew backwards, crashing into the passage wall. He grabbed the vampire by the throat. However, it was not fighting back as anticipated and appeared to be scared. Good.

'If you don't want me to break your neck and throw you into the sun, you'll tell me how to get out of this place,' Alexandre snarled.

The vampire stared back at him, a mixture of fear and anger in its eyes. It was a young woman. Alexandre relaxed his grip a fraction.

'My name's Zoe,' she said. 'I came to free you. I helped Maddy escape.'

'You did?' He didn't let her go just yet.

'I saved her twice. And now I've diverted the guards to get you out. Told them Sergell wanted to see them. They'll know I lied soon enough. We have to leave.'

Alexandre didn't reply. At this moment, he had no choice but to trust her, so he let her go, inclined his head and followed her through the corridors until they reached a ventilation shaft which led outside.

'What happened? Where is she?' Alexandre asked, looking around. They were standing on a snowy plain which seemed to stretch for miles in every direction. Far in the distance lay a small mountain range.

'There's no time to explain,' Zoe said. 'She's in danger. Follow me.'

Alexandre didn't need to hear anything else. They left the city behind them and swept along the snowy ground towards the cliffs.

CHAPTER THIRTY-THREE

CAPPADOCIA, AD 575

When they reached the blue-and-silver room, Mislav directed Aelia to one of the floor cushions. She sat with her feet tucked under her and watched as he made himself comfortable on a carved wooden chair in the corner. He observed her with a frank gaze and she lowered her eyes. What did he want? Why was he not drinking from her?

'You are an interesting human,' he said.

She didn't reply.

'Why don't you tremble and scream?'

Still she said nothing.

'Answer me. Why aren't you afraid?'

'I... I don't know. I suppose it wouldn't do any good if I was.'

He laughed. 'You are becoming the subject of conversation. You are desirable.'

Aelia blushed.

'Not in the way you think,' he said. 'You have a quality...' He broke off. 'Will you be mine? Will you agree to be only mine? No other will be allowed to take your blood. I alone will look after you, ensure you have everything you need.'

Aelia's mind began to race. What should she say? If she

became his alone, the infection wouldn't spread to the other demons. But if she agreed to be his, perhaps she could save her family. Perhaps he would grant them mercy. Even as she thought of it, she knew they would never really be free. Soon she would be dead from the blood plague and then her family would be at risk again. Her only real option was to continue on her original course.

'What would happen if I said no to you?'

His face darkened for a moment. 'I would be insulted. You would return to the stinking pit with the rest and be fought over by my companions. There would be no rest for you. My brothers and sisters would drain you dry.' He smiled.

Her heart pounded at his words. This was what she had come here for – to infect as many as possible. But now that she was clean and rested, the thought of going back to that room with the others, of waiting for the demons to come for her again and again, made her weak with terror. What should she do? She knew what she should do, but it would take every last bit of her courage to say the words.

'I can... I cannot be yours.' There, she had said it.

Mislav's smile melted onto the floor. 'I lied,' he said. 'You don't have a choice in these things, little human. But I was interested to hear what your answer would be. Part of me is angry... but part of me likes your courage. You will not return to your humans, but I'm sorry you would choose to return there rather than stay. You have disappointed me.'

Aelia was ashamed to feel relief that she would not have to face the claustrophobic darkness of the pit. But what did this mean for her? Would Mislav now keep her apart from the other demons? How would she then manage to spread the plague among them?

'This will be your chamber,' he said. 'And now... you are mine.' He came close, pushing her hair from her neck and bending towards her throat.

Aelia tried to think of other things as she felt the burn followed by the swoon. Her heart beat loudly and she felt her blood pumping and draining. This part was almost pleasurable, but she knew it would eventually be followed by pain and weakness. Soon, oblivion claimed her and all was nothing.

When she came to, Mislav was gone and the girls from the lake were in the chamber with her. One mopped her brow with a cool wet rag and the other stood by the entrance.

'How long was I asleep?' Aelia croaked.

Neither girl replied.

'Oh, I forgot. You're the mute twins,' Aelia said, her weariness interrupted by a spark of irritation. She closed her eyes again.

Mislav treated Aelia as his pet, sometimes gentle, sometimes impatient. He often spoke to her in soothing tones, trying to initiate conversation, but she was too exhausted to pay him any attention, beset by continuous fevers and terrible nausea. Disturbing images invaded her dreams – a demon horse, her family dead and broken, a waterfall of blood. She was barely able to distinguish whether she was awake or asleep. Then something happened to jolt her out of her stupor. As she lay wrapped in nightmares, she felt a presence in the chamber and when she opened her eyes, two male demons stood before her. What did they want? She hardly cared.

'Where is Mislav?' one of them barked.

'I don't know,' she whispered.

'You,' he said to one of the girls. 'Where is your master?'

'I don't know,' she stammered.

'Then we wait.' They stood unmoving.

Aelia thought they must be important. Their dress was formal, almost military, with dark cloaks pinned at their right shoulders. But she drifted back into sleep before she had time to wonder further.

Raised voices woke her.

'Get out of here,' Mislav said to the demons.

'You are not authorised to have her,' one of them replied.

'Whose dogs are you? Get out,' Mislav ordered, and turned his back on them.

'You are not authorised, Sir,' the demon continued. 'It has been decreed that—'

Mislav swore and overturned a table. 'Get out!'

The demons left, their cloaks swishing out behind them.

Mislav crouched next to Aelia and stroked her hair. 'They will not take you from me. They have no right. I claimed you first.'

Every caress of his hand sent shards of pain through Aelia's skull.

Moments later the demons returned, but this time, there were five of them.

'Sir,' one of them spoke. 'I take my orders directly from His Imperial Highness. The human is not yours alone.'

Mislav stood, seemingly in control, but Aelia saw him flick at the tips of his fingers with his long nails.

'His Imperial Highness? Why should he be interested in a weak and dying human?'

'We do not question *why* and neither should you.'

'Insolence,' Mislav hissed.

'I apologise, Sir. But we have our orders. We must return her to the pit with the others. She is not yours alone. You are not authorised.'

'Not authorised,' Mislav muttered. 'Very well. I will return her.'

Aelia suddenly felt a burning pain in her scalp. The room disappeared as she was dragged by her hair, like a sack of rubble, through the blackness of the rock corridors. Within seconds, she was lying in the darkness, her body battered and aching, her scalp on fire. She panted with the shock of it.

'Aelia?' Nonna's voice.

She couldn't speak.

'Aelia? Someone pass me the water,' Nonna said.

'There's none left,' came the reply.

'Then God help us all.'

And so Aelia found herself back in the reeking cave with her human companions. She didn't know how she kept going. She was weak, delirious, feverish and sick. Whether it was the infection or the loss of blood, she wasn't sure.

All the while, the creatures came for her again and again – males, females and even young ones who looked like children. She didn't know how long this had been going on. It felt like an eternity. There was no day and no night; only darkness or the dancing flames of torchlight. She was either burning up with fever or freezing cold with the shivers, her teeth chattering uncontrollably in her head. She realised she didn't have much time left. She could only hope she had done her job in spreading the infection throughout the demon population. She understood she would never see her family or friends again, but perhaps they were still alive and would eventually escape this hell.

Snatches of the demons' conversations wove through her subconscious. They loved her pliancy, her willingness to go with them. She now understood that human fear infused the blood with bitterness and that her subservience made her irresistible to them. But she was also a source of conflict between them and she caught fragments of terrible violent arguments. Aelia felt herself to be near the end. She couldn't eat, she could barely walk and her skin was mottled with a rash of sores. The demons didn't seem to care. They still wanted her.

As well as the others, Mislav still came for Aelia. He didn't mention his vicious treatment of her after the guard demons had ordered her back to the pit. But she had the feeling he was sorry for it. He gave her water and soothing poultices for her pustule-ridden skin. He tried to tempt her with delicacies, but her appetite was gone. She was dying. It wouldn't be long now, even though Mislav told her he wouldn't let her die, that he would save her. All she was aware of was her body doing its duty and infecting these monsters. Her mind had shut down and she didn't have the strength to feel anything other than an overwhelming wish to die.

Aelia lay on a tapestried chaise, the intricate pattern making her so dizzy she had to close her eyes. She couldn't remember them coming for her, or what they said or did. She was barely holding onto life now, her breaths coming in short shallow gasps. The voices of the demons seemed a long way away.

'I am going to do it.' She recognised the voice.

'You must not,' an unknown male voice replied.

'I will. You cannot prevent it.'

'You. Must. Not.'

'Such a shame she is so weak.' A female voice this time. 'This one would have satisfied me for years. Is there really nothing to be done?'

'She has some pitiful human disease. She'll be dead before the night is through,' the male said. 'I cannot let you do it.'

'Juraj, I'll rip your teeth out if you try to stop me.' Now Aelia recognised the voice. It was Mislav. Her eyelids creaked open and from her horizontal position, she saw the two males facing each other.

Juraj laughed. 'She's really got under your skin, brother. Forget her. There are so many others.'

'It is not your business.'

'Oh, but it is my business. It is all of our business and I cannot let you go ahead with your foolish plan.'

Mislav snarled and smashed into the dark-haired demon. They flew across the chamber and ricocheted off the ceiling. Juraj stood and dusted himself down.

'You're a fool, brother, to expend so much energy on a pathetic human.'

'I'm warning you, Juraj. Do not cross me on this matter.'

'It's too late, Mislav. It is already out of my hands.' He left the chamber with the female demon.

Mislav snarled in anger and hurled a small silver table across the room. It clanged against the wall and echoed into the silence.

Aelia didn't know why the demons had been fighting, but she realised it was something to do with her. Something she had done or not done. She couldn't think clearly and she hurt so much. It hurt to move, to breathe. *Please, God*, she prayed. *Take me to you now. I have done all I can. I do not think I can bear another second of this existence.*

CHAPTER THIRTY-FOUR

PRESENT DAY

Following Eren's directions, Maddy rode out of the village and soon came to a wider road. A truck rumbled along in front of her and she overtook it. A couple of cars came along. It felt strange to see normal traffic after her lone trek through the wilderness. A few more cars drove by, crawling through the treacherous weather. The snow had returned, more whirling flakes which flew into her eyes. Maddy blinked and squinted through the white haze, expecting at any moment to be dragged from the bike and taken back to the caverns... or worse. But after twenty minutes or so, she saw the blurred lights of a petrol station up ahead.

Hoping she had enough money, Maddy pulled into the station and stopped next to one of the pumps. She shrugged off the rucksack and dug around inside it until she found the notes. A man approached the bike and spoke to her in Turkish. He looked as though he worked here.

'Do you speak English?' Maddy said.

'Engleesh? No.'

'Here.' She held out the notes in her gloved hand. 'Petrol?'

The man held out his hand with his palm facing upwards.

He placed his other hand on the top and raised it up slowly and then lowered it. He was asking her if she wanted a lot of fuel or a little. Maddy nodded her head in comprehension and mimed back that she would like a full tank. The man nodded and began to fill up the tank. When he'd finished, he motioned to her to go into the building to pay. She nodded her thanks and went inside.

The brightness made her wince. She felt exposed under the lights, sure that she was in more danger here than out on the bike. Quickly, she scooped up some brightly coloured bags of snacks. She had no idea what they contained, but she might as well stock up now. She also bought a pair of cheap sunglasses, picking out a pair with the lightest lenses she could find. They would protect her eyes from the wind and snow as she rode. The woman at the cash register picked out the notes she needed but still left Maddy with a sizable wedge. Zoe had been generous with the cash.

Once back on the road, Maddy felt a little less worried. At least she wouldn't run out of fuel in the middle of nowhere. In her rearview mirror, Maddy saw a couple of motorbikes. Her heart sped up. She told herself not to panic. They were motorbikes, that was all. It didn't mean they were chasing her. She sped up just the same and overtook a van. Checking in her mirror, she saw the bikes also overtake the van. Dizziness swept over her and she swerved slightly before righting herself again. *Calm down*, she told herself. The van was slow. Anyone would probably have overtaken it. She put on another spurt of speed. The bikers matched it.

She would make sure to lose them. A lorry loomed up ahead, lumbering through the snowstorm like a great dark beast. She'd have to pass it, but she couldn't see if anything was coming in the opposite direction. She whipped her head around – the bikers were gaining on her. Accelerating, she pulled out into the middle of the road to overtake the lorry. Up ahead, lights flashed at her and she swerved in front of the lorry to avoid the oncoming vehicle.

Were the bikers still behind her? Were they going to collide with the oncoming car? She didn't look to find out. Instead, she slowed and eased the bike across to the right, to the other side of the lorry so it hid her from the bikers' view. As she did so, the lorry driver pressed down on his horn, mightily upset with her, as he had every right to be. After all, she had nearly killed them both.

Temporarily shielded by the truck, she turned off her headlight and pulled sharply off the road, heading out cross-country down a steep slope. Madison felt completely in control of the bike now; it was almost as though it had become an extension of her body, bending to her will. And, strangely, mixed in with the terror, a little bit of exhilaration broke through, surprising her. She didn't dare let go of the handlebars, but in her head, she stuck a middle finger up at the bikers.

A thick shivering stand of fir trees lay to her left and she veered towards it. It would be a good place to hide. Once they realised she was down here, she wouldn't be able to outride them. Reaching the trees, she stopped, turned off the engine and wheeled the bike into the densest part. Heart thumping, hands shaking, head swimming, Madison waited, any minute expecting to hear the whine of bikes. But all she heard was the distant swoosh of a car passing on the road.

Had she really lost them? For now, it seemed she had. Although they could double back at any time. Thankfully, the snow was still falling, covering her tyre tracks. If the bikers didn't spot the tracks in the next minute or two, they'd have a hard time following her. The darkness shielded her from the bikers, but it also gave rise to a more deadly pursuer, one she'd so far managed to evade. Surely dawn couldn't be far away. Tonight seemed to have lasted forever. She remembered she had Eren's phone and checked the time on it – 6.50 a.m. It was

later than she thought. Sunrise was close. Still no messages for
her, though, and there was no signal either for her to try calling
Alex again.

Either she could hide out here and hope for the best, or she
could try to get back to the hotel. Once it got light, those motorcyclists would find her more easily. And if she just sat here, the
vampires would surely come. Maddy made up her mind. The
road up there led pretty much straight to Ayvali. It was too
exposed to travel on but she could ride parallel to it, down here
out of sight.

Taking a breath, she started up the engine. Its roar flooded
the silent plain. Maddy took off. The night suddenly didn't
seem so long or dark. Morning was almost here. Maybe she
could let herself think she might see Alex very soon. The
thought was too good to imagine. She glanced behind her for
bikes or dark swooping shapes, but could see none. The snow
was easing again. Her tracks would stay visible now.

The engine noise lulled her into a kind of stupor. Maddy
was exhausted and the cold had once again penetrated the
marrow of her bones. She felt like she would never be warm
again. She hoped the hotel had a good deep bath.

The going was becoming more treacherous with mounds of
snow-covered rock, trenches, slopes, dips and copses to negotiate. Out of the corner of her eye, Maddy saw a dark speck in the
distance up ahead, moving through the snow towards her. Then
she looked again and realised there were several of them. And
they weren't motorcyclists. Dread clutched her stomach.

Maddy braked, her breath shallow and fast. Vampires.
They were vampires and they were coming for her. They might
not even want to take her back to the underground city. Perhaps
they had something worse planned. *No. Stop thinking that way.
Think what to do next.* There was no way she would be able to
outrun them, even on the bike. The only thing that could harm
them was daylight and that was almost here, but not quite. They

must have calculated that they would have enough time to capture her and take her back with them, or kill her or whatever it was they wanted to do before dawn broke.

All she had to do was delay them, so they were forced to leave before the sun rose. They would have to flee or they would die. But what could she do? What could save her? Fire? She had matches, but everything out here was covered in snow. Anyway, would fire even stop them? She glanced around, frantic. She only had a few seconds to act.

A mound of snow lay behind her, about two feet high and three feet wide – probably a snow-covered rock. Maddy jumped off the bike, unscrewed the fuel cap and kicked the motorcycle on its side. Petrol went everywhere, sloshing all around the base of the rock. She leapt up onto the rock, reaching into her backpack at the same time. The vampires were almost here.

As she landed on the rock, she pulled the box of matches out of her rucksack, but her gloves were too thick and she fumbled, dropping the box into the snow. She ripped off her gloves with her teeth and scrabbled around to retrieve the small box. Finally, her hand closed around it and Maddy took out a match. If she could surround herself with fire, keep the vampires at bay until the sun came up...

As the first vampire stared her in the eye, she struck the match and tossed it into the gasoline. The fuel instantly ignited and eager flames rose up around Madison in a burning wall of fire. That first vampire, a young male, was immediately engulfed in the flames and he screamed, flailing backwards into the snow. Maddy crouched, making herself as small as possible. The fire had formed a ring around the rock, flickering dangerously close to her. She hadn't anticipated it being quite so vicious and quite so hot. But she was glad of it, because, through the yellow and orange wall of fire, she saw that she was completely surrounded by vampires.

The frozen bite of winter filled his nostrils. Snow, a faint wisp
of woodsmoke and the sharp odour of martens and foxes.
Alexandre tried to ignore these peripheral scents and search
further afield. He heard the intermittent patter of loose scree on
the hillsides and the swish of an owl's wings as it swooped and
missed its prey. Where was she? Why couldn't they find her?

Zoe had told Maddy to head east and so she and Alex now
headed in that direction, but the snow was making things difficult to scent. He was also mindful that they would soon be
pursued by the Cappadocians. There was too little time.

'My mobile phone,' Alexandre said. 'They took it. Did
you—'

Zoe shrugged. 'Sorry, I never saw it.'

'We need to get to a phone so I can call the others. Maybe
Maddy's with them already. Come on.'

Alexandre and Zoe moved quickly through the desolate
landscape until they reached a small village, set into the side of
a hill in the typical Cappadocian style. All was silent in the dark
night. No lights, no movement, but Alexandre sensed the warm
pulsing blood of the sleeping villagers. He was hungry, but now
was not the time. One of the buildings looked like an inn or
restaurant of some kind. Alexandre crept around the back and
forced open the door as quietly as he was able. It still made a
loud cracking noise as the wood splintered, so he paused,
waiting to see if he had disturbed anyone. No one came and he
was glad. He could do without any kind of confrontation at the
moment. After a brief search, Alexandre soon discovered a
landline and he called Isobel.

'Belle, it's me.'

'Alexandre, thank God! I was beginning to get worried.
What's this number you're calling from? I've been ringing your
phone, but it's going straight through to voicemail.'

'No time to explain. Is Maddy with you?'

'No. But she's left messages on all our phones. She's escaped! Can you believe it? We're in a village called Akarsuli. She was here, but the couple who helped her said she's now making her way back to the hotel. So, that's where we're heading.'

'Good. We'll meet you there.'

'Are you all right, Alexandre? And who's "we"? Are you with someone?'

'I'll explain later.' Alex hung up. He'd heard footsteps on the staircase and he motioned to Zoe that it was time for them to leave.

CHAPTER THIRTY-FIVE

CAPPADOCIA, AD 575

All she could hear were her ragged breaths echoing on forever, curling around her and out into infinity. She was burning and freezing, too weak to throw up, no longer human, just a thing existing. A thin imperious voice cut through her pain.

'Why do you bring me this creature?' The question hung in the air for a few moments.

'Your Imperial Highness, I request a making.'

'You dare to come here requesting a making for something so pitiful.'

Aelia forced her eyelids open. She was kneeling, slumped forward, her forehead resting on an intricately patterned rug. From the reverberating sound of the voices, they were in a large room, possibly a hall. She didn't possess the strength to lift her head to see, but she needn't have worried, for suddenly she was hauled to her feet and dragged along the ground, her head lolling and her eyes flicking open and closed.

She saw the far-away ceiling, the frescoed walls, and felt the echoing space around her. It was indeed a hall and it was a hall fit for a king – lavishly decorated and thronged with people or demons, she couldn't tell, all richly attired in beautiful robes.

Their eyes darted back and forth from her to the end of the hall. She followed their gazes until her eyes found Mislav standing before a raised dais, his back to her. In front of him, seated on a glittering throne was a boy. He was beautiful, like the carved statue of a god. He wore an elaborate headdress, embroidered robes of blood-red and a shimmering golden cloak. His eyes were heavily rimmed with black kohl and he was staring directly at her, unblinking. She lowered her eyes once more to the carpeted floor.

'Your Highness,' Mislav spoke, his usual confidence gone. 'She will not last the day, but I pray you drink from her and you will know why I request it.'

'Very well. Bring her to me. But if you are wrong I will strip you of your privileges for wasting my time.'

Aelia felt herself propelled forward again, towards the boy emperor. They held her in front of him, but after a quick glance, she dared not look again. It was too unnerving to see those dead eyes in such a young face. His movements were all at once fast and slow, blurred but measured. She didn't quite understand it. The warm metallic smell of blood was all around him. Perhaps he was the devil, the ancient God from her childhood terrors, banished to live underground forever. She closed her eyes and yet again willed death to come and deliver her.

The boy emperor tipped his head back and then threw it forwards again, towards her throat. If she'd had the strength to scream she would have – this demon was not gentle. She felt the flesh on her neck tear and rip. The pain was sharp, excruciating. She wanted to cry out to her mother and her father, to a God who wasn't listening anymore. The swoon came. Hopefully, this would be the last. Hopefully, she would never wake up again.

Her eyes opened. So, she was still alive. But this time, something felt different. Her body no longer hurt. She felt… not quite normal, but almost. She was back in the blue-and-silver chamber, lying on the cushions.

'Thirsty,' she whispered. 'So thirsty.'

Laughter. Mislav's laughter.

'Thirsty,' she repeated. If she didn't get a drink soon, she would go mad. She sat up.

'Hello, little one,' he said. 'Here. For you.'

Aelia looked up at him, expecting to see him holding a cup. Instead, he pushed a young man towards her. The man was shivering in fear, but he leant towards her and closed his eyes. As he came close, Aelia breathed in the most wonderful sweet scent she had ever experienced. It was as though her whole body was infused with a need so great it couldn't be denied. Suddenly she was slaking her terrible thirst with something beautiful, something created just for her. She opened her eyes to see Mislav smiling.

What was happening? What was she doing? There was blood everywhere. But not *her* blood. Aelia's mind cleared and she realised she was drinking the blood of this terrified man and it was good. It was what she craved. It was as if her whole exis-tence had been leading up to this moment. As if she'd been waiting for this blood all her life. It answered all the questions, banished all the fears, gave meaning to life itself.

'No,' she whispered. 'No!' she said. '*No!*'

'Yes.' Mislav smiled. 'Now, you know. Now, you are one of us.'

Aelia pushed the unconscious man away from her and rose to her feet. She was strong and healthy again, her skin unblem-ished, her body new and perfect. She wiped her mouth and ran from the chamber, Mislav's laughter ringing in her ears. She ran and ran, wanting to tire herself into oblivion, but exhaustion didn't come. Thoughts of the blood pulsed through her mind, her need for it mingled with her disgust. How could she be one of them? This was not the plan. If her plan had succeeded she would be dead by now, in peaceful oblivion. Instead, an even worse fate had befallen her. She must be cursed. No one could suffer this much misfortune in one lifetime.

As she ran for miles through the tunnels and caverns, she came across nobody. It was as if she could sense where to go in order to avoid meeting anyone. Everything was clearer and sharper, as though her previous life had been fuzzy around the edges, but now she could see and feel with a clarity like nothing else. Aelia took herself to the farthest corner of the city and finally came to a stop at the end of a rock tunnel which led to nowhere.

Rolling up her sleeve, she looked at her arm, at the place where the infection had entered her blood. Where before the skin had been black, it was now like new – creamy and unblemished. The scabs and pustules too had disappeared. Her hair was lustrous and golden like never before. She hesitated before bringing her fingers to her mouth. Feeling her teeth, she discovered what she knew she would find – sharpened fangs, like the demons had. She was someone else's nightmare now.

She should cry. She should sob and wail and throw herself on the floor at the injustice of it. But she couldn't. Part of her was a little intrigued by the situation. Those other beings were evil, but she didn't feel that way about herself. She felt like *her,* only better. Would she continue to feel this way, or would the need for blood alter her and turn her into a monster? She listened to the air... Mislav was nowhere near. He had not followed her. Good. She needed some time to plan what she might do next.

CHAPTER THIRTY-SIX

PRESENT DAY

Crouched on the rock inside the circle of fire, Maddy swivelled her head to see vampires all around her, fangs bared and faces pale against the dark morning. There must have been at least ten of them, their features and figures distorted through the flames, like a hall of mirrors.

The rock beneath her feet now oozed with slush, as the snow melted in the fierce heat. Maddy's face glowed and she was terrified she might catch alight. But the fire was both her enemy and her saviour as it was all that lay between her and imprisonment or death. How long would the gasoline burn for? Would it last until dawn? For now, it looked as though the vampires were happy to play chicken with the sun. Was it her imagination or was the sky beginning to lighten?

Large sparks flew over Maddy's head and she squealed, convinced she was going to burn to death. She unwound Zoe's scarf and dunked it in the slushy water at her feet. Then she wrapped it back around her head and face, just leaving her eyes visible. She reached around to take the ruck-sack off her back, and from it she dug out the knife. It wouldn't do any good against them, but at least she felt a little better with a weapon in her hand, especially one with a good sharp blade.

With a lurching heart, she realised the vampires were now trying to douse the flames with armfuls of snow and she worried they would succeed. But their efforts seemed to make no difference – the fire burned just as fiercely. At least they hadn't tried to walk through the flames to get to her.

Just as Maddy formulated that thought, a dark shape came flying down toward her. She screamed, pointing the knife wildly upwards, fighting the urge to jump up and run away through the fire. One of the vampires had leapt over the circle. But the flames were so high, they almost formed a canopy over the top of Madison. The vampire instantly caught alight and he yelled out in agony and frustration, rolling away from her through the flames. Another one tried the same thing and Maddy stood up shakily, ready to defend herself again. Not that she would stand a chance, but she had to try.

Standing there, with the knife thrust out in front of her, Madison blinked and stared. She blinked again and turned to look around. The second vampire hadn't made it into the circle. In fact, she could hardly believe it, but they had *all* disappeared. Not one vampire remained. Was it a trick? She spun around again, trying to glimpse them through the flames. She stared upwards, terrified they were about to swoop down from the sky en masse like birds of prey diving in for the kill. But after a moment or two, she realised it was true. The vampires had fled. And now she saw the reason why, as a faint white disc crept over the far horizon. Dawn had arrived.

In a flash of hatred, Maddy hoped the vampires had been incinerated, that the sun had caught them out and that they were now nothing more than ash on snow. But Maddy's problems weren't over. As the flames roared and spat, the heat became unbearable. Her fingers and toes tingled and burned, her face flushed and her skin prickled. She dropped the knife and made herself as small as possible, hugging her knees to her chest and burying her face into her arms. She was going to be barbequed.

Maddy squealed as an almighty explosion almost made her lose her footing and go tumbling into the fire. The bike. It was the dirt bike. It had become an orange and black fireball behind her. Another explosion came immediately after the first and Maddy winced, cringing down to try to escape the flying, burning debris.

Why had she poured out so much fuel? The temperature was insane now, like a furnace. There was no snow left on the rock which gleamed under the heat, slick and warm. This was it. After everything she'd been through, it had all been for nothing. She was going to die out here. Alone in the burning snow.

A dull sliver of light pooled on the floor of the van. It would be safe to leave now. Morris's wrists and ankles had been tied up tight but he wasn't worried about that, for in the inside pocket of his coat sat his penknife. He wriggled out of the blanket Leonora had placed so carefully around him and he lay on his side. Then he jiggled and shook until the small implement slipped onto the carpet with a dull thud. Morris sat up and shifted towards the knife. His gloved hands were behind his back, but he managed to pick up the knife easily enough and flick out its blade. Next, he set to work scraping it against the twine on his wrists. The strands quickly flew apart and he was then able to cut through his ankle ties.

Leonora considered him slow-witted and Morris hadn't liked to deprive her of that notion. He was of the opinion that it was better to keep quiet and observe. That way you didn't miss anything and you didn't let things slip.

Morris rubbed his hands together and blew on them

through his woollen gloves. His body couldn't take the cold like it used to. He was getting on a bit now. Not too old to know what was what, though. He lifted the latch on the van door. Lenora thought she'd locked him inside. She didn't realise these vans were designed so you couldn't get locked in, and he hadn't mentioned that fact to her. Sloppy of her not to check these things properly. He climbed out slowly, no panic in his mind, no thought but the job in hand. Just take it one step at a time. Nice and steady, that's the way.

Contrary to her fears, Maddy didn't burn. She didn't melt or pass out or self-combust or any of the things she'd imagined so vividly. She just crouched there, uncomfortable and scared as the flames burned around her, waiting for something to happen or not to happen. She ate some of the food that Eren and Derya had given her and she sipped at some water, pressing the side of the bottle to her cheeks and forehead, trying to cool herself down, but the bottle was warm and did nothing to relieve her discomfort. She took out Eren's phone several times, but there was no signal at all and no new messages. For now, she was stuck.

Maddy waited and eventually the flames died down enough for her to leap across the circle and away from the flickering prison. It was a blissful relief to escape the fire and she immediately threw herself down onto the snow to cool her roasting body. She knew it would only be a matter of time before unbearable heat would be replaced with unbearable cold, but she couldn't help herself. The snow felt so good against her burning hot face and limbs.

She knew she couldn't stay sprawled in the snow for long. She had to keep moving. The bike was toast and her gloves were gone. Maddy dragged herself to her feet, dusted off the snow and began to walk, shoving her hands into her pockets. The bikers were still out there and she knew they could return at any moment, but she couldn't summon up any fear. Exhaustion lay too heavy on her. If they came, they came. She had a knife. This time, she'd use it.

The storm had ended, but the snow lay in deep drifts and every step was hard going. Her boots sank down with each stride and Maddy realised the bike would've been useless out here anyway. Her jeans were sodden and frozen and she could no longer feel her toes. Tiredness settled deep inside her bones and all she wanted to do was curl up and sleep. How long had she been out here running away from people? Or running to find people? She couldn't remember. She didn't care.

Madison squinted into the distance. The snow was white, the sky was white, the sun was white. Her mind went fuzzy. Sleep would clear her head. Just for a few minutes. A little nap and then she'd feel much better. She gave a half-smile as she sank down into the snow. This was all she needed. What a luxury to just lie down and sleep.

Morris left the van and walked back through the snow to the hotel. It was morning now, so he knew he was safe from Leonora and the others. They couldn't leave their suite and so he wasn't worried about returning. Once back at reception, he asked if there was somewhere he could buy a phone and hire a car. Leonora had been sloppy again and hadn't bothered to check his pockets, so he still had his wallet. Unfortunately, his phone was back in the hotel suite. The woman on reception said the nearest town for those things was a couple of kilometres away and that she could order him a taxi.

Two and a half hours later, Morris was driving out into the snowy wilderness at the wheel of a battered jeep. It was perfect for what he had in mind and he had hired it for a very reasonable price as it hadn't yet been valeted after its previous muddy excursion. Morris had kitted himself out in warm clothes and in the back sat a couple of bags containing essential survival provisions which he'd bought in town. After about twenty minutes, he stopped and turned off the engine. His new phone had a good strong signal and he punched in the number for Marchwood House.

'Hello.'

'Esther, love, it's me. I need to speak to young Ben.'

'You all right?'

'Yeah, I will be soon enough.'

Morris waited while Esther fetched the boy.

'Morris?' Ben's voice came nervous and hesitant on the phone.

'Morning, Ben. Leonora told me about your worries.'

'Really? Look, Morris, I—'

'What's your evidence, then?' Morris said.

'What? I don't know what you—'

'Come on, Ben. You must have found something pretty big to have told Leonora what you did. You think I've let you down in some way?'

'No... I... Is Leonora okay? You haven't—'

'Far as I'm aware, she's fine.'

'Look, Morris, you've been good to us and I didn't want to believe—'

'Ben. It's fine. Just tell me what you found.' Morris didn't have time for the boy's hesitation. 'Come on, Ben. Spit it out, lad'

'I... well, I found some notepaper in the recycling bin. The same paper that the note from the Cappadocian vampires was written on. I did some digging and discovered the notepaper is from the Old Bell. And I know that's your local pub. I'm sorry, but I had to tell the others.'

'That's okay, lad. Put Esther back on.'

'Morris?' she said.

'Esther, we've got a problem,' he said.

'Another one? Seems to me we've been having problems for days.'

'Well, this problem is bigger than the rest. I need you to do something for me. I need you to lock Ben up somewhere secure. Oh, and make sure you take his phone away and his laptop. Don't let him out under any circumstances. Do you hear me, Esther? Not under any circumstances.'

CHAPTER THIRTY-SEVEN

CAPPADOCIA, AD 575

The people trembled as she asked the question:

'Do you know the Lascaroi family from Selmea?'

It was the same all over the city. Everywhere she went, they all had the same reply: *no, we don't know who they are.* It made her sick to see these humans quail before her, looking at her like she was one of *Them*. She wanted to soothe and reassure the people that she was not a demon, that she was ultimately human with a human heart and a human soul, but the words stuck in her throat as she remembered the poor man whose blood she had drained. Was he still alive? She hadn't dared ask. The answer to that question was too terrifying to contemplate. Mislav hadn't mentioned him and for that she was grateful. He had also given her freedom to roam.

'We have all eternity to ourselves,' he said. 'Go and explore our underground empire. Return to me whenever you wish. Just do not leave the caverns. Daylight is your enemy. It will kill you. It is the only thing now that can.'

And so she roamed the city. She did not ever wish to return to Mislav. She didn't love him or need him. All she wanted was to free her family and to free the other people trapped in this stinking hell. The terrible thing was, the stink of the pit had now changed into something wonderful, like the scent of heaven itself. But Aelia knew why it smelt this way and the thought nauseated her. She prayed for the strength to overcome her physical need. She realised that, given the choice, she would suffer the torments of the plague again, rather than this unnatural existence. If they hadn't turned her, she would probably be dead by now – a fate she had accepted. *This...* this *demon* existence she did not accept. What was she to do?

One day, as she searched in vain for her family, Mislav came to her. She was startled and unnerved to see him again. The other demons still frightened her and she kept out of their way as much as possible.

'Tell me,' he said. 'How do you like your new life? Is it good? Are you happy?'

Aelia didn't reply. She didn't want to make him angry, but she couldn't lie.

'You must feed or you will grow weak.' He stroked her cheek.

'I've been trying to find my family. I know they came underground, but I can't find them anywhere. I'm worried. I couldn't bear it if they were—'

'You must learn to leave your old life behind. We are your family now. We are your brothers and sisters, your mother and father, your lovers, your children. We can be everything to you if you'll let us. You were chosen. You are special. Embrace your new life and you will be happier than you ever thought possible.'

'How can you be happy when all you do is kill and bring misery to thousands?' She couldn't help saying the words; they tumbled from her lips.

'You must let all your mortal preconceptions go. Those rules no longer apply.'

Aelia bit her lip to stop the next angry retort.

'I can tell it is hard for you, but in time, you will see I am right.'

Never, Aelia said to herself.

'Come.' Mislav held out his hand. 'We've been summoned.'

'What? Summoned where?'

'His Imperial Highness has called us to the great hall.'

'Why?'

'Let us go and we will find out.'

Aelia let herself be led by Mislav, towards the hall where she had been turned. What did this boy emperor want now?

When they reached the hall, moments later, it was already thronged with demons. For some reason, Aelia had wrongly assumed that it was only her and Mislav that the Emperor wanted to see, and she was relieved that it was not, that she could remain in an anonymous crowd in the background. The hall was packed, but there was no chattering, just the odd murmur or whisper and the swish of cloaks and gowns as the creatures entered the hall. The glittering throne on the raised dais stood empty. They were all awaiting the arrival of the Emperor.

The last time she was here, she had been weak and near death, but now she really had a chance to take in her surroundings. The space was huge, the ceiling carved into smooth arches, painted with figures and animals, oceans and countryside. They were all night scenes with the moon and stars glowing as though they were the real thing. As Aelia studied the paintings more closely, she saw that most were scenes of slaughter, of mortals meeting their end at the hand of a demon. She shifted her gaze from the paintings to the real creatures around her. They were so beautiful... until they fed and showed their true ugly selves. Those teeth changing their heavenly faces into the countenances of beasts. Was that what she had looked like when she'd fed from that man? Aelia shuddered.

On the outer edges of the hall, Aelia noted massive arched

recesses with pillars, again lavishly ornamented with carvings and frescoes. Standing in these arches were humans. She caught their delicious scent and tried to block it out. These were the humans who had been spared the pit – the village leaders, the people of note, the praetors and judges and their families. These humans were now slaves to their demon masters. Aelia noted their clean, well-fed appearances. They still dressed as befitted their human rank and most seemed settled. Her demon senses could identify fear, and these people did not seem all that afraid. Perhaps they had not witnessed the horrors she had seen down here.

And then Aelia's eyes alighted on a face which transported her back to a different time. A face which made her catch her breath in her throat. Anger followed shock and she felt herself hiss like a snake, attracting the attention of several demons around her. Mislav took her arm and looked questioningly at her, but she paid him no mind, for she had seen someone who demanded all of her attention. Standing to her far right, in one of the recessed arches, next to his plump mother and stern father, stood *Lysus*. He was older now – no longer a boy, but a grown man. Still handsome, still confident.

Before she had a chance to react further, she realised everyone was sinking to their knees. Aelia tore her eyes away from the boy who had betrayed her and did the same as Mislav pulled her down next to him. The hall fell deadly silent and she peered up to see the child Emperor now seated on his throne, his eyes resting on his subjects, demanding their full attention with a penetrating gaze.

At that moment, Aelia didn't care about the boy ruler. All she wanted to do was leap across the hall and sink her teeth into Lysus's throat. Her demon-self wanted to terrify him, to have him at her mercy and make him pay for ruining her life. She wanted to taste his sweet cowardly blood, to drain every drop in his veins before flinging his used body to the ground. The feelings rising up in her were like nothing she had experienced before.

Mislav's hand was still on her arm and he gripped it as if he could sense her intentions. She was possessed. She was enraged. She was ready to kill.

CHAPTER THIRTY-EIGHT

PRESENT DAY

Esther had locked Ben securely in an attic storeroom. She'd got him up there on the pretence of helping her to lift down some boxes. Once he'd realised what she'd done, he'd made a bit of a fuss, hurling himself at the door and carrying on; much good that would do him. Those old doors were solid, not like the modern bits of cardboard that passed for doors these days. He'd quietened down a bit now, thank goodness. She wasn't generally a nervy person, but it had put her quite out of sorts to hear him like that. Shouting and swearing. Not at all like the Ben she knew.

She put on her woollen coat and picked up her keys from the hook in the utility room. Gloves... she'd need gloves. It looked a bit nippy out there, but at least the rain had stopped. Esther let herself out of the back door and walked around the side to where she'd parked her Renault Clio.

Settling herself in, she started up the engine and swung the car around. Maybe a bit of Radio 4 would calm her down a bit. She switched it on but it was some unfunny comedy thing, so she turned it off again. Silence was better anyway. That way, she could get her thoughts straight and concentrate on the job in hand, on sorting things out once and for all. This was a minor setback, that was all, but luckily she knew the people who could supply her with what she needed.

The road into Tetbury was busier than usual. But that's because it was only a few days till Christmas. They'd all be getting their last-minute shopping, which is what she should be doing, but she hadn't had a moment, what with all this carry-on, with Morris up to his neck in it. He'd be all right. He could take care of himself. No, she didn't have any worries on that score. Her Morris was ex-army, hard as nails when it counted. But it was disconcerting nonetheless and she'd be glad when it was all over.

The last time Esther had been to the Old Bell was months ago, on her birthday. Morris had taken her for a half pint of bitter and they'd even stretched to a spot of lunch. Not as good as home-cooked, but nice for a change. Today, there would be no nice lunch. Today, she had more important matters to attend to.

Parking was going to be a problem. Long Street was bumper-to-bumper and the car parks would be chocka. She'd try round the back of the Bell although she didn't hold out much hope. As luck would have it, a white Mercedes was driving out of the hotel car park just as she was driving in. Esther pulled straight into the gaping space and turned off the engine. She got out of the car, smoothed down her coat, patted her bobbed hair and marched briskly across the car park and into the back entrance of the hotel. She had a lot to get on with today. No time for dawdling.

Alexandre and Zoe reached the hotel just before dawn. The four other Marchwood vampires jumped up as they walked into the hotel suite. Isobel threw her arms around her older brother and Jacques clasped his arm. They all eyed Zoe with suspicion.

'This is Zoe,' Alexandre said. 'She helped Maddy to escape... And she also helped me to escape.'

'Helped you to escape?' Isobel said. 'Escape from where? And you're absolutely covered in dirt! What happened to you?'

Alexandre told them a watered down version of events, leaving out the part where he had been beaten up. The others looked at Zoe again – this time with gratitude. Zoe stared at her feet.

'Alex, I can't believe you went there on your own,' Jacques said. 'Don't you trust us?'

'It's nothing to do with trust. I thought it would look less threatening if I went on my own. I thought I could reason with them.'

'It's everything to do with trust,' Jacques argued. 'And to make that decision without us was extremely thoughtless, not to mention arrogant.'

'I just did what I thought was right,' Alex replied. 'I feel responsible for Maddy. I didn't want to drag you all into it.'

'Arrogant!' Isobel echoed her twin.

The room fell silent and Zoe looked down at her boots again, embarrassed to be witnessing this family argument.

'Well, at least he's back now,' said Leonora.

Alexandre threw her a grateful glance. It was odd for Leonora to be the one to stick up for him.

'I apologise,' said Alex. 'I was wrong.'

Jacques smirked. 'Can we have that in writing?'

Alexandre gave him a look. 'So, is Maddy on her way here? Have you spoken to her? Is Morris out looking for her?'

Everyone fell silent.

'What?' Alexandre stared at them, a sick feeling in his gullet. 'What is it? Is Maddy all right?'

'As far as we know she's still on her way here,' Isobel said.

'Someone give me a phone. Do you have a number for her?'

'We've all been trying, but it goes straight to answerphone,' Freddie said.

'She probably can't get a good signal, that's all,' Isobel added.

Alexandre was swamped with feelings of helplessness again. 'She was on a motorbike, yes?' he asked.

'Yes,' Zoe replied. 'A dirt bike.'

'So she should have been here by now, right?'

No one answered.

'*Right?*' He shouted this time.

'Don't shout at us, Alex. We're on your side.'

'I'm sorry, Belle. You're right.'

'So, is Morris searching the route between here and Akarsuli? To see if he can find out what's happened?'

'The thing is, Alex...' Freddie began.

'The thing is, Morris has been deceiving us,' Leonora said.

'What are you talking about?' Alexandre blinked his confusion.

Leonora told him what Ben had discovered.

'So where is Morris now?' Alex asked, not quite able to believe what he was hearing. Of all the people to betray them, Morris was the last person he would've predicted.

'I locked him up in the van,' Leonora replied.

Alex slumped into an armchair and ran his fingers through his dark hair, still matted with mud from when he'd tunnelled into the city. 'I need to take a shower,' he said, making no move to get up.

'Maddy will probably walk through that door at any moment, brother,' Jacques said.

Alex stared up at his younger brother, willing him to be right, because if he wasn't there wasn't a damn thing he could do about it. Once again, he was stuck here until nightfall.

Esther walked out of the hotel, back to the car. She unlocked it and got in. The hotel car park was still full and a couple of cars hovered, waiting to see if her space was about to become free. They'd just have to wait a bit longer; she had an important call to make.

Morris answered on the first ring.

'Well?' he said.

'I got it, love, but it'll probably take me a few hours. Maybe even days.'

'We haven't got days.'

'I'll do my best, love.'

'And what about the lad?'

'Oh, you know – he made a bit of a fuss at first, but he quietened down eventually.'

'Good. Call me when you get something.'

'You be careful, Morris.'

'Don't worry about me. Just get what we need and I'll be home soon.'

It was quiet. How strange to not hear a thing. No wind or roaring fire. No motorcycle engine or crunching snow underfoot. Just silence. And she wasn't cold anymore. She remembered falling asleep in the snow. Her eyes were still closed and she felt afraid to open them. Was she dead?

'Hello, Madison.'

At the voice, Maddy blinked her eyes open and eased herself up into a sitting position. She was no longer out in the snow. In the dim light, an old woman stared back at her.

'Who are you?' Maddy asked groggily.

The woman had a wrinkled face and surprisingly bright blue eyes. Her hair was greyish blonde, loosely tied back in a low bun at the nape of her neck. She wasn't smiling, but still managed to seem friendly somehow.

'How are you feeling?' The woman had a strange accent.

'Umm...' Maddy thought about it. How was she feeling? Still tired, but pretty comfortable. 'Where am I? Who are you?'

'You're safe. My name is Sofia.'

'Yes, but where am I?'

'I found you asleep in the snow. Not the best place for a nap.' The woman gave a short laugh. 'I brought you here, to my home.'

Maddy stared around. It looked like a cave of some sort. She was lying on a mattress on the floor – a rock floor. The woman was seated on a boulder next to Maddy's mattress.

'I'm not back in that place, am I?' Maddy asked, suddenly panicked. 'Is this the underground city? Are you a vampire?' She didn't look like one, but Maddy couldn't be sure.

'Hush, hush. You're not underground or in any danger. And I'm certainly not a vampire, of all things! This is just a place I come to sometimes. You're free to leave whenever you wish, but it's cold out there and it will be dark soon. You might as well stay and share a little supper with me. I don't get company that often.'

Dark soon? She must have been asleep the whole day. She would surely be dead by now if it wasn't for this strange old woman.

'My phone... My bag... Do you have them?'

Sofia stood and crossed the cave floor. Maddy saw her retrieve the rucksack from a far wall. An energetic fire blazed in the back. So, that was why it felt so warm in here. Maddy suddenly remembered the other fire, the one which had kept the vampires at bay. And now, according to this woman, Sofia, it was night again. Would they return for her? Would they find her here? Wherever 'here' was. All those familiar feelings of panic and urgency descended upon her again.

Maddy pushed off the thick blankets and stood shakily. She looked down and realised she was wearing a shapeless dress of some kind.

'Where are my clothes?' she asked, taking the backpack from Sofia's outstretched hand.

'They were wet through from the snow. I dried them by the fire.' Sofia pointed to the wall where Maddy saw her coat and a pile of folded clothes on the ground.

'Oh. Thank you.'

'I made spinach and feta gozleme while you were sleeping. Are you hungry?'

Maddy didn't know what the spinach thing was, but something smelled good.

'I have to call my friends,' Maddy said.

'You call them. I need to go out for a short time, but I'll be back soon. Come and sit by the fire. Help yourself to food or you can wait until I return. It's up to you.'

'Thanks,' Maddy replied, rooting about in her bag. She found the phone and prayed for a signal, but there were still no bars. It was useless. 'Do you have a phone?' she asked Sofia. 'Or a car?'

'No.'

Great, it looked like she was stuck here for the night unless the woman showed her the way to the hotel.

'I really need to contact my friends. Do you know the way to Ayvali?'

'Ayvali? It's too far to go tonight. You can go there tomorrow.'

This was like déjà vu. She just couldn't seem to get to where she wanted to go. People were kind, but they didn't understand how desperate she was.

'Can't you just point me in the right direction?'

'It's almost dark. Wait until morning.'

'But you don't understand.' Maddy walked over to her and gripped the woman's arm. 'I have to get to Ayvali. I have to reach my friends. It's important. A matter of life and death.'

'Life and death, yes,' Sofia replied. 'You go outside and there will be death. Much death.'

Maddy let go of Sofia's arm. Who was this woman? And what did she know about death?

'I thought you said I could go whenever I wanted.'

'You may leave if you wish, but I advise you to stay if you want to be safe. I'll see you shortly. Or not. It's your choice.' Sofia wrapped a heavy cloak around her head and shoulders and walked towards a narrow archway which Maddy assumed must be the way out.

What should she do now? Should she wait for the woman to come back? And then what? Was she supposed to sit down and eat with her like nothing was wrong? She could leave now if she wanted. The woman had said that nothing was stopping her, but where was this place anyway? Maddy walked over to her clothes and hurriedly dressed. The material felt gorgeously warm and dry. Even her thick socks and boots which had been sodden. At least she had that to thank Sofia for.

The exit consisted of a narrow passageway. Maddy really hoped the woman hadn't been lying when she said they weren't in the underground city. But as she walked, she felt an icy breeze and after a few seconds, she stepped out of the cave and back into the snowy wilderness. Wow, this place really was in the middle of nowhere. Darkness had not quite fallen, but night wasn't far away. Sofia was nowhere to be seen. It wasn't snowing and yet Maddy couldn't spot a single footprint. Odd.

She turned in a full circle to take in her surroundings. Behind her, the cave was set into a steep hillside and on all other sides lay snowy plains studded with bushes, hillocks and trees. If she left now, she'd be wandering around without a clue. She tried the phone again. Perhaps the cave walls had been blocking the signal. But there were still no bars, so she shoved it back into her bag and returned to the relative warmth and safety of the cave, her brain ticking.

CHAPTER THIRTY-NINE

CAPPADOCIA, AD 575

Aelia's mind whirled like a top. Lysus was *here*. He was still alive. What should she do? Her first instinct had been to kill him, but she knew she would not. He probably knew what had happened to her parents and sisters. She would have to speak to him and perhaps torment him a little. It was just like Lysus to be safe with his parents while the rest of their village suffered in the pits. She made a low growling noise in her throat and felt Mislav's hand steady her.

Suddenly, as one, the demons rose to their feet again. The boy emperor had begun to speak but she wasn't listening. She was irritated at having to be here. She wanted to confront Lysus, not stand around impotently waiting. Her anger was already dissipating and she didn't want to lose its power. For once, she wanted to act with passion and feeling, but as the minutes passed she felt cool rationality overtake her, setting off a fresh wave of anger, this time, aimed at herself. Mislav's eyes bored into her face, his unasked questions making her want to scream.

Lysus's eyes were focused on the Emperor. He hadn't noticed Aelia and she wanted to keep it that way. She would meet him on *her* terms. She thought of their tryst all those years ago. So much had happened since that time; she wasn't anything like the naïve child she'd been back then. Aelia wondered if he had changed much, or if he was still the same selfish coward. She wished he wasn't quite so handsome. If anything, he was even better looking now than he'd been back then – his shoulders broader, his features less soft...

'Remove them from the hall!' a demon guard ordered.

Aelia looked around, confused. Remove who? When she turned back to look at Lysus, he was gone. She gasped. Where was he? His parents had also disappeared. And then she saw all the humans filing out of the hall.

'What's happening,' Aelia asked Mislav. 'Why are they leaving?'

'Quiet,' he whispered.

Once the last human had exited the hall, the room was sealed closed with a millstone. Aelia felt tension and anticipation in the air, but her mind was still on Lysus. She told herself to relax, that she would find him easily enough when she got out of here.

'You may wonder why you are here.' The Emperor's reedy voice cut through her thoughts. '... or you may already know.' His gaze swept the hall. 'We are in the middle of a crisis and we are running out of time. Something is occurring which I have never witnessed in all my years of existence.' He paused.

The demons remained silent, but the tension increased – a tautening of necks, a widening of eyes and the faint scent of... fear.

'My dearest sister has fallen asleep. And it is a sleep from which she cannot be woken.'

There were gasps from the hall, and mutterings ensued.

'But it is not only my sister. Three others of our number have also fallen prey to this slumber.'

Now the hall erupted into noise, the demons chattering

amongst themselves. Aelia tried to suppress her joy. It must be the blood plague. It must finally be spreading through the demons.

'Silence,' shouted one of the guards.

Instant hush descended on the hall.

'It begins with a terrible lethargy,' continued the Emperor. 'A weakness of the mind and body. Does anybody know anything of this? Do any of you have this illness? Come forward if you are afflicted and we will try to heal you.'

There was a pause and some hesitancy before several of the demons made their way to the front of the hall. Shock radiated from the others, who drew back as the infected creatures passed, worried they too would catch the illness. As they reached the dais, the Emperor gestured to his guards who led the demons away.

'Can he cure them?' Aelia asked Mislav.

'I do not know,' he replied. 'But he won't try. He'll expose them to try to prevent the spread.'

'Expose them?'

'To the sun.'

'Kill them, you mean?'

'Yes.'

Good, Aelia thought. But when she saw the faces of the infected creatures as they left the hall, a small wave of sympathy overtook her. She shook her pity away with images of the bloodbath and misery they had created down here.

'It is the mortals who have brought disease here,' the Emperor continued. 'They are succumbing to a plague which kills them within days. It is my belief that this human plague is the culprit.'

'Your Imperial Highness,' a voice rang out from the crowd. 'May I speak?'

The Emperor nodded and the demon spoke:

'How is this possible? We do not suffer human disease. It cannot be the plague. Surely it—'

'You tell me something I already know,' the Emperor interrupted. 'But this is happening. The impossible is happening.'

'What are we to do?' the demons began to cry out.

'Silence!' The Emperor waited until the hall was quiet once more. 'We must burn all human plague victims. We must not feed until we have purged this disease. Go now and eradicate the infection. It cannot be allowed to persist.'

The millstone rolled aside and the demons left the hall, Mislav at Aelia's side. For once, she wasn't eager to be away from him. She needed information. They hurried to the blue-and-silver chamber where he waved away his girl servants.

'This is most unsettling,' Mislav said, pacing the room. 'Do you feel unwell at all?' he asked sharply. 'Are you weak or tired?'

'No,' she replied with a laugh. 'And would I tell you if I was? You've already told me the infected demons will be put outside to burn in the sun. And what about the poor humans who have it? Will they really burn them too?' She felt so guilty. She had signed their death sentence by bringing the plague with her, but what other choice had there been?

'Burning is the only way to purge disease,' Mislav replied. He stopped pacing and gave her a sharp look. 'But *you*,' he said. 'You are different. Something happened in there before the announcement. I felt your anger. I had to restrain you. What was it? Has someone hurt you or threatened you? Tell me.'

Aelia paused a moment and sank down onto a cushion.

Mislav crouched before her. 'I have missed you these past days,' he said sadly. 'I wondered if you would ever return to me. I need a companion during this long life and you interest me more than most.'

Aelia couldn't look him in the eyes. He made her too

uncomfortable. She ignored his previous comment and decided to answer his other question.

'I saw someone in the hall. Someone from my human life.'

Mislav tensed. 'Someone who did you wrong?'

'You could say that.'

'What did this human do?'

'He used me and betrayed me. I was banished from my village and left to die because of him.'

'A man did all this to you? Then I will kill him.'

'*No!* No. That is not what I want. I must speak to him and find out why he did it. We were barely children at the time – young and stupid.' She couldn't believe she was defending Lysus. 'And I think he may also know what happened to my family. I need to find them and he may be the key.'

'It would be better if you left him to me.'

'No. Please, let me sort this out. It's... personal.'

Mislav grimaced. 'Very well. Tell me of this man and I will make sure he is not harmed during the plague burnings.'

'His name is Lysus Garidas. His father is... *was* the Praetor of our village, Selmea.'

'You are from Selmea?'

'I was, before they sent me away.'

'I know this Praetor Garidas. I spoke with him on many occasions before we descended. And your family? What is their name?'

'I am Aelia Laskarina of the Lascaroi family.'

'The name is not familiar to me.'

'My father is an artisan. A good man. We are not an important family.'

'They are most likely dead.'

She glared at him.

'I only speak the truth.'

'You don't know for certain.'

'If they were alive, you would have found them already.'

Aelia stood and turned away from him, battling to keep her emotions at bay. She would not accept his assessment that her family were gone.

'You are one of us now,' he continued. 'You will outlive them all. Better they are dead now than later.'

'Better for who? For *you*? Not for me.' She bowed her head and closed her eyes. 'I need to go. I wish to be on my own for a while.'

'Stay away from the others. You do not want to become infected.'

If only you knew, she thought. *If only you knew.*

CHAPTER FORTY

PRESENT DAY

The spinach thing on the griddle smelt incredible, but Maddy felt weird helping herself to dinner without Sofia here. Instead, she sat cross-legged on the mattress and delved into her rucksack, locating a huge pack of Turkish crisps that she'd picked up at the petrol station. She opened them, dug her hand in and pulled out a couple of cheese puffs. They tasted of margarine, but she didn't care.

This cave place was amazing. Completely hidden from the outside. But once you were inside, you felt kind of cosy and safe, with the fire flickering and casting warm shadows. A bowl of fruit sat on a ledge on one of the walls. Maddy ambled over and helped herself to a bright orange clementine. Hopefully, Sofia wouldn't mind. She wandered back down the passageway to peek outside again. It was probably dark by now.

Without the light from the fire, the passage was coal black. But outside, the moon shone huge and bright in the dark velvet sky. The snow clouds had dispersed and the air smelt sharp and icy. It was beautiful and peaceful. Maddy gazed out over the snow-covered landscape to see if she could spot Sofia returning, but all was empty and still. Maddy brought the shiny clementine up to her nose and inhaled its sweet tangy scent. It reminded her of Christmas. She realised she didn't even know what day it was and she hadn't thought to ask Sofia. Maybe it was Christmas Eve already. Or perhaps she'd missed Christmas completely.

Ben would be worried sick, but it sounded like Esther was taking good care of him. At least she had that to be thankful for. And Alex would be going mad trying to find her. He always made her feel so safe – not in a cheesy, lovey-dovey way, but in a life-changing empowering way. She missed him so much. It was a physical ache. How could she bear it if she never saw him again?

When Alex had come into her life, she had found an equal. An ally. It was them against the world. Someone to share everything with. She could tell him anything and he was funny too. They laughed so much together, at stupid stuff. Madison trusted him implicitly. She knew he would never let her down. And he was so completely gorgeous, she felt like she was going into free fall every time she saw him... every time she *thought* of him.

He'd even changed the way she thought about herself. Before Alex, she'd been pretty insecure. There had always been plenty of male attention, but it was generally from adolescent dickheads who wanted to get in her knickers. But, for some reason, Alex actually thought she was something special. She could see it when he looked at her – that he saw her, really saw *her*. Not just some girl who might be a good lay. He made her feel like she was worth something. Like she had the power to make his life better. And that feeling was incredible.

What was it with this place? It had made her go all philosophical. Maybe it was the several near-death experiences she'd just had, making her appreciate life and what was important. The other Marchwood vampires had also become like a family. Well, Leonora and Freddie actually *were* her family, which was pretty amazing if she stopped to think about it. Going from being an orphan to having all these new relations...

Suddenly, Maddy's thoughts veered off a cliff. Up ahead she saw a figure heading this way. It must be Sofia. She frowned. It looked like it was moving much too fast for an old woman. Shit. That wasn't Sofia. Shit, shit, shit. It was a man. A vampire. It had to be, it was moving so fast. Maddy stood frozen to the spot. What could she do? She couldn't outrun it. There was nowhere to hide. No escape. The clementine dropped out of her hand and rolled into the snow.

Madison did not show up at the hotel. Alexandre must have tried calling her phone about fifty times. It helped to make the minutes pass more quickly. Made him feel like he was *doing* something. But every ten minutes, when he tried the number again, it just went straight to voicemail. He quickly began to loathe that single ring followed by that click and then the automated Turkish woman's voice. That voice. He wanted to grind that voice into dust.

Zoe was getting to know the others. Alexandre could hear them chatting in the next room, but he didn't have the heart to join in and be polite. Even though he knew he owed her his life... and Maddy's. He would make it up to Zoe when this was all over. He would apologise for his rudeness and talk to her properly. But right now, he couldn't think straight, let alone make conversation with a stranger.

Eventually, as always, night followed day and Alexandre was freed from his luxurious prison. He left the hotel without waiting for the others. They had already agreed that as soon as the sun set they would go out and begin their search for Madison again. They would fan out this time, but keep close enough to sense each other in case of danger. Alexandre did not expend his energy on keeping track of the others. He knew one of them, at least, would have his back. Instead, he focused his mind and cast out his senses as far as they would go.

He travelled straight towards the village of Akarsuli. That was where she'd been when she contacted the others by phone. Back at the hotel, he had studied the route online. She had to be somewhere between the hotel and that village, unless... unless the Cappadocians had reached her first. But he couldn't think like that. Perhaps her bike had broken down and she was coming to the hotel on foot. That would explain why she was taking so long. He had to get to her before anyone else did, or before the cold and snow made it impossible for her to continue. Clearing his mind of all other thoughts but Madison, Alexandre channelled his energy outwards.

As he moved, it was as though he was blending with the air, travelling inside the icy breeze. Everything around him became part of his consciousness. He moved so fast he blurred into the landscape. He was the air, he was the earth and he was the sky. He was the creatures which lived and breathed and hunted and died. He knew he would find her. He knew it. It wasn't just *her* life at stake. It was *his* too, for how could he live an eternity without her? He couldn't.

Alexandre felt himself getting closer. He scented fire and came to a place which puzzled and scared him. He stood and contemplated the scene. Madison had been here, but there had been some kind of encounter. He smelled vampires. An awful lot of vampires. A lump of charred metal lay on an icy rock – the remains of a motorcycle. Please, God, don't let it be her bike. But he knew it must be. There was no trace of a body. No smell of burning human flesh. No blood. Next to the bike remains, he saw a circle of thin ice which surrounded a rock. He could not make any sense of it.

Jacques and the others were still some way behind him, but he knew they had him in their sights. Perhaps they smelled the fire too. Moving away from the scene, he closed his eyes and breathed in the night air. A faint aroma of heat and fire took him back towards the hotel, but via a different route than the one he had just travelled. She had walked this way and she had the scent of fire on her. She would be easy to track now. It was a palpable thing, this burning trail. He could only hope it didn't mean she was injured. What had happened back there?

His mind conjured up terrible images of the vampires taunting her with fire, like a wild animal for sport. Had they harmed her? Was she burned? In pain? He wanted to stop this train of thought. It was useless to think this way. He just had to find her.

Soon another scent mingled with Madison's, but Alexandre couldn't tell if it was human or vampire. The smell of fire smothered everything, making it hard to distinguish one scent from another. The trail now changed course, away from the hotel and away from Akarsuli, instead leading out into the open countryside. Into the wilderness, away from civilisation. Alexandre didn't allow himself to think what he might find at the end of the trail. He had the scent strong in his nostrils and he followed it.

The clean snow made it easy to pick out the trail. He was getting close now, he could feel it. The moon shone bright, almost as bright as day and he felt a surge of hope. He caught a tang of citrus fruit, a cooking aroma, warmth and... *Madison*. She was here.

A snow-covered cliff reared up ahead of him and she was there, standing in front of it, staring across the plain at his approach. A lone figure in the snow. Alexandre caught her fear, saw her sink to her knees. She didn't know it was him. She thought she was in danger. He slowed and called out her name. Then he finally came to a stop in front of her, crouched down in the snow and cupped her face in his hands.

'Alex,' she sobbed.

'Maddy, I can't believe it's really you,' he said. 'Are you all right? Are you hurt? Don't cry. It's okay now. Everything's okay.'

'Alex,' she whispered, her voice like warm honey, her arms reaching up to embrace him. He held her close, breathing in the scent of her skin and kissing her hair. She was here. She was real and he realised what he'd almost lost. Gently, he took her arms from around his neck and brought them down by her side so he could look at her beautiful, perfect, familiar face. Then he reached out and she tilted her face toward his hand. He stroked her cheek and drew his thumb across her bottom lip, leant forward and kissed her salty tears. Lifting her up, Alexandre felt her legs wrap around his body. She was here. He had found her. Safe.

She was saying his name, saying how much she'd missed him and how she loved him, and he wanted to lose himself in this moment and never have to think of anything else ever again. But Isobel and the others were coming. He could feel their approach. If he kissed Madison now, he wouldn't be able to stop. He sighed and relaxed his hold, lowering her to the ground. She stood in front of him, still gripping his arms.

'Alex,' she said. Was that *hurt* in her voice? Was she upset he had ended their embrace?

'Alex!'

No. It was *alarm* in her voice. And he suddenly knew why.

CHAPTER FORTY-ONE

CAPPADOCIA, AD 575

Aelia left Mislav in the chamber and resumed her favourite occupation of roaming the narrow twisting passageways of the underground city. It was mainly peaceful. She steered away from the pits and the more populated areas, staying to the outer edges on the upper levels, where there was darkness and silence. She could see perfectly clearly in the dark and barely had to think about where she was going. It was as though all she had to do was will herself forward and she could glide along the rock floor with little or no effort.

There was so much to think about. Aelia was happy that the plague was doing its job, but she also worried it would wipe out the human population as well as the demons. The main thing on her mind at the moment was to locate her family and keep them safe. She'd had no luck finding them on her own, so she would have to speak to Lysus. On realising this, her demon heart beat fast and she felt breathless with nerves. How ridiculous. He was just an idiot boy who had treated her badly. She was over him... wasn't she? Truthfully, the thought of seeing him again unnerved her. She hated him for what he'd done, but she could so clearly remember his warm kisses and the feel of his hands on her skin. If she'd still been human, she would have blushed at the thought. She knew he would remember it too, and this was partly what made her uncomfortable about meeting him again.

Aelia couldn't put it off any longer. It seemed time was running out for everyone. She didn't know how long she herself might have. The plague was in her system and although, as a demon, she hadn't felt any symptoms yet, surely it was only a matter of time. She would go to Lysus now before she changed her mind.

Moving down several sets of staircases, she eventually reached the ninth floor. This was where most of the demons' quarters lay. Although the creatures needed no light to see by, this level was ablaze with lanterns. The corridors were wide and smooth, the walls adorned with silk hangings and the floors polished to a gleaming honey glaze. There were no filthy human pits down here. The only humans were the demons' personal slaves who were not used for feeding, but for the practical tasks of tidying, dressing, washing and arranging. They were also charged with disposing of the used human bodies.

Lysus and his family lived on this level, but Aelia wanted to avoid running into either his parents or his demon master or mistress. She would have to wait until he was alone. As Aelia waited and watched, she saw that Lysus's mistress was a powerful demon with a whole suite of chambers. As well as human slaves, she had other demons to do her bidding. She was also blatantly ignoring the Emperor's command to refrain from feeding until the infection was under control. Aelia was pleased. If she was still feeding, that probably meant most of the others were too.

Aelia didn't have long to wait. The disease was taking hold and the demons were weak and sleepy. After a day of watching, she was able to walk unchecked into Lysus's tiny chamber. She stood in the open doorway. He was lying on his back, staring up at the ceiling, his arms behind his head. After a few beats, he glanced towards the door and hastily rose to his feet, bowing his head.

'Forgive me,' he said. 'I only lay for a few moments to rest. It will not happen again. I will continue with my work now, if it pleases your lady.'

He looked scared and Aelia felt a moment's pity for him.

'Lysus,' she said.

'Yes, my lady.' He kept his eyes on the floor.

'Lysus, it's me.'

'My lady?' He tentatively raised his eyes to meet Aelia's, his body still cowering.

Aelia the demon wore rich robes of deep blue and her loose golden hair fell in tresses over her shoulders. She knew she probably looked nothing like the simple young girl she had been three and a half years earlier.

'Do I... do I know you?' Lysus asked. 'You remind me of—'

'It is I, Aelia Laskarina of Selmea.'

Lysus drew in his breath and relaxed his stance a little.

'Aelia?' he said, as realisation slowly dawned. 'But you were... and now you are...'

'Yes. And yes,' she drawled, beginning to enjoy herself a little. After the build-up to seeing him again, this was not as terrifying as she had anticipated. She enjoyed seeing the various emotions skitter across his face – fear, shock, recognition and now something else – lust?

'You are a demon,' he said. 'And you're still so beautiful.'

'And you are still trying to manipulate me with your charming words.'

'No, no, I just meant—'

'I'm no longer interested in you, Lysus. I do not care what happened in the past. I'm not here for revenge or to forgive you. All I want is my family.'

He flushed with embarrassment and defensiveness.

'It wasn't my fault. I wanted to marry you, but my father said—'

'Did you not understand me when I said I wasn't interested in your explanations?' Aelia felt anger quicken in her chest. She moved to stand in front of him, bringing her face up close to his and curling her lip into a snarl. He took a step backwards and she leant towards him, her previous words forgotten as she remembered the hurt and humiliation, the separation from her friends and family, her fear and loneliness, the wasted years. It would be so easy to take her revenge now. No one would hold her accountable. She had the freedom to do it.

His heart beat loud in her head and she smelt his rich blood, thick with the bitterness of terror. It would still have tasted sweet to her and she bent, meaning to pierce his flesh and take her fill.

'I'm sorry,' he gasped, breaking her train of thought for a second.

Aelia hesitated. She still hadn't found out about her family. She would finish him after he told her what he knew. She moved her mouth from his throat to his ear.

'Where are my family?' she hissed.

'I'm sorry,' he stuttered.

'So you said. But what of my mother and father? My sisters? Where are they?'

'That's what I'm trying to tell you – I'm afraid... I'm afraid they are dead.'

'No!' She let go of him and stood swaying for a moment before sinking to her knees. 'Are you saying this to hurt me? To distract me?'

'I would never purposely hurt you, Aelia,' he replied. 'I swear. I may have done some awful things in the past, but I am not cruel. Not on purpose. I'm so sorry, Aelia, for everything.'

Warm blood tears dripped onto her cheeks.

Lysus still trembled, but he crouched down, put his arm around her shoulders and smoothed her hair.

'They were one of the first families to be taken,' he said. 'It would have been quick. I'm so sorry.'

'All of them?' she whispered. 'My sisters too?'

'I'm sorry.'

'But how can you be sure they are really dead? Perhaps they—'

'I saw them... afterwards. There can be no mistake about it.'

'Then there is nothing left for me in this life. There is nothing I want.' She felt empty, drained, nothing mattered anymore. 'I think I already guessed the truth, but I needed to hear it from someone who knew.' She sniffed and wiped her face, smudging crimson tears across her cheeks.

'How is it you are like this?' Lysus asked. 'A demon, like them?'

'This was not the plan,' she replied, drawing away from his embrace. She stood and tried to compose herself. 'I did not wish to become a monster, but it was beyond my control.'

'Maybe you could help me?' Lysus asked, standing. 'Help *us*?'

'I have already done all I can,' she replied, feeling bone-weary all of a sudden. Sick of everything. Her anger had vanished and she didn't have the energy to summon it up again. 'I will tell you what I have done and you can pass the knowledge to the other humans. Perhaps you will yet escape from this, even though it is too late for me and my family.'

'Tell me,' Lysus said.

Aelia gestured to him to sit on the bed. She sat too, cross-legged like a child. There she told him of Widow Maleina and the blood plague. She told him how she had infected herself and how this had now passed over to the demons, that they were finally succumbing to a sleeping sickness from which, she hoped, they would never wake up. That fairly soon, the humans who survived would be free to leave their underground prison.

'But what of the plague?' Lysus asked. 'Surely we will all be infected, living in such close quarters as we do.'

'The widow created it so it is only transferred through the blood. As long as they do not feed on you, you should be safe.'

'They never use me for that,' Lysus said. 'Not so far anyway.' He looked across at her and she felt something stir as his gaze connected with hers. 'I'm really sorry for everything,' he said. 'And not just because you're a demon who could finish me off with one bite.'

Aelia gave him a half-smile. She remembered why she had fallen for him in the first place, with his easy charm and sense of humour. He had little respect for the rules and that was still attractive to her.

He grinned back.

Suddenly she felt a shadow behind them. Lysus broke eye contact and looked up, the smile vanishing from his face. Aelia sensed Mislav in the doorway. For a moment, she worried he might have overheard her talking about the plague and she turned to look at him.

'This is the human?' Mislav asked. 'The one who upset you?'

'We have resolved our issues,' Aelia said. This wasn't quite the truth. She didn't think she would ever really forgive Lysus, but she found it didn't matter to her so much now. He wouldn't change. He was a silly arrogant boy with too much charisma and good bone structure for his own good. He could still make her swoon and it would be better if she kept out of his way and never saw him again.

'Your family?' Mislav asked. 'Does he know where they are?'

She shook her head. 'They are gone.'

'I'm sorry for your loss,' he said. 'But you will find it is better this way, in the long run.'

No compassion, Aelia thought. *Is this how I will become?*

'And so your dealings with this mortal are complete?' Mislav asked.

'I suppose so,' she replied, and looked across at Lysus with a twinge of longing at what might have been. She stood and went to join Mislav.

'Good,' the demon replied before turning to face Lysus. 'Boy, we do not need you anymore,' he said. And before she could stop him, Mislav crossed the room and snapped his neck. 'I will not allow a mortal to upset you,' he said to Aelia. 'If you are upset, I am upset.'

Aelia's mouth hung open as she stared at Lysus's broken body in Mislav's arms.

'What have you done?' she hissed. Aelia crossed the room and looked down at Lysus, his eyes staring emptily up at the dusty ceiling, where moments before they had danced with fear, then humour, then compassion.

'You've been crying,' Mislav said, tracing his finger down her cheek.

'Get off me, you MONSTER!' she shrieked, all control gone. Her family was dead, Lysus was dead and here she was – an immortal, destined to live in dark misery for an eternity with these evil, unfeeling devils. A few moments ago, she had almost given in to her demon nature. She was no better than they were. She deserved to die, but even the plague was no guarantee of death, just a long sleep during which she would probably have to endure centuries of nightmares. No. She couldn't take another second of this unnatural existence. She didn't want to think about consequences anymore, about wrongs and rights and destinies or duties.

Aelia backed away from Mislav who still held Lysus's limp body in his arms, puzzlement on his face at Aelia's furious reaction. He did not understand her. Would never understand how she felt.

She fled the chamber and retreated along the corridor. In a haze of grief and anger, she raced up the staircase to the floor above. She knew where she was headed, and now she had made the decision, she welcomed it. She couldn't wait. Up she went to the next floor, through the Emperor's empty hall, past the pits of suffering humans, up and up to the next floor, past demons and chambers, stables and food stores. All these things passed her in a blur of irrelevance. Until she reached the top where the man stood next to the millstone. The rolling stone which led to the outside world. She couldn't wait to breathe in the air, to get away from this stinking place of death and unnaturalness.

'Open it,' she ordered.

The man looked surprised. 'But—'

'Open it or I'll do it myself.'

The man shrugged and wheeled the stone aside.

She stepped through the opening and walked slowly down the steps into the gloomy cavern, whispers of fresh air swirling around her. She moved across the cavern towards the narrow passageway which led to the white cave on the outside. How long had she been down here? she briefly wondered. It didn't matter. She was leaving now and she would never return to this godforsaken place. Through the passage she walked, calmer now, humming a tune which she remembered her mother singing to her when she was a child.

And now, here was the place which led to freedom. She crossed the cave, saw the thick shapes of the pillars standing sentry-like outside. She blinked and took a breath and then she walked out of the cave and into the unforgiving brightness of the midday sun.

CHAPTER FORTY-TWO

PRESENT DAY

Maddy's eyes were wide. Focused on a point beyond Alexandre's left shoulder. He swung around just in time to ward off a flying kick from a female vampire with glittering eyes and bared fangs. Behind her came an army of speeding shapes.

'Get back!' he yelled to Maddy. 'Hide!'

The female vampire now had her arms around his neck. She was trying to snap it. He twisted around and slammed her down onto her back. She was up in less than a second, her palm on his face and her spike heel grinding into his foot. He picked her up and threw her into the cliff wall, dislodging rocks and stones and chunks of snow which rained down on her. Then he turned his attention to a male who was trying to get past him to Madison.

'Maddy, I told you to get out of here! Run. Hide. Now!' But he knew no matter how fast she ran, she would not be able to hide from them. She disappeared from view behind a rock while he tried to head off the approaching vampire. They traded punches and kicks and then began to grapple in the snow. He had the creature pinned, but didn't know how to incapacitate him. More vampires moved in. He couldn't fight all of them at once. They were going to overpower him and there was nothing he could do about it.

Alexandre felt another of them jump onto his back, prising him away from the one on the ground. He tried to shake him off, but he wasn't able to keep the other one pinned at the same time. He was losing control. And they were going to get Madison. He couldn't let them—

'Alex!'

It was Jacques!

Jacques and the others had arrived. He felt the vampire on his back disappear and when he turned his head he saw Freddie using some of the martial arts moves he'd been learning with Ben at an evening class. That vampire didn't stand a chance. Alex allowed himself a small grin, before returning to the job of subduing the vampire beneath him. The creature had its teeth bared and was trying to bite him. Alex stuck his hand into the snow and picked out some small rocks. He smashed them into the vampire's mouth. The rocks crumbled, but it gave Alex a couple of seconds to pick the creature up and sling him across the plain.

Alexandre counted at least nine attackers. He and the Marchwood vampires were badly outnumbered, despite Zoe having joined them, but he couldn't worry about that now. He saw his brother and sister and Freddie giving as good as they got, but he hadn't spotted Leonora yet. He hoped she was all right. Zoe stood nearby, blocking all attempts from the Cappadocians to get past her. Stopping them from getting to Maddy.

Suddenly, he felt another presence at the side of him.

'I should have killed you when I had the chance.'

Alexandre recognised that voice. He looked round. It was Sergell and he had Zoe by the throat. Suddenly, Alexandre was grasped either side by two vampires. He tried to shake them off, but they threw something around his neck. He felt cold metal burn into his skin and the power drain from his body. He growled and hissed, trying desperately to break free from his captors, but he couldn't loosen their grip and the metal chain around his neck was sapping his energy somehow. What was happening?

Next to him, Zoe's eyes were wide with fear, but Alexandre could do nothing to free her either. He felt worse than useless. What did these damned creatures want with them? And where was Madison?

'You've disappointed me, Zoe,' Sergell said. 'I gave you a home. I gave you eternal life and you betray me for a worthless girl and a group of weak fledglings. You picked the wrong side.' He flung her towards Alexandre.

Another of the Cappadocians put a chain around her neck and Alex saw that Jacques, Freddie and Isobel had also been chained. He locked eyes with his brother who shook his head in anger and frustration. Was everyone he loved to be persecuted or killed? He tried to wrestle the chain from his neck, but when he touched it with his fingers, the skin on his hands melted and a searing pain shot up his arms. What were these chains? Why did they burn so?

'Silver,' Zoe moaned. 'Silver chains.'

Alex hadn't known silver was harmful to vampires. He wondered why, and wondered how he could get the damned things off.

'Sir!' Sergell called over his shoulder. 'Sir, we have them subdued.' He was addressing another vampire. An ancient being who came towards Alexandre with evil and destruction in his eyes. This vampire shimmered with power, his marble skin and golden hair alive with it. He was no foot soldier but was dressed in ancient robes and a heavily embroidered cloak. Was this one of the Cappadocians he and his family had disturbed in that underground chamber all those years ago? It was very likely.

Not for the first time, Alexandre wished they had never unearthed that hellish city. These creatures should still be buried in the cold belly of the earth. They should have remained undisturbed. And he, Alexandre, should have died a natural human death many years ago, along with his family. Instead, he was here, chained in silver and unable to defend the girl he loved. The girl who would still be safe if it wasn't for him and his *condition*.

'Who are you?' Alexandre croaked, barely able to talk now. The chains had thoroughly incapacitated him.

'The girl?' The golden creature addressed Sergell, ignoring Alexandre's question.

'She is back there, Sir. In the cave.'

'Good. His Imperial Highness wishes us to bring them all back to the city. But the girl, you can kill.'

'No!' Alexandre choked on the word. The silver chain was like a burning brand around his throat. He had to do something to save Maddy before it was too late.

'But we would be better to finish them all now,' Sergell said. 'They are no good to us. They will not—'

'Would you like to tell his Imperial Highness what your thoughts are?' the golden one said.

'Of course, I would never presume to—'

'Fine,' his leader snapped. 'Then do as I ask. And bring out the girl. This chained fledgling seems to be fond of her. It would be amusing to watch him while you kill her.'

Sergell bowed and retrieved Madison from her inadequate hiding place. She looked defiant. Her chin set and her eyes blazing, trying to keep up with Sergell as he dragged her through the messed up snow.

'Please,' Alexandre begged. 'If you spare her, I will come willingly. I will serve you for eternity. I will be the best—'

'Quiet.' The golden vampire held up his hand. 'You had an

opportunity, but you did not take it. There is no plea bargaining here. It's too late. Do it, Sergell.'

The vampire ripped Madison's coat away from her neck, bared his teeth and prepared to rip her throat out.

The Marchwood Vampires moaned, a collective noise which reverberated throughout the snowy plain. Alexandre felt so much pain he couldn't bear it. How could he watch the destruction of the girl he loved? He felt disgusted at himself that he could do nothing, that he was too weak to move, to even try to save his love. All their plans to save her had come to nothing. He bowed his head, unable to watch, but his captors yanked it up and forced him to look at her.

This was it then. This was the end of his happiness.

'Hello, Mislav.' A voice rang out. A woman's voice, confident and mature.

Sergell stopped and turned his head to see who had spoken. So did everyone else. An old woman walked towards them, alone through the snow, her bright blue eyes fixed on the golden vampire. She was small with pale hair fixed in a bun at the back of her head. A dark woollen cloak was wrapped around her shoulders and she carried a basket on her arm.

She will be slaughtered, Alexandre thought.

'Sofia!' Madison cried out.

Maddy knew this woman? Alexandre's confusion dulled his pain for a moment.

'How do you know my name?' the golden vampire, Mislav, demanded of the woman.

'Well, that's no way to greet an old friend,' she replied. 'It is I, Aelia. Don't you remember me?'

CHAPTER FORTY-THREE

PRESENT DAY

Alexandre realised the arrival of this woman had delayed Madison's death. Perhaps all was not lost. If he could only get these chains off he would stand a chance of rescuing her from Sergell's fangs.

'*What?* What are you talking about?' Mislav growled at the old woman. 'Aelia was a young girl. You are old. How do you know about Aelia?'

'I know I have aged, but do you really not recognise me?'

'You have wandered into the wrong place at the wrong time, old woman, talking of things you know nothing about.' Mislav's eyes blazed with anger. He crossed the snow to where she stood and grasped her chin in his hand, staring into her face.

To the old woman's credit, she didn't flinch or look away.

'Mislav,' she said. 'I remember the-blue and-silver room, the hot springs and the icy waterfall. I remember the night you found me outside and my horse disappeared. Who else would know those things?'

Although his face was already pale as moonlight, Mislav visibly blanched. His cool composure evaporating into the chill night sky.

'Who have you been talking to?' he said. 'You are spouting rubbish. Old wives' tales and nonsense. I do not have time for this.' He snapped his fingers and one of his minions bared its teeth and crossed to where Aelia stood, preparing to bite her.

Alexandre was shocked at what happened next. The frail old lady tossed the six-foot vampire away from her and into the snow-covered darkness. Another took its place, but she gave out the same treatment. Mislav snarled and grabbed her. His fangs were millimetres from her neck, but she held him at bay.

'Bite me and I'll send you all back to sleep for another few hundred years,' she said.

Complete silence descended. Alexandre wasn't sure if he had heard her correctly.

'What do you know of the Sleep?' Mislav said. 'I demand you tell me.'

The woman gazed around at the vampires and their prisoners. Then she turned her attention back to Mislav.

'Do you really not know me, Mislav? Look at my face. Look beneath the wrinkled skin and greying hair.'

'You might share the same eyes, that is all,' he snapped.

'And they are not enough to convince you?' she asked.

'Perhaps you are a descendant. But that is not enough to save you.'

'Once, long ago,' she began, 'you fought the other demons to keep me. You had me turned by your Emperor. You thought I was your plaything. But I was a weapon sent to destroy you all.' Her voice rang out, strong and clear.

'A weapon?' He frowned. 'What are you talking about? Who are you really?'

'I told you, I am Aelia.'

'Aelia?' Mislav's voice softened. He put a finger under her chin and tipped her face up to the moonlight, staring at her. 'Can it really be you? But if it is, you have aged. How can this be? You were one of us.'

'I will tell you everything. But first *he* needs to leave Madison alone.' She pointed to Sergell whose fangs still hovered over Maddy's exposed throat.

Alexandre wondered how she knew Madison. But he was grateful for her request. Could he dare to hope Maddy was safe? Not yet.

'And all these chains need to come off,' she continued. 'Silver chains. How barbaric.'

'Aelia.' Mislav smiled. 'If it *is* you, since when do you order me around?'

She smiled back. 'Since I have the power to put you back to sleep for another fifteen hundred years. Chains. Off. Now,' she said.

Mislav nodded to his minions and, with gloved hands, they removed the clinking silver. Alexandre immediately felt his strength returning, the skin healing where the metal had bitten into his neck. Now he had a fighting chance once again.

'You need to tell me what you are doing here, Aelia,' Mislav said.

'I thought you said your name was Sofia,' Madison interrupted, her voice trembling.

'Silence, human,' Mislav barked.

Alexandre bristled at the way Mislav had shouted at her. He tried to catch Maddy's eye, but her attention was on the woman.

'My name *is* Sofia, the woman replied. 'It is Aelia, it is Sarah, it is Havva. My name has changed many times over the centuries.'

'Havva Sahin! I thought I recognised you.' Suddenly, Alexandre remembered this strange lady. She turned to face him.

'Yes, it is I. Hello, Alexandre. It's been a while.'

He remembered Havva's strange words of warning all those

years ago when he was still a mortal, remembered her telling him to heed the legends and leave the city undisturbed. But he had ignored her words as the ravings of a delusional old woman. And he and his family had gone on to unleash the demons from their sleep. But he had paid the price for not heeding her – for he had lost his parents and been cursed to live as a blood drinker for all eternity. He bowed his head in shame as she looked at him.

'Send your demons away, Mislav,' Aelia said, turning to the golden vampire. 'Come and sit. Hear my story, if you will. It is time you heard the truth.'

'His Imperial Highness is expecting me to return with these fledglings. My vampires can take them to the city while I listen to your story.'

'No,' she said. 'The "fledglings" will stay and hear my story too and then they will be free to go.'

'Aelia, you are trying my patience. I am pleased to see you, but I will not take orders from you.'

'You will, Mislav. Or I will send you all back into your coma and then I will destroy you while you sleep. For I have a plague in my blood.'

Aelia held her ground as Mislav lost all composure and grabbed her by the hair. She slid a knife from her sleeve and pierced the tip of her finger, holding the dark bead of blood up to his face. Mislav let go of her hair and took a step back.

'You are wise to keep your distance,' she said, 'for this blood will render you helpless as the proverbial kitten. Send your vampires away and when you return, you can tell his Imperial Highness that you just saved his kind from total destruction. I'm sure he will forgive you the loss of a few fledglings in return for his life.'

Mislav considered her words.

'She's a lying witch, Sir,' Sergell called out. 'I can finish her off if you'll let me.'

'No, Sergell. You and the others return to the city. I will follow shortly.'

'But, Sir, you surely cannot—'

Mislav turned his back on Sergell and stared at Aelia.

'I missed you when you left,' he said. 'I thought you might have destroyed yourself, walked out into the sunlight. You were not happy.'

'No, I was not.'

'Well?' Mislav turned to Sergell. 'What are you waiting for? All of you. Leave now. I will return soon.'

Sergell did as he was told. He took his small army of vampires and left them, disappearing into the night.

CHAPTER FORTY-FOUR

PRESENT DAY

As soon as Sergell and his vampires left the snow-covered plain, Alexandre rushed to Madison's side, joined by the others.

'Are you all right, Madison? Did he hurt you?'

'No, but I really thought that was it.' Her breath caught in her throat. 'I thought I was going to—'

'I know.' Alexandre interrupted her before she had a chance to say the word. He put his arm around her shoulders and brought her close to his chest, still shocked by what had almost befallen her.

'What do you make of the woman?' Isobel asked.

'She is Havva Sahin,' Alexandre said, almost to himself. 'I cannot believe it.'

'I thought Havva Sahin was human,' Jacques said.

'So did I,' Alex replied. 'And yet she is not a vampire either.'

'She saved me,' Maddy said. 'She rescued me from the cold and brought me here. This is where she lives. This cave behind us.'

Aelia's voice rang out. 'Come,' she said to Mislav and the others. 'Let us go inside. And there we shall sit and make a pretence at being civilised for a few moments. I will tell you my story and then you can leave.' She sucked the blood off her finger and walked into the cave, sheathing her knife. They all followed.

The cave was large and clean. Food had been cooking on a fire which had almost burned down to nothing. Havva, or Aelia as she now seemed to be calling herself, threw a log on the embers and settled down on a large boulder in the corner of the cavern. Mislav sat close by.

Alexandre followed Madison to a mattress on the rock floor. She sat and leant back into him and he kissed her head, entwining her fingers in his. But Alexandre did not for one second take his eyes off Mislav. This was a demon cut from the same cloth as the Byzantine emperor – a cold and emotionless being with no heart. Havva Sahin might feel comfortable talking to him, all cosy and chatty in her cave, but Alexandre did not. That creature had given the order for Madison's death. It took all of Alex's willpower not to reach across and smash his head into the fire, which was now blazing furiously. But he wanted to hear Aelia's story and guessed she wouldn't take kindly to vampires fighting in her home.

Everyone settled into a space, waiting for her to begin, but Alexandre suddenly realised that someone was not with them. That they had not been here from the start.

'Where is Leonora?' he whispered to Freddie.

'She said she had something to do. That she would find us later.'

Alexandre did not have time to wonder about this, as Aelia had begun her story. She was telling them of her entrance to the underground city, armed with a box containing the blood plague. As she continued with her tale, Alexandre found himself impressed by her selflessness and bravery; although she did not boast of her deeds and did not expect any pity.

Mislav's face showed anger and incredulity. It was clear he was not enjoying her tale at all.

Soon she came to the part where she had left the city in despair, expecting the sunlight to kill her.

'I just wanted to end my existence. To stop the sadness and mounting pain that swam in my blood and battered my skull at every waking moment. I had been told daylight was fatal to demons. Now that I was one of them, I knew I had no choice.

'But I didn't die. Something happened to me when the sun's rays hit. I passed out and when I came to, I felt different. More myself again. More human. The dry air made me thirsty. But strangely, I was thirsty for clear cool water, not for blood. And I felt hungry for food. For normal, human food. I thought I might be dead and that this was the afterlife. Or that perhaps I had lost my mind.

'I returned here, to the Widow Maleina's empty cave where I mourned her death along with the death of so many others. It felt so strange to be back here without her. I decided to walk back to the cave, like a mortal. I wanted to feel the warmth of the sun on my face, the desert dust on my skin and the breeze through my hair. I wasn't worried about meeting anybody on the journey. For everybody was trapped beneath my feet, living in terror. Not for long, though. The plague soon did its job and worked its way through the demons, rendering them all unconscious. And once that happened, the humans who survived were able to escape.'

'I cannot believe you did all that,' Mislav said. He looked at Aelia, partly in admiration and partly in anger. 'You ruined everything. You destroyed our whole civilisation.'

'There was nothing civilised about you, Mislav. You were all despicable.'

'You never took the time to see how wonderful our life was. You and I could have had everything.'

'I never wanted everything,' Aelia replied.

She turned to look at the others, all stunned by her story. She caught Alexandre's eye.

'What happened next?' he asked.

'Next? Well, when the demons finally slept their long sleep and the humans had emerged into the sunshine, I plucked up the courage to return to Selmea. Twenty thousand men, women and children had descended into the earth, but only six hundred and twenty-eight came out. It had been a massacre. I felt partly guilty as many had died, not by the demons' hands, but from the plague I unleashed.'

'But that wasn't your fault,' Madison said. 'There was nothing else you could've done.'

'So I keep trying to convince myself,' Aelia said. 'Anyway, I had a theory of which I couldn't be certain, but I didn't want to take any chances. You see, when I emerged from the city, I think the sun did something to my body. I felt it shock my system and I didn't want to risk the same thing happening to the demons. So, I told the survivors that under no circumstances were they to bring the creatures outside into daylight. The villagers argued and said it was the only way to truly kill them. But I believed the plague had altered them somehow and that exposing them to the sun would regenerate them.'

'You were right,' Alexandre said.

'Yes, but it was different with me,' she replied. 'You are still affected by the sun. I am not. You still need blood to survive. I do not.'

'So you've been alive all these years?' Madison said. 'That's insane. Weren't you lonely?'

'Yes. In the early years, this cave became like a prison, but I was too scared to leave. I had no family or friends. No society to become a part of. Eventually, I had to force myself to step out into the world and make a new life.

'After a few years, I met a man and we fell in love. We had children. We had to keep moving so people wouldn't grow suspicious. You see, I didn't age in the normal way. My husband did. And of course eventually, he died. My children died. My grandchildren died.'

'You put yourself through all that pain,' Mislav sneered. 'For what?'

'For love, Mislav. Something you never really understood.'

'There's nothing *to* understand.'

Aelia shook her head sadly. 'After a while, people still talked of the demons, but there was no longer anyone left alive who had personally experienced the horror of it. Centuries passed and I changed my name several times. I lived in many different villages. But I always returned here to the widow's cave for long periods to contemplate my existence and decide where to go and what to do next. I had also begun to age. Not at the normal human rate, but very slowly and imperceptibly.

'In the thirteen hundreds – or was it later? I can't remember, but no matter, the locals diverted the course of a river to bring it closer to their crops. The new course ran through the very same valley as the cave entrance to the underground city. I breathed easier after that. The demons were still deep underground and now the entrance was covered by a deep river. Memories of the demons passed out of history. Buried under the weight of time. They had become legend or perhaps a scary bedtime story. But there were still those who believed. Although no one ever knew the full story. Except me.

'At the end of the eighteenth century, I returned to the village of Selmea. By then, I looked much as I do now. I had an enormous family and managed to stay with them by leaving and then returning several years later as an aunt, or later as a long-lost great-grandmother. I always brought wealth with me and this usually eased their acceptance.' She laughed. 'That, and the striking family resemblance that had filtered down to my descendants.

'But then, in 1881, something happened that I never thought would come to pass. You know this part, Alexandre.'

She stared at him and he felt shame.

'I was living peacefully with my wonderful ancestors, the Sahin family. I was now known as Havva Sahin, and my "great-grandson" was the village elder of Selmea, then, and until this day, known as Zelmat. Alexandre, you and your family came and unleashed chaos. I warned you not to meddle, but it seems I underestimated your persistence. I never dreamed you would find the cave entrance beneath the river. But you certainly paid the price for that, didn't you?'

Alexandre gave a single nod and then bowed his head. Madison squeezed his hand. When he looked up again, he saw that Aelia looked tired. Reliving history had taken it out of her, but she hadn't quite finished the story.

'Harold Swinton wrote to me, you know.'

'He was my father,' Freddie said. 'I'm Frederick Swinton.'

'Yes. Well, while you were sleeping, he asked me if I knew how to revive you. I lied to him. I told him to keep you locked up in the dark. I didn't know then that you were capable of being human, of having compassion. I'm sorry for that.'

'You did what you thought was right,' said Alexandre. 'I probably would've done the same.'

'Looking at you, I see that maybe not all vampires are evil. Perhaps some of you can live with love in your hearts. But you are still young. Time may still warp and twist your soul into something terrible. It's the blood, you see. It changes you.'

'And so, what now?' Mislav said to her, rising to his feet. 'You say you carry the sickness in you. As far as I am aware, all I need to do is destroy you without spilling your blood. Then you can do no further damage.'

'You do not need to threaten me. I will do you no harm, Mislav. You are not the powerful civilisation you once were. Today's society will not tolerate your ungodly ways.'

'Today's society is worse than ever,' he replied. 'Have you

not seen what is happening in this modern world? We were angels compared to some of today's regimes.'

'Not by any stretch of the imagination could you be called an angel, Mislav.'

'I have heard enough,' he said. 'You cannot be allowed to survive, Aelia. You pose too much of a threat. Once his Imperial Highness hears of your existence, he will have you killed.'

'He will not succeed. You cannot destroy me with sunlight, nor chain me with silver.'

'We'll see about that, old woman.' Mislav glared at her, threw a look of contempt at the rest of them and disappeared so quickly, that none saw him leave.

Alexandre did not want to let him go. That demon was too dangerous to be left roaming free. There were four of them here, plus Zoe and Aelia. They could destroy him. If they went after him now...

He felt Madison's restraining hand on his shoulder. She knew what was in his mind.

'No,' she said. 'Not now.'

'*Now* may be the only time we have.'

'No. Please. Enough.'

Alexandre sighed but stayed where he was. He knew he would regret his decision.

CHAPTER FORTY-FIVE

PRESENT DAY

Now that Mislav had left the cave, the tension lifted, lightening the atmosphere a little. But Alexandre remained wary. Aelia was hundreds of years old, incredibly powerful and she carried the sleeping sickness in her body. No matter how nice the woman seemed, she was still potentially dangerous and the sooner they left this place the better. In fact, the sooner they left the country, the safer it would be for all of them.

But the Cappadocians were out there roaming free, an unknown quantity. What did they want? Would they come after them again? Would they target Madison once more to get to him and the others? Yes, probably.

Definitely.

He could not allow that to happen again. From now on, they would have to be on their guard at all times. But how could they live like that? Looking over their shoulders every minute of every day.

He would question Morris first – haul him out of the van and see what the man had to say for himself. Perhaps he knew what the Cappadocians wanted. If Morris was a traitor, he must have information on them.

'Are you okay, Alex?' Madison touched his arm.

'Yes. Sorry, I'm just trying to sort things out in my mind, but everything's a mess in there.'

'I know. It's all been crazy. I can't believe what's happened over the last few days. And I can't believe that Zoe's here. I'm so glad she decided to leave the city.'

'She saved us both.'

Alexandre and Madison looked over to where Zoe sat talking quietly to Jacques and Isobel.

Freddie's voice rose above their hushed murmurs. 'We need to find my sister,' he announced. 'I'm worried about her.'

'No need, little brother.'

'Leonora!' Freddie cried as she walked into the cave. 'Where have you been?'

'You missed all the fun,' Jacques said.

Isobel gave Jacques a look and walked over to her friend.

'Leonora, are you well?' she said. 'We were worried about you.'

'I'm fine,' she said. 'Listen... don't be angry...' She flicked her gaze across them all but would not make proper eye contact.

'What is it, Leonora?' Alexandre asked.

'I've something to tell you,' she said. 'but it sounds worse than it is.'

Alexandre had never seen her so flustered before. He couldn't guess at what was making her act so nervously, so ill at ease.

'I'll just go ahead and say it...'

By now, the cave was silent, everyone's gaze fixed on Leonora.

'I've been to see the Cappadocians.' She put her chin in the air and finally looked Alexandre in the eye.

'You've been to see them?' He was confused. Why would she put herself in so much danger? Had she been trying to rescue Maddy on her own? But that wouldn't make any sense. Maddy had already escaped.

'I wanted to try to make a truce with them.'

'A truce?' Maddy repeated. 'Let me guess what they said. Was it "no" by any chance?'

'Leonora, you could've been killed!' Freddie cried.

'You cannot make deals with them,' Aelia said. 'They do what they want. They do not care about anyone else.'

'I'm sorry, who are you?' Leonora asked, raising a dark eyebrow.

Aelia merely smiled.

'This is Aelia,' Alexandre said. 'It's a long story, but she saved Maddy. What did the Cappadocians say to your proposal?'

'Their Emperor arrived this evening,' Leonora replied. 'He is anxious to meet us. I said... I said we would go there tonight.'

'You said *what*?' Maddy choked out a disbelieving laugh. 'I hope you're joking.'

'It's a chance for us to put all this behind us,' Leonora continued. 'If we go home now, we'll always be in danger.'

Leonora's words echoed exactly what Alexandre had been thinking. Going to the underground city was the last thing he wanted to do, but it could be a way to end things once and for all.

'Do you really think we can trust them?' Freddie asked his sister.

'I don't think we have much choice,' Leonora replied.

'Well, I do not think we should go,' Isobel said. 'I really think it is the worst idea I have ever heard. We came to Turkey to rescue Madison. We have her back now, so we should just go home and forget this ever happened.'

'Belle,' Jacques said. 'I know it sounds like a crazy thing to do, but—'

'Crazy?' Maddy chipped in. 'It's the most stupid idea I've

ever heard. Those vamps were just on the verge of executing me. Alex, tell them what a terrible idea this is.'

Alex was torn. His instincts were telling him to get the hell out of this country and never return, but he knew that somewhere down the line he would regret not taking this opportunity, risky though it was.

'Alex.' Maddy shook his arm lightly. 'We're not doing this... right? It'll be a trap, you know that.'

'Maddy—'

'No! I can't believe you're actually contemplating going back there.'

'Madison,' Leonora said. 'It's the only sensible option. Alexandre understands that.'

'Leonora, it's the least sensible option,' Maddy replied. 'It's stupid and it's dangerous. You weren't here earlier. You didn't see them fighting. And that Mislav guy is the scariest thing I've ever seen.'

'I'm not going back there,' Zoe said.

'This is Zoe,' Freddie introduced her to his sister. 'Zoe risked her life to save Maddy. Zoe, as you may have gathered, this is my sister, Leonora.'

Zoe nodded at her.

Leonora glanced at Zoe and nodded back.

'Maddy, I'm sorry,' said Alexandre. 'I really think we have to go there. We should at least try to make a truce. Otherwise we're going to be looking over our shoulders forever. I, for one, do not want a repeat performance of the past few days.'

'Good.' Leonora smiled. Suddenly, her smile vanished to be replaced with a frown and then a snarl. She flew past Alexandre and out of the cave.

'Wait here,' Alexandre said to Maddy, before following Leonora outside, the other vampires on his heels.

Madison ignored him and hurried to catch up to where he

and all the Marchwood vampires had now gathered outside the cave.

Leonora had someone in a headlock, and it looked to Alexandre as though she might be about to break their neck. *Morris.* The caretaker was helpless to defend himself, becoming red in the face, unable to breathe. Where had he come from? How had he found them?

'What are you doing?' Maddy screamed at her.

'You cannot kill him, Leonora,' Isobel cried.

'Why not? He betrayed us. Ben found the evidence.'

'No!' Maddy yelled. 'Let him go, Leonora! It's Morris! What are you doing to him? It's *Morris.*'

The caretaker's mouth opened and closed ineffectually. It looked like he was about to suffocate.

'Maddy. The man is a traitor,' said Jacques. 'He betrayed us to the Cappadocians.'

'*What?*' Maddy said. 'Don't be stupid. He would never—'

'How did he get out of the van?' Freddie asked.

'Let him go, Leonora!' Maddy pleaded. 'He'll die if you don't loosen your grip.'

'He deserves to die. I'll break his neck. He won't feel a thing.'

'No! Don't you dare!' Maddy stepped in front of Leonora and glared at her. Leonora shot back a look of venom.

'Alex,' Maddy said. 'Make her let him go. Please.'

'Alexandre,' Leonora said. 'Tell Madison it is for the best if I do this.'

'No, Leonora,' Alexandre replied. 'Release your hold on him. Let's bring him inside and hear what he has to say.'

'We'd better hear him out, Nora,' Freddie added. 'He came here of his own free will. Maybe he knows something important. And if he's a traitor, we'll need information from him first.'

'Leonora, let him go,' Alexandre repeated, more forcefully. 'Or I will be forced to step in and help the man. Much as he may deserve a snapped neck, Freddie is right; we need to find out what he knows.'

Reluctantly, Leonora released Morris. He collapsed into the snow, struggling for breath. Maddy crouched and took his hand. 'Help me get him inside,' she snapped. 'He's freezing.'

Alexandre helped Maddy lift him to his feet and they all returned to the cave. As they made their way inside, Alexandre quickly told Maddy about Ben's discovery of the notepaper and how he suspected Morris of having dealings with the Cappadocians.

'I don't believe it,' said Maddy. 'I can see why Ben would be worried, but I think he's wrong. Morris and Esther are our friends. They're not traitors.'

'Leonora's the traitor, not me,' Morris gasped, still struggling for breath.

'What did you say?' Maddy said. They were now inside the cave and everyone was staring at Morris with suspicion.

'I said...' Morris cleared his throat. 'I said, Leonora's the traitor, not me.'

At his words, Leonora flew at him again, dragging him out from between Alexandre and Maddy and flinging him onto the rock floor. Leonora crouched over his body, her fangs poised above his neck. Alexandre knew she wouldn't listen to reason this time so he pulled her away from the caretaker. Fresh fragrant blood oozed from a gash in Morris's head and Alex had to swallow down a sudden urge to fall on the man and drink from him.

'Let go of my, sister!' Freddie yelled, flying towards Alex.

'*Enough!*' Aelia said. She hadn't shouted, but her voice cut through their snarls and yells like a blade. 'Children,' she said, once quiet had descended. 'Let this man speak.' She and Madison helped Morris sit up, his hand pressed to the wound on the back of his head.

'Are you all right?' Madison asked.

'I don't know. I feel a bit odd, if the truth be known.'

'I'll get something to dress your wound,' Aelia said. 'The rest of you, sit down or leave my home.'

They all did as she asked, except Leonora who looked as though she might go for Morris at any second.

'Leonora,' Alexandre warned.

'Very well.' She sat, leaning back against the rock wall, arms crossed, legs stretched out in front of her. 'But what that man said is ridiculous. As if I would betray my own family.'

'I thought Leonora locked you in the van,' Alexandre said to Morris.

'You can get out of a van easy enough,' he replied. 'Now, will you hear me out without attacking me again? I'm a bit old for all this rough and tumble.'

'We're listening,' Alexandre said.

'If you let me, I can show you something that might interest you.' He put his hand into his coat pocket and the vampires immediately leapt to their feet again. 'Easy does it,' Morris said. 'You lot are as jumpy as a bucket of grasshoppers. I'm a feeble old man – no match for the likes of you. It's just my phone, that's all.' He held out his mobile for them to see. 'There's a video on here you need to watch.'

'Pass it to me,' Alexandre said, coming closer to take it from him.

Morris handed him the phone.

'I spoke to Ben,' Morris said. 'And he told me about the notepaper that came from the Bell.'

'What notepaper?' Maddy asked. 'Is Ben all right?'

'Ben's fine,' Morris replied. 'I'll tell you the rest, Maddy. But first, press play on the phone screen, Alex.'

He did so and the others got up and crowded round to watch. They saw an image of Leonora walking into what appeared to be a hotel lobby. She sat next to two men and began talking to them. There was no sound on the video, so they couldn't hear the content of their conversation.

'It's CCTV footage from the Old Bell Hotel in Tetbury,' Morris explained. 'Esther got it for me. Look at the date on the bottom of the screen.'

'December 13th' Isobel said. 'That's the evening before we went ice-skating and Maddy disappeared.'

'I recognise one of those men,' Alexandre said, shaking his head in disbelief.

'They're vampires,' said Jacques. 'Cappadocians. We fought with them tonight.'

'But why would you have been talking to them back then?' Maddy turned to Leonora.

'No!' Freddie shouted. 'I don't believe it. You must have doctored the footage, faked it somehow!'

'I'm sorry, lad,' Morris said. 'Esther took a copy from the CCTV cameras at the hotel. You can go there and see the original files if you like.'

'Well, I still don't believe it,' Freddie said. 'I know my sister and she would never...' He turned to her, wiping away an angry red tear. '... Leonora?'

'I know it looks bad,' Leonora said. 'But I can explain why I was there. There's a perfectly good reason for it.'

Leonora's anger had disappeared and now she was flustered again. Alexandre had a sinking feeling in his stomach. He really didn't want to hear the explanation. He had a horrible feeling he wasn't going to like what she had to say.

CHAPTER FORTY-SIX

PRESENT DAY

Leonora glared at them defiantly. 'I know what you're all thinking, but you're wrong.'

No one spoke

'I'm not a traitor. I swear it.'

'I know you're not,' Freddie said. 'It's all just a mistake. Tell them you weren't there, Leonora. Put them straight.' He gave his sister an encouraging smile.

'Wait a minute, Freds,' Leonora said.

'What do you mean?'

She sighed. 'They're wrong to say I betrayed you. But I did go to see the Cappadocians.' She paused.

'Go on...' he said, his smile faltering.

'I thought... I *think* that if we join them—'

'Join them?' Jacques cried. 'What do you mean, "join them"?'

'Are you mad?' Isobel hissed.

Disbelief clouded Freddie's cherubic features.

'Just listen for a minute,' Leonora said, getting into her stride. 'If we join them, we'll be safe from them. We can live without looking over our shoulders all the time. We can finally be what we are – *vampires*.'

Alexandre stared at her like he didn't know who she was anymore.

'I'll be back later,' Zoe whispered to Madison. 'I won't go far. I'll just give you all some space... to sort things out.'

'Okay,' Maddy replied, and squeezed her hand. 'Don't go too far.'

'Leonora,' Alexandre said. 'Have you lost your mind? "Join them"? You would really consider living like that? Killing mortals and striking terror into everyone you meet?'

'Oh, don't be so dramatic, Alexandre.'

'I'm not being dramatic. I'm downplaying it if anything. You would be agreeing to become a monster.'

'I would be no such thing! But I wouldn't be agreeing to become anything if it wasn't for *her*!' Leonora turned and pointed a finger at Madison.

Maddy looked shocked, like she'd been hit. She took a step backwards. Alexandre looked from Leonora to Madison and back again. He didn't understand what Leonora was talking about.

'What do you mean?' Maddy stuttered. 'What did I do? How is this my fault?'

Leonora looked away from Madison and stared at the others. 'I always seem to be the villain,' she said. 'I'm only trying to look out for all of us. I want us to be safe and my name has been sullied before I've even had a chance to put forward my side of the story. That video condemned me before I had a chance to speak.'

'We're listening to you now,' Alexandre said.

'I know, but it's all coming out wrong. It looks as if I'm conspiring against you, but I'm not. I'm really not.'

'You said it was my fault,' Maddy said. 'I'd like to know why.'

'All right.' She fixed her eyes on Madison again. 'If you must know, I was looking for a way out. And I thought that by contacting the Cappadocians, I could negotiate a place for us in the underground city.'

'A way out of what?' Alexandre asked.

'A way out of Marchwood.'

'But Marchwood is our home,' Freddie said.

'It doesn't feel like my home anymore,' Leonora replied. 'That was *our* home, Freddie. *Ours*. We grew up there with mother and father. But now I feel like some kind of interloper. Shoved down in the basement, like a... like a... refugee, or a servant. And *she*' – Leonora pointed at Madison – '*she* is sleeping in our parents' bedroom like she has the right. It is outrageous.'

'So why didn't you say anything?' Freddie said.

'But what could I possibly have said that would sound reasonable? Could I have asked Madison to move out of that bedroom? Could I have spoken to you, Alexandre? Or you, Isobel? Would you have listened? No. You would have thought I was being petty and small-minded. And all the while my guts were churning with the wrongness of it. Having to watch while Madison Greene played at being queen of all she surveyed.'

'Shut up, Leonora!' Isobel said. 'How can you say such hateful things?'

'Exactly,' Leonora replied. 'I knew you wouldn't understand.'

Maddy's expression had gone from anger to shock to something else – humiliation? Alexandre put his arm around her. 'She is crazy,' he whispered in her ear. 'Do not listen. She doesn't mean it. She doesn't know what she is saying.'

But Leonora had not finished talking. 'No. If I said those things, it would not go down well at all. You would think I was being unreasonable. Freddie, why do you not mind that she has taken over our house? Why can none of you see how wrong it is?' She turned to face Madison again. 'How can you not see how selfish you are... with your whorish behaviour.'

Maddy felt a tear slide down her face. She'd had no idea Leonora felt this way. And how could she have known she had chosen Leonora and Freddie's parents' bedroom as her own. She would never have been so insensitive if she'd realised. Why hadn't the others said anything? She felt like an idiot.

'I'm so sorry, Leonora,' Maddy said. 'I didn't know. I really am sorry. I never wanted to make—'

'Do not apologise for her rudeness, Madison,' Alexandre said. 'She has no right to talk to you that way.'

'Don't you feel claustrophobic at Marchwood?' Leonora asked her brother. 'Like it isn't ours anymore? Doesn't it feel just a bit stifling to you? As though we're guests in our own house?'

'No.'

'Really? You're happy having the *Greenes*' – she sneered as she said the name – 'take over our home?'

'They haven't taken over,' Freddie said. 'And it *is* their house. Madison and Ben are family. The only family we have left. They own it. Legitimately.'

'And morally?'

'Look, Leonora,' Freddie continued, 'I love it there with them and with you. And I thought you did too. And, anyway, it's a big enough place for us all.'

'I'm not talking about square footage! All I know is I cannot stay there any longer. If I go back, I might do something I regret.'

'I think you already have,' Isobel said.

'I thought that if I helped the Cappadocians to get us all to come here, we could see how they lived and what sort of life we could have with them.'

'What sort of life?' Freddie almost choked. 'Leonora, I think you've lost your mind. And how could you plan all that without telling us? Without telling *me*? I'm your brother. We could have talked about it.'

'You would have tried to change my mind.'

'Yes I would, because it's a terrible idea. And please tell me it wasn't you who arranged to have Madison kidnapped.'

'That was not my suggestion.'

'But you didn't speak out against it. You helped them plan it?'

Leonora didn't reply.

'My God, you have become a monster.' Freddie ran his hands through his hair, a look of horror etched into his face.

'You put me... *us* through all this?' Alexandre said. 'Taking Madison away from me. Letting me worry myself sick about it and you knew all along. You planned it!'

'Leonora,' Jacques said. 'You do realise none of us would even be alive if it wasn't for Madison.'

'And Maddy is your blood,' Alexandre said. 'Have you any idea what you've put her through? No matter what you say, she is your family.'

'Madison is nothing to me,' Leonora spat. 'She is a common child with no breeding or class.' She took a step toward Maddy who was now crying freely. 'You had the good fortune to be sired by a distant relation, but there is nothing of the Swinton family in you. Nothing.'

'That's enough, Leonora!' Alexandre shouted. 'You have gone too far! Listen to yourself! I think you'd better leave.'

'So you would send me away?'

'Good God, Leonora!' Alexandre cried. 'No one wants this, but you've gone too far. You said yourself you do not want to stay at Marchwood. And as for blaming all this on Madison, you are too harsh. You have let things become distorted in your mind. If you had talked to us about your worries, we could have accommodated you, we would have listened and tried to help. Maddy loves you like a sister. She is always telling me how happy she is to have found you and Freddie. She is the image of you. She has your spirit.'

'She is obviously a more worthy image than I am,' Leonora said. 'She won your heart – something I was never able to do.'

'That is because you kept your heart hidden from me.' Alexandre had no wish to talk about this in front of everyone. He and Leonora had never discussed their 'almost' relationship before now, and he had not realised she still even thought of it.

'You must have known that I loved you,' Leonora said, stiffly.

'I did not,' Alexandre replied.

Maddy's eyes widened, looking from one to the other.

'Back then,' Alexandre continued, 'when we first met, I was enchanted by you, Leonora. I had sleepless nights with thoughts of you.'

Leonora shook her head and bit her lip.

'But you were cold to me,' he continued. 'You spurned my advances time and time again. I could say nothing. Do nothing.'

'That is not true.'

'You know it is, Leonora. And then, after we were turned, things went beyond that. We became friends, like brother and sister. That is why this betrayal is so shocking to me.'

'I did not betray you. I made a hard decision. You would never have agreed to come here willingly. We would have had to fight them. This way, no one gets hurt.'

'Except we did get hurt.'

'You are fine.'

'And do not pretend you did this for *us*,' Alexandre spat. 'You did it for yourself. And it was not your decision to make on our behalf.'

'Well, Alexandre, you are not the head of our household. In fact, Marchwood is *my* house. You are there as a guest.'

'So, it is to be like that,' Alexandre replied stiffly. 'Very well, I can see our friendship has come to nothing. I will leave Marchwood House if that is what you wish.'

'No... *No*, I did not mean... I'm sorry. Of course you must stay at Marchwood. I am leaving anyway. I had hoped you would all join me here willingly, but I can see I expected too much. Freddie is my brother and I hope he at least will change his mind and join me.' She turned to look at him. 'Come with me, Freddie, and I'll prove I'm right. Come to the city and see for yourself. It's going to be incredible. They're restoring it to its former beauty. It will be an adventure. A new life for us. Mother and Father would have loved to have had the chance to explore the city properly, without fear.'

'I realise this is nothing to do with me,' Aelia interjected, 'but you will find nothing but pain and misery in that city.'

'You are right,' Leonora replied coldly. 'It is nothing to do with you.'

'Thank you, Aelia,' Freddie replied. 'I believe you.' He turned back to his sister. 'There is no way on earth I would want to live there, Leonora. Not after what happened to us. And if you had heard Aelia's story, you would agree with me. I can't believe you're even considering it. And after what I've just heard from your lips, I'm ashamed to call you my sister.'

'Don't say that, Freddie! Of course I'm your sister. I will always be here for you.'

He turned away from her.

'Freddie! Don't be like that.'

'You need to leave, Leonora,' Alexandre said.

'No,' Maddy interjected. 'She has every right to be angry. Leonora, I'm sorry. I had no idea you were going through such a lonely time. We can sort it out. I'll move out of your parents' bedroom, of course I will. And I agree, that—'

'You are offering me crumbs,' Leonora said witheringly. 'Crumbs that are not yours to offer.'

'I still think we can sort this out amicably,' Maddy persevered.

'No, we can't,' Alexandre replied. 'I don't know if I can look at your face again, Leonora. You have made me so angry and so sad.'

'You're not sad. You're humiliated and disappointed because things did not go your way as usual.'

Alexandre stared at the vampire he'd thought was his friend and she had the grace to squirm slightly under his gaze.

'Who are you?' he asked. 'I do not know you anymore.'

'Then come with me, Alexandre, and you can get to know me. The real me. I will not hide my heart from you any longer. It is not too late—'

'Get out!' Alexandre shook with rage.

Leonora turned her gaze on the other vampires, but they either shook their heads or turned their eyes away from her.

'Don't send her away,' Maddy said to Alex. 'She's my family.'

'But she almost had you killed.'

'She loves you, Alexandre. That's why she did this; her heart is broken.'

'I don't need your pity,' Leonora hissed, 'or your condescension.' She cast a final scathing glance around the cavern and then was gone.

Maddy hurried after her into the snow. The moon still shone brightly, but there was no trace of Leonora. She shouted for her, but her voice fell away into the night. How had she misjudged the situation at home so badly? Strangely, she didn't feel angry at what Leonora had done to her. She felt sympathy. She understood the burn of emotions that must have been building and festering inside her, leading up to this massive outpouring. Maddy recognised the loneliness and helplessness trapped inside her ancestor. If only Maddy had realised earlier, they might have avoided all of this and reached a happier outcome.

Had Madison been as selfish as Leonora had said? Perhaps she had. Perhaps she'd been so caught up in her own personal love story that she hadn't considered anyone else.

'Stop it.'

She turned to see Alex standing behind her.

'Stop what?'

'Beating yourself up.'

'But Leonora had a point,' Maddy said. 'She must have been keeping so much emotion bottled up.'

'It still doesn't excuse what she's done.'

'No, but it explains it.'

Alex came and put his arms around her and she leant her head against his chest.

'Do you know,' she said, 'out of everything that's happened, I think this Leonora thing has been the most shocking.'

'I agree.'

'I feel sick about it.'

'Come back inside. She's gone and I don't think she'll be back anytime soon.'

Maddy heaved a huge sigh. They turned and made their way back into the cavern where Isobel and Jacques were trying and failing to console Freddie. Maddy took a step toward them, but Alex pulled her back.

'Leave it for a while. The others will calm him.'

She nodded. 'I should apologise to Aelia for turning her home into a battleground.'

'You go ahead. I have some apologising of my own to do.' He nodded in the direction of Morris who lay on the mattress, resting after his ordeal.

Maddy headed over to where Aelia was busying herself by the fire, decanting some food from a pan into a deep clay dish.

'Aelia, I'm sorry I brought so much trouble to your door.'

'Trouble always finds me eventually,' Aelia replied. 'I think I was born under a star called trouble.'

Maddy gave a small smile. 'And I haven't thanked you properly for saving my life – twice. Thank you. I'm pretty sure you saved the rest of us too. That vampire, Mislav, he would've had me killed and taken the others if it wasn't for you.'

'Like me, you have aligned yourself with trouble. You do realise your life will never be straightforward as long as you remain in the company of these creatures.'

'I know,' Maddy said. 'But I can't help it. My life is tied up with them. I could never leave.'

'Then all I can do is wish you luck. And hope that trouble never gets the best of you.'

'Thank you,' Maddy said. 'For everything.'

It was clear there was nothing further to be said, so Maddy headed over to where Alexandre was apologising to Morris.

'Doesn't matter,' Morris was saying.

'It does matter,' Alex replied. 'I feel terrible. You are our friend and I didn't believe you.'

'I've got some apologising of my own to do,' Morris replied, looking at Madison.

'What for?' she said.

'I had to get Esther to lock Ben up for a short while.'

'You did *what*!' Maddy clenched her fists.

'Don't worry, the lad's fine. But I couldn't risk him telling the vampires I'd escaped. Not until I had a chance to find out who'd betrayed you.'

Maddy didn't reply.

'That makes sense,' Alex said.

'Sorry for that,' Morris said.

'I *suppose* I can understand why you did it,' Maddy said. 'As long as he's okay.'

'He's fine.'

'So what do we do now?' Maddy said.

'Now?' Alexandre looked at her. Then he looked at Morris. Finally, he gazed around the room at everybody else. At their shocked, tired faces. 'Now... we go home.'

EPILOGUE

CHRISTMAS EVE

Out there, darkness cloaked the countryside and rain skittered against the drawing room window of Marchwood House. But inside, the lights blazed and the fire crackled, sending yellow sparks showering up the chimney. They were all curled up cosy and warm. Alex and Maddy on the sofa. Jacques, Isobel and Freddie playing Chance on the rug in front of the fire. And Ben (who had forgiven Esther for locking him up, and apologised to Morris for the terrible misunderstanding) was attaching their stockings to the fireplace. All was calm. There was one notice-able absence, but nobody mentioned her name. The only reminder was a discreet tinge of melancholy which hung imper-ceptibly in the air.

As well as Leonora's absence, there was another worry – the knowledge that this peace was only temporary. That this Christmas Eve was merely an illusion of happiness. For there were still those out there who sought to destroy it. Who would never leave them alone. But, for a short while, they would savour this brief reprieve and enjoy each other, for there had been too much fear and violence lately. Too much regret and too much worry. Tonight was a night for friends and for family.

Madison hoped Zoe was enjoying her Christmas too. Zoe had finally plucked up the courage to visit her husband and son. She was going to come clean and tell them what had happened. She was going to give her husband the opportunity to decide what *he* thought was best for their family. She hoped Zoe was as happy as *she* felt right now, here with her body pressed close into Alex. Maddy closed her eyes and smiled.

But Madison would not have smiled if she knew what waited outside.

From beneath a gnarled oak, it regarded them through the drawing room window. Only metres away, its stare cut across the darkness to the blissful scene within.

The creature gave a sad smile, echoing the emotions of the ones it watched and making them its own. Cold rain fell on its skin. It closed its eyes and savoured this long-awaited moment. After centuries of searching, it had finally found what it needed.

Over the past millennium, its only sustenance had gradually disappeared from the earth, until there was nothing at all for it to feed on. But now, miraculously, the creature had scented down what it craved and had traced it here. To this quiet corner of the world.

Still weak from hunger, it would need to rest, to prepare for the true hunt. But it had the sense that this would be an easy conquest. Did the creature detect a little vanity on the part of its quarry? It could use that to its advantage.

Inside, they were oblivious to what waited. The creature had always been able to remain undetected until it chose to reveal itself. And then they always took notice. Always. It had never failed to take down its prey, not in the several millennia it had roamed the earth. It always went for the coven leader and it was quite obvious who that was – the dark-haired male.

The creature cocked its head and listened for the vampire's name... yes, it had a pleasing ring to it... *Alexandre*.

A LETTER FROM SHALINI

Dear reader,

Thank you for reading *Taken*. I had a blast writing it, weaving all the Byzantine history in amongst the supernatural folklore and then placing Maddy and Alex slap bang in the middle. If you enjoyed book 2, you'll find more star-crossed love, ancient history and supernatural action in *Hunted* book 3 of the Vampires of Marchwood.

If you'd like to keep up to date with my latest releases, just sign up here and I'll let you know when I have a new novel coming out.

www.secondskybooks.com/shalini-boland

I love getting feedback on my books, so if you have a few moments, I'd be really grateful if you'd be kind enough to post a review online or tell your friends about it. A good review absolutely makes my day.

When I'm not writing, reading, walking on the beach or spending time with my family, you can reach me via my Facebook page, through Twitter, Goodreads or my website.

Thanks so much,

Shalini Boland x

KEEP IN TOUCH WITH SHALINI

www.shaliniboland.co.uk

facebook.com/ShaliniBolandAuthor

twitter.com/ShaliniBoland

goodreads.com/shaliniboland

ACKNOWLEDGMENTS

THANK YOU

To my superstar husband, Peter Boland, who helped me shape this story, made me endless cups of tea, bought me chocolate and saw me through many a writing-related meltdown.

To my wonderful beta readers: Amara Gillo – best mum in the world (who's devastatingly no longer in this world but who continues to inspire me every day) and Julie Carey, who can spot a missing speech mark at fifty paces.

To all my gorgeous friends and writing support network online from back when I first wrote this series a decade ago, including: Johanna Frappier, C. Reg Jones, B. Lloyd, Samantha Towle, Suzy Turner, Amanda Cowley, Robert Craven, Poppet and Sessha Batto.

To Zoe Marshall and Sergell Elioreg, who entered the 'Be a Vampire in My Book' competition and won!

To my wonderful publisher, Natasha Harding, for believing in the series and working her magic on these characters. I'm forever grateful for your talent and patience.

To the dedicated team at Second Sky. Jenny Geras, Ruth Tross, Jack Renninson, Sarah Hardy, Kim Nash, Noelle Holten, Melanie Price, Mark Alder, Alex Crow, Natalie Butlin, Jess Readett, Alexandra Holmes, Emily Boyce, Saidah Graham, Lizzie Brien, Occy Carr and everyone else who helped relaunch this book.

To Madeline Newquist for your fantastic proofreading skills. Thank you to designer Eileen Carey for an incredible cover.

To Jordan Spellman at Tantor Audio and narrator Henrietta Meire for creating fabulous audiobooks for the series.

To all my lovely readers who take the time to read, review or recommend my novels. It means so, so much. And to all the fabulous book bloggers and reviewers out there who spread the word. You guys are the absolute best!

To my incredible family who have been by my side from start to finish, you inspire me every day. Thanks for making me laugh, giving good hugs and being the best people I could hope to have by my side (or on the other side of that door while I'm writing).

Printed in Great Britain
by Amazon